8.99

When it's Love

Beverly Shearer

RISING
TIDE
PRESS

Rising Tide Press
PO Box 30457
Tucson, AZ 85751-0457
520-888-1140

Printed in the United States on acid-free paper.

Publisher's note:
All characters, places, and situations in this book are fictitious, or used fictitiously, and any resemblance to persons (living or dead) is purely coincidental.

Cover art by Jude Ockenfels

First Printing: January 2001

Shearer, Beverly
When It's Love/Beverly Shearer

ISBN 1-883061-29-6

Library of Congress Control Number: 00 133933

DEDICATION

Thanks to the women who read this work in its early stages and who encouraged me to continue.

And, as always, for the deepest inspiration
... *Taylor.*

The impact of her boot heels hitting the concrete shocked her knees and shoulders upward and made her jaws clash together so hard it was like a flashbulb going off behind her eyes. She staggered, then hit the garage floor flat on her back. Her stiff-brimmed Stetson rolled drunkenly under a parked car as she stared up at the narrow strips of florescent lights that paralleled their way into the distance. She stared in wonder, her trembling hand seeking the solid comfort of her pistol grip, for she had never before seen florescent lights, or concrete, or flashbulbs, or cars, parked or otherwise. It was just as well that her breath had left her as she hit, because she couldn't think to breathe anyway.

Her eyes shifted rapidly right and left, trying to focus on any one thing familiar. Despite the strange blue light, the square, cavernous room held the feel of darkness. She thought she could see the air that lay heavy all around. She pressed her lips tightly together in fear. Finally, her body forced her to gasp in a deep gulp of that stinking air. It burned the sides of her nostrils and the corners of her eyes.

A taste of metal trailed across her tongue and spread, stinging over the back of her throat. The unpleasantness suggested that she was alive. It also suggested that she had, for the first time, encountered something she knew was beyond her.

The cold lifelessness of the concrete rose through her thin brown coat and black cotton shirt, and she felt it heading straight for her heart. Pushing herself up on her elbows, she drew her legs up to sit in a crouch. She held still that way for a moment, waiting for the urge to vomit to subside. Her body rocked back and forth with her heartbeat, quickly, in short movements like the ticking of a tiny clock. Sweat beaded on her forehead and trickled down to catch in the thick brows framing her cold blue eyes.

She studied the black curl of her hat brim visible under the huge, green chunk of metal and glass. She wanted it back on her head—next to her pistol, it was her security. Better to be without pants than without her Stetson. But wanting didn't bring it closer, and she was ashamed to realize that she was afraid to reach out for it. She was afraid to stand up, afraid to sit down, and afraid she wasn't going to find a way out of this situation.

Scared and shamed—two things worse than death. She slowly eased her weight forward onto her knees, then whipped her hand out quicker than she'd ever drawn a gun. Thumb tip and fingertip gripped the thick felt and jerked the hat back to her side. She clapped the Stetson onto her head and pulled down tight till it pushed against the top edges of her ears. Now she could look around with a little more confidence.

Other than the soft brush of her hat against the floor, she hadn't heard a sound since she'd fallen. The stillness was a small part of the overall unnatural feeling of the place. She turned her head to the left and saw letters painted on the wall. The words were painted with a dirty yellow pigment and seemed to give off a dim light of their own. LEVEL ONE, she read and surmised that if there was a first level, there had to be others. And they surely couldn't all be this bad.

A faint tapping sound started up in the distance. Her ears strained toward it, her eyes automatically closing to block out the distraction of sight. The sound was familiar, rhythmic, the sound of metal against stone. A hammer on drill steel sounded like that. She nodded her head, unconsciously picking up the beat and copying it. It made sense. She was in a mine. Suddenly the world again made sense.

Standing, she looked around another time. She'd been in a mine before. She'd seen the ore carts on their rails and the guttering lights that hung from ropes stretched down the length of the shafts. She'd smelled the acrid scent of dynamite.

Yes, it made sense. What did it matter that these carts lined up sideways in long rows were nothing like she'd seen before and that there were no rails for them to ride on? What did she care that the lights burned cold without flame or that the smell was not quite dynamite? She could let these inconsistencies go because she wasn't that familiar with the workings of mining. Copper, gold, coal, or silver—maybe each one was different. But she knew it didn't make sense that the tapping of the steel was steadily becoming nearer. Regardless of how much she wanted to hold on to her notion of the familiar, the sound forced her to recognize it as quick-paced and sharp footsteps.

Across the way, an impossibly smooth column rose from the floor and joined up with the ceiling above her head. A silent stride took her to the column and she ducked behind it. The tapping came closer and was accompanied by a high metallic jangle. Again, she reached for her pistol. Cautiously, she tipped her head around the corner and took a peek.

"Jesus Christ!" The words came out before she could draw them back. Her manner of saying that phrase had never been mistaken for a prayer, but she'd never said them with such reverence. Wide eyed, she stared. She should have ducked back behind the column before she was spotted, but she was frozen.

The woman that walked toward her was dressed in a shimmering blue fabric that shone like light from a butterfly's wing. The dress was tight, too tight for walking, so the hem had to be pulled way above the woman's knees. So tight, the woman's breasts were pressed together and lifted up. She'd never seen such cleavage before and had never experienced vertigo from simply standing above another woman.

The tapping came from dangerously high, sharp heels that graced shoes to match the color of the dress. The woman walked past without realizing anyone was watching her. From behind the column, she caught her breath and waited a moment for the woman's back to be to her before she leaned around again. The view from the back was equally splendid. The shimmering blue fabric did nothing to conceal the curves of the woman's body; its purpose actually seemed to be the opposite.

The woman approached one of the "ore carts," a low, black one, and selected a key from the ring jingling in her hand. In a second, the door swung open and the woman folded herself into the seat.

Not knowing what could possibly happen next and denied the view of that dress, she again crouched down beside the column and waited. Suddenly the space was filled with the roar of dynamite and the loud rumble of a desert canyon thunderstorm. The noise drove her back on her heels and she almost fell backwards onto the cart behind her. The black cart holding the woman rolled past, leaving behind a faint trail of stinking blue smoke and a very startled cowhand. 🌵

One

The phone rang again. Melia closed her eyes and rested her forehead against the pages of her book. She knew who it was, and she knew if she didn't just give up and answer, Dana would keep calling until she'd filled the answering machine with progressively angrier messages. She tucked a loose strand of brown hair behind her ear and picked up before the machine kicked in.

"Hello," she spoke in a voice as flat and emotionless as she could manage.

"Melia, thanks for answering. I didn't call at a bad time, did I?" There was an almost laugh in Dana's voice that stopped just short of mocking Melia.

"No, you didn't." Melia kicked her feet under the covers. An angry, yellow-green eye peered up through the wadded blankets followed by a black paw with claws extended in warning. Melia pulled her foot away and grinned.

"So, can I come over?" Dana asked.

The smile left Melia's face. "No."

"Why not?"

"The night is not long enough to go into the reasons. Besides, I'm going out," Melia lied.

"You're lying." Dana did laugh this time, as if the picture of Melia going out of the house after dark was too hilarious to hold back.

Melia rubbed the two thin lines that formed between her dark eyebrows at the top of her long, narrow nose. She tilted her head down, making shadows form in the hollows beneath her cheekbones and her usually full lips were thinned with tension. "Dana, I don't need to hear this. I have better things to do."

"Like what? Reading one of those stupid, trashy novels?"

Melia closed her book and slid it under the edge of the blanket. The cold eyes of the gunslinger posed on the front cover glared up from under the brim of his black hat. She glared back, determined not to give an inch this time.

"That's not what I'm doing . . . and I *am* going out."

"Okay, then you must be coming to see me," Dana teased.

"You are so incredibly arrogant. What makes you think you know—"

"That's just it, Melia. I know." Dana deliberately softened her voice. "I know you better than anyone knows you. I know you better than you know yourself."

"Then you should know I don't want to see you."

"I know you're dying to see me. I know you're cold and you're wrapped in that red blanket . . . I know you're thinking how good it would feel to have my arms around you, holding you warm and tight."

"That's not right. I'm reading and I'm perfectly warm and I haven't even given you a thought all day."

"And you didn't think about me last night? When you slept alone? Are you going to tell me you liked that?"

Melia closed her eyes, knowing that her silence answered Dana's question. She couldn't lie about that, Dana knew she hated to sleep alone.

"So, are you going to let me in or should I use my key?" Dana prodded.

Melia sat up. "Your key? But, you gave me back your key."

"I gave you a key."

"Dana, I don't believe you."

"I love you, Melia. Do you expect me to just give that up?"

"Again, I don't believe you." Melia heard Dana exhale. It sent a vibrating sound through the receiver, raising the hair on Melia's neck. She knew that Dana was trying hard to control her temper. She whispered, "I'm just not ready to see you."

"If you don't put down that goddamn book, you'll never be ready. You need to quit going to those stupid fantasy worlds and try to live in this one."

"My reading doesn't hurt anyone."

"Yes, it does, Melia. It hurts me." Dana's voice was harsh.

Melia knew the pain was real.

"If you didn't read so damn much, I wouldn't . . . " Dana sighed, unable to finish her sentence.

Refusing to leave it unspoken, Melia finished the thought. "You wouldn't hit me?"

There was a moment of frozen silence on the line. "One time, Melia. One time and I've said I'm sorry a thousand times," Dana forced the words through clenched teeth.

"I know you're sorry, Dana. But it doesn't change things." Melia rubbed the bridge of her nose with her thumb and forefinger. A strong and steady pain was building behind her deep brown eyes.

"Yes, it does. It changes everything."

"No."

"I'm coming over."

"Don't!"

"We need to talk about this. I'm getting cold standing out here."

"Where are you?"

"Outside the coffee shop. On the corner."

Melia knew if she looked out her bedroom window she would see Dana standing there. Dana would be leaning against the booth, her tall muscular body looking so strong and confident, and her long legs crossed in tight black jeans. She'd be looking right back at Melia's window. She would raise one of her long, slender hands and push a blonde curl from her forehead, and smile just enough for Melia to see it through the darkness. Melia balled up her fist and pressed it against her stomach.

"If you come here, we won't talk. We never do."

"This time we will." Dana's voice caressed. Promising. Lying.

"I'm not dressed. I'm not—"

"It doesn't matter. I have to see you."

"We'll talk?"

"Yeah," Dana's laugh was velvet as she answered. "We'll talk."

The click of the phone ended their connection and Melia slowly replaced the receiver. She glanced down to her novel and it seemed the gunslinger's eyes had become even colder. Melia sensed a contempt that wasn't there before. She grabbed the book and flung it against the wall. It bounced off the bookcase and thumped to the floor.

"This time, we'll talk." Melia informed the long rows of books.

She backtracked the steps the woman had taken. The farther she walked, the more deserted the place appeared. Only occasionally did she pass another of those carts. She tried a few of the doors. All were locked.

Finally, in the long, gray expanse of the far wall, she came upon a doorway. She pushed against the smooth metal door, but it wouldn't budge. There was no handle to lift or turn, and she couldn't figure out how it was supposed to open. But she was encouraged that it also seemed to be without a lock. On the wall beside the door was a metal plate with an arrow pointing up. She shrugged and pushed it, knowing she wasn't going to get anywhere if she wasn't willing to try.

The whoosh of the door opening made her jump back on her heels. The doorway opened into a tiny room that wasn't big enough to hold anything she thought might need a door. As she stepped inside to check it out, the door closed behind her. Her first thought was that she had walked into a trap. She spun around and struggled to force down her panic. A slow and steady trembling began in her legs and worked its way up through her belly and into her hands. She blinked rapidly. Before her was another metal plate like the one outside the tiny room, but this one had an arrow pointing up and one pointing down. Another plate had two rows of numbered buttons. Her forehead wrinkled as she considered the buttons. Drawing her gun, she reached out and tapped the barrel on the number fourteen. It was her lucky number.

The floor dropped and, as quickly, sprang back up. She felt as if her stomach was still going down. She staggered back against the wall and gripped the rail that ran around three walls of the room. Gritting her teeth, she pointed her gun at the door and waited for the ride to end. Something was sure to happen then.

With another brief lurch, the small room stopped moving. The door whooshed open again and she jumped out into the outer room before she could be closed in a second time. Crouched against the wall, she quickly scanned the dimly lit aisles that stretched out before her. Silence. Nothing happened.

She was in one massive room, at least half the size of the underground chamber. The room was like a huge stable that was blocked out with individual little stalls. But there was a fine, pale green carpet on the floor and not the faintest smell of animals. Suspecting correctly that the stalls were meant for human use, she didn't let herself imagine what happened within them.

Her pistol held ready, she walked along the narrow hallways between the rooms, looking for anything familiar or comforting. There was nothing. This place had to be hell. The more she walked, the worse she felt. Her skin tingled and her nerves were on edge. But damned if she was going to get back in that little room with the sliding door that brought her here. Her stomach still threatened to turn over at the thought of it.

She reached the far wall before she realized it. By a trick of the lighting, the room had seemed to continue on into its reflection in the bank of windows. Stepping up to the glass, she slid her gun into its holster and looked out. A sudden wave of vertigo made her squeeze her eyes shut. In a far more disturbing illusion, the starry night sky seemed to sweep out both above and below her. She pushed herself backwards away from the window and sat down hard. When her head continued to reel, she lay on her back and opened her eyes. Picking a line between long, off-white ceiling tiles, she stared at one spot until the room stopped spinning.

"Jesus Christ, how far up did I come?" she whispered, her voice dry like sand pouring over stone. Weak as the sound was, it reassured her. "But it ain't possible. I can't be above the stars."

She crawled back to the window, and this time, looked up, instead of down. The stars were there, faint, but glowing a pale blue-white. They were distant, as far above her head as they had always been. She lowered her gaze some and looked out level from her vantage point. There were no stars floating at her height. So what was beneath her had to have another explanation.

Tipping her Stetson far back on her head, she peered down. Thousands of lights in a myriad of colors twinkled, flashed, and flowed below her. She felt the spin again, but resisted it. The beauty of the sight calmed her anxiety. Open mouthed, she stared transfixed as an understanding of what she was seeing crept into her mind. It was a town, a city, spread for mile upon mile on the earth somewhere beneath her. This town was enormous, bigger than her own Denver. It was bigger than New Orleans, the biggest city she'd seen. It was city upon city upon city. Down there, it must never be nighttime, not with all those lights.

"But how can they burn so many lights without catching afire?" As soon as she spoke, she thought of the cold, burning lights in the underground room. Somebody had invented something that gave off light, she surmised. But she was unable to conjure up the words to even guess at it all.

A thought took hold of her, a slow, growing suspicion that was too far-fetched to be believed, but was the only explanation her imagination could muster. She backed away from the window and walked along the nearest row of rooms. In the fourth one, she found what she was looking for—she lifted the book-like calendar from the desk and read the date.

February 24th. That much was right.

She dropped the calendar onto the desk and stumbled back to the windows. The glass was cold as she leaned her body full against the window, her palms pressed hard, trying to absorb the full meaning of what lay beyond her.

"Jesus Christ." With her lips near the cold glass, her breath fanned out white beside her cheek. "I busted through time."

∩   ∩   ∩   ∩   ∩

The alarm rang at seven. Melia reached out to slap it off and felt nothing but carpet. It took her a moment to remember why she was on the floor and naked. Before the annoying tone could awaken Dana, she found the clock's cord and unplugged it from the wall.

Dana's leg was between hers and her hand was warm on Melia's belly. The skin to skin connection felt so real, the only thing real about the woman next to her. Melia savored it, snuggling her thin body within Dana's strong embrace, until she realized that she was drifting back to sleep. Opening her eyes wide, she tried to imagine what kind of pattern the carpet had imprinted on her back.

Dana groaned as Melia pulled away from her and sat up. Melia took another blanket from the bed and added it to the one that covered Dana. She knelt for a moment, looking at the face, quiet in sleep, the force that drove the thoughts behind it hidden. Dana just looked like a woman. An ordinary, good-looking woman; young, with a slightly crooked smile, but with no special power. Melia imagined her in leather, a stiff black collar turned up to her long, fine jawbone. She imagined her in a faded blue shirt, a cowboy hat pulled down low over her forehead, the slight curl of her dark blonde hair tucked behind her ear. When Dana's deep green eyes were closed, Melia could imagine her as anything. When her eyes were open, Melia was lost and couldn't imagine anything but sex. Taking and giving. They never talked. Really, they had nothing to talk about.

Melia pushed herself upright and leaned for a moment against the long bookcase that covered one wall of the bedroom. She considered going to the spare room and working out, but she was afraid that the movement of the weight machine cables would wake Dana. Anyway, she was too light-headed. They had skipped dinner.

As she shuffled to the bathroom, she ran her fingers along the spines of her most precious belongings. Just to touch the books made her feel better about the day. It would be nice to ditch work, stay home, and read away the hours, but with Dana here that was impossible. She had to shower and get out of the apartment before Dana awakened or she would have to call in sick again. She decided to phone during her lunch break and try to convince Dana to be gone before she finished work. A good decision, but one Melia knew was pointless. Dana would stay until she got bored and that could take a week, a month . . . all Melia could say for sure was that she'd have little influence on the matter.

She wished Dana would at least get a job, it would surely help to relieve some of the tension that built during the long hours Melia was at work. Just her luck, the only thing Dana didn't need was money, and Melia suspected that Dana had never worked a day in all of her 33 years.

The shower was hot and Melia closed her eyes in the rising steam. Her pale skin stung from the heat and she felt it was purifying her. Not that she felt dirty . . . She put her head under and tried to relax as the water ran through her shoulder-length brown hair and over her back.

"I'll move," she whispered to herself. "I'll get an unlisted number." The words were a mantra she repeated each time Dana came back into her life. She knew there was no point in speaking them. There was no hiding from Dana, because Melia wouldn't quit her job, and Dana could always persuade the front desk to put her through.

Melia dressed quietly, donning her standard khaki pants, black button-up shirt and black Rykas. As she cinched her leather belt, she looked into the bedroom one last time. Dana hadn't moved. Melia saw her unfinished novel lying on the floor beside the bed, half under Dana's long leg. She debated the wisdom of retrieving it to read during lunch break. If Dana woke up and saw it in her hand, she'd be furious. There was no point in looking for trouble, she'd be better off stopping by the book stand in the hotel lobby next to her office building and buying another.

Ω   Ω   Ω   Ω   Ω

"Hey, Ms. Ellis."

Melia glanced across the marble-floored lobby at the security booth of her office building in the Denver Tech Center. The big glass box took up half of the entryway that opened from the street. "Hey, Aaron."

"You still reading those crappy Westerns?"

Melia held up her latest purchase and smiled. "You still reading those shitty horror stories?"

"Damn right. You should read the one I'm working on now," Aaron's eyes shone at the fear he was sure it would inspire. "It's got to be the goriest thing I have ever read."

"I don't know how you do it," Melia shook her head. "Working here in this empty building all night."

"It just adds to the spice."

Melia stepped up to the booth and contemplated the cover of the book Aaron held to the glass. A lurid painting of orange eyes beneath black brows and a blood-covered forehead made her cringe.

"Lovely."

"You're here kinda early, aren't you?"

"Yeah," Melia grimaced and let the expression speak for her. Though he knew just enough of her personal life to be a nuisance, Aaron unfailingly understood when not to question her any farther. "And you're here kind of late."

"I'm doing the two to ten this week. Covering for Alfie."

"Oh, is she sick?"

"No, she's trying to get pregnant. Her husband's tired of trying it in the daytime. He says no sperm in its right mind would be out before dark anyway."

"That is entirely more than I ever wanted to know about Alfie."

Aaron laughed at her distaste. "Well, you asked."

Melia grimaced again.

"Hey, your eyes are really red. They look like hell." Aaron smiled to take the sting from his words. "Want me to send out for some eye drops?"

"No, CompInnovations has a whole vat upstairs. In fact, all the water coolers on the fourteenth floor are really full of Visine," she teased.

"Ugh. Thanks for the warning. You want me to tell you what that stuff will do to your digestive system?"

Melia shook her head. "I've got to go."

"Exactly."

"Enough, Aaron," Melia pleaded. "I haven't eaten for a while, and if you don't shut up, I never will."

Aaron laughed. "Better get up there to your damn computer then. No bodily functions to concern yourself with there."

Melia nodded with mock enthusiasm and walked to the elevator. Closing her eyes to the bright lights of the lobby, she pushed the button by feel and waited for the elevator to lift up from the underground parking garage. A whole month of constant inversion kept Denver's brown cloud of smog pressed down against the plains, yet people still insisted on driving to work instead of taking the bus. During inversions, she only drove when she had no choice, and she didn't understand people's attitudes. When the elevator door opened, she avoided looking into anyone's face; she was afraid they would sense her disapproval.

The ride to the fourteenth floor was too quick. She didn't have time to do any more than reread the teaser at the front of her new book. Going on to the first page, she read it as she passed the reception area and threaded her way through the maze of cubicles. Each held a desk, a chair, a computer terminal, and a two-foot square bulletin board which held the only permitted personal belongings. Most of the booths she passed had the boards plastered with pictures and comic strips cut from the paper. A few held ribbons or plaques won as coding awards for programming. Melia kept her awards stuffed in the bottom drawer under the well-read emergency novels she hoarded for the days when she couldn't bring a book for lunch break. Her bulletin board was bare and her desk held nothing but her computer and a narrow black nameplate with "Melia Ellis" embossed in gold.

When she reached her cubicle, she put her book in the drawer, shrugged off her baggy, black-wool pea coat and draped it over the back of her chair. She sat down and, hooking her toes under the edge of her desk, leaned the chair back as far as it would go. Staring up at the ceiling tiles, Melia breathed in and out deeply, giving herself two full minutes of relaxation before turning on her monitor and spending the next eight to ten hours writing computer code.

She never saw the cool, blue eyes that stared down at her.

Two

Dana woke shortly before noon. She woke with a smile, as she always did after spending the night with Melia. There was something about that woman. Something deep in her dark brown eyes that always seemed to be looking so far away. Something that intrigued Dana, exciting her and challenging her. She burned just being in the same room with Melia.

Closing her eyes, Dana let Melia's image fill her mind. She was beautiful, in an off-hand way that Dana found hard to explain. Melia's brown hair had just enough of a wave to keep it off of her high forehead and she was forever trying to keep her long bangs tucked behind her ears when she was concentrating. Dana loved to break that concentration whenever she could, just to force Melia back into the real world where Dana lived.

Dana thought of the way Melia's muscles tightened when they made love, how her jawbone would tense, accentuating the hollows under her high cheekbones and causing her wide full lips to part slightly. She loved the look of Melia's neck and shoulders when Melia leaned her head back, how her slender muscles and sharp bones would strain against her pale skin . . . Dana pushed the image from her mind, cursing herself for not waking up when Melia did, and wasting the opportunity to make her stay home from work.

Dana stretched, her body half under the bed they had not quite reached the night before. As she bent her knee she felt something slide past her leg. Reaching down, she found a thin paperback novel.

"Didn't need this fucking thing last night, did you, Mel?" Dana sneered at the hokey picture of a black-clad gunslinger on the cover. She could not comprehend how someone as intelligent as Melia could enjoy reading such shit. Hefting the book, she considered pitching it across the room to see if she could throw it hard enough to make it break apart as it hit the far wall. Instead, she put it back on the floor and slid it under the night table.

Without sitting up, she took the phone from the bedside table and ordered pizza. She contemplated calling Melia at work, but decided on a quick shower instead. Melia was probably taking her lunch break now, anyway.

Stretching again as she stood, Dana enjoyed the feel of her body. She was comfortable nude, comfortable in the way her body looked, and her posture showed it. Many women took her attitude to be vanity, even arrogance, but to Dana it was merely satisfaction with what she'd made of the body she'd been given. She worked hard to keep herself two notches above being in shape, and that hard work allowed her an occasional excess, like eating pizza for breakfast, if that was what she craved.

Unaware that she was copying Melia's movements from earlier that morning, Dana dragged her fingertips along the books lining the bedroom wall. She stopped for a moment and studied the shelves. There were six rows of books and she estimated that each row held at least one hundred books. She shook her head in wonder. And there were two more bookcases in the living room.

Most of the books here were Westerns. Dana had never read a Western novel, but she'd seen enough John Wayne movies to think she'd experienced all possible plot lines.

As she turned to go into the bathroom, her attention was caught by a paper sticking out from between two of the books. It was the top edge of a greeting card. Dana pulled it out and read it. It was a tenth birthday card to Melia from her mother. She couldn't help but laugh at the picture of a cowboy-hatted, gun-toting duck that struck a menacing pose on the front of the card. Inside, Melia's mom had written, I hope you enjoy the books. Love forever, Jewel.

Dana knew that Jewel had died sometime when Melia was still a kid, but obviously she'd lived long enough to pass on the obsession with books to her daughter. Melia didn't know who her father was, and Dana doubted that Jewel even knew. She shrugged and closed the card. That kind of upbringing was as far from hers as imaginable, but she made no judgements. She wanted Melia, and that was all that mattered to her.

As she started to slide the card back between the books, she realized it was a marker. She'd seen Melia select books from the shelves, apparently her choices were not random. Melia probably started at the top and read her way through all of the books before starting over again.

"That woman is fucking nuts." Dana wanted to laugh, but the thought was just too bizarre. She could not understand such voracious reading as merely a hunger. To her, it was an unhealthy addiction. The amount of money Melia spent on books every year could probably buy her a new car and a substantial down payment on a decent house, instead of this old, cramped pseudo-Victorian, with its dingy one-car garage which held Melia's even dingier old Honda. Dana considered her impulse to return the marker to a different book on the shelf, but discarded the thought as too petty.

Melia's unnamed cat prowled the bedroom. As he dragged his side along Dana's calves, she laughed and picked him up, loving the feel of his fur on her naked body. The two of them had a love/hate relationship fueled by jealousy. When Melia was out of the picture, they got along fine.

"You want to shower with me?"

The cat purred.

"You want to share pizza with me?"

Dana thought the purr increased in volume. She walked into the bathroom and put him on the sink counter. She held his head in her hands and looked into his impassive yellow-green eyes.

"Now, we'll make a deal. I'll give you pizza, but when Mel comes home you get one scratch on the belly and then you disappear."

He lifted one side of his lips and showed a long ivory fang. His tailed twitched.

"All right then, no pizza." She let him go and hissed. He tore from the room.

∩   ∩   ∩   ∩   ∩

What had happened to her?

Yesterday was as clear as ice on a water bucket. She remembered everything said and done. The switch between her time and this one had happened without a ripple. One moment ran smoothly into the next. For the fifth time, she went over all that had occurred. She'd spent the night and most of the morning in Lily's room . . .

"Parker McCallem, you're gonna get yourself killed."

Parker looked up at Lily's reflection in the clouded mirror and smiled. She continued to clean her gun. Bullets and a blackened rag were spread across the top of the bureau. The small room was practically filled with Lily's feather bed.

"You could make more money workin' here with me."

"As a whore?" Parker laughed loudly. Her blue eyes sparkled under the dark shadow of her brows. She was in an ornery mood, but the feeling was good and her laughter so contagious that Lily couldn't help but join in.

"You're very good looking. If you just let your hair grow and dressed decently—"

"You mean, indecently," Parker interrupted.

"Damn you, you know what I mean." Lily pouted as she said the words.

Parker looked back at her and relented. She put down the gun and went to lie beside Lily on the bed. Pulling down the lace bedspread to expose the smooth white skin above Lily's breast, she smiled again.

"Don't you give me that starved animal look," Lily warned. "I'm sore from doin' it, and we need to talk."

"*We* don't need to talk," Parker trailed her fingers across Lily's warm skin. "Just *you* do."

Lily snagged her hand and held it on top of the bedspread. "People are startin' to suspect that you're in with that gang, Parker. They're gonna catch on that you're the stakeout man."

"Man?" Parker teased.

Lily slugged her in the stomach, hard. Parker closed her eyes briefly, but her smile didn't falter.

"You listen to me. You could make a good livin' here. And I'll take care of you."

"Sorry, Lily. I just don't believe in chargin' money for

it." Parker got out of the bed, adjusted her jeans, and slid on her boots.

"Oh, so that means you're not gonna pay me for all night?"

Taking out her wallet, Parker removed a few bills and put them on the nightstand. "I'm sayin', I'm not gonna charge *you*."

"You little shit ass!" Laughing, Lily scooped up the money and threw it back at Parker, who let it fall to the floor. "You think you're that damn good, huh?"

"I never noticed you turnin' me away."

"You're confusin' pity with passion."

Boots and all, Parker leaped on the middle of the bed and wrestled a screaming Lily into a bear hug. "That mouth of yours is gonna get you in trouble," she warned.

"It'll get you out of trouble if you listen to me."

Parker kissed her full lips hard. She waited for Lily to return the kiss before moving her mouth away. She held her nose against Lily's. "Now don't confuse that kiss with passion," she whispered. "I'm just tryin' to shut you up."

Only the tangled bed sheets prevented Lily from kneeing her in the crotch.

She'd actually given thought to Lily's words as she rode out of Denver toward the Rockies. Lily's place could be fun, it would surely be warmer than riding out this time of the year. And having Lily close at hand every day would be blissful. But Parker knew she was too selective in her bed mates to get along in that life. She was good in a fight and could handle her pistol better than most. Maybe Lily would consider taking her on as a bouncer. Her reputation as an outlaw would be a benefit in a job like that.

Parker rode her buckskin gelding hard, angling toward the foothills south of Boulder. The boys had planned a rendezvous this afternoon to discuss what she'd learned in town. They'd be none too happy at what she had to offer. Owen Lane's idea to rob the opera house was foolish. The take would be too low, the quarters too tight, and the back door too far away. The job was not worth the risk. She knew it was the kind of affair where someone ended up dead, and she had no desire to be involved in any more of those.

Parker rode along the trail with her black Stetson pulled low over her forehead. It was cold, her shoulders were stiff from hunching up against the wind, and she wasn't paying attention to her surroundings. She heard the ricochet of a bullet off a rock beside the trail and instantly knew it for what it was. Before the sound of the shot reached her, she was off her horse and belly down on the ground. But the next shot was already on its way and took her horse square in the forehead. It grunted, took a few more steps, then folded its legs and fell to the ground with a thud.

Squirming across the cold ground like a snake, Parker tried to get closer to the cover of a grouping of rocks, and at the same time, get a glimpse of whoever was shooting at her. She took off her hat and lifted her head just enough to peek through a crack between the rocks. It was hard to say where the shots had come from. A shallow gully ran across the road about thirty feet ahead of her position. Beyond that were a few clumps of sage brush and rock outcroppings like the one she hid behind. Suddenly, from the gully, a puff of someone's heated breath rose up white in the frigid air. She pulled her pistol and held it pointed at the spot.

Patience was always the sign of the winner in this kind of situation. Experience had taught her that the first to move was usually the first to die. Parker held her hat brim over her mouth and breathed down into the crown. Not more than ten minutes passed before she heard voices coming from the gully. She couldn't make out most of the words, but she gathered that at least three men were discussing whether or not they had killed her.

The man who believed she was dead abruptly stood and started to climb from his position. Parker couldn't believe her eyes.

"Jesus Christ, Owen," she yelled over the top of the rocks. "Don't you even look before you start shootin' at someone?"

Ready to push herself to her feet, she was startled to see Owen dive back into the gully and three rifle barrels come back up.

"Why, you sons of bitches. You meanin' to kill me?"

"I got enough of you, McCallem. I'm done with your talk," Owen yelled back.

"What in hell are you goin' on about?" Parker was genuinely confused. "Markie, what's he goin' on about?"

Markie kept his mouth shut.

"I'm talkin' now, Park. I'm done with you determinin' our jobs. I'm sick of you decidin' what goes and what doesn't." He punctuated his sentence with another shot. It went well over her head.

"Well, goddamn. Run me off then. Kick me out. You don't have to kill me before I get the picture." Parker held her gun steady as she spoke. Her pistol was a six-shooter. Even up against only three of them, she couldn't afford to waste a shot. She glanced over to her horse. There was a box of shells in her saddle bag, but there was no cover between the rocks and her horse.

"You're not leavin' this gang alive. You'd be to the law before I could drop a hat."

"Now what makes you think the law wants you any more than it wants me?"

"They always go easy on a woman," Markie offered.

Parker laughed. The sound was as cold as the air. "It's not too late to back out of this situation," she responded coolly.

"It is for me," Owen answered her. "I mean to kill you."

"I wasn't talkin' to you, Owen. I was talkin' to Bob and Markie."

"I'll kill the first man to step out of here," Owen warned. No one moved.

Parker looked around in desperation. Patience be damned, she had to move before this stalemate wore on too long. If they decided to rush her, she wouldn't be able to kill them all before they got to her. And knowing Owen, he would send Bob or Markie out to take her bullets while he waited to pick her off from under cover.

The gully the men hid in deepened as it approached the foothills, becoming a small canyon separating two bluffs. The gully was only one of several that branched off the canyon. As luck would have it, another one no bigger than a ditch curved around and came up behind and to the right of her. If she could keep her head down, she might be able to scoot back and get into that ditch. That way, she could take the ditch back to the fork and come up alongside the men and take them by surprise.

Without hesitation, she began crawling backwards. There was a tense moment when she thought she'd been seen. A volley of shots rang out, but none came near her. She assumed they were trying to break her nerve and flush her out of cover.

Parker's foot reached out over space and she gratefully pushed back and dropped into the ditch. She wiped her forehead and was surprised to find she was sweating. Even worse, her hands were shaking like they had on her first holdup. With such convincing evidence, she had to admit that she was scared. Thinking about what she had to do only made it worse, so she didn't allow herself to pause. In an awkward crouch, she ran forward to find the branch gully that would take her back toward Owen and the others.

But Parker was not the only one to think of that plan. When she turned the corner at the fork in the canyon, she came face to face with Bob Weeks.

She'd never pulled off a shot so quickly. Before Bob could finish his gasp of surprise at seeing her, she'd nailed him in the forehead. He stood for a moment, blinking as though the sun was burning too bright in his eyes, then he fell forward onto her. Panic rising, she struggled to push him off. He was not the first dying man she'd seen, but he was the first she'd killed. And he was her friend. She could smell the heat of his blood in the frigid air.

Loud shouting rose up from the other men's position. They knew she'd escaped from the rocks. She had no time to do anything but pull Bob's pistol from his hand and run. Her boots dug deep into the soft sand as she ran toward the mountains. If she could make it to the trees, she could lose them.

The walls of the canyon were soon well above her head. The fear that she was running into a trap overcame her fear of the men behind her. If the canyon were to come to a sudden dead end, she'd be unable to scale the walls before they reached her. If Owen knew this ground better than she did, he already might have climbed out of the canyon and could be stalking her along the rim. She'd be an easy target on the open canyon floor. Her steps faltered for a moment, but then she continued to run. She had taken her chance and there was nothing to do but play it out.

The base of the mountain rose before her. Parker's legs were as weak as water, but ahead she could see the welcome cover of a jumble of granite boulders. She wouldn't find a better place to catch her breath and assess her situation. She ran on.

A bullet plugged into the dirt just ahead of her. Owen yelled something and she figured that he had gained the rim of the canyon. Parker staggered and fell, and his next shot whistled through the air where she had stood. Rising to a crouch, she raced on and rounded the boulders before he took aim again. She turned and fired a blind shot toward the canyon's edge.

After the echo of her gun faded away there was silence. Parker tried to breathe quietly, but the cold air tore at her laboring lungs.

"Damn you, Lily," she said through panting breath. "Why couldn't you a' been more convincing?"

Parker turned and rested her back against the solid rock. There wasn't much time or many options left for her. She knew that if something didn't change the situation for the better, time was going to run out on her. The thought of some loner stumbling across her bleached and bare bones a hundred years from now pissed her off to no end. She turned back and emptied Bob's pistol in Owen's direction.

"I'm gonna get you, Owen Lane. I'm gonna live to spit on your grave," she swore up at him. She ignored his laughter. "You, too, Markie."

"Markie's gone. That yellow belly tore outta here the minute my back was turned," Owen yelled back. "But I'll get him, too."

Parker shook her head. "Jesus Christ, he must think I'm as stupid as he is," she muttered. If Markie had left the two of them even, Owen would never have admitted it. He wasn't brave enough to face her alone. The only thing Owen's lie could mean was that Markie was working his way around to get at her from behind.

Once again she turned, this time to scan the slope behind her for a sign of Markie. A slash of dull, red color along the edge of a boulder caught her eye. She raised her gun, but then realized that the color was a symbol painted on the rock. From this distance, she couldn't make out the design. She squinted her eyes and twisted her head to no avail.

"Shit, why die curious?" Giving one more look around to be sure she was in the clear, she scrambled up the incline and slid between the painted boulder and its neighbor. She had expected a shot to follow, but none came. That worried her more than anything.

The painting was about the size of her head. A small human shaped figure with a spiral tail shook a spear at something beyond the edge of the rock. His stubby legs straddled a circle at his feet. Three jagged lines like lightning came down from the stone sky. Parker grinned and shook her head. *Those Indians and their loco weed.*

A cold breeze came down from the mountain and chilled her through. Suddenly, it seemed that the spear the figure held was pointing, pointing to something behind her. Parker turned her head slowly. There in the exposed bedrock of the mountain was a narrow crevice just wider than her body. The light that angled in seemed to suggest that the crack opened into a small cave. Parker cautiously edged up to the opening. It was a cave.

The pale sunlight didn't reach in far enough to give her an idea of the cave's size. She picked up a rock and tossed it in. It directly struck the back wall, then fell to the floor of the cave without another sound. It was just big enough to hide her.

Parker crawled back down the slope a ways and, using her hat, she brushed her footprints from the dirt as she returned to opening. Let Owen find her now. She could sit and wait, protected from the cold, until they either gave up or got within her sights.

"Come and get me, Owen," Parker challenged, pulling her hat back down tight on her head. Not waiting for his response, she ducked and backed into the cave. Her last step was over open air and she fell backwards into darkness.

Three

Five o'clock came and went and Melia stayed at her desk, nodding at her coworkers' departing "goodnights" without looking up from her screen. Nothing she was doing was so pressing that she needed to stay, but still, she lingered. She didn't feel like going home. It had nothing to do with Dana; hopefully she had disappeared again anyway. Melia simply had no desire to be there.

Restless, she poked at the keyboard, knowing that all the programming she was doing would likely have to be redone tomorrow. After eight or nine hours in front of a computer monitor, she lost the ability to recognize her errors. She printed the screen and scanned the output with a high-lighter in hand.

In the middle of a line, Melia looked up, feeling that someone was watching her. She was sure everyone else had gone, but she turned her chair slowly and looked down the hall. No one was there. She stood on her toes and looked over the partition that separated her cubicle from the next one. The supervisors' offices were empty, the block of cubicles deserted. Shaking her head, she sat again and picked up the printout. A half a page later, she realized she had no idea what she had just read. Her concentration was broken, there was no point in trying to continue.

Melia sighed and got to her feet. She put on her coat and stuffed the printouts in her pocket. Struggling to hitch up her backpack, she felt a band of tension and fatigue tighten across her shoulders. As she left her cubicle, she impulsively turned away from the elevator and walked out toward the west windows. She stood and watched as the sun quickly dropped behind the mountains. There was no sunset. Just a gray, dirty sky becoming grayer. Looking down on the city, Melia wondered why she hadn't yet moved away. Even from this height she could see the filth and imagine the uncomfortable press of people. She should be on a mountain or on some lonesome ranch out on the prairie. Her life was wasted here in Denver.

She sighed again and leaned her head against the glass. A swelling headache pounded in her temple. *If* she could go home, she'd take a long bath, eat some pasta, and read until she nodded off. If she could go home . . . but with Dana there, they would fight or make love. Both prospects were simply too emotional for Melia to face right now.

A footstep scuffed on the carpet behind her. Perhaps it was her edginess, or the earlier feeling of being watched, but the sound startled her into a panic. She whirled around and stepped away from the window.

"Ms. Ellis, I'm sorry if I frightened you." A square-chested security guard stood before her. He nodded his crew cut in a short, apologetic bow. She thought she recognized him, but the name on his badge didn't ring a bell.

"Oh, it's okay. My mind was . . . elsewhere."

"I understand. I'm just making the once through."

"Once through?" She looked up into his good-natured smile.

"Just checking the building to make sure there's no one here that shouldn't be. We do it every night after business hours."

"Oh, yes. I've noticed Aaron doing that. I never heard what it was called." Melia pulled her coat tighter and smiled stiffly. Not sure how to end the conversation, she shifted away from him.

"Are you all right?"

"Yeah, I'm fine. I just remembered, I'm supposed to meet a friend at six," Melia lied.

He laughed. "Well, you're only twelve minutes late."

He had a nice laugh; the sound melted her uneasiness away. "Guess I'd better hurry."

"Oh, Ms. Ellis, before you go, I know you're sometimes here at odd hours. Were you in the office last night?"

"Mm-hmm." Melia nodded. "I believe I was . . ."

The guard smiled. His expression revealed a patient disbelief. In his opinion, people who could dig into the guts of computers and make them do what they wanted often didn't seem to share reality with the rest of the human race. "Yesterday was Sunday. Did you come in this weekend?"

"Oh, Sunday. This is Monday." She shook her head. "No, I didn't come in at all this weekend."

"Then it wasn't you."

"What wasn't me?"

"Oh, it's nothing. Just curious." He gestured toward the elevator as if to encourage her to go.

Melia gladly took his encouragement and walked away.

Once on the street, Melia was again at loose ends. She walked past her bus stop and continued down the street. From the pay phone on the corner she called for a cab to take her to Woman To Woman, her best friend Chris' bookstore. It was her favorite place in all of Denver.

The warm light from the store windows spilled into the street. The small building was an old house renovated to become a comfortable and inviting bookstore. Whenever she came here, Melia felt she was arriving at a cherished family home. She knew each of the clerks and at least half of the customers personally. They knew her as well, and the clerks often made purchase orders from publishers with her tastes in mind.

When she pushed open the door, she was greeted with a warmth she never felt when coming into her own home. Melia smiled and breathed in the sharp scent of sandlewood. The shelves along the front walls had books interspersed with lighted candles and small vases of flowers. The walls without bookcases were papered with bright posters of women authors and artists. Unobtrusive, soft music came just within hearing.

A muscular young woman with skin the color of strong, hot tea with a touch of cream looked up from behind the glass counter as Melia walked forward. She smiled broadly, revealing a narrow gap between her white front teeth and a sparkle of silver from her tongue. Her ears were outlined with rows of bright rings and her neck was laced with deep black, tribal tattoos. Despite the familiar markings, Melia stared at the woman for a brief moment before recognizing her.

"Langley, you shaved your head!"

"Yeah, how do you like it?" Langley smiled like some furless Cheshire cat.

"I've got to feel it before I can say for sure . . ."

Langley stood and leaned over the counter, offering her shining scalp to Melia. "I hope your hands aren't too cold."

"I took a cab." Melia cupped both hands to the sides of Langley's head and slid her palms back to her neck. One stroke was not enough. She continued to rub. "Mm, it's so smooth."

"Kinda sexy?"

"Not kinda', definitely. Wish I were so brave."

"Razor's still sharp," Langley teased.

A voice from the back of the shop called out, "Lang, are you trying to shave the customers again? If you're not careful, I'm going to make you wear a wig 'til that hair of yours grows back."

"She's so jealous." Langley winked and grinned.

"I heard that!"

Langley laughed. "She didn't hear anything. She always says that just in case I have a smart remark."

"And you usually do," Melia noted.

"Believe it or not, that's why she hired me. It was getting too stale and, I don't know, bookish,' around here."

"Should I resent that remark?"

"Well, if you spent any more time here, I'd advise you just to buy the place."

Melia reached over and playfully slapped the top of Langley's head. It gave a very satisfying smack. Laughing, Langley stood to her full six feet of height, effectively removing the top of her head from Melia's reach.

"You know, if I did buy this place, I would be your boss." Melia looked the woman up and down as if she were appraising her worth. "That puts a new light on it, doesn't it?"

"Gosh, then we could never have that ill-fated love affair we're always talking about."

"*You're* always talking about, you mean. I've accepted that you're just too much woman for me."

Langley struck a seductive pose that was somewhere between Mae West and Mel Gibson. Melia just shook her head.

"I guess you'll have to settle for whatever it was you came here for."

"I want to talk to Chris."

"Hey, Mel's here," Langley yelled to the woman in the back room, then turned to help a customer who approached the counter with an armload of books.

"Melia, come on back," Chris called out.

Melia walked into the back room, stepping over stacks of books and around cardboard boxes. The room was littered with Chris' "organized clutter." She was the only one who knew where to find anything back there. The clerks were afraid to even enter the room. Even more intimidating was Chris' computer system. Langley had helped Chris install so many high-tech add-ons that the rest of the staff insisted the computer had gained intelligence and was not only running the store but the whole Denver Metro area. Even Melia, who knew programming inside and out, was apprehensive of some of the hardware Langley had wired into it.

Chris dropped a handful of paperbacks and gave Melia a friendly squeeze. As usual, Melia felt swallowed up by the embrace.

"How's my little brain tonight?" Chris teased. She had a true respect for Melia's programming skills, regardless of the number of times she described Melia as a nerd.

"Oh, I'm okay."

"Hmpf. That must mean *she's* back in your life." Chris had no love for Dana and couldn't understand how Melia might. "Is she trying to shack up with you again?"

"I don't know." Melia leaned over and pretended interest in the titles of the paperbacks Chris had dropped. "We haven't really talked."

"And you shouldn't. You should kick her butt out." Chris' round face was turning dangerously red. "Or I'll send

Langley over and you won't even have to see her again."

"Please, don't start this," Melia asked. The conversation could only get worse. Not for the first time, Melia regretted Chris' ability to surmise all that was going on in Melia's life with little or no information to go on.

Chris glared for a moment longer, just enough to assure Melia that she meant what she said. Melia also had no doubt that Langley would be up for the confrontation. She was always up for confrontation.

"You got anything new?" Melia asked, hoping to redirect the conversation.

"Yeah, a new batch of erotica came in this morning."

"Oh, that's nice."

"Oh, that's nice," Chris mocked Melia's dry remark. "It is nice. I read an advance copy. It's a collection of all the best lesbian writers, and this stuff is really hot."

"Yes!" Langley shouted back. "So hot!"

Melia laughed and shook her head. "Well, erotica's not really my thing."

"Yeah, I know. You got that cowgirl thing going. Well . . ." Chris paused as she squatted on the floor and rummaged through a half empty box. She selected a book and held it out to Melia "How about both?"

Melia raised her eyebrows as she took the book. On the cover was a sultry-eyed woman in a black cowboy hat sitting astride a powerful steed. Melia was sold, without reading the blurbs or even the title.

"You like that picture?"

"God, yes."

"I know the artist. She works here in town and she told me she copied that from an old photograph in the museum archives. Can you believe a woman like that ever existed?"

"It's too much to hope for. It kind of makes me not

even care what the story's about."

"Well, it's a cowdyke in drag' story. Anyway, that's how the publisher described it. I thought you'd be interested."

"Yes, of course. I love Westerns, but the heterosexuality does wear thin after a while. This'll be a nice change."

Chris smiled at her excitement. "You know, you can come read it at my place. Molly's baking up a batch of bread today."

"No, I really should go home."

Chris breathed in deeply, crossed her heavy arms over her ample chest and glared at Melia for a long moment. Then, without a word, she went to the door and, after clearing away loose books and opened boxes, she pushed it closed. She gestured for Melia to take a seat on an unopened carton, then sat herself down in her computer chair. Melia felt her stomach sinking. It was time for The Talk.

"Mel, you know I care about you. We both know that you're a smart woman. And I think it's safe to say that we both know you're not too bright when it comes to relationships."

Melia tried to protest. "I don't need to hear this."

"I think you do. Now you're going to sit here and tell me why that woman is back in your house."

"I don't owe you an explanation, Chris. I don't owe you anything."

"No, you don't. But I do owe you." Chris' voice was low and emotional. The chair let out a worried squeak as she leaned toward Melia. "I wouldn't be a decent friend if I didn't at least try to make you sit down and look at this relationship and what it might cost you."

Melia slouched and put her forehead in her hand. She couldn't look Chris in the eye.

"I'm not judging you, Melia. I just want to hear you say what makes Dana right for you."

Melia opened her mouth to answer, then closed it

before speaking. How could she explain the pull she felt toward Dana? How could she describe the passion Dana inspired, the lust? And desire as strong as Dana's could be expected to include other strong emotions. Anger, violence —these were as much a part of Dana as the passion. But Chris had been Melia's friend since she was a little girl. She'd been there when her mother died. She was like a sister, and Melia knew she must try to answer.

"She loves me," Melia finally whispered.

Chris paused. "She has a strange way of showing it."

"Come on, Chris. You're not being fair." Melia straightened her back and tried to look calmly into Chris' eyes. "She only hit me one time."

"She only hit you one time," Chris repeated the words, her tone flat. She again breathed deeply before speaking. "As if one time was not one too many. But that's not all there is to it. For more than six months I've been seeing you come in here and I see the bruises on your arms or your neck. Lord knows where else."

"It's not her fault."

"God damn it!" Chris pounded her heavy fist on the desk, sending the mouse flying. "Don't you ever defend her that way."

"You don't understand the situation."

"You're damn right I don't. So this is your chance to enlighten me. Why do you put up with her?"

"It's just her intensity; she doesn't even know she's doing it. But she makes me *feel*." Melia felt her heart start to pound. She was afraid that Chris would hear it, or see the sweat beginning to form on her forehead. Her nervousness made the words pour from her. "She says I don't feel, I don't respond. It's not her fault. I ignore her. I read too much. She just wants to be close to me. She just wants me to feel love for her like she feels for me."

Melia stood and paced distractedly through the maze of boxes. Chris said nothing to interrupt her.

"I want it. I want to feel things, to feel life, as strongly as she does. She savors every damn moment. Everything is good to her, no matter how bad or strange. I want to feel that way. Like I belong in this world somehow." Melia rubbed her forehead before continuing.

"But I can't. I don't fit. I forget to look around me, I forget the people who are with me. I . . . neglect my relationships and they die. Well, Dana won't let this one die."

"This one needs to die."

Melia turned on her, shouting. "Don't you understand? Haven't you heard a thing I've said? She makes me *feel*. No one else has ever made me feel."

Chris stood and caught Melia in her arms. She stopped Melia's pacing and held her still, although she struggled against the confinement. Chris spoke as kindly as her anger would allow. "You're the one that doesn't understand, Mel. If you loved her, you would feel it. She wouldn't have to hurt you to make you pay attention. When it's love, you'd go to the ends of the earth to be with her. When it's love, no book could ever compete for your attention."

Melia refused to cry although her body shook with suppressed emotion. She stood in silence until Chris released her.

"Mel, I'm sorry. I know you didn't come here to be lectured." Chris brushed Melia's hair back from her face and tried to look into her eyes. Melia turned her head away. "I needed to say something. I needed to hear your reasons. I don't have to like them."

"You don't have to like her, either."

"And I don't. But I'll accept that she gives you something you need." Chris turned away. She picked up the book she had given Melia from the floor and handed it back to her.

"I'll buy this one for you."

"Thanks, but it's not necessary."

"It'll make me feel better. Please?"

"All right." Melia relented and let her hand touch Chris' arm lightly. "I do appreciate your concern. I just think it's misguided."

"I love you, Mel. We all love you." Chris spread her arms as if to include the whole city.

"I know you do." Melia cradled the book to her chest. "I should go now."

Chris let her walk to the door before she spoke again. "You need to know that if she ever hits you again, I will call the police."

Melia nodded. "Thank you," she whispered as she left the room.

Outside the snow had begun to fall. Melia walked blindly for several blocks. She reached a pay phone and stared up into the curtain of white as she dialed. As she let the cold flakes drop on her face, she waited to hear Dana's voice.

"Melia?" Dana answered. Melia convinced herself that the sharpness of her tone was from worry.

"Hey, girl. Would you like to pick me up?"

Dana laughed. "Anytime, love. Just tell me when and where."

"Now." Melia closed her eyes to keep the tears from rolling down her freezing cheeks. "Just here and now."

Four

As Melia waited in the falling snow half the city away, Parker woke with a start. Her head dropped off the pillow she'd made of her wadded-up coat and knocked against the beam. She had dreamed of rolling over and falling through one of the ceiling tiles. And falling and falling without end. She clutched the beam and stared wide-eyed at the wooden flooring above her, the disorientation short-lived but frightening.

Her legs were cramped from sleeping curled in a ball. It was impossible to stretch out in the corner where the beams came together. The hideout was dark. The dim light illuminating the room below her didn't shine up into her area and the silence told her she was alone. Pulling herself into a sitting position, she rubbed her legs vigorously. As soon as some feeling returned, she lifted the nearest tile and let herself down to the floor below. She was starving.

Her observations of earlier that day had taught her where to find food. Parker went to the nearest desk and started pulling open drawers. Her efforts were rewarded by the discovery of something called a granola bar. It looked none too edible, but it was sweet and her hunger didn't allow her to be choosy.

A thorough search of the next few cubicles provided her with a small stash of food. Beside each desk was a small metal can, lined with a strange sort of bag. She pulled a clean one away from a can and held it up to the light. It was like cloth, but thin and cold and she could see right through it. When she rubbed it between her fingertips, it felt almost alive as it tried to cling to her hands. She poked at it, and her finger went through, puncturing the material without a sound.

Not fully approving of the bag, she nonetheless dumped her supplies into it, then stood on a desk to stuff the bag up into the ceiling space. That done, she dropped back to the floor. At the end of the hall was a water machine. All day she'd watched it with longing, imaging she could smell it, and envying those who came to drink. She took a paper cup and filled it repeatedly. It reminded her of her other too-long delayed need.

Luckily, she had also observed that ritual. While carefully exploring the crawl spaces and peeking down through the cracks between tiles, she had witnessed a man standing before a white, stone-looking trough on the wall, relieving himself. Soon after, another man entered one of a small row of cubicles. Before he closed the door, she caught a glimpse of a strange chair made of the same white material. After a few minutes, she heard the rush of water and the man left the room. She was curious why the sitting-down thing had the benefit of privacy while the standing-up thing was out in the open for all to see. What if a woman had entered while the man had himself dangling out there? Parker grinned at the imagined reaction.

After drinking another cup of water she set out to locate the privy. Navigating wasn't too hard, although everything had looked different from above. She found the room without much trouble and had her concern about the ladies' virtues answered. Little signs on separate doors made it clear that the two genders would not accidentally meet.

Parker pushed open the door marked Women and entered. Her reflection in a long line of mirrors made her jump. The mirror image was remarkably clear. She could see every wrinkle and tear in her shirt and jeans. Lily's inexpert haircut drew a dark, jagged line across her forehead. It was so real that if someone was to stand beside her, Parker would have a hard time judging which was the genuine thing and which was reflection. She took off her hat and leaned forward, looking closely at the glass. Tanned skin covered her broad cheekbones and her strong, square jaw. Her lips had a suprisingly feminine curve that should have looked out of place in the rugged strength of her face, but did not.

Smiling to see herself so curious, Parker noticed little lines branching off from the corners of her eyes. "Never noticed that before," she muttered, not completely disappointed with how they made her look. The lines suggested she was older and wiser than her 27 years, but she suspected they had come more from squinting into the sun than any kind of wisdom.

Letting her smile fade, she inspected her stern and serious expression. She nodded coolly. Impressive. On an impulse she stepped back and dropped her hand, whipping her six-shooter out of its holster. Not really that quick a draw, but she was satisfied regardless. It looked good and the hand that held the pistol pointed right between her reflected eyes was rock steady.

After putting the gun back in the holster and clamping her hat back on, she pushed open the nearest stall. Before she dropped her pants and sat down she needed to figure out how the water was replaced. To her relief, the set up was pretty much self-explanatory. A little metal lever stuck out from the side of the works and when she pushed it, the water rushed in through an unseen pipe. A little roll of incredibly soft paper was kindly placed on the wall. She felt a momentary pride at the inventiveness of this future generation.

When Parker finished, she went straight to the row of basins along the wall. She knew their purpose and was looking forward to getting some of the stink of the underground room from her skin. There were two knobs that she expected would start the water. One knob had a blue dot on top and the other, a red dot. Her mouth dropped a little. It was too much to be believed, even in the future, but she suspected that they had somehow arranged to have hot water on demand, running right to their basin. She twisted the knob and was quickly rewarded with a steaming flow.

"Jesus Christ. I could get used to this."

Parker added some cold water to the hot until the temperature was perfect. Taking off her hat, she plunged her head under the spout and soaked her short, black hair. It felt so good that she decided to strip off her shirt and wash her whole upper body. What she wanted was a nice, hot bath, but this would certainly do.

Finished in the privy, Parker went back to the main room. Snow was falling silently through the darkness and she was drawn to the windows and the flowing lights below. Washed, fed, and rested, she could look on the city with less fear, but she was still satisfied to stay right where she was. No desire to go down among those lights lived within her. Still, she knew that ultimately she would have to find more sustaining, healthy food and someone she could talk to about her situation. She'd never done well with extended periods of isolation. With a shrug, she turned away from the window.

That river would be crossed when she came to it. No point in fretting about it now.

Her hair still dripping water, she paced back through the rows of cubicles. She came upon one familiar to her; she had spent several hours watching the woman who occupied it and she recognized its singular barrenness. It was a cold and unwelcoming place, even among the hundred lifeless cubicles that surrounded it. There was no personality here, no human warmth. Despite its lack of hospitality, Parker pulled out the chair and sat down. She put her knees together and scooted up to the desk. Her holster bumped against the side drawer and she shifted to move it aside.

A black nameplate sat on the back side of the desk, its golden letters reading: Melia Ellis. Parker picked it up; it was lighter than it looked, confirming her suspicion that the gold was not real. She scratched it idly with her fingernail. The woman, this Melia Ellis, seemed odd to Parker's eye, but it was hard to predict what would be normal in this time Parker found herself in.

Melia had been in no hurry to leave. Parker wondered what could be so bad out there that she would be willing to stay in this strange place long after everyone else had left. Watching, Parker had noticed Melia's habit of looking up from her work and gazing into a far off, invisible distance. Each time, she seemed to be waiting, for a sight, a sound, or maybe someone to look back at her. Parker found the expression to be painfully touching and hoped that there was someone this woman could go to for a response to her need.

The machine on the desk was lighted. The glass face of it had a thin line of color that tossed and fell constantly. Parker found herself mesmerized by the movement. It never seemed to repeat. She put a cautious finger to the glass and when her touch met it there was a quick pop and a sting.

Snatching her hand back, she stuck her finger into her mouth. The machine scared her and, this time, she believed that her curiosity had better give way to the fear.

Shaking her head to break the spell of that bouncing line, Parker stood up. The chair rolled back away from her and bumped the wall of the cubicle. Parker left it and resumed her pacing of the halls.

Down one hall at the end, she could see a light that spelled the word EXIT. She walked toward the door below it and saw more writing. "Fire escape," she read aloud. "In case of fire, use stairs." She turned the knob and pushed. The door was heavy, but it opened. The stairwell was lit with too bright, white lighting. Stairs reeled out both above and below her, and they seemed to have no end. Parker stepped forward to lean out over the railing and look down. She hoped to see the bottom of the spiral.

Behind her, the door closed with a clash. The sound echoed up and down the stairwell, bouncing into itself and seeming to increase. She whirled around and grasped the handle with desperation. The fear of being trapped made her heart pound against her chest. But the door opened without a struggle. Parker sighed and let it close more carefully. She wanted to explore the stairs and maybe check out other floors, but she had to know that she could return to the area she felt was her temporary home.

Parker was halfway down the first flight of stairs when she heard the muted click. Almost letting herself believe it was her imagination, she took a few more steps before the meaning of the sound sank into her brain. It was the same click she had heard when she had carefully closed the door to the fourteenth floor. But this sound had come from below her.

Edging quietly to the rail, Parker peered over it. The shadow of an unseen person moved slowly against the steps.

Even in shadow, she recognized the shape of a gun held in the figure's hand. Touching the butt of her own gun, she glided back up the stairs to her door. She could hear the careful footsteps coming closer. With a painful slowness, she silently twisted the knob. A slight scrape that she couldn't prevent sounded as she pulled the door open. She held very still and hoped the sound had not carried.

"Is someone there?" A male voice, quavering slightly, traveled up to her.

Parker had to smile. The man was as frightened as she was herself. At least she had the benefit of knowing what she faced. She stepped through the door and let it close quietly behind her. Not waiting to see if she'd been heard, she ran to the nearest desk and used it to reach the tile that lead to her hide-out. She was up and across the ceiling before the man could enter the room. Her bag of snacks in hand, she settled into her corner and listened to him prowl the hallways below her.

∩   ∩   ∩   ∩   ∩

Aaron took the elevator back to the lobby. The idea of walking the stairs made his neck hair stand up. He had heard sounds. He had even felt a presence. There was something lurking on the fourteenth floor, he was convinced of that.

Once in the security booth, he pulled the door closed behind him and, for the first time in his three years of working in the building, he turned the lock. Sitting on his stool, he fidgeted nervously, wishing that Roger would return from his walk to the third floor lunch room. Roger had a problem with low blood sugar, or so he said, using that excuse to visit the lunch room in search of something to eat.

Aaron turned in his seat, repeatedly scanning the lobby for movement as he chewed his nails. In a motion that had become habitual, he reached over and picked up the book lying on the counter. He had the book open to his mark before he realized what he was doing. He snapped the book closed and stared down at the cover.

"Tales of the Grisly Macabre," Aaron read. He took a deep breath and sighed. His shoulders relaxed. "And I wonder why I'm encountering phantoms on the stairs."

Suddenly the doorknob rattled. Aaron jumped to his feet, struggling to release his gun from its holster. Roger saw the pistol rising and dived to the side.

"What the hell are you doing?" he yelled from his position flat on the floor.

"Man, you scared the shit out of me!" Aaron responded, clutching his hand to his heart. He replaced his gun and unlocked the door. "Why did you do that?"

"Why did you have the door locked?" Roger got to his feet and brushed himself off. He pushed past Aaron and took his seat in the booth. He glared up at him, waiting for an explanation.

Aaron bent to retrieve his book from the floor. He tossed it onto the counter and shook his head. "You're gonna laugh at me."

"Yeah, probably. As long as it doesn't involve me getting shot."

"I just decided to take a hike on the stairs while you were gone."

"Worried about your fat butt again?" Roger interrupted.

"Very funny. You want to hear this or not?" Aaron waited for Roger to gesture for him to continue. "I was just coming back to the stairwell from getting a drink on the twelfth floor when I heard a door close above me. Halfway up the landing, I hear someone coming down the stairs toward me."

Intent on his story, Aaron didn't notice Roger's eyes growing wider as he talked. He went on. "I called to ask who was there. Stupid, I know. But then the door to the fourteenth floor closed again. I had my gun out, but I'd left my radio here so I couldn't call you. I went on up and looked around. I could . . . feel that someone was there. You know, watching me."

Aaron finally noticed Roger's attention. "You're not making fun of me. What's going on?"

"You say the fourteenth floor? CompInnovations' floor?"

"Yeah . . . what's going on?" He repeated.

"You know how Ms. Franklin from the penthouse is always here until after 10:00 on the weekends?" Roger waited for Aaron's nod. "Well, last night, a little while after she went down to parking, the elevator started up and went to the fourteenth floor. I thought for some reason Ms. Franklin had gone back up and pushed the wrong button or something. But just then, I see her drive by the front window."

"Maybe she pushed the button accidentally as she was leaving the elevator."

"Then why did it take so long for it to go up?"

"But there's no way anyone can enter the garage without a keycard. The computer didn't show an access record, did it?"

Roger shook his head. "And there was no one in the building when we did our once through."

"Maybe we'd better have maintenance check the garage access, make sure it's not screwed up."

"That's a good idea. But what would someone be doing, that they would still be here from last night?"

Aaron shivered and unconsciously checked the lock on the door. "I've been reading too many horror stories. This is getting spooky."

∩   ∩   ∩   ∩   ∩

Melia paced back and forth in front of the pay phone while she waited for Dana to pick her up. She had stopped crying; it was too cold to cry. Her feet were freezing—she hadn't dressed for snow—and she stomped them on the sidewalk at each turn. A truck approached, then passed her by. It was not Dana's.

She still held the book Chris had given her. With cold fingers, she fanned through the pages and considered moving under the streetlight to read until Dana arrived. The idea went from her mind as quick as it came. It was a bad idea. The street was safe, but not safe enough for her to stand there with her attention riveted on a book. Besides, Dana would be angry with her for doing it, and she already had enough reasons to hate Melia's voracious reading habit.

"It's time to put some effort into this relationship," Melia spoke aloud. She slid her backpack from her shoulder and stuffed the book inside. "Time to pay attention."

When it's love, no book could ever compete for your attention, Chris' words came back to her, but Melia pushed the thought away. What she knew about love could probably fit in an espresso cup, but she couldn't accept Chris' assessment.

"Melia."

Melia was surprised at the soft voice behind her. She hadn't heard anyone approach. Turning, she found Langley standing close behind her in a bulky green parka, snowflakes melting on her smooth, brown scalp.

"Lang, what are you doing out here?" she asked.

Langley shrugged. "Chris decided to close down early. She sent me home."

"You should wear something on your head, you'll catch pneumonia in this weather."

Rubbing a mittened hand across her head, Langley smiled broadly, causing two small dimples to spring into sight beneath her high cheekbones. "I don't have far to go and I've never felt the snow on my skull. I wanted to try it."

Realizing that Melia's hands were bare, Langley reached out and took them, wrapping them in the warm wool of her mittens. "God, you're freezing. Why don't you come to my place? I'll make some coffee to warm you up."

"I can't—" Melia began.

"That's all I mean," Langley interrupted. She kept her hold on Melia's hands, her dark eyes shining in the streetlight. "Just coffee. I won't ask you for anything else."

"Dana's picking me up. Soon."

Muscles over Langley's jawbone tensed, but she kept her mouth shut.

"Didn't Chris tell you she was back?" Melia asked with heavy sarcasm. "Why else did she let you go early?"

"No." Dropping Melia's hands, Langley took a step away from her. "I wondered why she was so angry. But, no. She didn't say anything. She didn't send me out here."

Melia stepped into the space Langley had left, bringing her body back close to the woman. "I'm sorry, Lang. That was rude and unnecessary."

Langley didn't respond. Melia could see that she was hurt. She looked away from Melia's face and Melia watched her eyes follow an approaching vehicle. Her expression grew even colder and Melia knew without turning that Dana had arrived.

The truck pulled to a quick stop and Melia heard the door fly open. "Hey, buddy!" Dana yelled. "Get your black ass away from her."

Langley flashed Melia a final, angry glance then turned and walked away. Dana ran up and grabbed Melia, physically turning her around.

"Hey, was that guy bothering you? Should I go after him?" Dana shook Melia until she looked up into her eyes.

"No. He was just asking directions." Melia didn't bother to correct Dana's mistake. Thinking a man was talking to Melia, Dana would feel protective. If she knew Langley was a woman, she would be threatened and suspicious.

"My god, honey. You're freezing. Get in the truck." Dana wrapped her arm around Melia's shoulders and led her to the curb.

The truck's heater was blowing hard and Melia gratefully opened her coat to the blast of warm air. Her body was shaking and she was not sure how much of it was due to the cold. For some unknown reason, she was frightened. The feeling made her think of the book hidden in her backpack.

"What were you doing out here on the street?" Dana asked as she drove the truck out into traffic. Her voice was neutral.

"I just left the bookstore."

Dana turned her eyes from the street and looked at Melia. She shook her head before looking away. Melia knew what she was thinking.

"I didn't buy anything, I just wanted to see Chris."

Dana smacked her palm against the steering wheel a few times before responding. "You know, Mel, I think this is the first time you've really come right out and lied to me."

Without giving herself time to think of her actions, Melia reached over and took Dana's hand. Her warm, soft skin was so comforting. Dana held her arm stiff, refusing to let Melia pull her hand any closer. "But it's true. We talked. And I didn't buy a thing," Melia whispered, leaning forward and brushing her cold lips against Dana's palm.

Dana made a fist. Melia immediately pulled her face away. Dana dropped her fist to Melia's leg and let her hand slowly open. Softly, she began to stroke Melia's thigh. "Sorry," she said softly. "I shouldn't have responded that way."

"It's okay," Melia assured her.

Dana grinned and looked back to Melia, ignoring the traffic flowing by. "You really didn't buy anything? You were in a bookstore and you bought nothing?"

Melia laughed. The feeling of it released a pressure in her chest. "Nothing."

"Wow, this is some kind of special day. We need to celebrate. Have you eaten dinner?"

Melia shook her head.

"We'll go to a great restaurant. We'll feed you hot soup until we get you nice and warm, then we'll feast."

"No," Melia stopped her. She leaned over until she could rest her head on Dana's shoulder. "I'll tell you another honestly true thing instead. I would much rather you take me home, crawl into the bathtub with me, and get me nice and hot."

"Fuck," Dana whispered under her breath, drawing the word into two syllables. Melia could feel Dana studying her face. "Did I pick up the right woman back there?"

Melia leaned over again and spoke close to Dana's ear, letting the breath that carried her words tickle the fair hair along Dana's neck. "Take me home, and I'll let you decide if you have the right woman."

Five

Her breath was loud. It and a slowly ticking clock were the only sounds in the room. Melia's eyes were closed. She tilted her head back, her mouth open, the feel of the air moving over her tongue and down to her lungs was incredible. She breathed fast and hard. There was not enough oxygen to keep her head from spinning. She clenched her fists, and in one hand found a corner of her discarded shirt and in the other, Dana's soft, short hair. She pulled.

The clock ticked faster. Her heart followed the beat, pounding in rhythm, then raced past it. Pleasure that was pain, then pleasure again, consumed her. Melia had lost all definition of sensation. Every touch, every twist and bite and caress forced her in the same direction. She could feel. She could feel the mouth, the teeth, the hands. The fingers on her body, in her body. She pushed against them and was pushed back, defenseless and struggling in the same instant that she reached for more. She was torn. Lying there, pulled apart by the opposing forces of pain and pleasure, fear and lust, love and hate, she reached out for each and drew them into her soul. The touch became gentle.

The peak she was rising reached a plateau. Her tendons tight, her muscles straining, gave way to a wave of calm. A sense of tranquility and a softer passion washed through her. She knew not to trust it. She knew it would not last. The light stroke of a hand up her belly and over her breast caused her to take a hard, shuddering breath. A stronger touch, low and deep, drove the air from her in a sharp exhalation. The hand closed around her throat and there was nothing more to breathe.

Melia knew better than to fight it. She knew where this was going, and as the pressure increased in her head, the intensity of sensation grew. Opening her eyes to the darkness of the room, she resisted her body's desire to struggle until she saw red replace the black before her eyes, and the pain became too much. She shook her head and tried to push her body up from the floor. The pressure of the hand tightened beyond agony, then released. There was never any danger, Melia told herself, just carelessness, an abandonment to an obsession that required more than mere emotion. Dana's body came down hard upon hers and anchored her to the floor. Dana's lips pressed against the pain in her throat, then whispered in her ear.

"Do you want it?"

Voiceless, she nodded.

"Are you with me? Are you here?"

Melia nodded again. And again. Her knees were slowly and firmly pushed apart. She moaned softly.

"Can you feel me?"

"Yes."

"Nothing but me?"

"Yes."

And it was true. She could no longer feel the floor beneath her. The ticking of the clock, the beating of her heart, they were gone. There was one being, one sensation spreading from within and without her, taking her where it demanded she go. Having long given over control, Melia was powerless, and she was taken.

$$\cap \quad \cap \quad \cap \quad \cap \quad \cap$$

Parker spent the day on her belly, looking down at Melia Ellis through a gap next to the light fixture. Unlike her efficiency of the day before when Parker happened to be watching, today, Melia's movements were erratic and it seemed she couldn't concentrate on her work. The distant look came more often and the pain of the longing was obvious. Parker struggled with her desire to go down to her when she saw Melia silently crying.

"What's wrong with you?" she whispered beneath her breath, the sound swallowed by the hum of the fluorescent lights and the conversations of the workers around them. Melia's despair gripped Parker's heart. Balanced on the beam, she tried to make the woman feel her concern.

Later, when Melia returned from her lunch break, Parker saw something that made her furious. Melia was wearing a high-necked, black sweater. When she sat at the desk, she absently pulled down the collar and rubbed her throat. A dark, blue shadow underlined her jawbone. The bruise was unmistakably that of a hand print. Suddenly, Parker was to her knees before she realized that she'd moved. Her fists were hard and the blood pounded hot in her veins. Catching herself before she stood, Parker forced herself to calm down. Her anger was going to get her discovered if she wasn't careful.

"What the hell kind of world is this?" Shaken, Parker stretched out again and pondered the question. She told herself that the situation was no business of hers. After all, she didn't even know Melia. But she was sickened by the thought that something like this could happen to a woman and no one seemed to care. In her town and in her own time, she wouldn't hesitate to challenge a man who had the nerve to do violence to a lady.

The day spun on and Parker continued to watch. The woman's way of moving, her light touch on the letter board, her soft voice when she talked into one of her machines, and her wistful expression, all became familiar. Parker felt an intimacy growing and had to keep reminding herself that it was one-sided.

By early evening all the other workers had gone, yet Melia stayed on. The awareness that the two of them were alone was burning like a brand in Parker's hide. She turned to lie on her back. Her hands were sweating and itching; she kept rubbing her palms on her rough denim jeans. The impulse to go down there was so strong, she kept making and breaking plans for encountering Melia without frightening her. But she knew she was stupid even to consider it. What the hell would she say? *Listen, I need to get back to my own time and I want you to get me there . . .* Christ, she'd be tempted to shoot anybody that came up to her and said the same thing.

Sudden footsteps and a man's voice drew Parker's attention back to the scene below. She carefully twisted around to lie again on her stomach. Parker could see that the woman was facing the entrance to her cubicle, but the man she was talking to was out of Parker's range of view. She listened to their words.

"Aaron, you're back to your shift?" the woman asked.

"Yeah. Alfie was successful so she took back the two to ten."

Their words made no sense to Parker, but hearing Melia's voice good enough. It was a quiet, flowing voice, one that made you want to bend your ear down and get as close as you could.

"Well, it's good to see you."

"Thanks. But to tell the truth, Ms. Ellis, I'm not too happy to see you staying late."

Melia leaned back in her chair and appraised the man before responding. "And what do you mean by that?"

"I mean," he hesitated, then let his words rush on. "There's something strange happening up here. Someone, *or something*, has been sneaking around on this floor." Aaron's face grew animated as he related his experience in the stairwell.

Melia laughed, then instantly clapped her hand over her mouth. Both of them, and Parker as well, were surprised at her outburst. "I'm sorry." She held her hand out and touched the man's sleeve briefly. "I didn't mean to make fun of what you're saying. I've just wondered for a long time when one of your horror novels would finally get to you."

The man chuckled. Parker realized that he was probably the guard who had almost caught her on the stairs. She shifted her body backwards in a vain attempt to get a look at his face.

"I guess I deserved that. I've teased you enough about the Westerns you read. But I really did hear something up here, and Roger's sensed it too."

"Roger? The big guy with the buzz cut?"

"Yeah, I'm sure you've seen him around."

Melia nodded. "Yesterday. I saw him yesterday and he asked me if I'd come in Sunday night."

"See? It's not just me and my horror stories."

Parker couldn't keep the grin from her lips. She'd been somehow cast through time just to make this man's life more interesting. What an idea!

The man continued, "So, if you're not working on anything too important, I'd feel better if you didn't stay late."

Melia stared at him a moment before responding. "You're serious about this, aren't you?"

"Yeah, I am. I mean, you don't have to listen to me. It's just my advice because you're a friend. I can't make you leave."

"No. No, I'll go if you think it's necessary."

"Or I could just hang around and make sure nothing happens. You know, if you need to work."

"I can finish it at home," she assured him.

Parker's grin faded and she started to feel a little irritated. Melia would have stayed here in Parker's view if this guy hadn't said anything. Having seen the bruises on her neck, Parker felt sick about her leaving.

"I just need to copy this program to disk," Melia said. She rummaged through her backpack, pulled out a book, placed it on the corner of her desk, then continued digging. After a moment, she took out a small, black square and fed it into the front of her machine.

Melia tapped a few letters from the board. The man leaned over Melia's back and Parker heard him whistle shrilly.

"Wow, what's this?" He picked up the book. Parker couldn't make out the title, but the picture was of a woman wearing a hat similar to her own.

"She's quite a babe."

Quickly, Melia grabbed the book away from him and smiled. "Don't you even think about it, Aaron. I haven't read it yet."

"I don't want to read it, I just want to meet the woman who modeled for that picture."

"She's probably not your type."

"Oh, one of *those* books, huh?"

"Yeah, but don't get any perverted ideas."

"Hey, those are the best ideas," he quipped.

Melia smiled again and put the book on the desk

beside her, out of the man's reach. "Now, get out of here," she said, her tone without anger. "I'll just copy these files and be ready to go. Why don't you do your once over and then you can walk me out."

"Once through. It's called a once through, not a once over." He gave the book one last glance, then walked away.

Melia shook her head. Sadly, the smile quickly faded from her face and her serious expression returned. It held as she sighed and tapped a number of buttons. Parker twisted her head around enough to look at the book lying on the desk. She wondered what the man meant when he called it "one of *those* books."

The woman soon finished her task and removed the square from the machine. She stood and pulled on her coat. Picking up the backpack, she dropped the square into it and stepped out into the hallway. The book was still on her desk. Parker tried to pull her attention away from it, she didn't want her interest to somehow remind the woman she'd forgotten it there.

"Aaron," the woman called out. "I'm going on down to the lobby. I want to grab a paper before the stand closes."

"All right," Aaron yelled from somewhere across the floor. "I'll meet you down there in a few minutes."

The woman walked away. Parker listened hard for the sound of the elevator door opening. She heard the hiss and immediately got to her knees. Pulling the ceiling tile aside carefully, she peered down and saw Aaron disappear into a walled office on the far side of the floor. Knowing she was a fool for taking such a dangerous chance, she nevertheless lifted the tile away and dropped to the desk below. She grabbed the book and was back up in the ceiling before he could have turned around. With its slick pages tucked safely away in her shirt, Parker crawled to her corner and waited for the security guard to clear out.

∩   ∩   ∩   ∩   ∩

"Give me a *News*, please."

Melia handed the man her money and went back to wait for Aaron at his security booth. Roger, the other guard, nodded to her from behind the glass. She returned the motion, then looked down at the paper she'd bought for Dana, and scanned the headlines. She never read the newspapers or watched the evening news, it was too depressing. Everything that happened seemed so sordid and unreal. Melia didn't want it to become a part of her life. But Dana read the paper daily and kept up on current events. Having learned to accept Melia's distaste, Dana no longer tried to keep her informed. No matter how potentially exciting certain information would be to share, she refrained from trying to draw Melia into it and only told her about events she thought would actually have some bearing on Melia's life. There was not a lot. It was another of the many reasons Melia and Dana didn't communicate.

Melia sighed and unzipped her backpack. Maybe this gesture would make Dana realize that Melia did think of her . . . As she slid the paper inside, Melia noticed that the book Chris had given her was gone. Remembering that she'd left it on her desk, she went back to the elevator and pushed the button for the fourteenth floor.

Aaron was not in sight when the door opened. The room was so quiet that she could hear the hum of the ventilation system. She'd never noticed it before.

"Aaron, it's Melia. Don't shoot me," she called out.

As she walked to her cubicle, she looked all around. Her surroundings were familiar, but there was just a touch of the strange upon everything. It was as if she was seeing the place with new eyes. Aaron's suggestion had gotten to her fertile imagination and immediately taken seed.

Smiling at her apprehensiveness, Melia buttoned her coat up over her chest and stepped up her pace. Entering her tiny space, she reached down for the book. It was gone. She squatted down and looked under her desk. Not there. She checked the trash can just in case and rattled the plastic bag.

"Oh, Aaron. You ass." Melia stood up, thinking she knew where her book had gone. "If you think I'm going to let you read that before I do, you are mistaken."

The moment the sound of her words died in the empty room, Melia heard the squeak and scrape of a footstep. She turned, expecting to see Aaron, a few choice expressions for him already on her lips.

No one was there. Melia stepped out of her cubicle and into the hallway. She turned in a circle, looking carefully around her. There was nothing, she could see no movement from over the top of the partitions. Unless someone was in another hallway and was crouched down, it appeared she was alone.

The hair on her neck and arms stood up in a slowly advancing wave across her skin. She turned another full circle. In the same way that a deer can sense the hunter's cross hairs, Melia was convinced that someone was watching her.

"Goddamn you, Aaron." She spoke in a voice that couldn't manage to rise above a whisper. "If you're doing this, I'm going to get Langley to kick your ass."

Slowly, she backed out toward the elevator. She didn't care if Aaron was watching and laughing behind his hand, she was not going to turn her back to the room. As soon as she did, he would probably jump out at her. When she hit the wall, she felt for the panel and pressed down without looking. As soon as the door opened, she quickly glanced inside to make sure no one was there. Just as quickly, she brought her attention back to the office. Not turning to either side, she stepped back into the elevator and pushed the door button, trying to force it to close.

The short ride to the lobby gave her just enough time to become furious. Aaron's smiling face at the open door of the security booth compounded her anger. She strode up to him.

"All right, give me the book," she demanded, her hand held out.

Aaron shook his head. "What book?"

"Don't play games with me, Aaron. I get enough of that at home. Just give me the book."

"Ms. Ellis, I didn't take—"

"Don't you Ms. Ellis' me! You know my name." Melia was right in his face, her anger making her uncharacteristically aggressive.

Aaron touched her shoulder cautiously. Roger tried not to stare from the booth.

"Melia, I don't know what you're talking about. I gave you back the book before I left the office."

"Yeah, well, I put it on my desk and when I just went back to get it, it was gone. And I don't appreciate you trying to scare me. I have to work here."

Aaron stared at her. Roger forgot himself and stared too.

"What?" Melia asked. She didn't like the looks on their faces.

"I . . ." Aaron started, then stopped himself, as if he had no idea what to say.

Roger stepped out of the booth. "Ms. Ellis, he was here. When you got back into the elevator, he came out of the stairwell."

"I have to check there, too." Aaron explained.

Melia shook herself. This was foolish. Now they were getting as spooked as she had been. She rubbed her forehead.

"What happened up there?"

"Nothing. I heard—thought I heard a sound. It was nothing." Melia smiled as she spoke. "Your story just got my imagination going."

"But the book is gone?" Roger asked.

"It's probably in my backpack. Maybe I just didn't look well enough."

"Here, I'll help you look." Aaron put out his hand to take her pack.

Melia took the strap and shifted it more securely on her shoulder. "No. It's in there. This is foolish and we're all letting ourselves get freaked over nothing."

"You're sure it's there?"

"Yeah. Where else would it be?" Melia pointedly looked up at the clock. "Hey, if I'm going to catch the bus, I've got to run. You guys have a good night."

"Yeah, right."

Melia patted Aaron on the shoulder and smiled. Before he could speak again, she moved past him and jogged across the lobby. Her bus approached the stop as she did.

Melia boarded the bus, happy to see that she had waited long enough past rush hour that the bus was not crowded. She sat down on the last seat and instantly unzipped her backpack. Holding it by the bottom, she dumped its contents on the seat next to her. Floppy disks, Dana's newspaper, a few folded sheets of printouts, and her wallet . . . the book was not there.

Melia slowly stuffed her possessions back into the pack and then leaned stiffly against the seat. She searched her mind for possible explanations for its disappearance. None were forthcoming.

Six

Two days later, Melia walked into her cubicle and the air was almost electric. She felt the oddest force, like her desk had been moved to sit under a high voltage power line. There was such a strong feeling of watching and waiting that Melia half expected to find someone sitting in her chair. But the cubicle was empty. And the book was lying on her desk.

Melia stepped back out into the hall, but stood staring at the book in disbelief. She hadn't expected it to be returned, she had convinced herself that she'd dropped it on her way to or from the elevator. Or that she'd left it at the newsstand when she'd taken out the money for Dana's paper. What she knew was that when the book vanished, no one had been in the office other than herself and Aaron. Yet here was the book.

"Excuse me, Melia. Are you okay?"

The woman had to repeat her words before Melia realized someone was speaking to her. Melia turned her head and saw her co-worker in the next cubicle staring over the gray partition and waiting for her answer.

"Oh, I'm sorry, Amy." Melia shook her head as if to shake off a distraction. She thought of a quick lie. "I was just thinking about some coding I worked out on the bus."

Amy smiled. "Melia, you put too much energy into this job."

"But I get so much out of it."

Amy laughed and started to sit back down. Before she could disappear behind the wall, Melia stopped her.

"Hey, you didn't happen to see anyone come in here, did you?"

"Uh, no. I'm sorry. Were you expecting someone?"

"No. I just . . . well, yes." Melia fumbled along, trying to come up with a plausible explanation for asking. Amy didn't notice.

"Oh wait. I was wrong," Amy said abruptly. "Bob dropped by. I suppose he gave you one of these." She waved a yellow paper.

Melia leaned forward and looked. The yellow inter-office memo was wedged between the keys of her keyboard. "Anything interesting?"

"Not if you got the same thing I did." Amy dropped out of sight behind her wall.

Melia took a deep breath and entered her cubicle. Without removing her coat, she sat at the desk and picked up the memo. She pointedly ignored the book that lay next to her hand. The memo was short and to the point; the Colorado Springs' branch office computers were down. A team was on its way, but there would be no way to access the data bases until repairs were made. Blah, blah, blah. Melia never accessed them anyway. If she didn't get the occasional memos outlining their problems, she would have completely forgotten that there was a branch office.

She crumpled the paper and threw it over her shoulder

toward the waste basket. The office was cold. Shaking the mouse to remove the screen saver, Melia leaned forward and drew her coat even tighter around her. From the corner of her eye, she could see that the pages of the book had a worn look, like they'd been thumbed through several times. She liked the look better than the cold, tight pages of an unread book. It was comfortable. Inviting.

Melia punched in her password and entered the system. She had e-mail, tons of it, and knew that 80 percent of it was crap. She waded through it every morning. Like most mornings, she read with her finger tapping repeatedly on the delete key. When her wrist brushed against the book, she jerked a drawer open and pushed the book into it.

Irritated, she killed the rest of her unread e-mail file. She stared at the blinking cursor. Two days and it looked as if the book had been read several times. The person must be a fast reader.

Melia slammed her palm on the desk. She couldn't concentrate with that goddamn book on her mind. There was no point in trying to dismiss it. She pulled the drawer open again, took out the book and put it on the desk on front of her. Melia studied the mouth of the woman on the cover. She had great lips. Sensual, Melia thought, though she really didn't know what it meant to say lips were sensual. They just looked as if they would feel good no matter what part of her they touched. Did the person who swiped the book think the same thing? Did the lesbian content excite them or offend them? Melia guessed the theme was not too offensive. Why read a book several times if it insulted your morals?

A feeling of distaste went through her. The thought of a man reading this book and becoming excited by the lesbian content sickened her. Never having been intrigued by the image of heterosexuals together, or that of gay men together, she couldn't understand the fascination. Suddenly, she had no desire to read the book.

Disgusted, she carefully lifted the book and turned to throw it in the trash, when a slip of paper slid from between the pages and fluttered to the floor. Surprised, Melia dropped the book and bent to pick up the paper. It was the torn half of a specials menu from the third floor lunchroom. The specials listed were for today. Melia turned the paper over and read the tight, delicate script written in red ink.

I'm sorry about taking your book. I could tell you I never stole anything in my life, but it would be a lie. I enjoyed it.

I don't know you, so I got no right to say this, but I think you're in a situation you'd better get out of. (I saw the bruises on your neck) Ain't no reason to take that. Someone out there will care about you more.

Melia quickly raised her hand to her throat. She had been wearing turtleneck sweaters and she knew that the bruises were well below the top of her collars. There was no way anyone could have seen them. Only two people could know about her bruises, Dana and herself.

This had to be some kind of a joke. Someone was playing games with her. It had to be Dana, but that made no sense at all. She had never come here to CompInnovations and, as far as Melia knew, Dana didn't know anyone else who worked here. And what would the point of it be? Dana didn't need to go to these lengths to frighten her, she knew how to do that by simply changing the tone of her voice.

Melia felt her body shaking and tried to blame it on the chill she felt in the room. She read the note again, looking for some code or hidden message she should be able to understand. All she could think of was Dana and the impossibility of her managing this. Besides, they were getting along. Dana seemed to appreciate Melia's decision to read less. They had spent some good time together, quality time. Maybe they hadn't talked much over the past few days, but they had spent time together without fighting.

The note in one hand and the book in the other, Melia got to her feet. She felt she was moving without conscious thought. She walked straight to the door of her supervisor's office and pushed it open, without knocking.

Bob looked up from his monitor and batted his eyes. "Melia," his concern was clear in his voice. "You look terrible. Are you okay?"

"No. I am not, Bob." Melia did not even consider telling him what was happening.

"Well, you go straight home. I'll call down to the garage to get you a ride." He reached for the phone at his side.

"No, I have a ride." Melia did not intend to go home.

"Okay, if you're sure . . ."

Melia nodded.

"Take as much time as you need," Bob encouraged. "You know, it's been a while since your last vacation." His forehead wrinkled as he looked down at his keyboard. "In fact, I can't remember when you *did* take your last vacation."

Melia cleared her throat. "Four years ago."

"And you've been here five years? Melia, is that our fault? Have we been taking advantage of you?"

"No, I just didn't feel the need to take time off. There was the interface programming for the Lockheed project and then the—"

"God, Melia, we couldn't have done that without you."Bob rubbed his eyes, then seemed to come to a decision. "Listen, you take the rest of the week off. When you come back on Monday, I want to see your vacation request on my desk."

"Bob, I can't really—" she tried to protest.

He raised his hand to silence her, then got up and walked her back to the door. Awkwardly, he patted the air somewhere near her shoulder. "If you can't be back Monday, just call and let me know."

Melia nodded, unable to argue with him. She walked back to her cubicle and picked up her backpack. She dropped the book inside it, the note went into her coat pocket. The crumpled, yellow memo was still lying on the floor. She lifted it and spread it out on the desk. It sealed her plan.

She picked up the phone and dialed her own number. Dana answered on the third ring.

"Yes?"

Great, Melia thought, she already sounds irritated. "This is Melia."

"Hey, Mel. Sorry I sounded abrupt. I thought it was a sales call. What's up?"

Melia's resolve faltered at Dana's apology. She was trying so hard, Melia was an ass to suspect her. "Um, listen. I've got bad news. I need to go out of town for the night."

"Overnight?" Dana's sharp tone returned.

"Maybe more. The computers are down in the Springs. Um, I'm on the team to fix them."

"Fuck. Why you? Weren't you on last time?"

"Well, some people are sick. They asked and I said okay."

"You volunteered?"

Melia could hear Dana slapping the phone cord against her leg. "No, they asked me and I just didn't say no. I didn't think it would be a problem."

"Yeah, you never think."

Melia took a deep breath. A knot of fear made a painful lump in her belly, but she forced herself to continue. Might as well dive in all the way. "I'm sorry, but I don't need to hear this. I'll be home tomorrow night, if I can. There's nothing more I can say."

There was a tense moment of silence over the line. "You'll stop here to get some clothes." Dana demanded.

"No. I'm sorry, I've got to go now. I can go one night without a shower and clean clothes." Melia knew that if she went home, Dana would find a reason for her to stay. And if she didn't find a reason, she'd create one.

Dana slammed the phone down. Melia slowly replaced her receiver and turned away. Damn Dana, and damn her own fear. The relationship was a mess, a trap. Melia knew she was a fool to have any hope for it. The resolutions she made each night, her promises to herself to try harder, to not make Dana so angry, to not let herself be so afraid of facing up to that anger . . . but her determination always faded in the light of day. She had to get out.

Melia stood in the middle of her cubicle, oblivious to the bustle of people at work around her, and momentarily at a loss to her next move. She thought of calling Chris and asking if she could stay over, but she was afraid of trying to explain what was going on. The note, the book, Dana . . . there was no explanation for any of it. Langley was an option, but if Dana ever got wind of her staying at another woman's apartment she'd be beyond fury. Of course, just knowing that Melia had lied about going to the Colorado Springs office would probably be enough to push her to violence.

The only option was a hotel room. Melia shrugged her pack onto her shoulder. The Hilton across the parking lot would do just fine.

On her way out the door, she stopped. An impulse had taken her. She went back to the desk and pulled open the bottom drawer. Five or six paperback novels lay among the papers. Choosing one at random, Melia placed it on the corner of her desk. She ripped a page from her yearly planner and wrote "Who are you?" and slid it between the pages. She placed the book on the edge of her desk. Dana believed that Melia would be out of town. If tomorrow the book was gone, she would know she was dealing with an unknown.

Ω   Ω   Ω   Ω   Ω

"No, no, no." Parker slapped her palm on the beam with each word. Jerking her Stetson off, she flung it hard. It flew across the crawl space and slapped into the far wall. She didn't care how much noise she made or if someone might hear. "Parker, how stupid can you get?"

She should have known the note would upset the woman. She should have known better than to even touch that book. Turning over on her back, Parker stared up into the darkness above her. It was a mistake, she told herself, making a move too quickly. She knew better, but she'd gone ahead and made a stupid mistake. Her desperation had gotten the best of her.

The shock of finding herself here and realizing she'd somehow changed times had begun to wear off and was being replaced by fear. What was she going to do? How was she going to get home? Hiding out in this crawl space wasn't helping her situation any. Sooner or later, she was going to have to trust in someone, and she had chosen Melia. There was no way she could face stepping out of this building on her own.

For the past three nights, she'd stood at the windows, staring at the streets below. From a newspaper she'd found in the lunchroom, she knew that this was Denver below her. That knowledge was more frightening than thinking she'd been thrown through space and not just time. Denver had been her town. She knew the streets, she knew the hiding places, she knew the best bars and bordellos. Looking down at the maze of lights, she knew she'd be lost before crossing the street. Everything she owned was lost, her name, her reputation, the money she had hidden back at Lily's, and Lily herself. The awareness of that caused an emptiness in her stomach.

Parker crossed her feet and pulled her arms over her chest, trying to hold in the essence of who she was. She was lost. She was lost and she believed there was no one to lead her home. Taking a stupid chance with that note had most likely blown the only opportunity she had found.

Depressed, Parker drew herself up and crawled over to the small platform she'd built in the corner. She retrieved her hat and pulled it down low over her forehead before lying down. Without the woman there to watch, there was nothing for Parker to do until the building closed. She would sleep and perhaps things would look better when she woke.

The quiet was what roused her each evening. The ceaseless, muted tapping of the hundreds of fingers on the letter boards was a sound that made her sleepy. It was like the fluttering of aspen leaves in a breeze. She could lean back, relax, and imagine herself in the forest, sleeping in a grove of aspens. When the next to the last person had left, and the last goodbye was said, Parker would wake up and immediately crawl to the space over Melia's desk. She would be there, her hands moving gracefully over the letter board and Parker could count on Melia looking up several times with that far off look she'd grown to admire.

Parker woke and remembered the note she had left in Melia's book. She rolled over and pulled up the corner of a ceiling tile and looked down. The room was darker than usual. The woman was always the last to leave and she never turned off this many lights. Well, in any case, it was a safe bet that there was no one else working late on this floor.

Stretching the kinks in her back, Parker stood as tall as the ceiling above her would allow. She needed to get down and get some exercise. Finding the kitchen on the third floor had been a stroke of luck, she'd eaten well since then. Trying to survive on the stuff she'd pilfered from the desk drawers would have been impossible. Parker crawled to her usual jumping down place over Melia's desk and dragged away the tile. Not bothering to look into the darkened room, she dropped onto the desk. Her boots hit hard on a stack of papers and slid out from under her. Parker tumbled forward off the desk and crashed into the chair, her forehead connecting hard with the back of the seat. She fell over and the force of her fall drove the chair on its rollers into the wall. The sound echoed through the long room.

Flashing lights danced before her eyes. She struggled to her hands and knees and shook her head slowly. Blood dripped from her forehead onto the carpet. She stared at the red spot growing between her hands until the flashing lights faded and she could see more clearly. What she saw, beyond the small stain of her blood, was a book. The woman had left her another book.

A surge of exhilaration swelled in Parker's heart. For some reason, this gesture gave her all the hope she needed to push aside her depression. Ignoring her injury, she lifted the book and held it to her chest. She sat back on her heels and smiled.

Suddenly, the door to the stairway banged open. A guard yelled, "All right, I heard you, I know you're here. You come out, now."

Parker staggered to her feet, keeping her head down below the edge of the partition. She looked up and saw the black rectangle of the ceiling tile she had pulled aside. There was no way she could get up there without being seen, no way the guard could miss seeing that black hole. She had to lead him away and still manage to keep herself hidden.

"Don't think so," Parker whispered. She leaned over to pick up her hat and almost fell. Dizziness gripped her and invited her to meet the floor again. She took a deep breath and forced herself to stay upright. Moving without a sound, she rolled the chair back over to hide the blood and pulled the scattered papers together.

She could hear the guard's quiet footsteps in the hallway parallel to hers. A strange crackling sound was followed by the guard's hushed voice. "I've got someone here, Roger. Fourteenth floor. Get your ass up here."

Somehow the man could call the other guard downstairs. Parker knew if she gave him time to arrive, she would be trapped for sure. She tucked the book in the front of her pants. Still in a crouch, she ran down the hall toward the stairs.

When she reached the end of her corridor, she reconsidered. If she went for the door leading to the stairs, she would put herself directly in the guard's line of sight. She had no desire to be killed, nor did she want to kill him. There had to be a way out, without giving him any proof that she was more than his overactive imagination.

The numbered lights above the elevator began to flash and the numbers lit up in succession. In a matter of seconds, the door would open with her in plain sight. The salty blood running down over her eyebrows stung her eyes and made them water. Parker quickly wiped her eyes with her sleeve and squinted. She saw the door to the women's room.

Without further hesitation, she darted to the door and grabbed the handle. She hoped that the lights were off inside, if not the guard would notice the door opening the same as if she'd set out a beacon. No time to worry, it was do it or die. The door opened to darkness.

Her familiarity with the room allowed Parker to run straight to the bank of sinks and climb up. The counter was lower than the desks out in the main room. She would have to jump up and push the tile aside, then jump again, grab the beam, and pull herself up. Normally, she would hardly consider it exercise, but tonight, she had to make four jumps to get it done.

Up in the ceiling, she instantly felt safe. She'd noticed that the people who worked below never seemed to pay attention to what was above them. If something was not in their direct view, it didn't exist. She hoped that the custom would hold true for her now and the guards would not catch sight of the missing tile before she could replace it.

Crossing the beams was difficult with her head still spinning. Parker kept to her hands and knees and crawled as quickly as she could to the dislodged tile over Melia's cubicle. Quietly, she slid the tile back into position. In the same instant that it settled into place, the lights flared on. Parker sat back with a sigh, all she could do was hope that the guards would not notice the blood she had left on the carpet below.

Parker slunk back to her corner and pressed the tail of her shirt against the cut on her forehead. In a few hours, when the guards had calmed down and started to convince themselves that she didn't really exist, she would get down and clean up the mess she'd left. Then it would be best to make a raid on the kitchen and steal enough food to last a few days. After this encounter, the less she moved around, the safer she would be.

She listened to the guards walking below and smiled. She would hate to have their jobs. A sliver of illumination came up through a crack by the beam near her head. She pulled the book from her pants and angled it into the light. Another Western. She hoped it would be as good as the last. Opening to the first page, she found the note. Even more than finding the book, this gesture gave her hope. Perhaps she had not been so wrong.

Seven

The next morning, Melia paused in the Hilton hotel lobby long enough to reserve her room for another night. She'd slept poorly, all night anticipating the ring of the wake up call she'd requested for 6:00 a.m. Then, she had paced the room, hungry and sleepy, until 7:00. The fatigue didn't matter since she was not going to stay at work. Her only goal was to get to the office before anyone else and check to see if the book had been taken. The "borrower" had all day yesterday to take it, and if the book was gone, it was sure to be someone she worked with and Dana would be cleared.

Melia ran across the parking lot between the hotel and her office building. This morning, the first day of March, was bitterly cold and the sun looked like a faded, frozen ball of cotton on the horizon. A gray-yellow haze shadowed the sky and the street already smelled of exhaust fumes. She kept her head down as she entered the lobby and quickly passed by the security booth. As she gave the booth a sideways glance, she was relieved to see that Aaron was not there. Hopefully he was not prowling the halls. She couldn't remember if his shift had already ended.

Melia hesitated as the elevator door opened on the fourteenth floor. Holding the heavy door open with one hand, she scanned the long, dark room. The offices and cubicles were empty and the lights were still off. She thought it was strange that the cleaning crew had not turned them on, but perhaps they had not made it to her floor yet. The faint sound of her footsteps whispered across the empty floor. Her fingers brushed the long panel of light switches, but she felt hesitant to flood the room with their glare. The thin sunlight coming through the east windows would provide light enough for her purpose.

After entering her cubicle, she noticed the blood stain on the floor. It was a dark smudge under the wheel of her chair that she somehow knew was blood. The spot on the light green carpet had been scrubbed at, but not removed, and her chair pulled over to hide it. Melia knelt down and studied the stain, putting her hands between her knees to resist her impulse to touch it. It seemed to be still wet. She imagined it still warm.

Unsteady on her feet, she stood. Her world was spinning out of place. Dana was not the only person in her life that had accused her of being out of touch with reality. She knew she used fantasy as a refuge more than was considered normal, but her job had always been a stabilizing factor in her life. Now, there was a blood stain on the floor. The stability was starting to crumble. Melia sat in her chair and slid it up tight to the comforting bulk of her desk.

The book she'd left there was gone and a folded scrap of paper had taken its place. No mystery was solved, but she felt a faint relief from proving that Dana was not a part of this strange exchange. Still, she was left the questions of whom the "borrower" was and how they knew about the bruises on her throat.

The blood stain didn't bear thinking about, not here, not while she was alone. Suddenly, the pale light of morning and the rows of empty cubicles took on an ominous feel. Melia touched the paper and felt her fingertips tingling. This, too, was more than she was ready to face. She put the note in her pocket unread. Outside, in the sunlight, she would take it out and read it.

As she pushed away from the desk, she realized that the previous day's printouts that she'd stacked on the corner had been shuffled around and creased. When she rearranged the edges of the papers on the desk to straighten them, the top sheet caught her eye. It had been stepped on. Melia held it up to the light and saw the clear impression of a pointed-toe cowboy boot. A shiver of fear went up her spine. She was sure that somehow the boot print and the blood stain were connected.

Now, even the silence of the fourteenth became threatening to her. It was somehow too quiet. It was the quiet of waiting and watching, the quiet of the hunter before the kill. Aaron's fear of ghosts and prowlers no longer seemed so far-fetched. Suddenly, she dropped the stack of papers on the desk and ran to the elevator. The door could not open fast enough, and when it did, it took an eternity to close.

"Now read this, it's the second note." Melia handed Chris the paper she'd taken from her desk an hour earlier.

Chris took the note and sat down on a box. They had met again in the back room of Woman to Woman, Chris arriving at the bookstore early after receiving Melia's anxious phone call. She unfolded the sheet and read. It was definitely the same handwriting as the first note.

My name is Parker. My last note was maybe too familiar. I was wrong to mention things that ain't my concern. I didn't mean to scare you. I am enjoying the book. My days and nights are long, and I'm glad to get away if only in my mind. I think you understand how that feels.

"Well, it's a weird story, but I don't really see anything scary about it." Chris shrugged and passed the note back. "If the person knows Dana, the thing about the bruises would be an easy guess."

"Don't start, please." Melia wadded the note in her fist and threw it on Chris' computer desk. "This is serious."

Chris cleared her throat, but said nothing.

"It's not just the remark about my relationship, it's the books, the blood stain and the boot print, just the whole feeling. It's the thing about getting away, if only in my mind." Melia uncrumpled the note and smoothed it out on the desk. "How does this guy know how I feel?"

"You don't know anyone named Parker?"

"No one."

Chris came to the desk and tapped her finger on the corner of the note. "This writing looks feminine to me. Maybe you're thinking of the wrong gender."

"Well, I certainly don't know any women named Parker."

"Don't just think of first names. Met any women with that last name?"

"No," Melia sighed and leaned back in the chair.

"What's Dana's last name?"

"Very funny. Her name is Sperry, and I've ruled her out."

"She's the one I would have bet on." Chris stood behind Melia and patted her shoulder. "I'm not trying be antagonistic. It just sounds like a game she'd enjoy."

"You're right, I can't deny it. She was my first candidate, too." Melia let her head tilt back to rest on Chris' belly. She closed her eyes as Chris rubbed her forehead with gentle fingers.

Chris suddenly laughed. Melia opened her eyes and raised her eyebrows.

"I was just thinking, it couldn't possibly be Dana

because she would have had to read a book. What are the chances of that happening?"

"And a Western at that." Melia smiled despite herself. But her apprehensions quickly turned her serious again. "It's got to be someone I work with. Lately, when I'm there, I feel like I'm being watched."

Chris abruptly spun Melia's chair around to face her. She knelt down and looked soberly into Melia eyes. "Mel, don't take this wrong, but I feel like you making more of this than is there. Someone is borrowing your books. Maybe they're ashamed to have anyone know that they like to read escapist crap like lesbian Westerns. Frankly, you're beginning to sound a little paranoid and that concerns me more than this mystery person does."

"But you weren't there, Chris. And that's it. No one was there. The book just disappeared. And now the blood stain on the carpet and the boot print on the printout." Melia's expression made obvious the depths of her concern. "Someone's trying to scare me."

"But why? Who would want to do that to you?"

"I don't know. Could it be some wacked-out stalker who just picked me at random?"

Chris didn't respond. Melia looked up at her. Chris was staring at her computer with a strange look on her face. "That's it."

"What?"

"The answer to your problem. It's right here in front of us." Chris leaned over Melia's shoulder and pointed to the small digital camera attached to her monitor. "All we have to do is hook this up to your computer, set out a book, and wait for this Parker to walk in and smile for the camera."

Early Saturday morning, as Parker slept soundly in her ceiling hideout, the book she'd taken from Melia's desk resting on her chest, Melia and Chris set to work at Melia's terminal. Chris loaded the video software as Melia plugged the camera into a port behind the computer.

"If you insist on the images being saved to floppy, you're only going to have about four hours of recording time before it's full."

"That's with saving an image every minute?" Melia asked. "If we make it every two minutes, we could get a whole work day."

Chris shook her head. "We're pushing it at a minute. How long do you think it will take someone to step in here and pick up a book? Chances are good that we'll miss 'em at this rate."

"I don't want to save to the hard drive. Uploading the software is bad enough. I don't want anyone on the network to find this and question me." Melia sat on the corner of the desk and glanced again at the carpet under her chair. She couldn't believe that the stain was gone, but she couldn't even find a shadow of where it had been. The missing printout with the boot print didn't surprise her, the cleaning crew had a policy that if "it's on the floor, it's out the door." The paper must have slipped off the desk when she dropped it.

Chris had merely raised an eyebrow when the evidence Melia wanted to present was missing. Melia knew that Chris doubted whole chunks of her story, but as long as she was willing to play along, Melia didn't mind. This camera would soon prove her out.

"What day and time do you want it to start recording?"

Melia thought for a moment. She couldn't give a time frame for when the last book had been taken, but the first had disappeared right after closing time. "Make it Monday from . . . three to seven. Two hours of the regular shift and two after everyone leaves."

"But nobody's going to come in while you're here."

"I'm not coming in Monday. I need to spend some time at home." Melia didn't elaborate. Chris would not care to hear that Melia thought she needed to spend time with Dana. She had not been home since Thursday morning, electing to spend last night with Chris and Molly instead of at the hotel. She'd called Dana. It was a short, tense conversation, and Melia had told her that she missed her, but not that she wasn't in Colorado Springs. Melia knew she was likely in for a huge fight when she got home tonight, but hopefully the fact that she was taking Monday off would soothe some of Dana's anger.

"All right." Chris keyed in the activation schedule and then ran a quick check to be sure the camera and software were functioning. "This ought to do it. Bring the disk to the store and we'll check out the images in the slide show viewer."

Melia gave Chris a hug and they left the cubicle. The tiny square of white plastic with its unblinking black eye was hardly noticeable where it attached to the top of the monitor. Hardly noticeable, even if a person knew what they were looking for.

∩ ∩ ∩ ∩ ∩

Just after dark that evening, Melia slipped her key into her front door and opened it quietly. The flickering blue light of the television was lighting the living room.

"I called the front desk at your office. They said you were out sick. So where have you been?" Dana asked before Melia had time to close the door behind her. Dana was sitting on the couch, scowling at the television.

Melia sat her backpack down by the door before responding. "Why did you call the office? You knew I wasn't going to be there."

"Hey, we're not gonna play that answer a question with a question game. I asked you where you've been."

"I'm sorry, but I told you where I was going. When I left, I wasn't feeling very well. I didn't tell the front desk why I was leaving, so they probably assumed it was because I was sick." Melia dropped her keys on the coffee table and pulled off her coat. "That's all I can tell you."

Dana muted the television and turned to face Melia. "You'd better not be lying to me."

Melia felt an unaccustomed anger and stood her ground. Her fingers gripped her coat collar as she looked back at Dana without blinking. "Or what?"

Dana narrowed her eyes. Melia could see her body becoming tense and already regretted her words. "Are you challenging me?"

"No, of course not." Melia's courage abandoned her. She dropped her coat on the couch and walked past to the bedroom. Dana followed her into the dark room.

"Looks like you're wearing new clothes."

Melia's fingers paused in unbuttoning her shirt. She'd forgotten to change back to the clothes she wore Thursday. She should have known that Dana would remember what she'd worn. "Yeah, I just bought some things, since I was there longer than I expected."

"That was a stupid waste of money. You could have come home for clothing."

"Dana, we've talked about this before. It's my money." Melia couldn't understand Dana's obsession with money, her parents had enough that Dana had never needed to work. Still, she watched Melia's spending like it was their pension fund and she was tossing it to the wind. "Besides, a pair of jeans and a couple shirts aren't going to break me."

Dana moved up close to Melia, using her personal

space as a threat. "You've got a smart mouth today, don't you?"

"I'm sorry." Melia reached out to put her hand flat on Dana's stomach. "Hey, I didn't want it to be like this. I missed you."

In the darkness, Melia could not see if Dana's expression softened, but she didn't move away from Melia's touch. Taking that as encouragement, Melia went further. "I thought about you every night. You know how I hate to sleep alone." Melia stood on her toes to kiss Dana under her jawbone. Melia thought she could feel a smile, but Dana kept her hands to her sides.

"And you did sleep alone?" she asked.

"Yes, I did. But I won't tonight."

Dana put her hands on Melia's shoulders and pushed her back just enough to make her lose her balance. "Are you sure about that? Do you think I've been sitting here waiting for you?"

Melia caught Dana's arm to steady herself. Dana took Melia's wrist, her fingers digging painfully into Melia's skin as she continued. "Maybe I already have a date tonight."

Her words were a challenge, but this was one that Melia was not afraid to take. She stepped up again and pressed her small body against Dana's and let the contact linger. Even through their clothing, Dana's body had a heat that instantly warmed Melia's cool skin. With her free hand, Melia lifted Dana's other hand and led her fingers to the fly of her jeans.

"Give me a chance to change your plans," Melia whispered.

Dana answered by grasping Melia's pants and tugging the buttons open. Melia kept her hold on Dana's wrist and encouraged her to slip her hand beneath the soft cloth of her underwear. Dana leaned her head down and took the kiss that Melia offered. Lips pressed hard together and tongues caressing, they forgot to breathe for several long moments.

Groaning softly, Dana broke the kiss. She released Melia's wrist, then pulled their bodies closer. Her fingers brushed lightly over Melia's hair. Melia moved her legs apart to welcome the touch. Dana instantly pulled her hand away and pushed Melia backwards onto the bed.

Melia lay there quietly, unable to see any more than an outline of the woman who stood over her. This was always a tense moment, not knowing what Dana would want, but the suspense was so arousing.

"Unbutton your shirt," Dana commanded, her voice husky with desire.

Melia undid the shirt as quick as she could. She had lost countless buttons to Dana's impatience.

"And the bra."

Dana didn't have to tell her, Melia had already unfastened the front hook. Dana leaned down and Melia was surprised to feel the gentleness of her hands as she slid her palms up Melia's sides and onto her breasts. Her lips followed, as gentle as her hands as she took Melia's nipple into her mouth. Her tongue encouraged the tip to harden and Melia pressed her body upward into the pleasure. Dana gripped her lightly with her teeth.

Melia's body reacted immediately to Dana's attentions. She had not lied, even past her irritation with Dana, she did miss Dana's strong body next to hers the nights she'd been gone. If they never had to speak, or stop having sex, they would get along fine.

Dana straightened and slipped her right hand up to the back of Melia's neck. Without effort, she lifted Melia's upper body and used her left hand to push the shirt off her shoulders.

Melia pulled her hands from the sleeves and let the shirt fall away. Dana lowered her back to the bed. Her hands became noticeably more demanding as they tugged at Melia's jeans. Melia lifted her hips and let her pants be removed. Dana reached back for her underwear and pulled them down her legs slowly, letting her hands glide along the smooth skin. Melia shivered, causing Dana to laugh softly.

Their habit was to make love on the floor. They had done it once on the couch and even a few times in the car, but they had never used the bed. Melia didn't know the reasoning behind it and Dana had never offered to explain that particular twist. Melia wasn't sure she ever wanted to delve into Dana's reasoning, about sex or anything else. She turned to the side and moved to climb off the foot of the bed.

"No." Dana grabbed her shoulder and roughly pushed her back down. She used her weight to hold Melia there.

"I'm sorry. What did I do?"

Dana laughed again and eased up on the pressure. "Nothing. Nothing, I just want you here."

"On the bed?"

"Yes, on the bed. Is that too weird of a request?" Dana's voice was playful, but Melia detected an edge to it.

"No. Whatever you want," Melia complied.

"Mm . . . whatever?" Dana spoke the word close to Melia's ear.

Melia didn't bother to respond to the teasing. Dana knew where she stood.

"Just tell me."

"I'll show you."

The edge in her voice was sharper. Melia breathed deeply in an effort to stay relaxed. Dana put her hands under Melia and turned her over onto her stomach. Melia lay sideways across the bed. Dana ran her palms down Melia's back, over her buttocks, and along the backs of her legs. As she swept her hands back up, her thumbs moved along the insides of Melia's thighs, lightly brushing against the warm wetness between her legs. Melia shivered again. Dana's touch left her body.

Melia closed her eyes and listened to the sound of Dana undressing behind her. She was patient, anticipating the feel of Dana's skin against her own. Dana lay down on top of her, her body covering Melia's and her weight pressing Melia into the soft give of the mattress. Dana took a handful of Melia's hair and pushed her face forward, exposing the back of Melia's neck to her kisses. She moved her body slowly, rubbing her breasts on Melia's back. Melia moved her arms away from her body and let them dangle forward over the side of the bed.

The compelling sensations of Dana's movements were so distracting that it took several minutes for Melia to realize that her hands were brushing against something on the floor. It was torn and scattered paper. She touched the cover of a book. A chill went through her.

"What the hell is this?"

Dana knew exactly what she was talking about. She reached forward and grabbed Melia's hand, pulling it away from the mess on the floor. Melia struggled to prevent Dana from twisting her arm behind her back. Using Dana's movement against her, Melia followed the force and managed to turn onto her back. Before Dana could drop her weight down and pin Melia to the bed, Melia brought both her knees up hard. One connected with Dana's arm but the other hit her squarely in the stomach. Melia put her feet against Dana's body and used all of her strength to push her off the bed.

Melia turned and scrambled to the other side, falling off the bed into the litter of paper. She reached the light switch near the bathroom door before Dana could pick herself up off the floor. The glare of the overhead light illuminated Melia's worst fears.

The back half of the bedroom was in chaos. Her books had been thrown from the shelves. Pages were torn out and scattered. Melia stood speechless, shocked into immobility. She was too shocked to protect herself as Dana approached.

"Melia, I'm really sorry. I've already planned to replace everything." Dana touched Melia's cheek. "I just got so angry when I thought you were lying to me."

"Why didn't you tell me when I—when were you going to tell me about this? Did you think I wouldn't find it?"

"I'm not that stupid, Mel. I was going to tell you when you were relaxed. You know, after we finished—"

"Oh? You had to fuck me first? Because you knew I sure as hell wouldn't do it after," Melia screamed into her face.

Fury contorted Dana's features. She raised her fist. Melia didn't cower or hesitate, not this time. She slammed both hands against Dana's shoulders, shoving the taller woman backwards. Dana stumbled, slipping on the papers, and almost fell down. Angry beyond reason, Melia came after her before Dana could regain her balance. She shoved her again, this time knocking Dana to the floor.

"Get out," Melia demanded, standing over her. "Get out of my house, now."

"Mel, calm down." Dana didn't move to get up. "I already apologized. I admitted I was wrong. What more do you want me to do?"

"I want you to put on your clothes and get out. I don't ever want to see you again."

"Melia, don't be so hard. I just lost it when I thought you'd lied. It won't happen again."

Melia crouched down at Dana's eye level and held her gaze. "I did lie. I didn't go to Colorado Springs. It was all a lie. Now get out."

The shock in Dana's face was priceless. But Melia could see her rage building as the words sunk in. She suddenly realized that she'd pushed too far and Dana would not be easily overpowered again. She stood and stepped away from Dana, grabbing the phone from the bedside table as she backed away.

"Leave now, or I'll call the police," Melia warned.

Dana laughed. The coldness of the sound chilled Melia's blood.

"Do you know how much damage I can do to you before the police even decide if they're going to come?" Dana got to her feet. She clenched her fists and Melia saw the tension move up Dana's arms and into her shoulders. Dana's muscles were taut and trembling. It was her turn to smile. "I can kick the shit out you and still have time to get dressed and be halfway to Boulder."

Melia pressed the speed dial as she continued to back away. Dana advanced slowly as they both listened to the quiet ring in the receiver.

"Hello?"

Dana's smile faded as she recognized Chris' voice. Melia lifted the receiver and spoke quickly. "Chris, how fast can you get here?"

Chris responded instantly to the fear in Melia's voice. Melia held the phone away from her ear so Dana could hear the answer. "Five minutes."

Dana was breathing heavily. She didn't back down. "The door's locked. She can't protect you."

"She has a key. I gave her the one I took from you last time we fought."

"Goddamn you." Dana was so angry now, her whole body was shaking. And when she was this angry, she never raised her voice. The sound was almost a whisper. "Goddamn you."

"Melia, this is Molly."

Melia heard the tiny voice and lifted the phone again. She kept her eyes on Dana.

"Chris is on the way. Try to stay on the line."

"I will, Molly."

"Did you call the police?"

"No, I don't want the police. I just want her out."

Dana surged forward and grabbed Melia by the throat with her left hand, shoving her back against the bookcase. She knocked the phone from Melia's hand and kicked it across the room.

Her only thought to breathe, Melia tried to pry Dana's fingers away. Dana leaned her weight into the hold. She put her face against Melia's, her eyes wide and wild beyond reason. The whole room seemed to vibrate from the violent shaking that seized Dana's body. Melia felt Dana's lips and teeth against her cheek as Dana spoke.

"I'll go, tonight. But I will come back here." She released her grip enough to allow Melia a painful gasp of air. "And the best thing about it is, you'll ask me back."

Melia shook her head before Dana gripped her again. Driving her hand up hard under Melia's chin, she banged Melia's head against the shelf. Melia still struggled with Dana's hand, trying to pull it from her throat as her vision began to darken. Desperate, she kicked at Dana, her bare heel striking against Dana's knee.

Dana grunted with pain. "Stupid bitch!"

Melia didn't see the movement of Dana's right fist until it connected with the side of her face. She saw an explosion of darkness and felt a burning heat that flashed from her cheekbone up to her forehead.

Melia's body slumped at the pain and the lack of oxygen. But Dana wouldn't let her fall. She hit her again. And again.

At last, Melia felt herself falling. She didn't know if it was real or if she was just falling into darkness until she hit the floor. Dana kicked her in the side and all Melia could do was curl into a ball and close her eyes.

"You fucking bitch," Dana leaned down and spat the words in her face. "You stupid fucking bitch—look what you made me do!"

Melia tried to curl her body tighter, to pull so deeply into herself that Dana couldn't find her. Escape was not so easy.

"I said, look what you made me do!" Dana grabbed a handful of Melia's hair and shook her head until she was forced to open her eyes. Dana's expression was still twisted with rage and the fist she held in front of Melia's face was smeared with blood.

Melia knew it was her own blood, she could feel it running down her cheek from a point of pain below her left eye. "I'm sorry . . ."

"Fuck you, Melia. It's too late to be sorry."

"Please, Dana . . ." Melia was ashamed at the pleading sound of her voice, but she'd never been so afraid for her life. She reached up cautiously to touch Dana's face. "What can I do?"

Dana slapped Melia's hand away. "It's too late to do anything. You already called her, you can't change that now."

Chris.

Dana caught the brief flash of hope in Melia's eyes and laughed. "Didn't help you much, did it?" She released Melia's hair and stood. Just when Melia thought she was going to kick her again, Dana walked to the other side of the bed and leisurely began to dress. Melia stayed on the floor, forcing herself to not look up at Dana.

"I'm not leaving because I'm afraid of Chris. In fact, I'm tempted to stay here and make you watch me kick her ass, too." Dana strolled to the closet and took out her coat. "Wouldn't that be humiliating when you took me back? You'd never be able to look her in the eye again."

"I won't take you back." Melia's pained voice was barely audible. But Melia knew she spoke the truth this time. There was a cold certainty inside her unlike anything she'd felt in her life.

"Yeah, whatever. We'll see when the time comes."

Melia tried not to tense her muscles when Dana came to stand over her again. Dana squatted down and kissed Melia on the forehead. Tasting the bitterness of her own blood, Melia closed her eyes.

"I'll call you," Dana whispered.

When Melia found the will to open her eyes again, Dana was gone.

Eight

Depression settled over Parker like a suffocating blanket of snow. The injury on her forehead continued to shoot agonizing pain down behind her eyes and it seemed that she could never get warm. During her last trip to the lunchroom to gather her stockpile, she'd stolen two tablecloths for covers, they did nothing to keep out the chill. When she tried to move around enough to get her blood flowing, the headaches quickly immobilized her.

The woman had not returned. Parker was afraid that she'd gone for good. She thought about the woman constantly, about the things she wished she'd written in the note, about who the woman was going home to, and even the possibility that she was dead. Parker didn't want to believe it, but what else would prevent the woman from coming to work? The two days that no one at all had shown up had given Parker hope that she would return with the others. When she did not, Parker believed the worst.

Parker stared at the cover of the book. She'd leaned it against the wall so she could look at it as she lay there. It hadn't been as good as the first book, the one about the women, but she had finished it the first day. Now, she couldn't read anymore, her eyes tired too soon and the words were not worth the throbbing pain.

From down below, Parker could hear the quiet of lunch time. Though a few of the workers stayed at their desks, most went out to eat. When they started coming back and the noise level increased, she suddenly felt hopeful. Perhaps the woman had other responsibilities this morning and she had come back now. Steeling herself against a probable disappointment, Parker struggled to escape the covers. She didn't trust herself to walk the beams but crawled instead. Several times over the last two days she had almost fallen through the ceiling.

When she had felt better, she'd used her knife to cut small notches in the edges of the tile above the woman's cubicle. The gaps gave her tiny windows which allowed a full view of the room. She had cut carefully and didn't think her handiwork was visible from the floor.

Over the woman's desk, Parker put her eye to a notch. Her depression held firm, the woman was not there. She dropped her head, and sighed heavily. Crawling back to her corner no longer seemed worth the trouble. She lay there for a few minutes, gathering up strength to push herself beyond her apathy. Just as she drew herself up to turn around on the narrow beam, something caught her attention. It took her a moment to realize what had changed in the scene below her. When she finally made the connection, she almost cried and laughed in the same instant.

A book was leaning against the Melia's machine, propped between the letter board and the machine's square base. The way it stood there on its edge made it hard to spot from above. But Melia had, at sometime, come and left her another book. It was their way of communicating. A thread that linked them. A thread that Parker would wind up closer and closer until she could bind the woman to her with unbreakable knots. She started to reach down to pull away the tile before she realized what she was doing. She stopped abruptly and held her hand tightly to her chest.

With a smile on her face, Parker tilted her head to study the book. It was another one about the West, she could see that from the painting on its cover. Melia didn't seem to read anything else and Parker knew that this fascination would weigh heavily in Parker's favor.

As far as Parker was concerned, the subject of the books Melia left for her no longer mattered. What stirred her up and kept her hopeful was the possibility of a note tucked within the pages. Parker hoped that Melia had written a response. She was feeling so restless, she needed to feel that some progress was being made in getting herself out of this predicament and back to her own time. What she needed was someone intelligent enough to help her figure out what had happened. And Parker had a strong feeling about Melia that went well beyond her growing physical attraction.

Hell, for all she knew, time travel was commonplace in this age. After all, she'd witnessed wonders at least that improbable just in this building and these people took all of them in stride. It could be that every night Melia left the office, she used some machine to take her back to Parker's world. Or even beyond this time and into the distant future. Although it would ensure that Parker could make it home, deep inside she hoped it wasn't true. She just didn't want life to be so unpredictable.

The end of the work day took forever to come. Parker was too excited to sleep, which made the day seem even longer. She tried to rest, hoping that her head would improve enough to allow her to read. She lay there thinking of what she would write for the woman, planning it all out until she realized that she would need to respond to the note Melia might have written. The waiting was agony. Still, the anticipation felt better to her body than physical exertion, it did wonders to keep her blood pumping and her thoughts spinning.

The tapping of fingers faded slowly, then suddenly died. Parker strained to hear the final footsteps walking away and the elevator making its last trip down. When all was silent on the fourteenth floor, she continued to wait, though it was even harder now. She had to give the guards time to come up and inspect the large room. Foolishly, they kept to a pattern and their habit was to check this area as soon as the workers left. Without fail, they arrived at the same time each night. Less predictable were their night long checks, they could pop in at anytime, and did so more frequently since Parker had scared them. But tonight it wouldn't matter. She would slip down, get the book, and go right back to her hideout. Later, after writing her own note, she would return it, tucked in the pages of the book she had now. She didn't have any other reason to be moving around tonight. Her food supplies were holding out and she could drop directly down into the women's room any time the need arose. The guards never entered that room after their initial check of the floor. Apparently they didn't think ghosts or prowlers would need it.

The security guard came and went. Parker forced herself to lie still, counting five hundred heartbeats before crossing the ceiling to Melia's cubicle. When she arose her head felt clearer and she had more control of her body. Parker suspected that her inactivity was crippling her more than the injury to her forehead.

Although she was in no hurry and felt no fear of being discovered, it took Parker less than thirty seconds to drop down, pick up the book, and haul herself back up into the ceiling.

∩   ∩   ∩   ∩   ∩

Monday night came, and Melia couldn't wait for Tuesday morning to return to her office. She'd changed the locks on her doors, changed her phone number, the only thing that hadn't changed was her conviction. She was done with Dana. There would be no more coming back.

And it wasn't just the destruction of her books or the bruises darkening her left cheekbone and eye. Melia had waited for Chris to say "I warned you" as they sat in the middle of her bedroom, among the torn pages, making a long list of novels Melia would need to replace. Chris had never said a word that was not kind, hadn't looked at Melia in any way that was not compassionate and loving. This increased her conviction. As they worked together, Melia had watched Chris and thought of Dana's threat. Maybe Melia could flirt with danger and risk her own well-being, but she could not allow her actions to endanger her friends. No sex was that good and sleeping alone was a small price to pay for their safety.

Melia had gone home with Chris after her fight with Dana on Saturday night. She refused to see a doctor, knowing that her lies about how she got the injuries would be too easily seen through. She would not report Dana, although she didn't understand her own resistance to making Dana face the consequences of her actions.

Feeling guilty after two full days of Molly's spoiling, Melia needed to get out for a while. And as Monday wore on, Melia could not stop herself from thinking of the camera silently storing a picture every minute. She couldn't wait for

Tuesday morning. She could not possibly go to the office, pick up the disk, and finish her shift before going to the bookstore to view the images.

By seven o'clock the disk would be full, and if the book was gone, she would know. Five after seven Melia was in her car, headed for the Denver Tech Center. Twenty minutes later, she left her car in the underground garage beneath her office building.

Melia was intent on getting her hands on the disk and didn't even consider that security would question her actions. To her surprise, the elevator stopped at the lobby instead of going directly to the fourteenth floor. When the door opened, she saw Aaron hurrying across the lobby toward her.

"Hold the elevator please, Ms. Ellis."

Without responding, Melia held the door open.

"Jesus, what happened to you?" Aaron came up and leaned in to peer at her face.

"A fender bender," she lied. "No seatbelt."

"Ouch. How's your car?"

"Oh, it was a friend's car." The lies left a bad taste in Melia's mouth and she hurried to change the subject. "Seen any more spooks?"

"Shit. Like you wouldn't believe. But it's been quiet since Friday."

The elevator door bumped against her hand and, noticing it, Aaron stepped inside. He lifted his hand to the panel.

"You're going up to the fourteenth floor, right?"

Melia heard his stress on the words "fourteenth floor." She nodded. He punched Fourteen and stood back from the door.

"I appreciate the escort, but I really don't think it's necessary. I just need to grab a disk and leave."

"I don't mind."

I do, Melia thought. "Really Aaron, I'd prefer to go by myself."

"Melia," Aaron said sincerely. "Please, let me check first. Okay?"

"Yeah, whatever." Melia cringed as she said the words. That was Dana's expression and Melia had never thought to hear it come from her mouth.

The elevator reached the fourteenth floor and Aaron stood directly in front of Melia as the doors parted. He placed his hand on the butt of his gun as he scanned the room. Melia had to smile. He was the picture of a gunfighter poised for a shoot-out. Finally satisfied, he stepped aside and gestured for her to go ahead.

"I'll be right back," Melia promised.

"I'll wait here."

Melia hurried down the corridor to her cubicle and met disappointment. The book was still leaning against the monitor, precisely where she had left it. Melia stopped in the doorway. She hadn't considered this . . . the possibly that the book would not be taken had never entered her mind.

"Damn." Melia smacked her fist against her leg and went on into the room. She moved the book and popped the disk out of its drive. Uncertain, she slapped the disk on her palm as she debated her next move. She would have to try again. Unfortunately, Chris hadn't shown her how to set the timer for the camera. She could probably figure it out on her own, but Aaron would not stand there for long without coming to see what was keeping her. It meant she would lose another day. The thought was frustrating. The situation had grown beyond a tantalizing mystery or a thing of curiosity, it had become a challenge. Waiting one more day was unacceptable.

"Damn it!" Melia doubled her fist again, this time striking it down on the side of the book. It flipped up, then fell to the floor. A scrap of paper fluttered to the carpet with it. Melia knew instantly what it was—the same as the first time—she found the note by accident.

A thrill went through her. Would this note bring any sense of resolution? Would it give her reason to fear? She picked up the book and looked at it more closely. It was not the book she'd left Sunday night, but the time before. Her bait had been another lesbian book and this was just a regular Western novel. Melia slid the book in her coat pocket and knelt to take the note.

Same handwriting, same red ink. The note was very short. Melia held it up to catch the light and read

Thank you for the book (books) but I'm mighty disappointed you didn't write. It don't seem polite. If I offended you I am sorry. If you don't want to talk to me don't leave anymore books. I haven't seen you for a few days. I hope you're all right.

"Oh." Melia rubbed her forehead. She'd forgotten the note. Planning to write one while she was at the office Saturday, she'd been so involved with helping Chris set the trap that it had completely slipped her mind.

"Melia? You all right over there?"

"Yes, Aaron. I'll be right there. I'm almost done." Melia pulled a sheet of note paper from her desk and scrawled a single line: I'm all right, thank you. She leaned it against the monitor where the book had been.

Melia didn't know the wisdom of what she was doing, but it was only polite. Clutching the disk that would surely answer her questions, Melia jogged back to the elevator and a relieved Aaron.

"My god, Melia. We've been through the disk twice."

Chris pushed her chair back and covered her bloodshot eyes with her hands. "There's nothing there."

"There has to be." Melia felt like screaming. She wanted to jump up and stomp around the room, tearing out her hair. How, after their best laid plans, could there be nothing on the disk? It was just wrong.

"It's the minute between images," Chris stated, not for the first time. "I was afraid it was too much time."

"But they had to pick up that book, look for a note, write one of their own, and then leave the other book. How could they do all that in under a minute?"

"I give up. It is a ghost."

"Very fucking funny. I don't need to hear that." Melia lifted her cup of lukewarm tea and drained it. She flexed the muscles in her stiff shoulders and said the words Chris did not want to hear. "I'm going to go through it one more time."

Chris groaned. "You're on your own, hon. I can't sit through this again. I'm going home and see if I've been good enough lately to deserve a massage."

"You don't mind if I—"

"No, you go ahead. Lang will close down in about an hour and a half. Feel free."

Melia stood and gave Chris a hug. "Thanks. For everything."

As they hugged, Chris lightly rubbed the tense muscles of Melia's lower back. "You coming back to our place tonight?"

"No, I think I'll go home."

"I hate to think of you by yourself." Chris pulled away from Melia and looked down into her face. "You know, I'm sure Lang would be happy to put you up for a night or two."

"With your blessing, no doubt." Melia pushed Chris away and slapped at her playfully.

"Blessing, hell. I'm going to go tell her it's a condition for keeping her job."

"Don't you dare, Chris. Teasing aside, I really don't want to lead her on."

"She's a big girl."

"That's for damn sure."

Chris laughed and swept Melia up off the floor. Melia felt like Scarlet O'Hara in Rhett Butler's arms. "But we're all big girls next to you."

"Put me down, you oaf." Melia kicked, but Chris held her tight as she walked to the front of the store.

Langley looked up from her magazine, barely managing to keep the bland facial expression that suggested she was used to seeing women carried around the store like jumbo bags of dog food.

"This thing called me an oaf. Can you believe that?"

"Mm . . . no." Langley tapped her pen to her lips and looked thoughtful. "I'd say you're more of a lout than an oaf. But the line is pretty thin there."

"Okay! I'm sorry. Put me down, you lout." Melia demanded.

Chris immediately sat her on her feet. She pointed to Langley. "Now this is a woman who knows her vocabulary. Synonyms and antonyms inside and out. She's my thesaurus."

"Lucky you." Melia told Langley. She left them grinning at each other and went back into the back room.

The bookstore quieted after Chris left. Melia clicked through the images, one after another, almost ready to accept that there was nothing to be seen. An unexpected touch on her arm made her jump.

Langley took a step back and smiled. The light from the moniter glinted from a small, silver stud through her bottom lip. She placed a steaming cup of tea near Melia's elbow.

"Just thought you needed a warm-up, since you're working so hard in here."

Melia took a grateful sip of the hot, sweet tea. "Thanks, Lang. I do need a break. This is just a waste of time."

"Do you mind if I ask what you're looking for?"

Melia considered the wisdom of telling the story to anyone else. Finally, she relented and motioned for Langley to take a seat next to her.

"I really can't go into the whole story, but I was trying to catch someone coming into my office after hours." Melia tapped her finger against the image of her cubicle.

"Are they stealing from you?"

"No, just borrowing books. But I don't know who it is and it's making me crazy."

Langley chuckled, a low, warm sound that brought a smile to Melia's face. "Like a second grade secret admirer, huh?"

"I guess you could put it that way." The notion was certainly less sinister than what Melia had come up with.

"Is that the book they're supposed to take?" Langley pointed to a small triangle on the extreme edge of the screen.

Melia's eyes widened. She had not noticed the tiny corner of the book in the image. "Yes! Then I can just look . . ." Clicking rapidly through the images, she forgot Langley sitting beside her.

"There," Langley pointed again. "It's gone."

"What time?" Melia looked at the time stamp at the side of the image and answered her own question. "Five fourteen. And the other returned at what time?"

She kept clicking the mouse. Without any sign of movement or the suggestion that a human hand had neared the desk, a book was replaced. "Five forty. So they left to write the note."

"I hope you don't expect me to understand that."

"No. I'm sorry. Just thinking out loud."

Langley patted her shoulder and stood. "I'll leave you to it. It's time for me to get ready to close."

"Thanks so much for spotting the book, you gave me something to go from."

Langley shrugged. "Sometimes the only way to get the big picture is to look at the details."

Melia smiled up at her, then remembered with a pang how rude she'd been to Langley on the street while she waited for Dana to pick her up. She remembered Dana's racist remark and thought with regret how insulted Lang must have been, yet Langley had been nothing but kind to Melia. "Listen, Lang. I need to apologize for last week. I didn't mean—"

Langley raised her hand to stop Melia. "It's done, Mel. I don't need an apology. I've already heard the only thing I needed to hear."

"Which is?"

"Dana is out."

Melia rubbed her forehead, the characteristic gesture making her wince as her fingers crossed the bruise that spread above her eye. "So, Chris told you all about it?"

"No, she told me Dana is out. Looking at you, that's all I need to know." Langley dropped her head and tugged at the rings in her earlobe. "In fact, knowing that she's gone is the only way I can look at you without going off."

"You're still angry."

"Hell, yes, I'm still angry."

"I'm—"

Langley looked up quickly and the expression on her face stopped Melia. "Don't you dare say you're sorry, Melia. I won't hear it, and I won't hear you defend her."

Melia pressed her lips together to keep the word from being said. Reaching out, she took Langley's hand.

"Well, it's true, Lang. She's gone," Melia paused, not sure how to continue. "But I'm not really looking for—"

"Neither am I. I like you, I like to flirt with you, but I'm satisfied to keep it at that." She gave Melia's hand a squeeze then pulled free. "If anything more is meant to happen, it will."

Before Melia could respond, Langley turned and left the room. Melia could hear her humming as she did up her paperwork.

Melia turned her attention back to the computer. There was a time frame of nearly a half an hour. The book borrower had stayed in the building to write the note and return the other book. There was no way that a person could do that and not encounter Aaron or another guard as they did the once through. Tomorrow night, she would ask Aaron who had stayed late. Problem solved.

Melia leaned back and put her feet on the desk. She had such a sense of satisfaction that she toyed with the idea of inviting Langley out for dinner and a drink to thank her. It was her attention to detail that had given Melia her lead. She smiled smugly at the computer screen.

"Details." She studied the screen, seeing her office space from an unusual angle. It was still nothing to be thrilled about, regardless of the perspective. Being drained of all color by the black and white camera made it appear even colder, she hadn't realized how much the bland shade of her cubicle walls warmed the space up. It was left austere and barren with nothing but shadows and lines of varying tones of gray to separate the objects.

Melia leaned the chair forward, staring at the frozen instant in time. There in the image was something else she hadn't noticed before and wouldn't have noticed without Lang's suggestion. Her heart beat hard as fear welled up in her chest. She was afraid to click the mouse, afraid to move to the next moment in time. If this detail changed, she just didn't know what she would do, what she would think. She clicked it. The long edge of shadow that darkened the corner of her keyboard disappeared. Clicking back she could see, distorted, but still clear, the shadowy outline of a person's body leaning over her desk. But it wasn't possible. Not at that angle. There was no way a person standing in her cubicle could cast a shadow in that direction. It had to be coming from above the desk, from the ceiling.

∩   ∩   ∩   ∩   ∩

Dana sat at the bar, her head hung low, staring into the ashtray at the bright red ring some lipstick lesbian had left around a white cigarette butt. She was drinking whiskey sours. She'd had a few; the bartenders knew how many and just when to cut her off. Her temper was too well known for her to get away with much. But that was why Dana had come here instead of another bar that might give her the benefit of the doubt. She knew she didn't deserve it. She had fucked up. Big.

Between six and seven, she'd gone to Melia's place. Her key didn't fit anymore. The windows were all locked and the cat had even glared at her through the screen. She'd stood there, watching him gloat, thinking that if she'd have killed him instead of touching those damn books she wouldn't be standing outside at that point. They'd probably be at the pet store picking out a puppy and Melia would still love her.

"Shit. Who am I kidding? She never loved me." Dana tipped back the drink and drained it.

The young, crop-haired bartender didn't bother to look up at the sound of Dana's voice. With only two weeks on the job, she already knew lovelorn and was just not interested in hearing it anymore. Dana's empty glass hitting the bar was another thing. She responded to that instantly. Whisking away the glass without waiting for Dana to order, she poured an extra long shot.

"Last one, Dana," she said as she slid the drink over with one hand and scooped up Dana's cash with the other.

"So, why is it that you know my name, and I don't know yours?" Dana looked up into the bartender's face for the first time that evening. Dana's eyes appeared cold and sober, although the bartender knew that she was well beyond legally drunk.

"You don't know my name because you don't have to stand here with your hand on the phone, ready to call 911 because I'm sitting where you are drinking. And because you never asked."

"I'm asking now." Dana studied the set of the woman's small chin as she tried to look tough, determined. The effect was wasted on Dana, they both knew she was tougher.

"My name's Benny."

"Well, Benny. Do you think I could use that phone you're so fond of?"

"Why not? AA is a local call."

Dana's jaw tightened and her hand gripped her glass until her knuckles whitened. She glared at Benny, waiting for her thin face to become as white as Dana's knuckles. Suddenly, unexpectedly, Dana laughed. "Christ, you're good for business, aren't you?"

Relief washed over Benny. She smiled. "Sorry, sometimes I can't help myself. I say things before I think."

"Hey, I got the same problem."

"So I hear." Benny sat the phone down on the bar in front of Dana. "Go ahead. I'll be right back."

"Wait. You know the number to any book stores?"

Benny laughed. Her response was to toss the phone book on the bar next to Dana.

Now that is a normal woman, Dana thought. Melia would have been able to rattle off ten or twelve numbers. She thumbed through the yellow pages until she spotted the bookstore with the largest ad. Barnes & Noble. Stupid name. But they were open late. She dialed the number and ignored the pleasantries of the clerk who answered.

"You got any Western books?" she asked without preamble.

"Well, yes. We have the largest sele—"

"How many?"

The clerk stuttered for a moment, a little harried by Dana's brusqueness. "Um, about 300 titles. Both current and back list."

"Yeah, whatever. I'll take them."

"You—you want all of them?"

Dana rubbed her forehead, unconscious of the gesture she'd picked up from Melia. She couldn't understand why people had to be so damn slow. "One of each will do. Now do you deliver?"

"I—I have no idea. I'll have to talk to my manager."

"If you have a manager that can answer my questions, then why the hell am I talking to you?" Dana shouted. She ignored the faces that turned her way. "Give me the goddamn manager."

The clerk put her on hold without another word. Dana clenched her teeth as she suffered through an interminable rendition of an orchestra playing "Come To My Window." Sipping her drink through her teeth, she tried to keep herself from exploding.

"May I help you?"

Dana inhaled and exhaled slowly before replying. "If you can get me a copy of every Western book you have in stock and deliver them to the address I specify, you can help me. If you can't, I want to talk to the person who can."

"I can't do that, and before you say anything, no one here can. If you would be so kind as to come to the store and make this order in person, we might be able to help you."

"I see. Kind of like you need to see the color of my money."

"Something like that. I'm sure you understand. It's not every day that we get a request like this."

"Hey, it's not every day that I make a request like this." Dana tilted back her drink then wiped her lips with her forefinger. "How late are you there?"

"If you're serious, I'll stay here as late as you need. When can you get here?"

"When I get there." Dana heard the manager's voice continue as she replaced the receiver, but whatever she had to say didn't matter. She hung up. Benny swept by and picked up the phone and Dana's empty glass.

"When do you get off work?" Dana asked abruptly.

"Bout a half an hour."

Dana stood from her barstool and dug into her pocket. She fished out a wad of bills. Benny raised her eyebrows, but said nothing. "I'm too drunk to drive. In a half an hour, you come outside and look for a light blue four by four. If I'm still here, I'll give you two hundred dollars to drive me downtown."

"Are you serious?"

Dana pushed a hundred dollar bill into her hand. "I'm serious."

"Then I'm off work. Right now." Benny turned away, undoing the short black apron that rode low on her hips. "Carla, I'm out of here."

Carla, a tall blonde who had been pointedly ignoring Dana all evening, rushed over to her. She tried to pull Benny aside so that Dana could not hear what she was about to say. "You can say whatever you got to say in front of me." Dana leaned her elbows on the bar and smiled. "I'm harmless."

"And I'm the Virgin Mary," Carla snapped back. She turned to Benny and stroked the short, black hair at her temple. "Do I have to warn you about her again? I already told you, she's bad news. You can't seriously be thinking about leaving with her."

"Two hundred dollars? You bet I'm seriously thinking about it."

Carla whipped back around and glared at Dana. "Go get a prostitute, you asshole. Leave her alone."

Dana laughed. Benny couldn't prevent a grin from coming over her face.

"This is all the respect I get after my years of faithful patronage? Listen," Dana told Benny. "When your mom gets finished lecturing you, meet me in the parking lot."

Weaving through the growing crowd of women, Dana left the bar without looking back to see if Benny would follow. She knew she would. In five minutes she was there, grinning eagerly and revving Dana's engine.

"To the bookstore, Benny," Dana commanded, leaning back the passenger seat and folding her arms behind her head.

"Which one?"

"I don't know. Something with a barn in it?"

"Gotcha. But it's not downtown."

"Look at me, Benny." Dana turned her head and let Benny stare into her eyes long enough to get nervous. "Do I look like I care?"

Benny swallowed and Dana was impressed that she managed a smile. "Not at all."

"Not about anything you could say or do. Now let's go if we're going."

"You got it." Benny let the engine growl and pulled smoothly out of the parking lot.

At the bookstore, Dana's platinum card and her last name got her everything she wanted. The manager ordered cappuccino in heavy ceramic cups for her and Benny while they sat and watched three serious-faced clerks remove books from the shelves and pack them into boxes. After about fifteen minutes, Dana was bored. She rose from her seat and stretched.

"I'm getting sober, Benny. I don't like it."

Benny looked up through the steam rising from her cappuccino. "You really going to buy one of everything?"

"No. Just the Westerns."

"This is just bizarre. I've never seen anyone do something like this." Benny nudged a nearby stack of books with her toe. One of the clerks quickly moved the books to the safety of a waiting box.

Dana shrugged. "You want something?"

"Other than two hundred dollars?" At Dana's nod, Benny thought for a moment. "I'll take a t-shirt. Something like a souvenir of this."

There was rack of t-shirts across the room. Dana caught one of the clerks and made him pick out a couple of shirts in Benny's size. She watched, enjoying the smile of delight on Benny's face.

"These can be delivered before five tomorrow?" Dana asked, waving her hand at the growing pile of boxes. Somehow the manager knew that it was not a question. She nodded her assurance.

"Good. Benny, get me the hell out of here. I've seen enough books to last me a lifetime."

Benny stood and looked for a place to put her still half full cup of coffee.

"Just take it."

"But it's not—"

"Just take it. Christ, what are they going to say to you?" Dana walked past her, headed for the door. "Hurry up before I decide that I'm sober enough to drive myself."

Benny gulped down another swallow of the coffee and sat the cup carefully on the floor. She grabbed up her t-shirts and ran to follow Dana. Dana had the doors to her truck unlocked by the time Benny caught up with her. She handed her the keys.

"Where to now?"

"I said, at least fifty times, that I'm getting sober. Take me to a liquor store."

"All right." Benny pushed Dana's door closed behind her. She stood for a moment, then tapped on the window. Dana looked out at her. "Put on your seat belt."

Dana shook her head and laughed. "Get your ass in here and drive me to the liquor store."

Benny ran around the front of the truck. She got in and reached over Dana, pulling the belt down over her shoulder and clipping it closed. Her hand, not so casually, brushed Dana's side. Dana shook her head again and leaned back. She closed her eyes and relaxed as the truck rumbled down the street. Despite her claim of sobering up, before a block and a half had rolled under the wheels, Dana fell asleep in her seat.

A tapping on her shoulder woke her. She looked out the window and had no idea where she was. The lights of the truck shone on the cracked concrete steps of a weathered apartment building. She looked over at the young woman pushing lightly on her arm.

"This doesn't look like a liquor store."

"Been there." Benny held up a long, brown bag. "I got whiskey. I hope it's okay. I broke that hundred you gave me."

"That looks fine." Dana took the bag and pulled out the bottle. Without even a glance at the label, she unscrewed the lid and took a long drink. Benny wrinkled her nose as she watched Dana swallow.

"So where are we?"

Benny shrugged uncomfortably, no longer playing the part of the self-assured dyke from behind the bar. "You were asleep. I brought you to my place."

"Your place?" Dana asked dryly. She turned a critical eye to the run-down front of the building. "So, people actually do live in places like this?"

Benny looked away, clearly hurt. She turned off the lights. They sat for a moment in the darkness, silent. Dana passed her the bottle, but she shook her head.

"So, you want that other hundred now, or were you expecting me to leave it on the nightstand?"

Benny stared out through the windshield, her body stiff. Nothing moved but her lips when she spoke. "Damn, why do you have to be so cold?"

"I don't know." Dana took another drink and leaned back in her seat. The metal of the door frame was cool against her arm. "I really don't."

Benny didn't respond. Dana contemplated her profile. Her features were delicate, soft and feminine, despite her too-obvious attempts at toughness. She looked like a porcelain cameo of a very young woman. And she was just a woman. Inside, they were all just women. And it was so easy to hurt them, so much harder to heal. Dana made the only gesture she knew. Taking out a handful of bills, she then reached over and tucked them into the front pocket of Benny's jeans. It was much more than the hundred she owed her, but it was not enough. The one thing she had to give was never enough.

Dana made a fist, then stared down at her knuckles. She couldn't see the faint bruise on the back of her hand, gained from striking Melia's cheekbone, but she could feel it there. She shook away a sense of regret before it could overwhelm her and looked back to the woman beside her.

"Well, what the fuck, Benny. We got whiskey, we got t-shirts to wear, why not?" Dana smiled sadly and patted Benny on the leg. "Take me to your place."

Nine

When Melia returned to her cubicle the next day, she felt the same feeling of being watched, but now she was sure where it was coming from. She might as well have stayed home for all the work she'd done. She kept her fingers on the keyboard and her eyes on the monitor screen, but her mind was not on programming. Her thoughts raced over her options. Should she alert security that someone might be up there? Should she hide and wait for them to jump down for another book? The first option was the most intelligent, but Melia already knew what she was going to do. She wanted to go up there. She had to go up there. And she had a plan to do it.

What she hadn't considered was her coworkers' reaction to the bruises on her face. She spent half the day repeating the lies. Even though each person who asked seemed to leave her cubicle with a sense of relief, she couldn't guess how many of them believed her. But she'd never discussed her personal life and they had long since stopped trying to draw her out.

The most nerve-wracking moment came when her supervisor called and asked her into his office. Melia dreaded each step toward Bob's room, but he had not said a word about her face. He only repeated his demand for her vacation request and she had fled with the promise to have it in his e-mail by the end of the shift. At random, she picked the last week in March, sent the message, and then promptly forgot about it.

When the office cleared out at five o'clock, Melia stayed in her chair. Like clockwork, Aaron showed up to do his once through of her floor. He didn't speak as he left the elevator and Melia pretended not to notice as he went directly to the restrooms and checked each in turn. Not until he approached her cubicle did Melia act as if she were aware of his presence.

"Hey, Ms. Ellis."

"Hello, Aaron." She turned her chair and faced him. "Is it that time already?"

"Yep. You know Melia, you're the only one they have to pry out of here like a bad tooth. What is it about this job that won't let you go home?"

"It's exciting. And challenging." Thinking of what she planned to do, she couldn't resist adding, "And it gets more exciting every day."

"I guess you're lucky. Excitement in my line of work is never good. The more bored I am, the better."

Melia grimaced and shook her head. "I don't envy you."

"Well, it used to be better when I could read. Now, I'm so spooked here that I haven't read a book in almost a week." He held out his hand and she could see a minute tremor. "Withdrawals."

Melia laughed and reached into her stockpile of books. She was careful to pick one without a lesbian theme. "Try this. It's not horror, just a nice, peaceful, string em up or shoot em down western. I guarantee you *will* be bored."

Aaron started to shake his head, one of his glib put-downs of the genre on his lips, but then shrugged instead. He took the book. "Why not? Just don't tell a soul."

"Not a word," Melia promised. "Listen, before you go, did anyone stay here late last night?"

"From this floor?"

"Um . . . I don't know. Just did you see anyone here?"

"God, Melia. Don't start that spook shit again, I'm just getting calmed down from the last encounter."

"The blood stain?"

Aaron drew back in confusion. "Blood stain? What in the hell are you talking about?"

"Oh. I'm sorry, I think I'm confusing this with some movie . . ." She gestured at her face and added, "Since I conked the dash, some things aren't so clear." Melia was appalled at how quickly the lie was concocted. She was getting far too good at it.

"Don't even do that to me." He affected a shudder. "But, to answer your question, no. No one was here last night, but you. Missing something again?"

"No." She let it rest at that.

Aaron shrugged. "I'd better get on with it."

"You know, I think I should be able to find something to do out there. I believe I'll just go for a drive."

"Good for you. Can't hurt you any." He laughed at his own joke and Melia smiled weakly.

"I hope not." Melia stood and pulled on her coat. He stepped back as she walked from the cubicle. She passed him and he walked the other way.

"I'll see you tomorrow," Melia called out when she reached the elevator.

Aaron didn't look back, he just waved his hand and continued down the hall. Melia punched the button for the lobby, then stepped out of the elevator as the door was closing. She rushed to the restroom door and carefully pushed it open just enough to slip through.

The darkness in the room was complete. Not even a sliver of light came through any cracks around the door. She imagined she could hear her heart beating in the stillness. She hadn't realized that sound from the other room didn't carry into this one. There was no way she would know when Aaron left the floor. Melia touched her fingers to the wall and used it to guide her steps away from the door. When her thighs bumped against the long counter of sinks, she put her hand down and checked to make sure the counter in front of her was dry. She turned and boosted herself up to sit and wait.

After an immeasurable amount of time had passed Melia remembered the night light on her watch. She pushed the button and was amazed at how the tiny light burned her eyes. It was only five fifteen. Melia convinced herself to wait until five thirty, surely Aaron would be long gone by that time. Closing her eyes, she swung her legs back and forth and tried to concentrate on something besides the waiting.

Fifteen minutes in complete, soundless darkness proved to be an eternity. Melia could hold out no longer than seven. The fourth time she checked her watch it was five twenty-two and she knew that she had to get out of this room or scream. She smiled at her unusual impatience, normally she could have placed herself in any of a dozen different worlds and been content to wait out the night. But what was normal anymore? What she was considering was certainly far from normal behavior.

Expecting the counter to be higher than it was, Melia pushed herself off and hit the floor with a jarring thud. She reached out for the wall and had to suppress a moment's panic when she could not find any solidity around her. Fingertips extended, she shuffled forward until her hand touched the cool metal of the door. Grasping the handle, she jerked the door open. There was no longer any thought of secrecy, she had to get out and she didn't care who might see her go.

Out in the office space, the overhead lights were turned off. Still, the room seemed brightly lit to Melia's unaccustomed eyes. She leaned against the near wall and blinked until she could see clearly. The long room was again hers alone.

Melia looked to the ceiling. She had never paid it the slightest attention before. Even when her brief morning meditations drew her eyes upward, she never noticed it. But there were the tiles, dividing the ceiling like a huge board game and hanging nearer to the tops of the partitions than she would have imagined. If she stood on her desk, she could probably reach high enough to brush her fingertips against it. Another boost would be necessary for her to move the tile aside.

As she walked to her cubicle, she considered her options. Her chair was on rollers and she had no interest in trying to maintain her balance while simultaneously trying to keep the chair from rolling off the desk. Her trash can was metal and would give her another foot and a half, but that was probably not enough for safety. Not knowing what the ceiling tiles were made of and how heavy they were, she thought it best to get high enough to put her shoulder into lifting it. As she passed by other cubicles, she looked for a chair without rollers. She had to go into her supervisor's office to find one. She picked up the small wooden chair and lugged it back to her space.

After stacking the chair and the trash can on her desk, she stepped back and evaluated the setup. It looked risky. If she fell and broke her arm or leg, it was not going to be easy to come up with a plausible reason why she had been climbing to the ceiling. She pulled her desk chair out and dropped into it. Second thoughts were chewing away her determination.

"Tell me one sensible reason why you're doing this," Melia spoke into the quiet of the room. "You have no clue what you're going to see up there and, chances are, you're not climbing into an entirely safe situation here."

Her toe touched the place on the floor where she remembered seeing the blood stain. If there was a person up there, they could be injured. But why would they hide in the ceiling instead of getting medical attention? There was only one reason she could imagine; the person, this Parker, was a criminal, hiding from the police. Perhaps an escaped convict. Melia swallowed hard and suddenly felt the pressure of the ceiling, so close to her head, bearing down even stronger. She scooted her chair back up to the desk and pulled the telephone into her lap. She could alert security with the press of a few buttons. They would be here in probably less than a minute.

Feeling reassured with the phone at hand, Melia went back to her contemplation. The convict scenario was likely, but the reasoning had its flaws. Why would the person take so many risks and draw so much of her attention to their presence by stealing books? Why would they write such cryptic notes, sure to engage her curiosity, if they wanted no one to discover them? How could they know her feelings, her longing to distance herself from the real world and let time just pass by on its own? The notes and the hand that wrote them were what was drawing her in.

"Damn you," Melia whispered, addressing both herself and the person who might be up there somewhere. She had to know, she could not come here every day and not be possessed by the knowledge that she had backed out of knowing the truth. Damn her cowardice, damn her uncertainty, she was going up there.

Without allowing herself to hesitate, Melia replaced the phone on its corner of the desk and stood. In case she did fall, she pushed the desk chair out of the cubicle and into the hallway. The desk, the wooden chair, the trash can; in three easy steps she was at the ceiling. Her makeshift staircase was high enough that she had to lean a bit to keep from knocking her head against the tiles. She put her palms to the resilient material and carefully pushed. The tile was lighter than she imagined it would be and it moved away easily, revealing a darkened crawl space that was at least four and a half feet high. She would never have dreamed that there was that much space between her ceiling and the floor above.

Melia turned in a cautious, slow circle, taking care not to tip over the trash can. Above was much darker than below, but Melia could make out the far walls and a few details in between. Unlike the room below, this space was partitioned off into several enclosed areas. Narrow beams criss-crossed the ceiling and held the tiles; the base of the floor above was exposed wood over thick metal beams. The wiring connecting the florescent lights ran in tangles and bunches toward a mass of electrical connections on the north wall. In the nearest corner, Melia saw several dark shapes. None seemed to be the size of a human body, and with that reassurance, she decided that she would begin her search there.

By hooking her elbows over the beam she'd been leaning against, Melia was able to pull herself into the space without much effort. She struggled to mount the beam and stay on it, resisting the temptation to put her hands out on the tiles beside her to catch her balance. As easy as the tile had been for her to move, she knew they would not support her weight.

Moving in a careful crouch, Melia made her way to the corner. She could see that someone had placed boards across the beams to build a small platform. Stepping off the beam, she squatted on the edge of the platform, unsure of how to proceed. Was wanting to know more about the person who hid up here a good enough reason to invade someone's privacy? She didn't even know what she was looking for. There was no way to deduce anything from the items she could see.

A thin, brown coat caught her eye. It was folded into a compact square and was probably being used as a pillow. Melia picked it up and unfolded it. It was very plain, with nothing to suggest if it had been made for a man or a woman. The size didn't tell her anything either. Without realizing what she was doing, Melia lifted the cloth and smelled it. There was no scent of perfume or sweat, but the sharp bite of wood smoke was obvious to her nose. Not allowing herself to hesitate, she reached into one of the front pockets and emptied its contents onto the rough, wooden floor of the platform.

Two scraps of paper, an empty granola bar wrapper, an old-fashioned box of matches, and a very small pocket knife. Melia recognized the papers immediately, they were the two notes she had written in response to the book borrower. She returned the objects to the pocket. The other was empty. Melia folded the coat slowly and leaned forward to replace it. When she straightened, she felt the hard chill of metal against the back of her neck.

"Just put your hands out, and lean on down again."

The rough, whispered words made the hair stand on Melia's arms. She had no doubt that the pressure against her neck was the barrel of a gun. Carefully, she leaned forward with her weight on her toes until she was about to lose her balance, then stopped. The pressure of the gun barrel increased until she was forced to drop her knees to the boards and put her forehead to the floor. She stretched her hands as far out to the sides as she could reach.

"Don't you move. Don't you make a sound." The voice commanded.

The gun was removed from her neck. Melia felt the platform beneath her shift as the person moved around and to the front of her. She held her breath and listened carefully to every sound that was made as the person retrieved their coat and rustled through the pockets.

"I—I didn't take anything, I—"

The gun barrel tapped lightly against the top of her head. "Don't make a sound."

Melia took a deep breath and tried to keep her muscles relaxed. Her back and legs had already begun to complain of the strain of her position, but she knew she should not shift even slightly to relieve the pain. Biting her lip, she mentally kicked herself for her stupidity. She had known the possibility of getting into trouble by coming up here, but she had not expected to be found out so quickly, or to be faced with a gun.

"Okay, I'm gonna have you do somethin'," the voice whispered again. "You do just what I say."

Melia felt as if ice water was filling her stomach, but she tried to nod to show that she understood and would comply. The person moved farther back, out of her reach.

"Keep your hands where they are and lift your head. I want you to look at me, then put your head right back down."

Her fear increased. She knew she shouldn't speak, but couldn't help it. She kept her voice as quiet as she could and still be heard. "I don't want to look at you. If I don't see you, you don't have to kill me."

A quiet chuckle followed her words. Melia had thought she was as frightened as humanly possible, but the sound proved that fear had even deeper levels.

"Sounds like you think there's some kinda rule to this. If I mean to kill you, it don't matter what you see or don't see."

Melia didn't respond. The low roughness of the voice made it impossible to discern the speaker's gender She kept her head to the boards. At least a minute passed before the person spoke again.

"All right, you lift your head, but keep your eyes closed."

Melia had no trouble keeping her eyes closed. Her curiosity had finally been tamed. She lifted her head as high as she could without moving her hands from the floor. The position was even more painful.

"Son of a bitch." The voice broke from its whisper and Melia knew the person was a woman. She waited, her face reddening as she realized what had caused the outburst.

"Go ahead, put your head down," the woman finally whispered.

Melia put her forehead back to the floor and sighed in relief. Unaware of her own movement, she drew her hands in nearer to her head to ease the tension in her shoulders. Silence wore on, making time pass slower than it had even in the darkness of the restroom. Melia waited as long as possible before speaking.

"Are you Parker?" There was no response, but Melia heard a slight movement. Something slid across the boards and bumped her hand.

"Is that yours?"

Melia opened her eyes a slit and turned her head to look. It was her book. She nodded.

"I'm Parker. Now you're gonna have to look at me."

"Why?"

"Curiosity."

"May I move?"

"After you look, you can get down on your belly."

There was no help for it. Melia couldn't stay in this position much longer. She would have to move and likely get shot anyway, she might as well get a look at the woman who had become an obsession to her over-active imagination. She moved her hands and pushed herself up. Opening her eyes, her breath caught in her throat.

The woman sitting before her was incredible. Melia couldn't have imagined her any better, couldn't have put such a perfect face to her fantasies. The woman's broad shoulders and strong body fit perfectly in the clothing she wore and her outfit looked like she'd just stepped out of a cigarette advertisement. She sat cross legged, her black hat pulled low, and her gun casually pointed at Melia's heart. The small red line of a cut ran across the skin above her eye. The woman was smiling a half-smile, and her white teeth were bared in an animal's snarl.

Melia had the oddest sense of familiarity looking into her face. There was something about her, perhaps her mouth, that Melia found almost intimate. She had seen those lips recently, but they somehow didn't match the coldness of the rest of the woman's features. So, this is Parker, Melia thought to herself, she looks just like a woman named Parker should look. And if she could look past the danger evident in those eyes, or if they had met in any other circumstance, Melia would not hesitate to try and fire her interest.

Not until Parker raised one eyebrow in question did Melia realize how long she'd been staring. Glancing back at the pistol in Parker's hand, Melia carefully got down on her stomach and turned her face away.

"Now what do you s'pose I'm gonna do with you?"

"Talk to me," Melia suggested, trying unsuccessfully to keep the quaver from her voice. "Tell me why you are here."

"Well, shit. I was hopin' you'd tell me that."

Melia didn't know how to respond, but she knew she didn't like the sound of the words. If Parker was mentally unbalanced, all of the rules could go out the window at any time. But Parker had already told her that there were no rules. Melia kept quiet.

Parker moved suddenly and Melia felt the woman standing over her. She tried not to cringe as Parker stepped past her.

"Don't you move."

Melia didn't hear the sound of Parker's footsteps, but out of the corner of her eye she could see her bent over, walking easily across the narrow beam to the ceiling tile Melia had left displaced. Parker glanced back at Melia then knelt down to replace it. She looked down at the desk below.

"Shit!" Parker lashed the word out, then smacked her hand on the beam. Melia thought of the chair and trash can she'd left on her desk. Parker turned and walked back to where Melia lay on the platform. She again stood over Melia, this time with one booted foot to each side of Melia's body.

"You don't make this easy." Parker sounded irritated. "I can't just leave you here, I can't let you run away, but I didn't mean for it to be this way."

Melia didn't know if she was expected to understand the words, but their tone was ominous. With slow movements she hoped were imperceptible in the darkness she pulled her hands in nearer to her shoulders. If she could get her hands under her she could push up fast enough to roll over and break through one of the tiles. She could only hope that she wouldn't crash into something below that would disable her and keep her from running to the elevator. Tensing her muscles to prepare herself, her heightened senses enabled her to pick up the sound she thought was the soft brush of leather.

Parker shifted her weight and Melia froze. She didn't know if the gun was now pointed at the back of her head and was glad that she couldn't see. At this range, there was no way Parker could miss and Melia had no desire to see it coming. All she could do was hold her breath and wait for what would happen next.

Ten

Suddenly, Parker's hands were touching her sides. The strong fingers moved under her hips and lifted her body from the boards. Parker held her easily with one arm wrapped around her waist while the other moved around to undo Melia's belt buckle. Panic overcame Melia. She reached down, trying to push Parker's hand away. She struggled to turn her body over and push herself forward, away from Parker's touch. Parker knelt down and quickly tightened the hold of her arm around Melia's stomach, drawing Melia up on her hands and knees and holding her there with her body pressed tight against Melia's. She quickly pulled Melia's belt from its loops.

"Don't do this—I'll scream," Melia warned as she continued to struggle. She couldn't break free from Parker's hold, but she didn't care about the gun any longer. She would not lie here and allow herself to be raped.

"You scream one time and it will be your last. I don't think that's really what you want." Parker dropped her weight on Melia's back until she'd pushed her to the floor. She lifted her body away, then shoved her knee between Melia's shoulder blades. "It ain't what I want either."

Parker wasn't even breathing hard from the exertion. Melia felt like a bug pinned to the floor. "What *do* you want?" Melia asked anxiously

Parker took Melia's right wrist and pulled it behind her back before answering. "I want you to be quiet. I want some time to talk to you." She put the belt around Melia's wrist then brought her left hand back. She tightened the belt roughly, cinching Melia's hands together. "And I want you to trust me."

"Then why are you tying me?"

"Because I don't know if *I* can trust you." Parker released the pressure of her knee and patted Melia's back. The touch felt awkward. "But, if you keep still and be patient for just a couple minutes, I promise I'll let you go."

Parker leaned over, bringing her face in line with Melia's, apparently so Melia could see the sincerity in her eyes. It was there, as genuine as anything Melia had ever seen and she was as reassured as she could be in this situation. She nodded, the rough wood scraping her cheek. Parker patted her shoulder again and moved out of sight.

Melia heard the thump as Parker's boots hit her desktop and then there was silence. She imagined that Parker was moving the things from her desk so that no one would know where Melia had gone. Her heart started beating harder, painfully hard, as she realized that Parker could do whatever she wanted. If Melia disappeared, no one would ever know what happened. Aaron believed that she'd left the building and Melia hadn't told Chris or Langley or anyone what she had found on the computer images. She felt tears threatening, her eyes burned as she fought to hold them back.

The fear of death was in her, she'd never felt this before, not even when Dana had attacked her in her bedroom.

She tried to force herself to believe there was a way out of this. Parker's words were said with conviction and her facial expressions encouraged trust, but those things didn't mean a lot under the circumstances. This was a woman who wore a gun openly and lived hidden in the crawl spaces of an office building. Her voice was soft, but her touch was rough and she easily taken control of the situation. Control of Melia. She closed her eyes and hoped that there was a way to talk herself out of this predicament.

"Good deal."

Parker's voice made Melia open her eyes. Melia said nothing, waiting to see if Parker had lied when she said she would release her. She had not. Pulling the belt loose, Parker took one of Melia's hands and rubbed it brusquely. Melia brought her other hand forward and put it under her left cheek.

"It didn't hurt you?"

Melia shook her head.

"Why don't you get up, move into the corner?"

Melia couldn't tell if the words were a suggestion or a command. She did it, glad to have her feet under her again and her back safely against the wall. Parker sat down in front of her, just out of reach and blocking her escape. Melia drew her knees up and held her hands clasped tightly together in her lap.

"You look really scared."

"You wouldn't be?"

"Don't you think I am?" Parker asked with a smile.

Melia shook her head again. "Not at all. I think maybe you enjoy this."

"If you're so scared, why did you come up here?"

"I've been asking myself that. Even before I decided to, I was asking that."

"How did you know I was here?"

Melia was unsure of how to answer. She didn't know if the answer would make Parker feel compromised and that she needed to silence her. But if Parker thought that Melia had a picture of her and it was out there in someone else's hands, Melia would have some point to bargain from.

"If you tell the truth, it don't take that long to answer." Parker shifted her body. Melia could plainly see the grip of Parker's gun not far from her long fingered hand resting casually on her thigh.

"I want to tell the truth," Melia quickly promised. "I was just thinking if it was smart for me to."

"Lyin' would be stupid. The truth ain't gonna hurt you. Not here anyway."

Melia nodded. They had said nothing about embellishing the truth "I set up a camera on the computer. I saw you coming down from the ceiling."

Parker's face went blank as a stone. Melia had no clue how interpret the expression.

"I have it on disk."

Parker's look didn't change. She reached up and rubbed the bridge of her nose with her thumb and forefinger. "Maybe you'd better say that again," she finally suggested.

"Digital images. There's a little camera on the edge of the computer. It takes a picture every minute and saves it to disk. I—we put it there Sunday evening."

Parker didn't respond to her hint that she was not the only one to know about the pictures. She continued to rub her nose, her look showing increasing incomprehension.

"I guess you don't know much about computers?"

Parker laughed. "You got that right. But I've seen a camera and there ain't nothing like that down there. Your little room ain't hardly big enough for a camera. Now, I'm givin' one more try at the truth."

It was Melia's turn for confusion. "It's the truth. I have nothing to gain from lying."

"Maybe you ought'a show me that picture."

Melia's heart sank. "I don't have it. It's in a friend's computer."

"That thing on the desk is a computer?"

Melia blinked. There was no way Parker could be unsure of what a computer was, no way she could have been hiding up here so long that she didn't know that. She nodded.

"And your friend has one of those things, too? With my picture on it?"

"Yes."

Parker abruptly clenched her fists and struck them on her thighs. The movement made Melia cringe, it was so like something Dana would do. She felt the blood drain from her face and hoped the room was dark enough that Parker wouldn't see her increased fear at the thought that here Dana was again, only this time holding a gun.

"Well, you got one up on me. And I don't know just how I'm s'posed to do this, but I gotta talk to you. I can't try and wait for a better time."

"Parker, I don't know what's going on here, but I hope you *will* talk to me." Melia tried, with limited success, to sound encouraging instead of terrified.

Parker scooted herself closer to Melia, coming so close that her knees touched Melia's legs. Melia tried to lean back, but she was already pressed against the wall. Parker kept her right hand to her side, but her left came forward and rested on Melia's thigh. Parker narrowed her eyes and spoke intently.

"I'm gonna tell you something that even I can hardly believe. I don't 'spect you to get it all right away, but you gotta try and believe me. Just give me time to talk it out and don't judge me too soon. You swear to do that?"

"I'll try," Melia whispered. Parker's eyes were so intense, her body so close that Melia could almost feel the jangling tension of her nerves.

Parker nodded satisfaction with the answer. She tightened the lips that looked so familiar, clearly looking for words. "Well, you know anybody that dresses like this?" Parker waved her hand down over her body, letting Melia take in her appearance from her boots up to her hat.

"On TV and, I guess, at the rodeo."

"So, it's common?"

"No. Not any more. But I read books where people do."

"Yeah, that's right." Parker picked up the Western she'd taken from Melia's desk. "So when did people dress like this?"

"I don't know. I would guess the 1800s. Maybe the early 1900s. But not women."

"Right again." Parker smiled slightly. Melia was again struck by the image of an animal baring its teeth. "But this woman does. And I can't say much about the 1900s, but this happens to be just what I wore in 1862."

There was a moment of cold silence. Melia's next move surprised even herself. She grabbed the book from Parker's hand and held it away. "God damn you," she said bitterly, burning with resentment and suddenly not caring how dangerous Parker's apparent madness was to her. She was being mocked. Somehow this woman knew of Melia's sense of being born into the wrong time and was playing a sick game with her. "Are you and Dana setting me up?"

"Dana?" Parker's confusion could only be a part of the act.

"Don't you fuck with me," Melia pointed her finger at Parker, her hand shaking uncontrollably.

"I ain't fucking you," Parker retorted. "I didn't even touch you that way."

Melia was surprised to see a darkening of Parker's face. Though it could be anger, she suspected that Parker was blushing. She decided to push the small advantage she sensed. "I'm not staying here and listening to this." Melia got into a crouch and made to move past Parker.

Parker whipped out her left hand and shoved Melia back into the corner. The strike came so quickly that Melia didn't have time to put her hands down to break her fall. Her head hit the boards beneath her with a force so hard that she was stunned. Parker's right hand didn't appear to move, but the gun was somehow in her hand and pointed at Melia's face.

"Jesus Christ, don't make me hurt you." Parker's face was dark, now clearly with anger, and her eyes filled with tears.

"Let me go," Melia pleaded.

"You're stayin'. You're listenin' to me and you'll answer my questions." Parker put the gun right to Melia's nose as she spoke and Melia could hear the rough edge of rage and desperation in Parker's voice. She had pushed her luck way too far.

"I tried to start this nice and I tried to start this easy, but now I can't. I been watching you and I thought you were a real smart woman. You're not provin' yourself to be." Parker's hand shook with her fury and Melia feared the pressure of her finger, white-knuckled against the trigger of the gun. "Now you listen. You nod or you shake your head, but you lay right there and you keep your mouth shut. You got that?"

Melia nodded. She doubted she could speak even if she was pressed to, her throat was dry and her jaws seemed welded together.

Parker sat back a little, but kept the gun where it was. "I didn't mean for any of this to happen. I was ridin' along, havin' a perfect day. I didn't ask to be here, but here I am and I mean to find out why. You understand?"

Melia nodded unsurely, then decided that shaking her head was a better answer. She did not understand. Parker didn't mind her confusion.

"Do you travel through time?"

Melia stared at her, trying to decide if she was serious in asking that question. Parker's look was sincere. God, Melia thought, a heavy feeling in her chest, the woman is insane.

"Answer me," Parker demanded.

Melia shook her head.

"Nobody does?"

Melia shook again.

"I did. February 24, 1862, I rode away from Denver and I ended up here." Parker pushed her hat back and drew her face close enough for Melia to feel her breath against her cheek. "And you think I'm crazy, don't you?"

Melia couldn't pretend. She nodded. A strand of her hair brushed Parker's forehead near the cut over her eye. Parker gently brushed it away.

"So do I. But here I am." Parker pulled the gun from Melia's face, but she didn't return it to its holster. She sighed and looked away from Melia's eyes. "I been watchin' you," she repeated. "Somehow, I thought you would understand. I was hopin' you could help me."

Melia shook her head. The only help she could suggest was a visit to a psychiatrist and she doubted the suggestion would be warmly received.

"Is there any way I can convince you? I just want you, or anyone, to believe me. Even if there ain't nothin' can be done to change it." Parker waited for a moment, then remembered that she'd commanded Melia not to speak. "Go ahead and talk. I'll listen to you."

"Parker," Melia started. Her voice cracked and she had to lick her lips before she could continue. Parker watched her movements intently and Melia suddenly felt that her attention was focused on more than just the suspicion that Melia would try to bolt. The realization did nothing to diminish her fear. "I'm not the person who can help you. I don't understand these kind of things. I don't know what happened to you."

"I told you what happened. I came through time. I just fell and fell right into that underground room. I thought it was a mine, but then that woman came and she got into that cart and I *never* seen nothin' like that before. I had to get out of there and I found that room that moves and it brought me here. I sneak around the building all right, but I looked out that window and it scares me bad."

Melia listened as the words poured from Parker. The conviction she put in her voice persuaded Melia that Parker's delusion was not pretended. She really believed that she'd traveled through time. Parker continued.

"I don't think I can leave this building. I know that's Denver out there, but it changed. I don't know that town no more. I've tried looking down from here to find the old places, Lily's Red Dog, Charlie's, but nothing's left."

Melia had a sudden idea, not one that would prove Parker's claim, but would at least get them out of this crawl space and into an area that Melia might be able to escape from. If she could just get near the phone, she could push the call button for the guards. "Where were you born, Parker?"

"In New Orleans."

"Did you have a birth certificate?"

Parker shook her head. "I don't know. What's that?"

"It a paper that says when a person was born. Was there a courthouse in New Orleans when you lived there?"

"Of course."

"Well, I can search the records on the computer. I can find your birth date, and that would prove your story."

"Or prove if I was lyin'?"

Melia nodded. It was pointless to deny that possibility. Parker wasn't stupid.

"That's fair. Cause it ain't gonna happen." Parker lifted the barrel of the gun back to Melia's nose. "You lyin' to me? Can you really do that?"

"It's easy. I'm not lying."

Parker holstered her gun and gestured for Melia to rise. "Let's do it."

Melia got to her feet and brushed past Parker. She stepped onto the beam and her balance wavered. Parker took her arm and held her firmly until Melia steadied. Taking Melia's other arm and moving behind her, Parker gently pushed her onward.

"Just go, I'll help you move on."

Their position was awkward, but Melia was able to walk to the right tile without mishap. Parker's hold was firm, her hands warm and strong on Melia's body. Her touch seemed to tingle right through Melia's clothing. The woman was powerful, both in body and presence. Melia turned her head to watch as Parker released her and pulled away the ceiling tile.

"You smell good." Melia's words surprised herself. The thought had come to her suddenly, but she hadn't expected to say the words aloud. Parker stared at her, at least as surprised as Melia herself.

"I do?"

"Uh, yeah. Kind of a natural smell. No perfume. It's good."

Parker smiled, a full one this time, and Melia could see a sparkle in her eye. Melia's words had made her happy and Melia felt a pang of regret that Parker's mind was apparently betraying her so badly. Life was really unfair.

Parker dropped herself down the hole and stood on Melia's desk. She reached up and silently encouraged Melia to lower herself. Parker caught her by the waist and eased her down. Before Melia could move, Parker turned her around and cautiously felt the back of Melia's head. Melia held still as she brushed the hair aside and rubbed her head tenderly. The kindness was unnerving.

"No bump, I guess," Parker said. "I'm sorry anyway."

Melia tried to step away, but Parker turned her again. They stood face to face on the top of the desk. Parker gripped Melia's waist firmly, but gently, holding their bodies just inches apart. The look of intensity returned to Parker's eyes.

"I thought about how I'd meet you. I thought about what I'd say and how I'd convince you to help me."

Melia stared at Parker's lips as she spoke. Her eyes were dark and too intent for Melia, she felt they could hypnotize her. But her lips, soft and curved, held Melia just as spellbound. She fought not to fall.

"I wrote it all out, I practiced sayin' it. I just never expected to feel so threatened. I didn't know I'd be afraid of you."

"You're afraid of me?" Melia whispered, amazed that this cool, composed woman could fear anything.

"Yeah, I am. You don't know how much I've lost. How much I can still lose."

Melia shook her head. She was falling. She had to break the seduction of the lips so close, the eyes, the scent of her. The woman's charisma was overwhelming.

"I don't know. I don't know if I can help you."

"I'm just askin' you to try."

Melia nodded and lifted her hand cautiously. She took Parker's wrist and moved her hand from her hip. Parker turned the movement into a gesture for Melia to step down from the desk. She kept her other hand on Melia's back until she was safely to the floor, then jumped down beside her. Parker rolled the chair close for her before stepping away to stand at the entrance of the cubicle. Melia sat and pulled herself up to the desk.

Watching Parker from the corner of her eye, she pulled the phone close. Parker didn't show the least bit of alarm, as if she didn't realize that the telephone could be a danger to her. She either played her part very well, or had truly gone so far into her delusions that she'd forgotten the possibilities of technology. Melia pushed the mouse on the pad to wake the screen.

"I just need to log on, then I'll need your full name." Her network connection was only a few keystrokes away. She accessed the New Orleans' city records database and turned to Parker.

"Parker Ellen McCallem," Parker said slowly. She watched fascinated as Melia typed the letters onto the screen. She corrected Melia's spelling of her last name.

Melia entered the data and leaned back, while in the same motion, she lifted the receiver away from the phone. Lines of names and dates scrolled by on the computer screen.

"If I'd typed a year, this would have been faster," Melia informed her. She casually pushed the pound sign and 09. The guards would instantly get an alarm and in a few seconds, their computer would show them exactly which floor and room it originated from. Melia replaced the receiver. In the same instant, Parker jabbed her finger against the screen.

"There," her voice was triumphant.

Melia looked to where Parker was pointing. The line read: Parker Ellen McCallem, born August 12, 1835. There were no other matches for that name. Melia stared at the screen. Her mouth went dry. It could not be possible. She looked up into Parker's eyes. The relief, the vindication, the joy in her expression could not be faked. Melia panicked.

"Death certificate. There has got to be a death certificate." Quickly, she typed in the request. Seconds passed and the computer came up empty. No certificate on record.

"I'm not dead yet," Parker said, as if that explained it all.

"This can't be. You had to know this, you had to have gotten into the computer and . . ." Melia's words failed as she looked at Parker's face. She knew she was grasping for straws, and was saying things that she herself could not believe. This woman hadn't even known what the phone could do.

"Oh my god, Parker, I called security."

"What? What does that mean?" Parker turned as if the threat was right behind her.

Acting on impulse, Melia turned and pulled open her desk drawer, grabbing a book and shoving it into Parker's hands. "Go," she urged her. "Get back up there right now. You have to trust me. I'll come back as soon as I can."

"What—" Parker put her hand to her gun.

Melia touched her arm lightly, her eyes begging for Parker's compliance. Parker let her hand fall from the pistol.

"Don't ask me, just go. Now!" Melia shoved Parker toward the desk. Parker's expression grew even darker, but she jumped onto the desk and pulled herself up to the ceiling. She looked back down at Melia.

"I'm sorry," Melia called up to her. "I won't give you away. You can watch me. If I say anything about you up there, you can hear me. You can shoot me first."

Parker said nothing. Her eyes held Melia's for a long moment before she replaced the tile. Melia felt that the gaze had not left her.

Turning to look over the partition, Melia saw the numbers lighting up, they were almost to her floor. She hurried out into the hall where she would be seen the instant the elevator door opened. She got down on her stomach in the aisle and tried to lie as if she'd fallen. Her heart beat hard as she waited.

The door opened. Nothing happened. Melia gritted her teeth and forced herself not to look at the elevator. After a few seconds the stairway door burst open and Melia heard someone leap from the elevator at the same moment.

"Melia!" Aaron shouted. "Roger, Melia's down there. Cover me."

Melia almost cried at the concern in Aaron's voice. Not knowing what danger he might face, he still thought of her safety first. She hoped she was doing the right thing, protecting Parker. The woman could be waiting for each of them to get in her sights before killing them all.

"Melia."

She felt his hands touch her carefully. Letting herself be turned over, she kept her eyes closed until Aaron rubbed her cheek lightly. She groaned and looked up and past him.

"Melia, what happened? What's wrong?"

"I—I don't know," she whispered. "I feel sick."

"I thought you left the building, what are you doing here?"

"I decided to go to the bathroom before I left." Melia was glad she could say the words without lying too much. "I was leaving . . . I guess I blacked out. I came to my desk, called you, and I . . . just went black."

"Roger, come in. It's okay." Aaron unbuttoned the top button of Melia's shirt. "Damn Melia, I hate this floor. You scared the shit out of me again."

"I'm sorry. There's nothing to be afraid of." Melia hoped the words were loud enough to carry through the ceiling tile.

"I think you must have a concussion from that accident," Aaron decided. "Did you see a doctor?"

Roger kneeled down beside them. "Should I call for an ambulance?"

"Yes."

"No." Melia countered Aaron's opinion. "I just want to go home. I'll call my doctor tomorrow."

"You can't go like this. I'm not going to let you get on a bus in this condition."

"I brought my car."

"Well, I'm sure as hell not going to let you drive."

"I—I'll call a friend." Melia wished she could kick herself for not thinking this out better. Now she would have to involve someone else in this lie. There was no way she could call Chris. She would take her directly to the hospital and have her brain scanned one thousand and one ways before the night was over.

"Tell me your friend's number," Roger offered. "I'll have him come right away."

"Her," Aaron corrected without thinking.

Impulsively, Melia gave him Langley's number, remembering that it was her night off from the bookstore. He went to her desk and dialed. Melia closed her eyes and listened to him explain the situation. He returned after only a moment.

"She'll be here right away."

"Let's go down to the lobby and wait for her to come," Aaron advised. "Can you walk, or should I carry you?"

"Oh, I can walk." Melia assured him. She didn't want to take the charade that far. Getting to her feet, she swayed a little and Aaron took her arm. He didn't speak as they walked to the elevator. Melia was glad, her mind was busy trying to figure out how to explain all this to Langley and prevent her from telling Chris.

Ω   Ω   Ω   Ω   Ω

The woman was an actress. Parker vowed to remember that as she watched the scene play out below her. The whole thing was confusing. She didn't know how Melia had alerted the guards or why she'd changed her mind at the last moment. The information on the computer must have made her at least consider that Parker was telling the truth. And the computer must have been how she'd called the guards to come. Parker opinion of computers fluctuated, apparently they could be both bad and good.

Melia kept glancing up at the ceiling as she told her story. When the guards were looking away, she tried to smile or nod Parker's way, probably to assure her that she would keep the secret. Parker hoped it was true. She could not stop Melia from leaving the room with the men and once they were out of sight, Melia would be safe to say anything she wanted.

The man named Aaron helped Melia to her feet. They walked toward the elevator and out of Parker's limited view. She got to her feet and tried to quickly and quietly follow them along the beam above. Parker could not see them as they waited for the elevator door to open, but she put her ear down and listened. They didn't speak.

Contemplating the thought of dropping into the room as soon as they started down, Parker reached out for the tile. She could get into the stairwell and race down to the lobby where she'd seen the guard booth. But then what? She couldn't get into the ceiling from the stairwell. Every time she changed floors she had to drop from the ceiling space and take the stairs up or down. The first and only time she'd been in the lobby, she'd gone down to that floor and started to open the door before seeing the guards standing and talking in the booth. It was just luck that they hadn't spotted her. There was no way that she could follow them. No way she could be forewarned if Melia sold her out.

One thing was in her favor, the guards would be busy and concerned with Melia for awhile until she either left or told them the story. Parker had just a few minutes to get rid of the evidence of her presence. Hurrying to her corner, she stepped across the tiles, jumping from beam to beam. She spread out her coat and put the new book and the old one inside. Wadding up the table cloths, she added them and her small stock of food. She buttoned the coat and folded the sleeves in, tying them together to make a tiny pack. The three boards that made up her platform would be harder to move.

Parker decided to take only one and leave two behind. She would put one in each of the partitioned areas so it would not look like they had ever been used together. When she moved them, she put them standing up against the wall in the corner. In the dim light, they could be easily over-looked.

With her stuff loaded in her arms, Parker moved awkwardly to the tile directly above the door to the stairs. She had the tile pulled aside and had dropped her things before she realized her mistake. There was no desk below her and if she got down here, she wouldn't be able to replace the tile. She wasn't thinking clearly. Lowering the board, Parker knew that she was taking too much time. The guards could return at any point. She kept glancing at the elevator light to make sure it was not rising. If they were on the stairs, she wouldn't know until the door opened.

Parker replaced the tile and moved over the nearest cubicle with a desk. She jumped down, scooted the tile back into position and ran to her pile of belongings. Scooping them into her arms, she pulled the stairway door open and loped up three flights. The door to this floor opened onto a long hallway broken by evenly-spaced doors to private offices. There was a small reception area, but despite these differences, the layout of the floor was the same as the one where Melia worked. The restrooms were in the same area and the counter was high enough for her to reach the ceiling.

Once in the upper space, Parker placed the board across the beams and deposited her things on it while she searched the dark area. She found a narrow gap between the wall and a cluster of pipes where she could hide her pack. Before she stuffed it into the gap, she took out the new book. Might as well read, she reasoned. It would do her no good to just sit and worry.

The private offices below were all locked. Since she didn't have to bother with doors, the locks couldn't keep her out, but they would prevent anyone from sneaking up on her. She picked a tile at random, making sure only that it was not an office with a window, and lowered herself down. The chair in the office was padded leather, and the small lamp burning on the desk cast just a wide enough circle of light for her to read by. Leaning the chair back and putting her boots on the desk, Parker tried to relax her shoulders. Feeling a little more at ease and secure, she opened the book. After a few lines, she smiled broadly. It was "one of those" books.

Eleven

Langley kept casting sideways glances at Melia as she drove her Jeep up the freeway. Melia was unaware of the looks. She rested her forehead on the glass and tried to take in all that had happened to her this evening. Believing Parker's story was too much of a stretch, even with Melia's wild imagination. There had to be some explanation, some psychological delusion like technophobia or something that sent this woman over the edge. But who was she really and how did she come up with the name Parker? And why didn't the real Parker McCallem, born 1835, have a death certificate?

Melia sighed deeply and considered that record keeping before computers had been a pretty chancy process. Even now, there were continual horror stories of the computer deciding that someone who was still living had died or vice versa.

Born in 1835 or not, Parker sure fit the image. Melia reviewed the woman's appearance in her mind. She dressed for the part, her jeans and boots were well worn, and her hat had seen better days. Melia had gotten a very good look at the gun as it was pressed to her nose, it was not modern and didn't seem to be factory-made. But these things could be arranged, anyone could copy clothing from old patterns and the gun could have been purchased from an antique gun dealer. One detail bothered her. The box of matches she found in the coat pocket was undeniably old, the picture on it looked like an illustration from an old catalog. Matches were such a small detail, who would possibly think of something so minor, especially if they were deranged? And why would they need matches? Parker didn't smell like cigarette smoke and, living inside a high rise office building, what else would she need them for?

Melia thought again of Parker's coat and how it smelled faintly of wood smoke. Although her common sense continued to deride her, she was beginning to feel convinced. She looked ahead into the distance and considered what believing Parker's story would mean. Deep in thought, it took Melia a few seconds to realize that Langley's Jeep was gradually drifting to the side of the road. She grabbed the dashboard and yelled as the tires caught the shoulder and jerked to the right. Langley twisted the wheel and pulled the vehicle back to the pavement.

"What are you doing?"

"I'm sorry." Langley gripped the wheel tightly and stared straight ahead. "Uh, I was just looking at you, making sure you're okay."

"Yeah, I'm fine. Barring getting killed on the freeway."

"You're fine? Okay, you're blacking out, but you're fine." Despite her scare, Langley again focused her gaze on Melia. "I still have a mind to call Chris."

"I'm not blacking out."

"What's that? Seems I heard a different story just a bit ago."

"I can't tell you what's going on."

"You know what I think? I think that fucking Dana hurt you inside. You could have a concussion—or even seizures." Langley's face twisted with anger and hatred. "You know, a person can have one and not even remember it happened."

"I don't have a concussion and I'm not having seizures."

Langley didn't argue. She looked once over her shoulder and changed to the outside lane. The Jeep picked up speed.

"Hey, you're going to miss my exit."

"We're not taking your exit. If you're going to be having seizures, I'm taking you straight to Chris' house."

"I am not having seizures." Melia wrapped her hand around Langley's biceps. She tried to speak in a commanding tone. "Get back in my lane."

Despite her anger, Langley grinned. "You're so cute when you try to be butch. But I'm still a lot bigger than you."

"All right, goddamn it. If you get into to my lane, I'll tell you what's going on."

"You promise?"

"I'll tell you everything I can."

"Everything you can? I don't like the sound of that. Does that include any blacking out or seizures?"

"Yes. But there aren't any." Melia hurried to add.

Langley pulled back into the slow lane. Melia's exit was less than a mile ahead.

"You remember the disk that I was viewing at the bookstore the other night?"

Langley nodded. "This is about the book thief?"

"Well, yes. But no, the person is not a thief." Melia wrinkled her forehead. That statement was probably not accurate. Parker seemed to be thriving and she certainly wasn't paying for anything. "So, I was supposed to meet this person and give them the disk."

"The disk? With nothing on it, but the view from your computer?"

Damn. Langley was too sharp and Melia too stressed and exhausted for this game. "Well, yeah. Just to prove there was nothing on it. Anyway, I was supposed to meet them after hours. I didn't want the security guards to know, so I pretended to leave. When the person didn't show, I realized that there was no way I could get out of the building then without the guards knowing. So, I called them and pretended to have blacked out in the bathroom."

Langley chewed her lip for several moments and Melia could hear the quiet clicking of Langley's tongue stud against her teeth. Melia pointed out her exit and it wasn't until they left the freeway and drove on for a few blocks that Langley responded to Melia's story.

"Okay. What I've got is: a secret meeting, an unknown person, exchange of computer disks, and the need to hide the meeting from security." She counted off the points on her fingers. "What it all adds up to, in my mind, is not pretty. Mel, are you spying?"

"What?"

"Are you a spy? Are you selling computer secrets or something?"

Melia laughed and she could see that the sound reassured Langley more than any protests of innocence. "No, Lang. I'm not a spy, but you are so sweet to think of that. It sounds much cooler than what is really happening." Melia stopped herself. Was it really? She'd met a person who was about to persuade her that she'd come through time. What kind of spy could hold a candle to that? Melia loosened her seat belt and turned sideways to look at Langley.

"Um, listen Lang. I'm not really telling you the truth. I'm not telling you everything. But I swear, beyond these bruises, I'm perfectly healthy and I've never had a seizure in my life. I've never even fainted."

"And what you're doing is safe?"

Melia couldn't answer. Langley turned to look at her and Melia couldn't even muster a smile. Langley pulled the Jeep into a gas station parking lot and let it idle.

"Mel, you're not answering me," she finally said.

"Well, it's safe so far. I'm all right." Melia shrugged. She fought to keep her expression clear of the memory of the gun sight pointed down her nose or the feel of being on her stomach with her hands tied behind her back, waiting for a bullet. But Parker had untied her, shown her concern, and allowed her to leave. Was she safe? It seemed the only way to find out was to put herself back into the situation and that reasoning was beyond common sense. Melia glanced up as Langley grasped her hand.

"Look, Lang. All I can do is promise that I will be careful. And I promise that if I get into trouble, I'll come running straight to you, and you can turn me over to Chris."

"Don't think I won't," Langley warned. "In fact, I still think I should, right now."

"Please don't. Someday this will make a great story and I'll tell both of you, but at this point, I just don't have to energy to face her."

"God, I know that feeling."

"So you'll give me a break?"

Langley took a long breath and nodded. "Just one. Just for now." She put the Jeep in gear and pulled back onto the street.

Melia's small house was at the end of a long row of small houses in an old and dying neighborhood just north of downtown. Driving along her street, she always felt she was sliding back in time to when these houses held eager, new families and their dreams. Now, they held only the people who could not afford better, or like Melia, who tried to cling to a sense of the past. Even with the neighborhood's run-down atmosphere and bleak prospects for the future, this house was her home, and she loved it.

Langley pulled her Jeep in at the curb. Melia turned to thank Langley for the ride, but Langley was looking past her out the window with a puzzled expression.

"What the hell is all that?" she asked.

Melia turned to look. The front stoop of her house was covered with packages. Small cardboard boxes filled the steps and spilled out onto the sidewalk. For some reason, she knew it was Dana's doing and the thought filled her with dread. This could not be anything good. Her impulse was to slide down below the level of the window and hide. So she did.

Langley's confusion grew. "Why are you hiding?" she whispered, although there was obviously no one near to overhear.

"I just have a feeling. This is not good."

"This is not about the thing at work, is it?"

"No. That I am sure of."

Langley raised her eyebrows. She caught onto the implications of Melia's unspoken thought. Opening the door, she said quietly, "You stay here, I'll check it out."

Langley walked around the front of the Jeep. Melia eased the window down and could hear Langley's footsteps going up the walk. The sound faded, then disappeared as she walked onto the grass. Melia peeked up over the door's edge and saw her shadowed form slip around the side of the house.

Sliding back down in the seat, Melia covered her face with her hands. Dana was unbelievable, she had no sense of decency. Melia was getting a taste of what Dana really thought of her and the taste was bad. Dana believed money could change anything. She probably did something stupid like buying every book in a store, without even giving a thought to whether Melia would have picked them for herself or not. Melia was insulted at Dana's efforts. Sure she had probably spent a lot, still it was nothing but a shallow attempt to get back in Melia's bed. A soft tap on the window made her sit bolt upright in the seat and slap at the door lock.

"Just me." Langley had the courtesy not to grin at Melia alarm. "Coast is clear."

"Was that necessary?" Melia asked as she popped open the door and glared up at Langley.

"Huh. For all I knew, you'd blacked out."

"God, would you please give that a rest?" Melia stomped past her and kicked at the nearest box. There were about fifteen of them and she had a mind to leave them out and let the neighborhood kids steal them.

She went to the door and unlocked it. As she pushed it open, Langley came up behind her, already carrying one of the boxes. The cat tore out the door, ran between her legs, and took off down the sidewalk. Melia had been ignoring him too much lately. She'd bought him an automatic feeder, but it didn't pet or scratch itchy ears worth a damn.

For a moment, Melia was surprised to find that there were no messages on her answering machine. Normally, Dana would have called ten or fifteen times by now. She remembered that, on Chris' insistence, she had changed her number. The hassle of needing to do it disappeared in her relief at having it done. Langley dropped the box on the floor near her and went out for another. Melia tossed her keys on the end table and followed her out.

They were both breathing hard by the time they finished hauling in the boxes. Langley shut and locked the door as Melia went into the kitchen and grabbed a couple of cold beers. Langley flopped out on the couch and drank deeply.

"Ugh, I feel like it's delivery day at the bookstore. I hope you don't expect me to price and shelve all these."

"I don't know what I'm going to do with all of it. I can't keep them."

"Why not? She owes you."

"It just wouldn't work. They're like a bomb waiting to go off. She's got the timer set and she's just waiting for the walls to blow down."

"Are they going to?" Langley's black eyes peered over the edge of her can. She had the kindness to try to keep her expression neutral.

Melia just sighed and looked at the wall. No, this ploy was not going to work, but resistance wasn't going to be easy. Dana would be persistent, then angry, then violent. Melia knew that Dana's feelings of remorse wouldn't last long.

"Have you thought of a restraining order?"

Melia wrinkled her nose. "I don't know. I thought you could only get one if your life was in danger."

"Good god, Melia." Langley's neutrality flew out the window. She sat up straight, clutching her can, and frowning at Melia. "What does she have to do to make you feel like you're in danger? After she kills you, it will be a little too late."

"She's not going to kill me."

"Famous last words."

"If you knew her at all, you wouldn't say that. I know her and she's really not a bad person. There's just something I do wrong that sets her off."

"Maybe I know her better than you think."

"What does that mean?"

"It means I've asked around. She's been banned from most of the bars in town, her relationships look like friendly-fire casualty lists, and she's been arrested for disturbing the peace."

"And you were never young, Lang?"

"I'm young, now. I don't have a resume like that and neither do any of my friends. And we're considered the bad seed." Langley rubbed the fine stubble on her head as she spoke. Melia grinned. She'd seen a few of Langley's motley friends and could believe that they'd earned that name. While their hair came in various lengths, it was guaranteed to be no color nature intended, and their bodies had more piercings than a renaissance tapestry. They terrorized the coffee shops with confrontational poetry and politics and Melia envied them for their audacity.

The conversation died and Melia was content to sit and enjoy the peace. She didn't want to argue with Lang, but she had to admit that it did feel good having her here. She wondered why she had never before invited her up for a visit or dinner. Probably for the same reason none of her friends except Chris and Molly had ever been to her home. But it wasn't all Dana's fault. Melia lacked the social skills to feel comfortable inviting anyone. Maybe that could change.

Melia looked at Langley and saw that she was beginning to nod off. She had a long drive home ahead of her and Melia was tempted to let her sleep for a while there on the couch. But that was selfish. The drive wouldn't get any easier the later Langley stayed.

"Hey," Melia said to get her attention. "Are you hungry?"

"I could eat."

"I don't know what I've got in the fridge, I haven't been home much lately."

"Let's order pizza." Langley sat up and reached for the phone book on the end table.

"You know something? I feel good with you here." Melia blushed as she said the words, but she felt it was right to tell her. "I feel good."

"I'm glad, because I'm staying." Langley became absorbed in the contents of the phone book and avoided looking into Melia's eyes. "That is, if it's okay with you."

"Sure. I think I'd like that."

Looking up, Langley grinned and then leered evilly at Melia. "And who knows, maybe I'll get lucky and you'll black out again."

While Parker put down her book and explored the cupboards and closet of her private office and Langley slept soundly on Melia's couch, Melia sat bathed in the thin, blue light of her computer screen, searching the Internet for any evidence to bolster Parker's claim. Melia set out with the notion of proving her a psychotic liar, but soon realized she was as eager to believe Parker's story as Parker was to convince her. The possibilities were fascinating and so much more appealing than anything else in Melia's life.

After an hour spent in every database she could locate with facts of New Orleans' history, she was no farther along than when she'd punched in Parker's name on the computer at work. Apparently neither Parker, nor any other member of her family, had spent enough time in New Orleans to make a name for themselves. Melia tried the Denver city records and came up blank. No births, no deaths, no scandals of any family named McCallem. She flexed her cramping fingers and tried to remember everything that Parker had told her. There had to be something she'd said that would put her in Denver in the 1860s.

Melia leaned back and closed her eyes. Parker had mentioned looking down at the city and trying to find her landmarks. The name Charlie came back to her mind. Shaking her head, Melia discounted it. There had been several bars named Charlie's or some variation in the Denver area, most notably a gay bar that just happened to have a country and western theme. Not encouraging. The other name was

Red Dog. Parker hadn't said if it was a bar or a restaurant or a hotel, but if it had existed, Melia should be able to find it in the historical commerce listings.

Melia grinned when the information reeled out on her screen. There was a brief description of the Red Dog and its years of operation. The wisdom of naming a whorehouse the Red Dog was beyond Melia's reasoning, but the place had obviously done quite well for its owner, a Lilian Dupont. She reputedly was able to relocate in posh San Francisco when the whorehouse was burned down in a 1864 fire that started next door in Chatham's Dry Goods. So, there was one point in Parker's favor. Melia ran "Charlie's" and found that both a bar and a tannery with that name existed in the time frame Parker mentioned. Melia gave her another point.

"How long did it take you to find all this information, Parker?" Melia asked the patiently blinking cursor. "Or did you, honest-to-god, fall into a parking garage out of the clear blue, 1862 sky?" The story was too ridiculous to invent. No one would believe it.

Melia was beginning to believe it.

Ω   Ω   Ω   Ω   Ω

Langley didn't do mornings and for the first time in her life, Melia was late for work. It was not the day for it. As soon as she stepped off the elevator, she was waved over to the reception desk.

"You've got a visitor, conference room one. They've been waiting," a red-haired secretary, whose name Melia could never remember, informed her.

"Shit." Melia said the word under her breath. "Who is it?"

"Don't know, probably government by the look of the suit. Rough looking number. But she refused to leave any information." The secretary stressed the fact of the refusal and raised her eyebrow at Melia. "No one here has any clue. And why you were asked for specifically, I can't say."

Melia looked around the room and found at least half of all eyes upon her. She turned back to the reception desk and tried to pull herself deeper into her baggy coat. She felt herself shaking. But she'd done nothing wrong.

"So, what have you been doing all those late evenings in here, Melia? You haven't gotten yourself into trouble have you?" Though the words were prying, Melia sensed a genuine concern.

"No. I haven't done anything." Melia took a deep breath and wondered if she should go to her cubicle and drop off her backpack and coat, or if it was best to go straight to the conference room. She didn't want it to seem like she had something to hide. Trying to remember if she had any disks in her backpack, she walked slowly down the hall to the conference room.

When Melia entered the room, the woman's back was to the door. A long, mahogany-stained wooden table filled the room between them. The woman stood relaxed at the bank of windows and didn't turn as Melia eased the door shut. Her stance was confident and revealed that she had power and was secure in it. Melia had a few seconds to take in the cut of the dark, charcoal-gray suit. It was expensive and Melia agreed with the secretary in the opinion that she was government. The woman turned and Melia stepped forward, holding out her hand, ready to introduce herself. She stopped in mid-step, knowing that her face revealed the shock she felt. Without the hat and the outfit, Parker was hardly as recognizable, but the shape of her mouth and the cut on her forehead gave her away.

"I reckon you're surprised to see me." Parker smiled as she spoke.

Melia was without a response. She felt an up-welling of emotion, and was not sure which would crest. Fear, betrayal, and anger all battled within her. She'd let herself believe Parker's story and she'd been played a fool.

"Nothin' you want to say to me?"

Her anger peaked. She had plenty to say.

"You bastard. You incredible, stinking bastard. How could you?"

Parker batted her eyes. Melia would have none of the pretense anymore.

"Whatever the hell your game is, and whatever agency you're with, I'm not talking to you. What you did, what you— you hateful asshole." Melia's tirade dissolved into speechless fury.

"Whoa, wait a minute now. You got no call to—"

"Shut up, just shut the fuck up. I'm not talking to you until my supervisor and my lawyer are here."

Parker stepped around the table and reached for Melia's arm. Melia shook off her touch and turned to leave. Parker abruptly pushed her aside and moved to the door. She turned the bolt and stood leaning against the frame.

"You're not leavin'."

"You can't do this. I have rights. You can arrest me, but you cannot hold me here against my will."

"The hell I can't." Parker opened her jacket to reveal the gun tucked into the waistband of her slacks. Melia automatically stepped back.

"Oh god. This is unreal." Melia dropped her backpack on the floor and sat at the end of the table, putting her head in her hands. "I don't know what you think I've done, but I don't even work with classified materials. I'm not some hacker and I don't have any national security secrets for sale."

Melia didn't look up as the woman moved over and sat in the chair beside her. She didn't know the game, and she had no idea what to expect. Parker reached her hand out to Melia's, but stopped short of touching her.

"Melia, I guess I've upset you by comin' here. I'm sorry. But I have to tell you, I don't understand a thing you're sayin'."

"Please, don't play with me. I'll answer your questions because I've honestly got nothing to hide." Melia raised her eyes to Parker's face. Her look was a plea for mercy. "But stop the games. Just tell me who you are."

Parker leaned back in the seat and sighed. Her long fingers tapped nervously on the tabletop. Melia stared at their reflection in the polished wood. They suggested a repressed energy that was waiting to break out of the woman's composure. As if it helped her to maintain her patience, Parker used her other hand to rub the bridge of her nose while she spoke.

"Now, I figure what's got you thrown are these clothes. They're not mine. I stole them from an office on the seventeenth floor." Parker lifted the thin, silk tie from her chest and held it out to study it. "I was thinkin' I looked pretty damn sharp, but you're actin' like it's a threat to you."

"What do you mean, you stole them from the seventeenth floor?"

"They have these private rooms up there, not like your rooms. You got little stalls and they have closets and washrooms hooked right onto their rooms. I found these clothes and they fit me okay. I figured I could fit in and come down to talk to you without anyone thinkin' I don't belong."

"You're not with the government? You're not here to arrest me or interrogate me or—"

"I just meant to talk to you in a place you'd feel safe. I never wanted to convince you by putting a gun to your head." As if to prove her words, Parker took the gun from her belt and laid it on the table between them. "I don't usually move so fast. I try to take time to think these things out before leapin' in, but I gotta admit, I'm feelin' pretty desperate here."

"Why me?" The question surprised Melia. Now that it was asked, the answer seemed imperative.

Parker actually blushed. "I don't know. I just saw you and I liked your face. You seem like someone I could trust. And, I don't know, your eyes are always lookin' somewhere else, seein' things I don't think other people can see. I thought maybe you could look at me and maybe believe what I was sayin'."

"Oh, Parker. How can I believe you? It's impossible."

"I know. I've thought long and hard about it. I know it's impossible." Parker put her elbows on the table and copied Melia's earlier posture. Melia touched the pistol with her fingertips, then slowly pulled it toward herself. Parker heard the movement and spread her fingers to look through them, but she didn't try to prevent Melia from taking the gun.

"This is a Colt. It's a very old gun," Melia studied the manufacturer's mark on the barrel.

"No, it's just two years since I got it. It was my father's and he'd had it just a year. It's their new model."

Melia shook her head. Parker certainly had the talk down. She didn't miss a beat.

"Do you have your matches with you? Can I use one?"

Parker nodded and dug through the suit pockets until she found the small box. She handed them to Melia without comment.

The box was decorated with a flowery, ornate script. It proclaimed the matches to be the proud offering of the Senate Match company. There was no date on the box, nor was there a bar code or any of the safety information that assumed a person was too stupid to know that matches could burn.

"Where did you get these?"

"I don't know. Probably Chatham's. They give em away." Parker pronounced the name as "chat-hams."

"Chatham's? What's that?"

"The dry goods store. The one on Sixth Street." Parker looked at Melia, the questions finally making her curious. "Why are you askin'? It feels like you're testin' me. Is there a Chatham's on Sixth?"

"No. Not now anyway." Melia pushed back the matches. "Maybe I am testing you. But it's not easy. Anything I can find out on the computer or from old papers, you could have found out too. How do I know how long you've been working this out?"

"But why? Why would I pretend to be from another time? Why hide out like a rat in this building?"

"I don't know." The gun was still closer to Melia's hand than Parker's. She felt a little more safe to speak her mind. "Maybe you're mentally ill, Parker. Maybe you do believe it yourself and just can't remember inventing the story."

"I remember everything."

"I can't argue with you." Melia stood and paced the width of the room. Parker's eyes followed her steps back and forth. Melia came to a sudden stop and fired a question at Parker. "Did you know Lilian Dupont?"

Parker laughed and blushed again. "Lily? Madame Dupont? Sure I know her, I knew her when she was just plain, ol' Lily Baker."

"And she ran the Red Dog?"

"Yep. She finagled the seed money from some old miner. Didn't take her long to pay off his investment and own it free and clear. She makes good money there."

Parker's use of the present tense didn't strike Melia as feigned. Parker thought of Lily as if she were still living.

"So where did she go when the Red Dog burned?"

"What? The Red Dog never burned."

"Yes, it did. When Chatham's caught fire . . ." Melia stared at the confusion on Parker's face. Clearly she didn't know that the Red Dog had burned to the ground. The reason why came to her suddenly. "Wait a minute. When did you say you came through time?"

"Just over a week or so ago. I lose track of time here."

"No, I mean what was the year?"

"1862."

"That's why you don't know. It burns—burned in 1864. Two years after you came here."

"Lily?" Parker rose halfway from her chair, then sank back as she realized there was nothing she could do.

"She escaped. She moved to San Francisco."

"How do you know that?"

"I read it last night on the computer." Melia stared at Parker, looking at her with a new perspective.

She believed. She was absolutely convinced that Parker was who she'd said she was. A living, breathing woman from a time that Melia had visited only in her imagination. Unaware of the motion of her hand, Melia found herself touching Parker's cheek. She was warm, she was real.

"Jesus Christ," Parker whispered, her emotion sharpening the words with intensity. "I can see it. I can see it right there in your eyes. You believe me."

Melia nodded. Parker leaped from her chair and swept Melia into her arms. She whooped loudly and swung Melia around in a dizzying circle.

"Hey, stop!" Melia warned. "People might hear you."

"I don't give a damn. You believe me." Parker let her down and stood back, a full smile showing the appeal of her lips.

Melia returned the smile and their expressions brought warmth to the room. Melia could have basked in that glow all day, but another question remained to be asked.

"Yes, I believe you. But what do we do now?"

Twelve

Parker looked down into Melia's deep brown eyes, so relieved that she had gotten through the doubt and fear and finally believed. The world broadened out before her. No longer did it seem bound by the confines of the crawl spaces. Now, Parker had someone to talk to, someone who might help her find her way back home. Melia was smiling and Parker had not realized that she could be so beautiful.

But there was the question, still hanging on the air. What would they do now? How could Melia be any help in solving Parker's problem? Time travel was as foreign to her mind as it had recently been to Parker's. Despite the worry of that issue, Parker was happy. Just to know that she was not alone was enough to give her hope. She held Melia's hands and led her back to the long table. They sat beside each other and Melia never once took her eyes from Parker's face. Becoming a little self-conscious under that regard, Parker shyly reached up to pull her Stetson down before remembering that she had left it up in the ceiling when she'd changed into the suit. She needed it now.

The plan with the suit had been chancy, Parker had been nervous when she donned it. It was a man's suit, no question, and Parker had never seen a woman wearing one quite like it. But it fit her well, almost as if it had been tailored for her body, and she thought it made her look like she did belong in this time. The red-haired woman she'd talked to when she asked for Melia was cold, but seemed to take her outfit in stride. Parker had never dreamed it would have such a negative effect on Melia. Apparently, only the bad guys wore clothing like this. Parker wondered why there were so many of them in the building.

She shifted uncomfortably in the chair, not aware that her movement pulled the cloth against her shoulders, revealing the power of her body and making her look self assured. That was the last thing she was feeling at the moment. In fact, after the heavy material of her shirt and jeans, the thin clothes made her feel practically naked. And she just knew that her breasts could be seen through the white shirt. She made sure the jacket was buttoned.

"How did you . . . get here?" Melia finally asked.

"I'm not sure. I got an idea, but I can't explain it. I mean, I can tell you everything up to the point of fallin' down here, but it don't make sense to me."

"Can you tell me? I really don't think I can understand, but I want to hear the story." Melia put her elbows on the table and put her hands under her chin. Parker could see a light of excitement in her eyes, she looked like a kid waiting to hear the story of Christmas. They had both forgotten their surroundings.

A firm knock on the door brought Melia back to the present. She stood abruptly, putting herself between Parker and the door. Parker grabbed the gun and shoved back under her jacket. Remaining in her chair, Parker pushed away from the table and put both feet on the floor. The knock repeated, a bit softer. Melia glanced at Parker and Parker nodded.

"Come in." Melia had to clear her throat before she could speak the words.

"I locked it," Parker whispered. Melia hurried to the door and twisted the bolt just as the knob turned.

The door opened and a very tall, very thin man with an Adam's apple so sharp it hurt Parker's throat when he swallowed, stood nervously in the doorway. His large-knuckled fingers were clasped together. "Is everything all right, Melia? I just heard that someone was asking for you."

"Oh, yes. Everything is fine." Melia pasted on a hearty smile and Parker wondered how she was going to handle this one. Experience had shown that Melia could think fast on her feet. Melia turned to Parker and Parker smiled as well.

"This is my supervisor, Bob Conner. Bob, this is Ms. McCallem."

Parker stood and held out her hand as Bob walked forward to greet her. Parker tried not to make her handshake too firm for his comfort.

"Uh, Ms. McCallem. If this is an official visit, it really must be cleared through, uh, management before you speak to an employee. Well, that's just, uh, company policy." Bob tried to sound stern while not giving offense. Parker wondered how he stood so straight without a spine.

Not sure how to answer his statement, Parker raised her eyebrows and looked at Melia. Her response, or lack of it, made Bob swallow hard. A little bead of sweat trickled down from under his thin hair.

"Oh, I'm afraid there's been a misunderstanding. Ms. McCallem and I are acquaintances. We met at . . . the Historical Society. Last year. She's from New Orleans."

Parker smiled and nodded Bob's way. "That's right," she drawled.

"Ms. McCallem is just here in town on business. We were discussing work on a historical project, she was hoping I could do some research for her."

Bob nodded at each statement, turning his head from one to the other of them as they spoke. Parker had the feeling that he was not too smart and wondered how he could be in a position superior to Melia. It just didn't make sense, but she'd seen that plenty in the world.

"I am truly sorry to bother her at work, but time has been so messed up for me lately," Parker tried to keep her expression serious as she said the words. She caught Melia's quick grin as she picked up on the joke. "This is the first chance I've had to talk to her."

"Oh. Well, that's no problem. Melia knows she can pretty much make her own hours." Bob beamed as he looked at Melia. Parker could see respect and a friendly affection in his expression. "She has done so much for us. I'm sure she'll be able to meet your needs as well."

"I surely hope so."

"Well, I'm sorry I interrupted you. I was just, uh, well it was misunderstanding about who you were and why you were here."

"No offense taken," Parker assured him. She smiled warmly as he shuffled back to the door and slunk out.

Melia's shoulders sagged. "My god. I have lied more in the last week than I have in my entire life."

"You're pretty damn good at it. I'd suspect you been practicin'."

"I read too much."

Parker pushed her chair up to the table. She stood behind it, her hands resting on the high back. "He's right, though. I shouldn't be botherin' you now. I just wanted to talk, to convince you, and let you know that you are safe with me."

"I feel safe." Melia said the words with more emphasis than Parker expected. Yesterday's encounter had been frightening, and Parker felt bad about it. She studied Melia's face, hoping that the woman was not lying or pretending again. With those marks on her cheek and eye, Parker had to wonder what safety meant to Melia. Before she could think about what she was doing or consider the wisdom of bringing up the topic, she reached out and brushed her fingers over the bruises. Melia tried to step back out of her reach, but before she could move away Parker took her arm.

"Is this safe?" Parker continued to touch her skin, her fingers as gentle as she could make them.

Melia held her body stiff, but she didn't resist Parker's touch. She looked at the wall beyond Parker's shoulder.

"No. It wasn't. But it's over now."

"Are you sure? Maybe I can help you out?"

"No. I've ended it." Melia finally lifted her hand and pushed Parker's away. "How did you know about the bruises on my throat?"

"I told you. I been watchin' you. It must have been hurtin' you, you rubbed it a lot when no one could see you." Parker put her hands in her pockets. It was hard, not touching her. "But that was last week. This seems to be worse, not better."

Melia didn't respond. She was clearly disturbed by the topic, but Parker couldn't let it go. The thought of any woman being ill-treated like that made her furious.

"I could talk to him, make sure it don't happen again," Parker offered.

"It's not a him. It's a her and I told you, it's over."

"A woman? A woman did that to you?" Parker could not hide her astonishment.

"Yes. In this day and age, women can do just as many hateful things as men can. I suppose you never hit a woman?"

Parker felt her face turning red. The blood pounding up through her veins was painful. She hung her head. "Just you. Just yesterday." The words were hard to get out. She was a hypocrite, lecturing Melia that way. "I can't say how sorry I am."

"You didn't hit me." Melia's voice was certain.

"Yeah, I did. Up there." Parker gestured up to the ceiling. "I pushed you down."

Melia laughed. The sound shocked Parker into looking up. "You compare that to this?" Melia asked. "You scared the shit out of me, but you certainly didn't hurt me."

"Still, it was wrong."

"That's a great attitude. It's refreshing for me." Melia's voice had returned to a lighter, more normal tone. "Keep it." She picked up her backpack from the floor and slung it over her shoulder.

Parker raised her palms. "What should I do now? When can we talk?"

"It will be lunch break in a couple hours. Maybe we could meet then."

"Should I go back?" Parker tilted her head to indicate the ceiling. Melia shook her head.

"No. As long as you're here and dressed for the part, maybe you should go out and look around. I hate to think of you stuck up there."

Parker was so appalled at the suggestion that she took an involuntary step back. Her fists clenched so tight that the knuckles popped. She tried to cover her fear, but Melia noticed instantly that something was wrong.

"What's the matter? You've gone white as a ghost." She put her hand on Parker's shoulder as if to steady her. Thin creases appeared between her eyebrows. "Is it your head? That cut does look bad."

Parker was unable to admit her fear. It was humiliating. She took the excuse that Melia had given her and nodded. Melia stood on her toes and studied the wound. "It needs cleaned. You're headed for an infection."

"I washed it," Parker started to explain.

"Well, that's not enough. I'll check the first aid kit and take care of it when we meet for lunch." Melia stepped back and looked thoughtful. "There's a break room down by the third floor cafeteria. Do you know where that is?"

"Cafeteria?" It was a new word to Parker's vocabulary.

"The lunch room?"

Parker nodded.

"Why don't you just go down there and wait? You can read a book or take a nap and I'll meet you there at noon."

"Well, there's one more thing." The embarrassments of the day were never going to end. Parker turned out her pockets and dropped the contents onto the table top. The few coins she had jingled among the odds and ends and pocket lint. "See anything there that'll work for money?"

Melia came to the table and looked, smiling at the unfamiliar images on the coins. One she picked up and studied with fascination. "Is this gold? Real gold?"

"Yeah, it's a twenty-dollar piece. I should have a five-dollar one, too. Will they take that?"

"Not likely. They'd never believe it was real. But it certainly would pay for lunch and a whole lot more." Melia handed the coin back to Parker. "Put them back in your pocket. I can buy lunch. You can pay me back with your story."

"Deal." Parker scooped up her things and stuffed them back into her pockets. Melia gestured to the door. Parker opened it for her and smiled down as Melia passed her. The time would surely drag until lunch, but at least she was assured of Melia's interest.

"Come on, I'll walk you to the elevator," Melia offered.

"Oh, I'll be takin' the stairs, thank you." Parker tried to keep her voice casual. She hoped to god that there would come a day when she could show Melia that she wasn't afraid of every little thing. Until all this happened to her, she thought of herself as a brave and capable woman. Hopefully, she'd find a way to get that confidence back.

Ω　Ω　Ω　Ω　Ω

Melia found Parker in the break room. She stopped in the doorway. Parker hadn't noticed her yet and Melia took the time to better acquaint herself with Parker's appearance. Her opinion didn't change. Parker still seemed cool and confident. She sat in a low chair with her legs crossed, her back straight, looking both relaxed and ready at the same time. Her black hair was just long enough to cover the back of her neck. It stopped short of reaching her eyebrows in the front. Parker's expression was serious as she read, her head up and her jaw held tight. Her eyes moved smoothly across the page. Melia remembered how those eyes had looked at her from under the edge of the hat brim.

Parker turned the page and unconsciously reached up to adjust the hat she wasn't wearing. Melia smiled as Parker instead ran her fingers through her hair several times. The gesture was the only suggestion of nervousness in the woman's body. Melia doubted she would be as poised if she were in the same situation. Most of the things in Melia's everyday life, things she completely took for granted, must seem strange and unbelievable to Parker. Did she know about airplanes or televisions? Would she believe that people had gone to the moon and back? Melia hoped that Parker could assimilate all of the information that would be facing her, because the possibility of finding her way back to her own time seemed improbable.

Parker smiled a little at something she read. Melia still shivered at the expression. The smile looked so feral, so much like a hungry animal. Melia had seen the same look when her cat sat at the window, obsessively watching birds feeding on the lawn. Parker's full smile was the opposite of this expression. It brought warmth and humanity to her features, and made Melia want to believe every word she said.

Melia walked to Parker's chair and stood waiting for her to look up. Parker noticed her after a moment and gave Melia that smile.

"I'm sorry to keep you waiting."

"Not a problem. Feels good to be out among people." Parker turned her head and looked out the door as she spoke. "Although, an awful lot of you are strange these days. I can't believe some of the clothes I see people wearin'."

Melia smiled and wondered what Parker would make of Langley. "Well, you look very nice. Kind of formal, but I like it."

Parker leaned forward and shrugged her jacket into place. "You know, I kinda like it too. I s'pose I should take it back though."

Melia nodded. "But there's no rush." She sat on the arm of the chair next to Parker and dug in her backpack. "I brought some antiseptic wipes and a band-aid."

The look from Parker was one of incomprehension.

"It's medicine and a bandage, for your head."

"Oh." Parker brushed her hair away from her forehead. "I really think it's fine."

"It was your blood on my floor, wasn't it?"

Parker blushed. "I'm afraid so. I lost my footing and hit the back of your chair on the way down. Sorry."

Melia winced at the image conjured up by Parker's words. "How did you get it cleaned up from the carpet so well?"

"I didn't. I scrubbed at it for a while, but I was feelin' kinda sick and dizzy. I guess the folks that clean up got rid of it."

"Shall we go to the bathroom and get this taken care of?"

Standing, Parker gestured for Melia to go ahead of her to the door. They walked to the restroom in silence. Inside, Melia told Parker to sit on the counter while she washed her hands and ran a paper towel under the hot water. She gave the towel to Parker.

"Put it over the cut for a minute."

Parker looked like a kid. She sat impatiently, swinging her long legs back and forth under the counter. Melia tore open the package with the antiseptic wipe and approached her.

"This ain't gonna hurt, is it?"

"Of course, it will hurt."

"You say that so cold," Parker complained. "Never had kids, have you?"

"No, and I don't expect to." Melia thought way back to when her mother had been alive and taking care of her. She recalled what had made the hurts easier for her. "I'll blow on it for you. That will cut the pain."

Parker wrinkled her forehead and squinted her eyes as Melia brought the wipe close. Melia quickly dabbed at the cut. Parker squirmed, but managed to keep quiet. Melia stood on her toes and put her mouth close, blowing a steady stream of air onto Parker's forehead. She rested her hand on Parker's leg to keep her balance. Parker stopped wiggling and her face relaxed.

"That does work," she exclaimed. "How'd you know that?"

"My mom." Melia couldn't keep the smile from her face. How Parker could be so complex and yet so innocent was beyond her. Tearing the wrap off the band-aid, Melia pressed it over the cut. Parker tried to look up and see it.

"It's a bit lighter than your skin, but it's not that noticeable." Melia pointed to the mirror behind Parker. Parker turned and examined the small strip above her eyebrow. It covered the cut, except for the very edges still visible beyond its borders. She turned back and put her knuckle under Melia's chin.

Melia held still as Parker used the pressure to tilt her face up. She suspected Parker was going to kiss her and she didn't know quite how to respond. Stepping back was an option, but not the one she wanted. She waited.

Parker's expression was serious. "I wish I could take care of you so easily."

Melia stood for a moment, speechless until she realized that Parker had lifted her chin to look at the marks on her face. Knowing this, she did choose to step away. She busied herself with collecting the torn wrappers from the counter.

"I guess that means you're done talking about it. I'll let it go."

"Thank you." Melia tossed the scraps into waste basket and left the room, not waiting to see if Parker followed. But she did, and she stayed a step behind Melia as they walked to the lunch room. Forcing herself to shake off the mood that had overcome her, Melia smiled up at Parker as they entered the busy room.

Melia picked the table and after watching Parker study the menu and grow increasingly puzzled, she ordered for them as well. Parker seemed content to let Melia take charge. This was her time, after all. Melia felt like she was entertaining a visitor from another country and let herself get into thinking about what she would like to introduce Parker to first. The Museum of Natural History would be a great start. And she would have to meet Chris.

"What you thinkin'?" Parker looked over the rim of her coffee cup. She held her mouth close to the edge of the warm ceramic and Melia felt herself caught for a moment by the contrast of the black cup with Parker's lips. She forgot whatever it was she had been thinking.

"I just—I'm ready for your story." Melia took a sip of her cola and make herself look up into Parker's eyes.

"Whew," Parker dropped her head a little and scowled. "I been doin' some thinkin' about this and I got to admit, I'm a little worried about what you'll think of me."

"You're not going to tell me that it gets stranger than traveling through time?"

"Well, when you put it that way . . . but you gotta realize, life is different in my time. There ain't a lot a choices for women like me and, well, I never wanted to be a whore."

Parker paused and Melia let the thought sink in. It wasn't clear if Parker was saying she was not a whore, or she was, but not by choice.

"I'm a thief, Melia. An outlaw," Parker put down her cup and tapped her fingers on the table. She was staring at a point below Melia's chin. She didn't seem to want to raise her eyes to Melia's. "Just barely though. I wasn't really involved in so many hold-ups. Mostly I just scouted the jobs and collected my pay after."

"Mostly?" Melia was unsettled. Knowing that Parker was stealing to survive on the floors of a high rise was somehow more acceptable than the thought of her actually prowling the streets for a victim. "Did you . . . have you ever killed anyone?"

"Uh, this question, I wish you didn't have to ask it." Parker's face tightened and the lines near her eyes became deeply shadowed. "But you'd be a fool not to wonder and it wouldn't be right for me not to tell you."

Melia knew the answer from Parker's expression. A chill went down her back as she thought of sitting across the table from a murderer. How ignorant had she been crawling up into that crawl space?

"I never killed an innocent person, but I've regretted killing anyway. It's not . . . it's not good. Not a good feeling and I don't understand how some folks go out looking for the chance."

"Why did you do it?"

Parker sunk lower in her chair. Melia could see it was hurting her to talk about it, but if she wanted Melia's help, she was going to have to face up to her questions. Telling the truth wasn't going to give Melia any power over her, she could hardly turn her in for a murder committed in a previous century.

"Him or me. Reflex, I guess. I should'a hit him or something." Parker rubbed her jaw. The story was affecting her strongly and Melia suspected that, from Parker's point of view, the killing had happened recently. "I was scared and I had the gun in my hand. I didn't even think."

"He was trying to kill you?" Melia knew the answer shouldn't make any difference, but it did. Self-defense and cold-blooded killing were in two different leagues.

"He was tryin' to kill me. He was my friend and he was goaded on by someone else I thought was my friend." Parker took a deep breath and once again was able to look Melia in the eye. "And I'm thinkin', they're the reason I'm here."

Melia put her hand out to cover Parker's as she saw the waitress nearing their table. Melia was startled when Parker hooked her pinkie finger over Melia's and held her hand there. She didn't even seem to realize that she'd done it as she watched the waitress put down their plates and smiled gratefully up to her. Melia caught the brief look of disapproval in the waitress' face melt away at Parker's smile. It was that good.

Melia eased her hand away as Parker scanned her plate. The look of anticipation on her face was charming, Melia had to hide her own smile behind her hand.

"You know, this is the first cooked meal I've had in the longest time." Parker was beaming. "I don't even know what it is, but it looks fine."

"It's a club sandwich," Melia explained, pointing out each item. "Those are french fries and that is a pickle."

"Well, goddamn. I know what a pickle is." Parker picked it up and crunched down hard. Her forehead wrinkled at the sour taste, but she immediately took another bite. She nudged the corner of the sandwich and leaned over to speak quietly to Melia. "Now, am I s'pose to use a knife and fork with this?"

"No. Just pick it up." Melia demonstrated with her cheese burger.

"And what have you got?"

"Good old beef. I try and eat it at least once a year." Melia put the burger back onto her plate and cut it in half. She offered the half to Parker. "Most the time, I eat Asian food. Lots of vegetables."

"Asian food? You mean, like Chinese food?" Parker laughed at the thought. She had no idea that Melia was serious. Melia let it slide. Parker picked up a handful of fries and munched them one at a time. She looked down at them critically, then reached for the salt shaker.

After about the tenth shake, Melia couldn't stand it any longer. She grabbed Parker's hand and took the shaker away. "God, woman. You're going to kill yourself with that."

"I like salt," Parker explained.

"Moderation. Have you ever heard of moderation?"

"Nope. Salt don't hurt you anyway." Parker offered Melia one of the salt-encrusted fries.

Melia could hardly hold back her shudder. Parker laughed again and stuffed it in her mouth. She chewed it with exaggerated gusto, enjoying the look on Melia's face.

Wanting to know more, but regretting the need to steer the conversation back to their topic, Melia shook her head and tried to regain a serious expression. Parker caught on to her look instantly. Melia was sorry to see that Parker lost her enthusiasm for the food.

"I been double crossed, Melia. That Owen Lane. I never could trust him, but we'd gone along since we were kids. I knew he kept money from me, but I never expected him to want to kill me."

"Who was Owen Lane?"

"We were in a gang together. Might have gotten a name someday, if he hadn't decided he could do it better without me. So, I was s'pose to meet em and he set up an ambush instead. I had to run for the hills." Parker stopped to take a long drink of her coffee. She looked out over the lunch room and Melia realized she was seeing something that was still fresh upon her mind, regardless of how long ago it seemed to Melia. Parker went on.

"I was 'bout away, but I was thinkin' of killin' them all. It made me mad, you understand? Well, Bob popped up, right there in my way and his gun was in his hand, my gun was in mine. I didn't even think or feel or nothin'. I shot him and just kept runnin'."

Parker's hand was gripping the handle of her cup tight and her eyes filled with a wild look that caught Melia off guard and made the hair stand on her arms. Unconsciously, she leaned forward, absorbed in the story and the woman telling it. The reading she done all her life had prepared her for this moment. The action was a clear image in her mind. She could almost smell the gun powder filling the lunch room.

"I got to the hills and that's when I found the cave. It was just big enough to hide in, I thought, and nobody could sneak up on me there. I did think of snakes, but I figured the odds were better inside than out, so I jumped in there. That's when I fell, and I landed here."

Melia blinked. The abrupt ending came as a surprise. "That's it? That's all there is to it?"

"What do you want? What's s'posed to happen when you fall through time?"

"I—I don't know. I just expected there to be some . . . something. A flash of light or your life passing before your eyes or something."

"That's it. Just like falling in a hole."

Melia couldn't accept that. People walked in caves all the time. If there was a danger of being spit out in another era, surely she would have heard about it happening before now. "It couldn't have been a regular old cave. There had to be something more."

"Well, there was something more. It was a cold chill, I don't know. It fetched my hair up, but hell, February in the Rockies will do that any time." Parker shivered at the remembrance of that cold. "And there was that Indian drawing. It's what made me notice the cave."

"An Indian drawing? What was it?"

Parker took a french fry and dipped it in Melia's ketchup. On her napkin, she drew a figure that looked like a lizard with a spear. "Well, it's tail is s'posed to curl like so." Her finger made a spiral in the air.

"I've never seen a petroglyph like that." Melia scratched her head as she studied the sketch. A possibility nudged her brain. "There's a legend, a Native American myth, that says the first people came through a hole in the earth from another world. I don't really remember it, but I could look it up. It's a thought."

"But I'm not in a different world."

"Hey, don't expect me to make perfect sense of this. I don't know anymore about time travel than you do."

Parker sniffed and leaned back in her chair. "Less, I'd say. Since you never done it." She stuck out her chin and reached up to push her hat back. She caught herself in the motion and stopped before her hand reached her head. "Damn. I miss my hat."

Melia put her head down and smiled. She missed it, too. There was just something about a woman looking out under her hat brim that caused Melia to melt.

The lunch room was rapidly clearing out. Melia glanced up at the clock and frowned. It was time to return to work already. She hated to leave Parker, the story was still too fresh and questions remained to be asked and answered. Parker noticed the frown and stood up.

"Want to walk me home?" she offered. Melia rose and put her hands into her pockets.

"I hate to think of you staying up there. You know, there's a hotel next door. I could put you up for awhile until we got things straightened out."

Parker didn't speak, but she shook her head emphatically.

"If it's the money, you've got more than enough in that one gold coin to pay me back."

"No, it's not the money." Parker brushed past without another word and Melia was afraid she'd offended her. She hurried to catch up with Parker.

"Um, I'm sorry. I'd still like to walk with you."

"Let it go," Parker demanded. "We'll take the stairs."

By the time they reached the seventeenth floor, Melia was winded. She considered herself to be in good shape, but compared to Parker, who didn't seem to breathe any harder than normal, she felt like a slug. They left the stairwell and ducked unnoticed into the restroom.

"Why are you staying here instead of down on the fourteenth?"

"I thought it'd be best to keep moving. Don't want to attract attention." Parker lifted her foot onto the counter and stepped up easily. Melia stayed on the floor, looking up at Parker as she removed a tile.

"How will I find you?" Melia called up as Parker boosted herself into the darkness.

"I'll find you."

Melia was not satisfied with the answer. Something inside her was not willing to let Parker go. "Promise me. Promise me that you won't disappear."

Parker leaned back over the hole. Her smile spread slowly across her face. "Listen, I just got you. I'm not done with you yet." She leaned way down, so far that Melia was afraid she would tumble out of the ceiling. Reaching her hand to Melia, she said, "I promise."

Melia stretched as high as she could and shook Parker's hand.

Thirteen

Standing in the fourteenth floor bathroom, Melia stared up at the ceiling. Her nerves were wound up tight and her stomach coiled in knots. For the last day and a half, Parker had made no effort to contact her and ignored the note that Melia left with the paperback on her desk. The woman seemed to have disappeared as suddenly as she'd come.

But Melia was sure she was still in the building, and she was sure Parker had no idea of the danger she was in.

Melia paced the small room, the rhythmic scuffing of her shoes on the tiles was somewhat soothing, but did little to make a dent in her anxiety. She ignored the looks she received from the women who came and went. They watched her distraction and were not too surprised or worried at it. It was Melia, after all, and while everyone admitted she was a brilliant programmer, no one had ever praised her level head and sensibility. It was obvious that she was worried, but not ill, so they left her to simmer with her thoughts in privacy.

Melia had watched from her desk as the surveillance cameras and equipment were unloaded from the elevator and stacked near the positions they would take up as they guarded the floor. Wires snaked dangerously along the halls and potbellied workmen lounged and waited for the computer crew to leave at three this afternoon, as scheduled. Still holding the memo that asked her politely to leave the building early, just this once, she'd seen the men pointing and plotting the route the wires would take along the ceiling, hidden behind the ceiling tiles. A cold chill gripped her as she thought of Parker up there sleeping peacefully, either on this floor or the seventeenth, unaware of the danger she was in. Melia had to find a way to warn her.

At two o'clock she'd gone into the bathroom, fully intending to crawl into the ceiling to make sure Parker was not there or warn her away if she was. While standing on the counter, she'd realized that she was too short to reach the tile. There was no way to bring in the chair and the trash can to build another rickety pyramid. Seeing all that, someone would surely question her, eccentric reputation or not. Now, it was almost three o'clock and she would be shooed off the floor soon. She was ready to scream in frustration. Parker would never recognize the cameras for what they were, and once she was spotted, the search would not end until she was found, and would likely involve the police.

Melia had gone through her options at least five times, but found herself going through them again. She could enter the bathroom of each floor, taking along her chair, and climb into every ceiling to scout for Parker, or least shout up there and hope only Parker would hear her. Another option was to hide in the lunchroom and hope that Parker would go there this evening for something to eat. The safest option was to talk to Aaron and tell him the whole unbelievable story and hope that he would let her take Parker from the building without involving anyone else. It was smart, but she knew he would never believe the story or ever trust someone who would tell it.

"So much for your promise," Melia muttered. Tears threatened and she told herself they were only out of concern for Parker's safety. She stopped pacing, pushed back her hair, and looked steadily at her reflection, trying to imagine how she appeared to others. Was her gullibility written clearly on her face? Leaning closer to the glass, she glared, trying to take on the cool and composed expression that seemed to come so easily to Parker's face. The look was not natural, it was completely out of place on her.

At three o'clock, she left the restroom and went to her desk for her things. She was not going to be the last one out. It felt odd and unfinished to leave so soon. She puttered, picking up disks and putting them back, shuffling papers, and rearranging the books in her drawer. The high, grating sound of a drill finally forced her from the cubicle and into the elevator.

The crowded elevator crept downward, stopping every floor or so to load and unload people. Melia envied their business as usual attitudes, until she made the connection. The other floors were apparently not yet affected by the installation. She had to leave there by three, but the rest of the building was still open to her. The least she could do was go to the third floor and wait in the break room for inspiration to strike.

The small lounge with its nests of low-slung chairs and the empty dining room beyond were free of construction. Melia slouched in the nearest chair, her back to the door and her chin to her chest. It was because of the suit. Anyone who could afford to leave clothing like that lying around would certainly have the pull to get security cameras installed. Aaron was probably happy. It had to have been his pull that got the construction started on her floor. Parker was smart enough to avoid the fourteenth, the fact that she'd not touched the notes were proof of that. But the seventeenth would be next, if it, too, wasn't being outfitted with cameras at this same moment.

Minutes ticked by and Melia's frustration increased. Sitting and waiting for inspiration was a waste of her time, but the absence of any plan of action fed her inability to move. She made herself sit up straight. There had to be something, at least one thing she could try, something that would make her feel she'd given it her best shot before she was shooed from the building. There was an answer to every problem, she knew that from experience. The trouble was keeping her brain quiet enough to receive it. Melia breathed slowly and deeply.

Visualizing herself on the bathroom counter, reaching ineffectively for the ceiling, was what started her on the way to an answer. Knowing that she could never reach the tile, she made her imaginary self stop and consider what was around her. There was something in the room that would enable her to climb to the ceiling. It was so obvious, she'd overlooked it. The toilet seat, the toilet tank, the walls of the stall were a ready-made staircase, just waiting for her to notice. Melia grinned and hauled herself from the chair. Maybe Parker wasn't here, but Melia could try a few floors before she had to leave. She would do her best and that was all anyone could ask.

Melia took a step forward, almost walking out from under the light touch that rested briefly on her shoulder. An instant surge of relief passed through her body with her breath and she turned gratefully.

"Oh, thank goodness. I thought I—" Melia's words caught in her throat.

Dana raised her eyebrows and tilted her head forward. Her voice was silk. "I love the sound of pleasure in that, but your face is telling me those words weren't meant for me."

Melia couldn't hide her shock. Strangely, she had never expected Dana to come for her here.

"God, have I ever told you how easy you are to read?" Dana walked around the chairs and stepped up to Melia. "You didn't expect me to come here."

Melia moved back. Dana matched her steps, her movements casual, like she was trying not to threaten. Melia was threatened all the same. Dana didn't wait for a response.

"But that's why I came. Just to show you, just to make you think about it. I could have been here every day. I could have harassed you in a thousand ways." Dana smiled, an easy, gentle smile. One she had to know Melia would have paid good money for in another time. "But I didn't. That says something, doesn't it?"

The wall came to Melia's back and she was stopped. Dana didn't take the last step, leaving Melia a narrow margin of safety between their bodies. Dana's green eyes were glittering like diamonds. Her pupils looked tight and hard. "You don't make any sense. You're here. You're harassing me."

"I'm not harassing, I'm informing. I haven't been here, and that was my choice, but I had to let you know I still love you."

The words turned Melia's stomach. She would be content to never hear them said again in her lifetime. When she spoke, her voice was like ice. "You are unbelievable. You can turn the most beautiful sentiment into pure shit."

Dana sucked her breath through her teeth. Her smile changed, becoming sharp and strained, but it didn't leave her face. Melia squinted her eyes as Dana calmly and carefully lifted her right hand. She slapped her palm lightly on the wall next to Melia's head and leaned forward. "I think we need to talk," she said with simple directness.

"No, you are going to leave, right now. Or I'll call security."

Dana shrugged off the threat. "I understand why you're saying that, Melia. But I'm not going to give you any reason to call them. I'm not here to hurt you."

"When were you ever with me to hurt me?" Melia responded with heat. "But, you know, I sure as hell hurt."

"Give me a chance, Melia. I was wrong, I'll find a way to make it up to you."

"It's over."

"It will never be over." Dana finally lost control of the smile. It disappeared and there was no evidence that one had ever graced her features.

Melia ducked her head and tried to slip her body away from Dana's hand against the wall. Dana's reflexes were quicker and she was able to put her left hand out. Too late, Melia realized that she'd come to a stop next to the bathroom door. Dana gripped the handle and shoved the door open. She used her body to push Melia into the room. Once inside, she let Melia move away without following her. Leaning against the door frame, she watched Melia's retreat.

Surprised that Dana let her advantage drop so easily, Melia put her back to the counter. She would be ready this time. The shock had worn off and Dana would not overpower her without a fight.

"I'm sorry." Dana's voice was sincere and the words rang with cold clarity against the tiles of the floor and walls. "I mean it when I say I'm not going to hurt you. I just can't let you go without hearing me out."

Her hands rubbed lightly on her thighs. Melia watched the rhythm of their movements on the tight denim. Dana was nervous and her hands always gave her away. Soon, she would need to touch, the feeling would become a compulsion and then a danger. Without warning, the image of Parker's elegant fingers, so contrary to the roughness of her manner and dress, came to Melia's mind.

"You got the books?" Dana asked. Her voice was deeper, becoming hoarse.

"Yes. I'm sending them back."

Dana shook her head. "You do, and I'll burn the fucking store down."

"Jesus Christ, Dana!" Melia was horrified. The thought was beyond contemplation.

"I'm joking. Come on, lighten up." Dana took a step forward, but stopped as Melia raised her palm. "You can do what you want with them. Donate them to the library or a shelter. I only meant for them to make you feel better. If they don't, give 'em away."

The sincerity was back. Dana was playing it well, better than Melia had ever seen. The performance was impressive.

"Am I supposed to believe you've changed?"

"No." Dana moved toward her again. Ignoring Melia's shift away from her, she walked past her and leaned on the counter an arm's length away. "No, I haven't changed. Not yet. But I'm changing."

Melia held her tongue. Let Dana believe what she wanted to believe.

"Melia, this is hard. Please, don't make it harder."

A sound of frustration broke from Melia's lips before she could stop it. Dana's fingers twitched and she began flicking her fingernails against her jeans.

"Dana," Melia started. She turned to face the woman she thought she had loved. It was gone, there was no going back. The words to express her certainty would only infuriate Dana, and Melia couldn't find it in herself to blame her for the anger. If she was in Dana's place, she would be hurt and angry as well.

Dana took advantage of Melia's hesitation. "Don't say it now. Don't say anything." She placed a soft finger on Melia's lips. "I know what you're thinking."

For some reason, the touch was not repulsive to Melia. She wanted it to be. She wanted to be sickened the same way she'd been when Dana said the word love. The touch still swayed her. Dana sensed the response and struck with it. Running her fingers back along Melia's jawbone and around to catch in Melia's hair, she pulled her face up to encourage Melia to look into her eyes.

"Let me show you how much I care about you," she whispered.

The emotion Melia had hoped for came rushing in. Dana saw the revulsion in the same instant Melia experienced it. Her face twisted. And in Melia's hair, her fingers twisted. She jerked forward, pulling Melia off balance and shoving her head down to the level of her knees. As Melia staggered forward, Dana pushed her toward the open door of the nearest stall. Melia took a sharp breath and screamed.

∩   ∩   ∩   ∩   ∩

Parker heard them talking. She recognized that voice, it could bring her smiling from the deepest sleep. Turning to lie flat on the hard boards, she stretched long, wiggling her bare toes. Where she was, and the situation she was in, didn't come to her right away. She'd been dreaming of an excursion in the mountains, with warm sunshine and Melia. Closing her eyes, she let the voices tickle the edge of her awareness. Her relaxation was short lived. The tension in Melia's voice finally reached her.

Flipping over on her belly, Parker pulled at the edge of the tile with her fingernail. Melia was standing against the counter, intently watching someone who stood directly below

Parker's bed. The other woman was speaking now, her voice was harsher than Melia's, but Parker could feel the power of persuasion in her tone. It was the voice of a gambler, someone who played life close to the vest, and Parker hated the woman instantly. Her impression didn't change as a tall, blonde woman walked into view and stood next to Melia.

When she reached out and touched Melia's lips, Parker instinctively knew who she was. The urge to kill compressed her chest and her heart pounded with raw fury. Parker closed her eyes and let go of the tile. It was not jealousy. Anyone with any decency would feel the way she did right now. She wanted to just leap down to the floor and rip the woman away from Melia. What she would do after that, she couldn't say, but it wouldn't be pretty. Parker forced a breath to expand her lungs in an attempt to clear her head. Melia was a grown woman, she would decide her own path and Parker wasn't the one who had to walk it. Parker could be cold. She could give less than a damn for Melia's choices.

But the scream changed everything.

Parker had the tile torn from its frame before she realized she'd moved. Without a care for being seen, she grabbed the beam and dropped herself to the floor. Her bare feet hit the floor hard and the sting slammed straight up the backs of her legs. Parker fell to a crouch, her hand slapping her thigh where her gun should have been. It was on the boards, well above her head.

Parker hesitated. The woman's back was to her as she shoved Melia into the stall. Parker's landing had been silent, at least soundless enough that it was not overheard past their struggle. Just as Parker straightened up and took a noiseless step toward them, the woman slammed the door and pushed the bolt. Melia's cries were abruptly stilled. Fighting to keep her head clear, Parker tried shut out the sound of the woman's voice. Her hard, vulgar words were like rape, like filthy, obscene hands pawing at her flesh. Parker battled with her panic, barely keeping herself from ramming her body against the door, just to get inside and stop that voice. But she knew she couldn't break the door, and trying would only reveal her presence. The woman had no idea that she was not alone with Melia, and Parker had to use that to her advantage.

She knew how the latch worked. It was sturdy, but not meant to do much more than hold the door closed. Parker drew the small knife from her pocket and flipped open the longest blade. It was too short for a weapon, but long enough for what Parker meant to do. The women continued to struggle. The sound of tearing cloth impelled Parker to the door. Kneeling, she put her blade into the crack and pressed it against the top edge of the metal bar. A press down and a short twist of the blade moved the bar a fraction of an inch. Parker ignored the movement within and hoped the women would not push back against the door until she could work the bolt free. Two more sharp twists and the door swung inward slightly at Parker's touch. There was no more hesitation.

In a motion as smooth as if she'd rehearsed it, Parker drove the door open and into the woman's back. Before she could fall forward, Parker grabbed her by the hair, turned her away from Melia, then rammed her head directly into the tiled wall. Her forehead connected with a satisfying thunk. She went limp. Parker took a handful of the back of her jacket and held her upright as she drew her head back for another strike. Melia clung to her arm.

"Don't kill her. Don't kill her," she pleaded, her eyes wild and full of fear. Parker realized Melia was so frightened that, at that moment, she had no idea who Parker was.

Parker dragged the woman out of the stall and toward the door. The woman was still breathing. Parker pulled her head back roughly and examined her face. There was no blood, but a deep, red swelling was already beginning to grow just below her hairline. Parker leaned her against the wall and took a perverse satisfaction in gripping her by the throat to hold her there.

Pulling the door open a crack, Parker peered out into the break room. It was deserted. She took the woman by one sleeve and her collar and dragged her to the elevator. It had already been stopped on this floor and the door opened as soon as she pressed the panel. Parker dumped the woman on the floor and pushed the button for the top floor. She didn't care how long it took someone to find her.

Melia was huddled, shaking, in a corner of the stall when Parker returned to her. She screamed and struck out wildly when Parker touched her shoulder.

"Easy. Easy there," Parker soothed. She let Melia's hands push her backwards, not resisting the woman's need to push her away. "It's me, Parker. She's gone now."

Melia couldn't, or wouldn't, respond to the words. Her shirt was torn halfway down the front and a smear of blood was still wet on her chin. A red, half-circle of indentations showed where the woman had bitten into Melia's lower lip. Crouching next to her, Parker gritted her teeth and put her arms lightly around Melia. Melia pushed and hit at her, knocking Parker back into the wall. Parker kept her arms locked around her, but loose enough that Melia could move. After a minute of struggling, Melia felt that Parker was not fighting her. Her breath tore ragged in her throat, she looked up at Parker and comprehension came slowly to her face.

"Park—" her voice broke and the sound was an ache in Parker's heart.

She had hesitated enough for one day. Without another word, Parker lifted Melia into her arms and stood.

Effortlessly, she carried Melia to the counter and sat her there just long enough to climb onto it herself. She reached up and pushed away the tile above them. Taking Melia by gentle hands to her waist, Parker boosted her up into the darkness. Melia grabbed onto the beam and Parker helped her scramble upward to the platform.

Parker pulled herself up easily. She went straight to Melia, who had again crouched down in the corner. Firmly, but gently, she pressed Melia's shoulders, encouraging her to lie down on the boards. When Melia was on her back, looking up with eyes that still glittered with fear in the darkness, Parker lowered her body, full length to Melia's, covering her and pressing her into the security of the hard wood at her back. A sob broke from Melia's throat. Parker put her lips to Melia's ear and whispered words with no meaning but safety.

Melia's body shook so hard. Parker tried to hold her in a way that Melia would feel her strength and know that she was safe now. Parker kept her voice low and comforting and lightly brushed her fingers in the hair at Melia's temples. Melia cried, pushing her head into Parker's shoulder, wetting her shirt with her tears. When she finally reached up and wrapped her arms around Parker's back, Parker felt such a rush of emotion she thought she would never need to breathe again.

When Melia's shaking slowed, Parker lifted her weight from Melia's body. Melia gripped her tightly and Parker compromised by moving to the side and resting with half her weight on the boards and the other half on Melia. Melia turned to keep her face at Parker's shoulder. The scent of her hair was overwhelming. Parker had never smelled anything like it, not even a flower. She tried to breathe through her open mouth, but the soft brush of hair against her lips was just as devastating. She turned her face away as best she could before she was tempted to kiss the soft skin above Melia's eyebrow.

After long moments of their breath as the only sound, Melia spoke softly into the cloth of Parker's shirt. Parker bent her head down, but she couldn't catch the words Melia was repeating over and over again. Touching a finger to her chin, Parker tried to gently move Melia's face away from her shoulder. Melia resisted and Parker stopped the pressure.

"I can't understand you."

Melia sighed. Her eyes closed tightly, she moved her face away and said clearly, "I'm sorry. I'm so sorry."

"Don't be," Parker reassured her. "It wasn't your fault."

Melia shook her head and whispered the words again.

Parker took the opportunity to examine Melia's lip. As best she could tell by the faint illumination that filtered up into the ceiling, the cut had stopped bleeding and the blood that had covered her chin was wiped away. Parker knew it was probably staining her shirt. For some inexplicable reason the thought made her heart hammer and her face become hot.

"I'm sorry," Melia kept repeating. The sound was like a chant. Parker wondered what would make her stop, what words she could say to break the circle of Melia's thoughts. She knew what she wanted to do, how she wanted to silence those lips. But she would not do it, no matter how tempting it was. Now was not the time.

"Stop." Parker put her fingers gently over Melia's mouth. Melia kept moving her lips, now saying the words without sound. The movement tickled Parker's fingers and she swallowed hard. "Please stop. Look at me."

Melia stopped abruptly, but she didn't open her eyes. Parker slid her fingers to Melia's jawbone and turned her face up. Melia's forehead creased. Parker had no way of knowing that she was copying the other woman's earlier gesture. But

Parker didn't push. She let her fingertip brush back and forth along the studs in Melia's earlobe. Melia opened her eyes and looked directly into Parker's concerned gaze. The expression on her face mystified Parker.

"Where's your hat?"

Parker reached over Melia into the corner and retrieved her Stetson. She jammed it down on her head and showed Melia her smile. "I wasn't dressed yet," she explained.

"I didn't recognize you."

"Yeah. Well, it was a scary time. You're safe now."

"I—I know." Melia seemed surprised by the words. "I don't think I've ever felt this safe."

Parker grabbed onto the words, finding a deeper meaning within them. Could it be this was why she was here, to protect this woman? She had almost driven herself crazy searching for the reason her life had taken this turn, but she'd come up empty time and again. If she had purpose, if she was not just the butt of some devil's joke, she could make it. She could handle whatever changes were in store for her.

"I won't let her hurt you again."

Melia smiled. The sadness of it brought tears to Parker's eyes. As soon as the words were out of her mouth, she knew how empty they were. She was here, stuck in this building, and she couldn't keep Melia beside her. Remembering how it felt to drive the woman's head into the wall, she wished she hadn't let Melia stop her.

"That's such a kind thing to say."

Melia didn't say anything about Parker's inability. Her tone carried no contempt because she didn't know the extent of Parker's fear. Parker gritted her teeth. It was fear and nothing more keeping her here. She'd gambled with fear before, when the stakes were high enough, and she'd always come out all right. Feeling Melia's fragile body pressed warm against hers, feeling the desire to hold her and protect her . . . well, the stakes were rising. But what was Melia feeling, and did she even want to be protected?

"Is she . . . your lover?" Parker knew the answer and didn't want to hear it confirmed. Yet, she couldn't stop herself from asking.

"No. Not anymore. But she doesn't seem to believe that."

"What she does to you," Parker paused. She was getting into deep water and, depending on Melia's answer, she doubted she could swim it. Never could let well enough alone. "How she hurts you, do you—did you like it? Did you want it?"

Melia closed her eyes, and though her face was only inches from Parker's and her heart beat right against Parker's breast, she was gone far beyond Parker's reach. The white of her teeth gleamed as she bit her bottom lip. Parker watched as her mouth moved several times, but her thoughts remained unspoken. Suddenly, her eyes opened again and she looked at Parker with an perplexed expression.

"No. No, I did not like it," Melia voice grew stronger as she spoke. She seemed amazed at her own confession. "I never did. I just thought, I thought that's how it had to be."

Parker fought the disgust that threatened to twist her mouth. Holding her teeth hard together, she whispered, "Never. It never has to be that way. Love ain't like that."

"I'm not talking about love."

"But you said she was your lover."

"In the sense that she stayed with me, she made love' to me, she was my lover."

"You mean, you didn't love her?" Parker felt her body temperature rising as she spoke. She didn't know how Melia could not feel the way she was burning.

"Never."

Parker had never before felt such a blood lust. She would have been shocked to see how savage her smile appeared as she thought of her hands on that woman one more time. Somehow knowing that Melia didn't love her took any value from the woman's life. Parker remembered telling Melia that she didn't understand how anyone could kill for pleasure, but she was beginning to get the idea.

Melia's body unexpectedly tensed beside her and for a moment, Parker was afraid she'd read her thoughts.

"What is it?"

"You can't stay here anymore." Melia gripped Parker's arm as she spoke. "You're in danger."

Parker grinned and shook her head. "Nah, she didn't see me. She didn't know where I came from. Probably doesn't even know what hit her."

"It's not just her. They're putting up security cameras. They're going to find you."

Her grin faded. She had no idea what Melia was saying, but the look of concern on Melia's face was worrisome. "I can hide." The attempted reassurance in her voice sounded flat.

"These are cameras that can catch you walking. They can take pictures of you, of the whole building, all through the night. Just like a movie."

"Movie?"

"Oh, I don't know how to explain. It's just, like a picture of someone that shows them moving, walking and talking, and everything."

"I want to tell you that's impossible. But I don't know what to believe any more." Parker rolled away from Melia and stared at the floor above them. "Seems anything's likely to be possible."

"They can catch you. They *will* catch you."

"Well, what the hell am I gonna do?"

"You have to leave here."

Parker tried to laugh and failed. Melia was on her side, watching intently. Parker sat up and reached for her boots and socks. She slipped them on and wrapped her gun belt around her waist before answering.

"I just don't . . ." She dropped her head in shame. "I can't."

Melia touched Parker's leg just above the top of her boot. She seemed unsatisfied when Parker didn't look up into her eyes. She raised up and moved close, sitting cross legged before Parker. Parker thought back to the day she'd caught Melia in the crawl space on the fourteenth floor. Their positions were exactly reversed. She wondered if Melia realized it and if she felt the shift in power.

"They'll put cameras on every floor. They'll find Dana, I don't know what she'll say or what she knows, but it's one more suspicious thing added to all the rest. They'll find you."

"Dana," Parker repeated the name to remember it. Melia dug her fingers into Parker's leg.

"Listen to me, Parker. You probably saved my life down there. At the least, you saved me a lot of pain and humiliation."

The bare honesty in Melia's voice made Parker finally look into her eyes. The distance, the sense of far-off longing that seemed to haunt Melia, was gone.

"Something inside is making me feel so safe with you, I want you to feel the same." Melia leaned forward as she spoke, instilling in her voice an intensity Parker found hard to resist. If she knew how beautiful she was at this moment, she would know that words were no longer necessary. "I want you to trust me. Let me help you."

The stakes had gone as high as they'd ever been in Parker's life. No way could she resist gambling for them.

Fourteen

Dana opened her eyes. She was on her back and the world was swaying drunkenly. Two strips of bright light ran along the ceiling above her. They would not stay in focus. When she tried to squint, her forehead throbbed with an agonizing pressure.

"She's coming to," a man commented from beyond her vision. She tried to turn her head back to look, but a latex-gloved hand touched her cheek and prevented her from twisting around.

"Hold on, don't try to move. We'll be at the hospital in a few minutes." The hand stayed at Dana's cheek. The contact was enough to keep her still.

"What happened?" Dana whispered, not sure that the sound was loud enough to carry over the muted sound of a siren, but she couldn't put any more strength behind it.

"I was just going to ask you that. Can you tell me anything?"

Dana thought for a moment. She wasn't even sure what day it was or where she'd been. All she could think of was Melia, but that was all she ever seemed to think about lately. An image came back to her in slow motion. She was standing in the back of an elevator and Melia was walking toward her, her head down. Dana remembered facing the corner, hoping Melia wouldn't spot her. Then, the ride down, staring at the lean, familiar lines of Melia's back, the wave of soft hair at her neck. Wanting to touch her, but waiting. Waiting for the right moment. Determined not to screw it up this time. She remembered Melia leaving the elevator on the third floor. She stepped forward to follow . . . and nothing.

"I was in the elevator," she stated. It was the best she could do.

"Yes, you were found in the elevator. Do you know if you were assaulted?"

She started to shake her head. The pain stopped her before his hand could.

"Any history of seizures or fainting?"

"No."

"Dizziness?"

"No."

"Use any drugs?"

Dana tried to pull her cheek away from his touch. She didn't answer the question.

"We can tell by the blood tests at the hospital. It'll be easier for us to help you if you tell us everything you can now."

"I told you everything I can. I don't remember."

"You don't remember if you're using drugs? Cocaine, methamphetamines?"

"Get your fucking hand off my face." Struggling to pull her hands from under the light blanket that covered her, Dana shrugged her shoulder up to push him away. She freed her hand and fumbled with the buckle of the strap that crossed her midsection.

"Hey, you can't take that off until we're stopped." He

reached over to prevent her from sitting up, but stopped short of touching her.

"Then stop. I want out. I'm refusing treatment."

"I can't let you out until the hospital accepts you."

"Bullshit."

The driver of the ambulance took a quick look back at her. The man next to her gave him a pleading glance. "Hey, if there's been a crime, we have to notify the police."

"You are so full of shit." Dana sat up and swung her legs over the side of the stretcher. The pain in her head was raging but bearable. It didn't seem that she was going to pass out and that was good enough for her. "There's no crime and I have the right to refuse treatment."

"Maybe you got a concussion there. You really should—"

"You really should shut up. You're getting on my nerves."

The man clenched his jaw and glared at her. When the ambulance pulled up to the emergency room entrance, Dana didn't wait for him to open the door. She grabbed the latch and stepped down as carefully as she could. The thin sunlight made her eyes burn and the pain in her head increase. Hopefully, she could hold it together to get to a phone. Seeing a doctor was a smart idea, but it was going to be her doctor, not one that would ask her any questions about her choice of recreation. She straightened her back and walked away.

$$\cap \quad \cap \quad \cap \quad \cap \quad \cap$$

The ambulance was pulling away from the office building as Melia and Parker entered the parking garage from the stairwell. Checking her watch on the way down, Melia had been surprised to learn that it was barely after four o'clock. The encounter with Dana had distorted her sense of time. She'd hoped it would be already dark and that it would make the ride to her house easier on Parker's nerves. Glancing at Parker as they walked in silence, she was struck by her composure. No one would believe that the woman was afraid.

Parker had her hat jammed down to her ears and her chin jutted forward. She appeared immovable, as strong and steady as a mountain. In one hand, she carried the last book Melia had lent her like it was a treasure. Her other hand was covered by her coat; she'd folded it over her arm to conceal the pistol at her side. Walking with a comfortable stride, the only thing that betrayed her nervousness was the rapid shifting of her eyes. She continuously scanned the area around them, and Melia couldn't imagine what sense her mind was making of the things she saw.

They came to Melia's battered, old Civic and Parker stood beside her as Melia took out her keys and unlocked the door. Melia got in and leaned over to unlock the passenger side. Parker was still standing there.

"You've got to go to the other side." Melia tried to keep her smile from showing anything but reassurance.

Parker walked to the other door and Melia popped it open for her. Parker shifted her body nervously before taking a deep breath and plunging into the seat. Her hat jammed against the headrest and fell into her lap.

"Here, let me see if I can fix that." Melia pounded the top of the rest, trying to push it to its lowest position. Parker leaned away from her. "Okay, try now."

Parker put her hat back on and leaned back cautiously. The headrest still pushed against the brim. Parker pulled it off and held it over her stomach.

"This car wasn't made for hats," Melia said.

"I s'pose nobody wears a hat like this anymore."

"Not in Japan, anyway."

Parker looked confounded. Melia let it slide. There was too much to explain, if she started, there would be little else they could do.

Melia put on her seat belt and motioned for Parker to do the same. Parker slid the buckle around and Melia helped her insert it into the clasp between the seats. The feeling of the strap across her chest seemed to increase Parker's apprehension.

"It's gonna be so bad, we got to be tied in?"

"No." Melia patted her leg then lifted Parker's hat. Turning, she put it in the back seat. "It's just the rules."

Parker rubbed her chin and peered out through the windshield. Melia put the key in and didn't think to warn Parker before turning over the engine. At the sound, Parker jumped and jammed her feet hard to the floor.

"It's okay, it's normal. It's just a gasoline engine."

Parker's firm chin looked even firmer yet. Her composure was cracking, but her fear was revealed only by the paleness of her face. Melia let the car idle until Parker's muscles began to relax.

"I guess they didn't have gasoline engines in your time." She kept up the conversation to show Parker that the situation was normal for her and nothing to fear. "How about steam engines?"

"River boats." Parker grated the words through her teeth.

"River boats?"

"New Orleans. I rode a river boat, with a steam engine. Blew up a week later."

Bad topic. "Uh, well, there's no fire and no pressure in this engine. It can't explode like that. Really, it's safe."

Parker kept her response to herself. Any more hesitation on Melia's part would only prolong Parker's discomfort.

"Okay, I'm going to go forward now." Melia put her hand on the gear shift. Parker clenched her teeth and nodded.

Melia had seen that motion before. It was the same tense nod given by a bull rider when he was ready to leave the chute. She hoped this ride would be considerably smoother than that.

Melia kept an eye out for Parker's reaction as she drove up the ramp and out onto the street. Rush hour, which always seemed to come early in Denver, had just begun. The streets were filling fast, but Melia kept her speed slow and constant. Parker sat with her back stiff, one fist clenched in her lap and the other gripping the armrest. When Melia reached down to again pat Parker's leg, Parker looked at her hand in alarm.

"Hadn't you better hold on to this thing?" She asked, the tension in her voice escalating.

Melia put her hand back to the wheel. It was awkward. She felt like she was in a 1950s driver's safety film. "You ride a horse, Parker?"

"Sure, I do."

"I did a little, when I was a kid. At first, I wouldn't let go of the saddle horn, I gripped it like my life depended on it. But then, I couldn't use the reins." Melia kept her hands on the wheel and her eyes on the road as she spoke. "I finally got comfortable enough to let go and just hold onto the reins. When you ride, what do you do with your hands?"

"Well, I don't know." Parker squinted her eyes and thought about it for a second. "I guess I usually hold the reins in my left hand, so my right's free to do whatever."

"That's how I am with driving a car. I've been doing it so long, I don't usually need both hands."

"All right, I get you." Parker licked her lips.

Glancing over, Melia caught the motion. She had to whip her eyes back to the road to stop herself from staring. Those lips were an absolute fantasy. From the corner of her eye, she saw that Parker was slowly easing her back against the seat. The conversation was helping.

"Your name is a little unusual, Parker. I've never met a woman with that name before."

"It's a family name. I'm what ain't usual." Parker finally took her eyes off the road and looked at Melia as she spoke. Melia struggled not to fidget as Parker studied her profile. "I'm the only girl my family remembers havin'. There was always boys, at least four generations. I was s'posed to be Parker Allen."

"And you are?"

"Parker Ellen. My mother insisted on that much bein' womanly." Parker rubbed her palm along her thigh and almost grinned. "I don't see it did much good."

At that comment, Melia couldn't keep her eyes on driving. Turning her head, she smiled broadly. "I think it's worked out just right." She breathed deep as a light redness rose up Parker's neck and covered her cheeks. The blush seemed so out of character, it was captivating. Melia looked away and was suddenly glad to hold both hands to the steering wheel.

They reached the freeway and Melia hit the on-ramp, ready to be off the road and home. Parker's tension returned as their speed increased.

"Jesus Christ," she whispered as her knuckles tightened.

"It's just a few minutes, Parker, and we'll be there. Try to breathe, okay?"

Parker hissed air through her teeth and the sound gradually became a word. "S-s-slow. Can't you slow down a bit?"

"Uh, no, I'm sorry. Not yet. I have to go fast on this part." Melia could see that Parker's eyes were wide and she was trying to keep everything that rushed by in focus. A Porsche flew past them on the left. Parker gasped and Melia never heard her exhale. "Parker, close your eyes. Just try to close your eyes and lean back."

Parker shook her head in a short, stiff motion.

"I'm serious, do it." Melia put a command in her voice. She had to get a hold on Parker's fear now before she decided to leap from the car or grab the wheel. "Lean back."

Parker finally exhaled a shaking breath and leaned back a fraction of an inch.

"Good. Close your eyes. Just try it for a second."

Parker squeezed her eyes shut like she was expecting a blow.

"Now feel it. You can feel the vibration, but you can hardly tell we're moving, right?"

Surprised, Parker nodded. She opened her eyes for a second, as if to check that the car was still traveling along. They closed again quickly.

"Now think about your trip on the river. Did it feel good? Were you afraid?" Melia eased into the passing lane as she spoke. Their speed increased imperceptibly. The faster she could go, the sooner they would be off the streets and into the safety of her home.

"It was, it was good. I was just a kid." Parker licked her lips again and her voice smoothed out, the fear diminishing. "You know kids, they ain't smart enough to know when to be scared."

Melia understood the comment, but it was not true of her. She had always been afraid. Not until she was an adult did her anxieties begin to be dominated by her curiosity. "What did you do? What did you see?"

"I just watched. I stood at the rail and watched the trees go rollin' by. We were goin' upstream, up to St. Louis. We were goin' west from there, goin' to California."

"You didn't make it there?"

"No." The emotion drained from Parker's face and it became a mask. "My mom and my little brother died on the way. My dad, he lost his heart. We just ended up in Denver. That was the end of it."

"I'm sorry," Melia whispered. She put her hand over Parker's and gave it a squeeze.

Parker shrugged. "It was a long time ago." She laughed a little, but the sound was without humor. "I guess it's a real long time ago now."

Melia moved back in the slow lane and signaled for her exit. The unreality of Parker's situation returned with a sense of shock. It was strange how she could ever feel that it was normal to have the woman sitting beside her, breathing the same air she breathed. All at once, she wished she had someone to talk to about all this. Chris. She always thought of Chris.

Melia kept one ear open to the sound of splashing in the bathroom as she waited for Chris to come to the phone. She'd gotten Parker to the house and inside without incident and the only thing Parker wanted of the choices Melia offered was a hot bath. Gathering Parker's clothes from beside the door, she'd promised them to be washed and dried by the time Parker finished the bath. Parker had laughed and asked how long Melia thought she be in there. Melia just smiled. Parker had a lot to learn.

"Hey, Mel. I been missing you."

Melia smiled again. The voice was like a soft, warm hug. "Hey, Chris. Things have been a little strange for me lately. I really would like to talk to you."

"God, it's not Dana again, is it?"

"No, not really. Actually, not at all. But there's someone I'd like you to meet."

Chris was seized with coughing. Melia thought it sounded like she was choking on something she'd been drinking. When she was able to speak again, she was not at all happy.

"Goddamn girl, don't you think you're moving a little fast here? You just got rid of one and, I'm sorry, but your taste in women sucks."

"It's not like that, Chris." Melia paused. She didn't want to admit, not even to herself, that it was possible it was "like that" and she was in too fast and too deep already. She rushed on.

"I can't explain it on the phone, but she's got a story you've got to hear. I need your advice." Melia couldn't say too much, she hadn't even discussed this with Parker. "I need to see you."

"I can't today, Mel. It's inventory and tomorrow I've got a shipment coming in. Can you bring your little friend down here?"

Ignoring the sarcasm in Chris' voice was easy, Melia knew it was a cover for her concern. "Um, that's not good right now. But it's no crisis. Can we talk this Sunday?"

"That would be great. You sure it's okay? Would it help to talk to Lang? You know, she's almost become my clone."

Melia heard a snort of disgust in the background. Langley hadn't missed that one. Chris went on.

"I was just about to send her up anyway. I have a load of books I'm sending back to the publisher. I picked out a few I thought you'd like, I can keep them at the wholesale price."

Melia thought of Parker's enthusiasm for the books she'd been borrowing. Enough had survived Dana's rampage to keep her busy for a long time, but a new book was not something Melia could pass by. She needed to start rebuilding her collection and damned if she'd do it with Dana's books.

"That's great. Just keep track of the cost and I'll bring you a check this weekend."

"Actually, I got some new catalogs coming in with the order tomorrow. If you could look over the titles and give me some advice on the Westerns, I'd call it even."

"Perfect."

"So, I'll send Lang up." Chris called Langley over and started giving her instructions before Melia could respond. "She'll be up in about an hour. Bye, love."

"But—"

Chris had hung up, either not hearing or simply ignoring Melia's attempt to protest. Melia replaced the receiver and hoped that Parker would not be upset. The thought that this was her house and Parker wouldn't question her right to do whatever she wanted never crossed Melia's mind.

Parker's clothing folded over her arm, she went to the bathroom door and paused. What was the propriety of Parker's time? Would she be appalled that Melia thought of entering the room or would she think Melia a prude for hanging outside the door? She knocked softly. There was a heartbeat or two of silence, then Parker responded.

"Come on in."

Melia pushed the door open and held out the clothing. She kept her eyes on the floor, but she wanted to look. She really wanted to look. "See? All clean, all dry."

"You're a miracle," Parker teased.

Melia heard the water run from her body as she stood in the tub. The soft whisper of the towel being pulled from the rack followed. By the sound of Parker's voice, she had recovered from the drive and her composure had returned. Melia's suffered by contrast. Parker took the clothes from her hand and she finally allowed herself to look up.

Parker stood wrapped in the huge towel, still dripping with water. Her black hair was shining with water and slicked down flat to her head. When wet, her hair reached past her eyebrows and pushed against her lashes. It looked so smooth and Melia could smell her shampoo in Parker's hair.

It smelled better than it did in her own.

"These pants never felt this soft. It's good," Parker commented. "Thank you."

Melia nodded. She couldn't think of anything to say that wouldn't sound inane. Parker waited. Melia knew she was expecting her to speak or leave or something, but Melia felt like she could do nothing but stand there and look up at Parker.

"You all right?" Parker asked, leaning down a little to look straight into Melia's eyes.

"Yes," Melia assured her, the spell only partially broken. She didn't want it to break at all. "I just thought, maybe I could give you a hand. Maybe dry your hair?"

Parker smiled a bit and nodded. It wasn't her full smile, but Melia was realizing that she liked this one, the animal one, just as well. It certainly had its appeal. Backing away from Melia, Parker sat on the edge of the deep bathtub. Melia took a small towel from the rack and followed her, stopping when her legs touched Parker's knees.

Parker leaned her head toward Melia's chest. Water dripped from her hair onto Melia's toes. Melia unfolded the towel and pushed back Parker's bangs. Parker closed her eyes as Melia roughed the towel through her hair. The smile never left her face. Melia couldn't imagine her own expression. She hoped it wasn't too naked, too obvious, too entranced. Feeling like she did when she was contemplating crawling into the ceiling for the first time, she wondered why danger so easily compelled her. Dana was hardly gone and she was already considering this, already wondering, imagining what Parker's fine, long hands would feel like on her skin. What her lips promised without saying a word. She wanted to kneel down, to put her head in Parker's lap, to be still and submissive, and let Parker decide. Her hands stopped their movement and the air filled with tension.

Parker's smile faltered. Her lips tightened into a thin line and she reached up to take the towel from Melia. Melia let her hands fall to her sides. Parker stood, unfolding her body slowly, and Melia forced herself not to take a step back. Watching her right hand as if it was not a part of her, she saw it moving, reaching out to pull the towel from Parker's body. Just as she touched the material, her fingertips brushing the soft heat of Parker's skin, Parker grabbed her wrist and held her hand away. Melia closed her eyes, not wanting to see whatever expression was crossing Parker's face. She imagined it was contempt. She deserved it.

"You've movin' a bit too fast," Parker whispered. Her voice cut through the steam that still clouded the small room. It carried none of the tone Melia expected. It spoke concern. "You don't know me very well."

"No." It wasn't enough to say, but it was all Melia could manage at this moment.

"You do this often? Is it just this easy for you?"

Melia understood Parker's unspoken meaning. If it's this easy, it can't mean much.

"I'm sorry. I don't know what else to do. I feel . . ." Melia stepped back until she reached the wall behind her. Leaning on the cool tiles, she stared at Parker's feet. "I don't know how to express myself. This is . . . easier than trying to explain what I feel."

The towel dropped to the floor. Melia held her breath and slowly let her gaze rise up Parker's long legs and stop. Her palms flattened against the wall and she again fought with the desire to drop to her knees.

Parker reached down for her clothing and slowly, deliberately pulled on her underwear and then her jeans. Melia watched her button her fly, the suppleness of her fingers drawing a warmth from deep within. Parker walked to stand before her.

"You got somethin' to say to me? Am I doin' somethin' to make it hard for you to talk to me?"

You breathe, Melia thought. *You breathe and your heart beats and your blood flows through your body and I want it. I want it all, all of you, and I can't speak.* She looked into Parker's eyes and prayed that at least a glimmer of that emotion was visible. Dana said she was easy to read. She prayed it was true.

"Jesus Christ," Parker whispered and the strain in her voice made it all so clear.

Melia could see it now, the way Parker's eyes burned into hers, the way her chest rose and fell with the quickness of her breath. She had no more words than Melia did, she was just as torn. Parker's hand rose. It brushed across her cheek and took her earlobe between thumb and forefinger. The metal of Melia's earrings bit into skin. Parker pulled lightly, not enough to move Melia's head, not enough to hurt, just enough to make Melia's lips part and her breath catch in her throat.

Parker kissed her. Not abruptly, but as if the kiss was unavoidable, like the inevitable movement of the earth. Melia tasted Parker's lips and they were everything they promised and more. The moisture from Parker's upper body seeped into Melia's shirt as she wrapped her strong arms around to pull Melia close. Melia touched Parker's sides, then slid her hands up over the powerful muscles of her back. She couldn't get close enough, she couldn't press enough of her body against Parker. Like Dana had done, Parker pulled Melia's bottom lip into her mouth, but tenderly, with a gentleness that made the touch beyond any comparison.

Parker broke the kiss. Melia tried to reach back into it, but Parker was too tall and held her too still.

"I know what you want," Parker whispered. "But I gotta know what you feel. I can wait for you to tell me."

"What if—what if I can't?" Melia didn't cling to her, but let Parker step back. She again pressed her palms against the wall. "What if I can't ever say what I feel inside?"

"Then maybe it's only lust. Maybe that ain't what I want."

"What do you want?"

Parker let her eyes travel the length of Melia's body. The half-smile returned. Melia felt her legs go weak. But just as swiftly as the smile came, it disappeared.

Parker's face became grave. "I want to go back. I want to go home."

Fifteen

Langley whistled as she packed the books from her Jeep to Melia's house. She was happy to be here. Seeing Melia anytime, for any excuse, just did that to her. Grinning, she thought of the disappointment Chris would feel if she knew Langley had promised Melia to keep their friendship platonic. Chris worked so hard to find ways to push them together. Langley was flattered. Melia was like Chris' pot of gold and she treasured her and guarded her as if she was priceless. Langley shared the opinion, but she had to wonder what she'd done to fall so deeply into Chris' favor.

Shifting the books to her other arm, Langley rang the door bell with her elbow. From inside, Melia called out that it was unlocked. Stepping through the door, Langley was immediately aware of a long look of pure poison directed right at her. Her appearance often got her those kinds of stares, but she had not expected to feel it from Melia's house, not today. For a moment, she was convinced that Dana had returned.

A woman in a worn, black cowboy hat was sitting slouched on Melia's sofa, her legs crossed and her arm resting casually on the cushion next to her. Langley couldn't see her eyes from the darkness under the hat's wide brim, but she knew just where the woman was looking. The woman's lips were pulled back from her teeth and Langley didn't know if she was sneering or smiling. Lang felt a cold that reached deep into the pit of her stomach. She knew this wasn't Dana, there was something about this woman that unnerved her like Dana never had.

The woman didn't move or speak as Lang walked up and put the books on the end table. Melia was in the kitchen and the smell of coffee filled the room. Langley stood awkward in her parka, wishing Melia would come to meet her. Perching herself on the edge of the chair farthest from the woman, she nodded briefly and looked away.

When Melia entered carrying three steaming cups on a tray, the atmosphere of the room changed completely. The look shifted from Langley as the woman turned her eyes to Melia and smiled. The change was so abrupt, it was shocking. Langley pulled her coat tight around her and studied Melia's face.

She didn't seem to feel the sudden release of tension. Smiling nervously at first the woman, then Langley, she appeared unaware of the force that emanated from the woman. It wrapped Melia in her circle and stopped short and cold just as it reached Langley. Langley felt a tickle of wariness brush the skin between her shoulder blades.

"Did you introduce yourselves?" Melia asked.

Langley shook her head, knowing she should feel foolish, but knowing under no circumstance could she have offered that woman her hand.

"My name's Parker." Her voice was quiet.

Langley heard trail dust, she heard rough whiskey and long nights under the stars. She swallowed and wondered what Parker would hear when she spoke her own name. Melia saved her the worry.

"This is my friend, Langley," she said, with an unexpected touch of pride. Standing next to Langley, she rubbed her head with a warm hand.

Parker leaned forward, a slow, fluid motion that had Langley widening her eyes so not to miss a movement. She pushed her hat back from her forehead and her eyes were blue as ice, but not at all cold. Putting out her hand, she invited a handshake. Langley took the firm grasp and she felt the change inside like a switch had been flipped. There was no reason to be afraid, this woman could be trusted with her life. Langley took her hand back and it was shaking. She was being manipulated, she knew it, but didn't know how to fight it.

"You're not from here, are you?" Langley was relieved that her voice was steady. As soon as she asked the question, Melia's hand tightened on the back of her neck. Langley looked back at Melia. She was staring at Parker and her face was pale.

"To tell the truth, I'm from New Orleans. But I been in Denver awhile now," Parker drawled, settling back in her seat, her eyes never leaving Melia's face.

"And how did you meet Melia?"

"At work," Melia offered the answer quickly. Too quickly. It was obvious she was hiding something. She left Langley's side and sat down on the couch an arm's length from Parker.

"So, you work with computers too?"

Parker laughed hard. "Hell no," she answered with emphasis. "I don't know the first thing about 'em. I ain't sure I want to."

Langley grinned at the outburst. She couldn't understand that feeling. "I don't know how I would survive without them. I'm an Internet addict and a hardware junkie."

Parker frowned slightly and the conversation lagged.

Langley picked up her coffee cup and pretended to be interested in the smell of the rising steam. She knew better than to press the question of who Parker was, she wasn't going to get the truth anyway and she didn't want Melia to feel she had to lie.

"Take off your coat, Lang," Melia finally suggested.

"Uh, no, thank you. I really should be going."

"Not yet," Parker said abruptly.

Langley wasn't sure if the words were meant to be an order or a challenge. She almost stood involuntarily, defensively. She managed to stop herself, but her muscles remained tense and ready for anything.

"Hey, I'm makin' you uncomfortable." Parker leaned forward again. This time, she took off her hat and placed it carefully on the coffee table between them. "I know I'm starin' at you, I'm sorry."

Langley looked to Melia, who didn't seem to have any more of an idea what was going to happen than Langley did. She looked back at Parker. Parker smiled. Langley felt her shoulders relax. Her body responded to the expression without conscious thought. The woman was manipulating her again.

"I'm just tryin' to place your tribe. I know Blackfeet sometimes shave their heads, but I never seen markings like yours."

Unconsciously, Langley raised her hand to touch the black-inked tattoos that circled her neck. Melia laughed. The sound was light and welcome in the tension of the room.

"Oh, she's not Native American, Parker. I mean, she's not Indian."

Parker's eyebrow raised a fraction, but she said nothing.

"Why would you assume that?" Langley asked, thinking Parker was taking her cowboy role a bit far.

"Well, your skin's not black, but it's not white either. And I didn't reckon there could be another reason why you look like that," Parker replied without insult. Melia laughed again. Her pleasure made Langley finally feel like she belonged here with Melia as much as Parker did.

"My father is black, my mother was Vietnamese. The tattoos aren't related. While we asking, why do you look the way you do?" Langley balanced her coffee cup on the arm of her chair and leaned back. "I think we're both riding the fringe of society. My appearance is a little more radical than yours, but our objectives are probably not that different."

Parker narrowed her eyes and stroked her thumb along her chin. She shook her head, the gesture a little questioning, a little doubtful. "I'll be damned if I got any idea what you're talkin' about."

"Politics," Melia interjected. "It's all just politics Lang, and you know how I hate that."

"Sorry, Mel." Langley apologized and lifted her cup again. She ducked her chin and stared into the creamy, brown liquid, careful not to look up too soon, leaving them time to exchange the glances she could feel across the distance. Melia was trying to protect Parker from the questions, as innocent as they seemed, and she was not doing well at hiding her anxiety. What did Parker have to hide?

Langley closed her eyes and tried not to let her worry show on her face. First impressions were leading her to believe this woman was another Dana and her charisma was even more threatening than Dana's blunt superiority. The hope that she was reading more into their relationship than existed was naive, Melia had a one car garage and there was no other vehicle parked on the street in front of her house. Langley was hurt. She was disappointed and she was again feeling afraid.

"I'd better go," she said abruptly. She couldn't stay here and remain silent. Melia's relief at the words was like a slap to the face. Langley stood.

Parker got to her feet as well. Langley lifted her chin and matched Parker's cool gaze. Her face was without emotion, a poker face, Langley supposed it would be called. She was good.

"Listen, partner," Parker drawled. "Hold on just a minute."

Parker rounded the end of the coffee table and stepped up to Langley. As she moved, she held the heel of her hand braced against her wide leather belt, her fingers curled at her hip. The denim of her jeans had been worn in that area and Langley's imagination led her to believe it was from the holster of a gun rubbing against the fabric. She felt so young.

"I got the feelin' I offended you," Parker's voice was low, almost like she was trying to keep the words from Melia. "I don't mean it. You're . . . not like anyone I ever seen before."

Langley nodded. "I understand."

Parker gripped Langley's shoulder and leaned close to her face. So close that Langley could see the fine lines beside her eyes and smell Melia's shampoo in her hair.

"I can guess what you're thinkin'," Parker's voice was even lower, almost a whisper. "I'm not gonna hurt her."

Langley tilted her shoulder down and back, away from Parker's touch. She didn't attempt to speak quietly. "I've heard that before."

Parker withdrew her hand and stepped back. She gave Langley a brief nod and stood as if waiting.

"Let me walk you out," Melia broke in.

"Don't bother." Langley did try to keep her voice from sounding harsh, but didn't really care if she succeeded. Parker picked up her hat and her coffee cup and left the room, making sure that the door to the kitchen closed behind her. Melia touched her arm.

"You're angry with me."

"No."

Melia stood in front of Langley, but she wouldn't look up into her eyes. Taking the ends of Langley's coat, she attached the zipper and slowly pulled the tab up to the center of Langley's chest. Langley breathed deep, trying not to respond to the pressure of Melia's hands against her body.

"What can I say to you, Lang?"

"What makes you think you have to say anything?" Langley pulled away and walked to the door. Melia followed her. The gesture relieved a little of the hurt in her chest.

"I'm sorry that was uncomfortable. I want you to feel welcome here." Melia gripped the doorknob to prevent Lang from opening the door. "She's just really out of her element and . . ."

Lang waited a moment, but Melia didn't finish the thought. Whatever was happening, whoever Parker was, Melia was already in over her head.

"She really fits your image of the perfect woman, doesn't she?"

Melia seemed shocked by the statement. "Why do you say that?"

"Because I know what you read. You've probably been looking for someone to fit that character. I just hope you're judging her by more than her appearance."

Melia finally met Langley's eye. She shook her head. "I can't even begin to tell you about her. But I will someday, as soon as I can."

Langley felt the pressure in her chest returning. She couldn't stop herself from reaching out and taking Melia by the arms. Fear poured from her in a rush of words. "Melia, come home with me, right now. Just leave her in there, you can call and tell her I insisted, or there was an emergency or something. I don't feel good about this, I just can't leave you here with her."

"And I can't leave her here. You don't understand. She's not Dana. She hates Dana as much as you do," Melia spoke with a strange intensity that was so unlike her. "Lang, I feel so safe with her."

"Then why do I feel like I'm never going to see you again?"

"Lang! That's ridiculous." Langley was surprised to see tears fill Melia's eyes. "Don't ever say that."

Langley pulled Melia into her arms and held her tightly. Bending her head down, she put her cheek on the top of Melia's head. Her hair was as soft as always, but the familiar smell was now disturbing. Before Melia could move to return the hug, Langley broke away and let herself out the door. She closed it hard behind her and ran down the sidewalk. She never looked back to see if Melia had tried to follow.

Ω   Ω   Ω   Ω   Ω

"Now, I like that woman." Parker told Melia emphatically. "You ever gotta make a choice between friends, you keep that one."

Melia stood at the kitchen door, surprised at Parker's advice, especially after hearing Langley's apprehensions about Parker. "Why do you say that?"

"She's a smart one. Didn't you feel her?" Parker straddled a chair and rested her elbows on the table. "She was sittin' here and there wasn't a thing said that she didn't weigh out and measure. Every time I looked at you, every time you looked at me, she was learnin'. If she wasn't your friend, she'd be trouble."

"She doesn't trust you." Melia took the chair across from Parker. Her nerves were on edge from Langley's emotional departure.

"I told you, she's smart."

"Are you saying you're a danger to me?"

"As far as she's concerned, I'm a danger to you and her both. She's in love with you."

Melia looked down at her hands. Their trembling was mirrored by the feeling in her stomach. Everything she did, every choice she made, ended up affecting other people's lives. She couldn't take the responsibility. "You're wrong."

Parker shrugged and leaned back. She stretched her arms above her head and flexed her fingers. "You know what I like? Standing up straight and walking on a solid floor." Her voice was light and teasing. Melia felt Parker was trying to draw her back from her slide toward depression. She let herself be led away.

"And what about food? You say you've missed real food?"

"Christ, like you wouldn't believe."

"I think I have some steak in the freezer and I've always got potatoes." Melia went to the refrigerator and began digging for supplies. "You people were the meat and potatoes type, weren't you?"

"I can't hardly speak for everybody, but I sure can vouch for my appetite." Parker followed Melia across the kitchen, rubbing her belly under the denim shirt. She put a cautious fingertip to the package of frozen meat. Lifting her eyebrows at the depth of the cold that touched back, she managed to hold inside any comment.

Melia smiled as she peeled the potatoes over the garbage disposal. God, she wished she could have shared this sense of wonder and learning with Langley, it was an experience not to be missed. Someday, she would be able to explain it all and relieve the fears she believed were groundless.

"Where do you get your fire?"

Melia patted the top of the range. "Right here, but it's electric. No actual flames or anything."

"That's too bad, I was hoping I could do something. I'm pretty damn good at fire startin.'"

"We can eat in front of the fireplace in the living room. You can do the honor."

Parker rubbed her hands together and grinned. Melia pointed out the window to the small woodpile in the backyard. Parker whistled as she headed for the door. Suddenly she stopped, her hand still on the latch.

"I don't know the days, Melia. You work tomorrow?"

"No, tomorrow is Saturday."

"So, you'll be home all day?"

"Yes, unless you need some time alone. I can—"

"No. That's all right." Parker rubbed her lips with a fingertip.

Melia remembered Parker's kiss and the feel of it on her lips. She wished they were comfortable enough that she could close the distance between them and be back in Parker's arms. The woman's sudden quiet frightened Melia. She searched for something to say to bring the smile back to Parker's face.

"You know, tonight I can look on the computer and see if there is anything out there about what's happened to you. If there's any information at all, I can find it," Melia promised.

"You'd do that for me?" Parker asked, her eyes lighting up with the possibility of it.

Melia smiled. Parker had no idea the things she would be willing to do for her.

Ω   Ω   Ω   Ω   Ω

Parker had gone to sleep with the blue light of Melia's computer screen filling the room. She'd pulled the blanket over her head, the light gave her a headache, but she didn't think that sleep would come. Living up in the ceiling of Melia's office building had set her body's clock all backwards. She was used to staying up most of the night, only waking a few times during the day to go and soak up the sight of Melia. She'd peeked out over the edge of the blanket several times, still not too used to the way Melia's face looked as seen from a different angle than above. One thing she was sure of, Melia was beautiful from any perspective.

Letting the blanket fall back over her eyes, she had remembered how Melia felt lying beneath her as she'd comforted her this afternoon. Her body seemed so small, so fragile, but so much a woman. The memory had made Parker stir restlessly on the couch. Melia's chair squeaked and Parker forced herself to hold still. She didn't want to disturb Melia, she had to know whatever Melia could find, even if she didn't understand where that knowledge was coming from and how Melia could find it. "Accessing a database" sounded complicated, maybe even a little painful, but Melia was willing to do it and the least Parker could do was let her be while she tried.

Now, the room was dark. The only light anywhere in the house was the pale bars of the orange-tinted light shining down from the poles that lined the street. No one was out there moving, but still the lights burned. Just waiting, she guessed, never knowing when someone might come along and need them.

The smell of wood smoke from the fireplace had faded. The coals were gone and cold ashes filled the grate. She was awake. Turning on her side, she considered rekindling the fire. Not that she was so cold, just that the sight of the flames had brought her a peace she hadn't felt since coming to this time. Even confined there in its little bricked-off box, it seemed the only wild and natural thing she'd encountered in this world.

Melia had left her wine glass on the table. Parker slid the long, delicate stem between two fingers and lifted the glass. Tilting it to catch the edge in one of the bars of light, she examined the mark Melia's lips had left there. She touched it with her fingertip and the faint lines smudged away. Leaning her nose over the glass, she breathed in the scent, imagining the sweet, woody smell as a taste on Melia's tongue. She was awake. Sleep was as far from her as her own time.

Parker got up and paced the room. The clothing Melia had lent her to sleep in was not much good at keeping her warm. Melia had called them sweats, but still Parker shivered. Folding her arms across her chest, she walked back and forth between the kitchen door and the entryway. On her sixth or seventh pass, she realized that the door to Melia's bedroom was open slightly. Silent as a shadow, she found herself at the door, her hand on the knob, pushing it open even farther. When the crack was as wide as her chest, she stepped through and stood with her back against the wall.

The bars of light were thinner here, Melia had the shades turned tight, but there was enough light for Parker to make out her form. Melia was lying on her side, facing the door with her knees pulled up almost to her chest. She looked cold and small under the light blankets. Parker couldn't see her features, but still she stared, her throat becoming dry. She licked her lips.

With a suddenness that almost stopped her heart, the feel of Melia's kiss came back to her. Her lips had been warm and tingling all evening, but she hadn't let herself think about the kiss and what it meant. The naked desire on Melia's face had been almost frightening. There was a hunger there, and a depth Parker had never experienced. She felt that Melia could devour her, could drink her soul right out of her body. Her movement toward Melia had been beyond her control and it seemed Melia's desire was directing her to do whatever Melia wanted.

Until Parker kissed her. Then her power had returned with a rush and she knew that Melia was a slave to her hands, to her lips, to the strength of her body. She could take what she wanted and never stop until she had her fill. If she could ever truly be filled.

Parker bit her lip in the darkness. Wanting nothing more than to take the few steps that would lead her to the bed, Parker struggled to push down her desire.

Desire.

She scoffed at the thought. It was too weak. What she felt was lust. Lust, and nothing less. It didn't seem right. Melia was no Lily.

Clenching her fists, Parker considered the difference. Living a whore's life made a woman ready for anything. Parker knew she could come to Lily and get what just she wanted. Lily didn't need talk, she didn't need mornings, she didn't need the promise of an unbroken heart. But what was Melia expecting? Had things changed so much that every woman was like Lily? Parker had to know. She couldn't use Melia to satisfy her craving without knowing if Melia needed more.

Melia had said it was easier for her to use her body to express herself than to speak the words. Parker shared that feeling. Even as a kid, she could never express herself. She learned to use her fists when she was angry or frightened. When she'd taken her father's gun, learned to shoot it, and wore it plainly on her hip, she had even less of a need to speak. People stopped expecting her to.

But what was Melia feeling? Parker knew her own emotions for Melia were running too deep to be explained away simply as desire or lust. She wanted more than the release of passion, she wanted something to bind them together. Something for her to hold onto like an anchor in this storm. Something to tie her to this time if there was no going back. Could that need for connection be the emotion Melia couldn't express? Or was Parker alone in that longing, misunderstanding Melia's passion as more than it was? She felt she had to know before she emptied her soul into Melia.

The wall was hard and cold against her shoulder blades. She'd been pressing herself into it, unaware that her tension had tightened all the muscles in her body until she reached the point that her nerves felt like they were going to snap. Straining her ears for the sound of Melia's breathing, she hoped to use the relaxed rise and fall as way to ease her own stress. She couldn't hear it, and before she used that as an excuse to draw nearer to Melia's bed, she stepped sideways to retreat back to her bed in the living room.

"Don't go."

The sound was a hushed whisper, not more than a breath she'd lent imagined words. Parker stopped and gave herself to the count of five to decide if it was only her mind playing tricks on her. Melia shifted, her knees pulling down as she turned to lie on her back.

"You can't sleep?" Melia asked, her voice only a fraction louder. Just loud enough to be real.

"No."

"Aren't you cold standing there?"

"Yes."

Melia laughed. It was a quiet, delighted sound, painful to Parker's agony of desire. What Parker hoped and feared Melia would say, she said.

"Come over here and get in."

Parker couldn't move. She couldn't say yes or no, she could only try to keep herself standing on shaky legs.

"It's okay. We'll just talk." Melia said the words with a twist to her mouth that Parker didn't understand. Melia curled onto her side and pushed herself to the far edge of the bed. She touched the wide space that would separate Parker from her and pulled back the corner of the blanket.

As silently as she'd entered the room, Parker crossed the floor and eased herself down onto the bed. Leaning against the pillows, she sat stiffly, as if she needed to resist their comfort. She slid her feet under the covers and held her breath as Melia pulled the soft material up to cover her legs. That done, Melia moved her hand away, respecting the distance she had set up between them.

"I'm glad you came, I hate sleeping alone." Melia's voice was tranquil, apparently she felt none of the turbulent emotions that were tearing at Parker's composure. She explained her reasoning like she was telling Parker a bedtime story. "I've been that way all my life. My mom and I lived alone. We were very poor and we lived in a one-room apartment. Every night of my life with her, I felt her there in the room, and since she's been gone I've always missed that presence."

"She's dead?" The words came out too abruptly, sounding too harsh and revealing Parker's discomfort.

"Yeah, when I was eleven. It was hard growing up without her."

"I'm sorry," Parker offered, both for the loss and her brusqueness.

"You know, I've told never anyone that before. The reason why I hate sleeping alone."

"Why did you tell me?"

"I don't know. Maybe because I want to feel real to you. All this must seem so strange, so weird."

Parker turned her head toward Melia. Melia was studying her face and Parker wondered what she could see. "I know you're real. I know, too well."

Melia narrowed her eyes. "What do you mean?"

Parker moved her hand under the blanket. It crossed

the space between them and stopped as her cold fingers encountered the skin of Melia's hip. She was naked. Melia inhaled a sharp, tense breath.

"I mean . . . this."

"I don't know that I can talk to you yet," Melia whispered. "To tell you what I want."

"I was just thinkin' about that. But right now, it don't seem so important."

Melia held herself still, making no move toward, or away from Parker. "But will it be in the morning?"

Parker pulled her legs up even tighter and wrapped her arms around her knees. She felt colder than she had standing by Melia's door and her words were inflected by the chill. "Will I even be here in the mornin'?"

"What do you mean by that? Where will you go if you leave here?"

"I don't know."

"Oh god, you mean, like falling again?" Melia eyes were again wide open.

Parker nodded. Melia instantly slid across the bed. She pressed herself tight to Parker and wrapped her arms around her waist. Parker felt herself relaxing inch by inch into that embrace. She bent her head down and found Melia's soft hair against her cheek. The fear kept her from thinking of her desire for Melia.

"Don't be afraid," Melia said the words as if she hardly believed Parker's fear was possible. "I think I might know what happened to you and it won't happen again unless you try to do it. You won't just fall."

"What do you know?" Parker lifted her head and tried to see into Melia's eyes.

"It's just like I thought, there's an Indian myth. There are things called *sipapu*. The Hopi Indians believed that the first people came to Earth through a hole between worlds. It must actually span time as well. Anyway, these holes are scattered all across the west and southwest. You must have stumbled into one."

"So, if I stepped in another one, I could go back?"

"Theoretically. I mean, possibly. Of course, no one I asked even thought it was possible to move through time with one of these holes. But they kept open minds and played the what-if game with me."

Parker looked past Melia into the darkness. If there was a chance, any kind of a chance, she'd have to take it.

"I e-mailed a man in Cortez. He said he would fax a map of sites he knows about in the Four Corners area."

Parker shook her head and brought herself back to the conversation. The words Melia spoke were nonsense to her, but she understood about the map. "I don't need a map. I was just there, I know where it is."

Melia stiffened and drew back from Parker. Parker was too excited to notice her reaction. She could still see the way the canyon led to the base of the mountain, she knew how far she had ridden from Denver, and she knew the angle she'd taken toward the foothills. She could find that cave. Desire was forgotten in her elation.

"Will you take me there tomorrow? I'm sure I can show you right where we need to go."

In the dark, Parker could not see the expression that crossed Melia's face.

Sixteen

The expression on Parker's face was heart breaking. Melia looked up at the sprawling three-story luxury home and its expanse of manicured lawn. "Are you sure this is the right place?"

Parker slapped her hat against her thigh and breathed out her exasperation. "If I can ignore all of this and just look at the mountain beyond, I'd say it's the right place. But I can't even see where the canyon was."

"Well, they probably filled it in." Melia leaned on the fender of her car and stared across the highway at the subdivision that swept from the foothills up the side of the mountain. She was glad she didn't have to see it through Parker's eyes. It was ugly enough to her and she was used to the spread of civilization.

"Jesus Christ! Goddamn you all," Parker yelled as she kicked her boots through the rocks lining the shoulder of the road. She threw her hat to the ground and it rolled to a stop on Melia's foot. She paced back and forth, a cloud of dust rising up around her. "Stupid sons of bitches."

Melia leaned over. Picking up the hat, she dusted it off and placed it on the hood. She was glad she insisted that Parker leave her gun at the house. Her anger was strong enough to make Melia believe Parker would have taken a shot or two at the houses and she could hardly blame her.

"Hey, it's not the end of the world," Melia almost faltered as Parker shot her a look of pure disgust. "I mean, there are the other places on the map."

"In Utah? How in the hell am I going to get to Utah?"

"You could ask me to drive you."

Parker came to a stop, her back to Melia. Her boots crunched in the gravel as she turned and looked at Melia skeptically. "You'd do that?"

Melia laughed. "Of course. It's not that much to ask."

"You have any idea how far it is to Utah?" Parker's tone sounded as if she couldn't believe Melia knew what she was getting herself into.

"Yeah, Parker, I know. We could leave on a Friday and be back by Sunday evening." She lifted Parker's hat and, copying the motion that was Parker's habit, pushed it down tight to her ears. She grinned. "Easy."

Parker's mood was instantly brighter. She stepped up and tugged the hat from Melia's head. Smiling as she put it on her own head, she leaned down to Melia's eye level. Parker crowded Melia until she was forced to lean back against the cold metal of the car. "And how god-awful fast would you have to get this thing goin' to do that?"

"No faster than you've already gone." Melia assured her.

"That s'posed to make me feel better?"

Melia took back her ground. Pushing herself from the car, she stood so close to Parker that her breasts brushed against Parker's coat. "It just means we can do it."

Parker took several slow breaths, but declined to respond to Melia's words or body.

"I'll do whatever I can to help you, Parker." Even if it meant Parker would eventually leave, Melia felt she needed to do what she could to bring them closer together. She touched her thigh against Parker's and spoke honestly. "Simply because I can't resist you."

Parker immediately tried to step back and Melia grabbed her belt buckle to prevent her. Parker's eyes were squinted against the sunlight that had broken through the perpetual cloud cover and Melia was drawn in by the rugged and natural look of the lines near her eyes. The wind blew a strand of Melia's hair up to brush across Parker's chin.

"I ain't meanin' to force you."

"I know. That's not what I meant."

Melia's words drained the tension from Parker's body. They shared a smile and Parker let her thigh rest against Melia's.

"You know, when I used to watch you through the ceiling, you seemed so distant. You got that look in your eyes that was just so far away." As she spoke, Parker pulled Melia's hand in to hold it between their bodies, close to her chest. She touched a finger to Melia's cheek. "I don't see that anymore. It feels like you're with me all the time."

Melia took a moment to let Parker's words sink in. Parker was being so open that Melia could feel her emotions as well as she could feel those inside herself. She felt so alive, so aware, and for the first time in her life, she couldn't remember when she'd last opened a book. "I am with you. Even when we're not together, I think I'm with you."

"That bother you?"

"Oh, yes."

"In a bad way?"

Melia shook her head. She didn't want to speak, she knew Parker was going to kiss her and she wanted to be ready. Parker leaned her head down and their lips met with a soft touch. Melia closed her eyes and felt the warmth of Parker's breath on her cheek. Parker teased her mouth open and licked her tongue lightly along the inside of Melia's lips. Melia held still. When Parker's tongue brushed across her teeth, Melia closed her lips and sucked it in deeper. Parker increased the pressure of her mouth on Melia's and Melia felt the tension in Parker's thighs. Still holding Parker's belt, she pulled their bodies even closer together.

A truck blew by, buffeting them with the wind of its passage. A long, belated honk followed the gust of air. Parker lifted her mouth away and watched the back of the truck as it disappeared over a rise. Melia missed the contact already.

"Not too private here, huh?" Parker asked, as she looked again into Melia's eyes.

Melia shook her head. "I'd love to take you home with me."

"I think that's a damn fine idea."

Parker traced Melia's smile with her finger. Melia was dizzy with desire and wished they hadn't driven so far from her house. She wanted to continue this seduction before Parker changed her mind and again decided it was too soon for them to make love. Putting her hand on Parker's hip, she slid her fingers up under the jacket and around to rub the strong muscles of Parker's back. Her hand encountered cold metal. Parker reached back and pulled her hand away.

"Parker! I told you not to bring that gun."

Parker grinned and managed to look a little shame-faced. "I'm sorry. I didn't plan to. I'm just none too comfortable without it."

"If the police caught you, you'd go straight to jail."

Melia tried her best to look stern. " I don't think we could explain why you have no identification."

"Okay. I said I'm sorry." Brushing her hand across Melia's cheek, Parker smiled. "Now you gonna take me home or not?"

"Get in the car."

Ω   Ω   Ω   Ω   Ω

Her luck had finally changed for the better. Dana didn't know what made her try the back door, she knew Melia's tendency toward absentmindedness had taught her to double-check the locks as she left, but Dana had turned the knob and the door popped open. She stepped into the quiet kitchen and locked the door behind her.

Nothing had changed. There were no dirty dishes in the sink, not even a cup on the counter, everything was in its proper place. It looked like the kitchen from a catalog and she would swear the room hadn't been entered since she left. Opening the refrigerator out of habit, Dana wasn't surprised to see that it was almost empty. Melia probably hadn't gone shopping since throwing Dana out. She took a cold beer and held the bottle to her forehead as she pushed through the kitchen door. Now, she could see evidence that the house was lived in.

The boxes of books she'd sent were stacked along the wall near the entryway. Not one of them had been opened. Dana shook her head, not knowing what Melia expected from her. She flopped out on the couch, kicking aside the blanket folded on one end.

Dana twisted off the cap and took a long drink of the beer, then sat half up, more than a little surprised. Melia had lit a fire in the fireplace. That was a rare occurrence, Melia hardly ever felt that the pleasure of a fire outweighed its effect on the brown cloud. As the suggestion of what a fire meant sank into the pit of her stomach, her eyes scanned the room. She wasn't sure what she was looking for, until she realized that she wasn't seeing it. There were no books scattered around the room. Melia normally had three or four going and kept them spread around to be close at hand whenever she felt the urge. There was not a single book off the bookcase.

Putting her beer bottle on the coffee table, Dana stood. Her shoes made no sound as she walked slowly to Melia's bedroom. She pushed the door open, but didn't step inside. The long, now-empty bookcase that lined one wall made her feel an unaccustomed sense of shame. She looked away.

How could you tell if a bed had been slept in by one person alone? Dana asked herself as she stared at the neatly-made bed, the comforter stretched tight across and tucked in cleanly. There were two pillows, nothing unusual, Melia always kept two. She hated to sleep alone and Dana had come home late many times to find Melia snuggled around them.

Holding her shoulder away to prevent it from brushing the side of the bookcase, Dana walked over to Melia's bathroom. There nothing to see, nothing out of the ordinary. No extra toothbrushes or towels. No unfamiliar clothing in the clothes hamper, no strange hair in the hairbrush. She was being a fool, an obsessive, jealous fool. That knowledge didn't prevent her from checking the closet, but the only clothing that was not Melia's was her own.

A smile crossed her face. She'd left quite a bit of clothing here, sweats, jeans, a few jackets. Melia hadn't thrown them out. That meant something. Actually, that meant a lot. If Melia was truly through with her, she would have thrown them out. Dana put her hand under her shirt and rubbed her stomach. She felt better. Much better.

Giving the fact that there were no books on the nightstand no importance, Dana stretched out on the bed, the smile still on her face. There would surely be a fight and plenty of cruel things said, but Dana would hold out and keep her temper under control. Melia wanted her here and it was Dana's responsibility to make her admit it.

∩ ∩ ∩ ∩ ∩

Anytime Parker felt brave enough to open her eyes, she would look over at Melia's profile and feel blessed. Time and luck had been playing her like a pawn for too long now, but she couldn't say what had happened was all bad. She'd found Melia and the impossibility of it made her desire even sweeter. In those brief moments of looking, before the blur of the landscape streaking by the glass beyond Melia's face made her queasy, she stared hard to see just what it was in Melia that stirred such strong feelings. Obviously Melia was pretty, in a completely unconcerned way. She didn't act like she tried to be alluring, not even feminine, she was just what was inside herself and didn't seem to be affected by what others might see in her.

Parker loved that Melia moved as if she was unaware of her body. There was no posing, no dishonesty. Despite her ability to lie when the need arose, Melia seemed to be dangerously open with her emotions. Parker imagined that almost any actress would kill for the ability to express such feeling with just a glance or a wave of their hand. The skill would be useful on the stage, but being right up next to it was almost overpowering. Melia's desire had a force and a will of its own. Parker's good intentions couldn't withstand it and she no longer cared to continue the struggle.

Melia's mind was another thing. Parker was felt it was

always working, studying things probably too deep for her own comprehension.

Melia drove with one hand on the seat beside her leg. Parker wished Melia would reach over and take her hand or touch her thigh. It was what she wanted to do herself, but was afraid of distracting Melia from her driving. Melia took her eyes from the road whenever she could and, whenever she caught it, she returned Parker's stare. Parker couldn't handle both those depths and the sensation of movement, she was dizzier looking back into Melia's eyes than if she stared out at the cars passing by.

It was a long way back to Melia's house, yet Parker was amazed at how quickly they arrived. She'd tried to keep in her skepticism when Melia said they could travel to and from Utah in a weekend, but she'd doubted Melia really knew what was involved. Now, she believed the trip could be done, she only had to figure out how to make it without being sick the entire time.

Melia pulled up to the large door that opened the house up to the car. Parker still couldn't believe that people kept those things inside, it seemed dangerously foolish. The door opened itself by some sort of magic or communication between the car and the house. Parker hadn't asked Melia for an explanation, she figured the confusion of the explanation wasn't worth the knowledge she might gain from it. Some things were better accepted and ignored.

The car room was dark when the door closed behind them. Parker released the buckle and strap, but made no move to get out of the car. She felt in pieces, like parts of her had been left alongside the road and would need some time to catch up with the rest of her. It was hard to walk when she felt like this, hard to get all her limbs working together.

Melia didn't seem to mind. She turned off the engine, but kept the soft sound of her music playing. Parker leaned her head back and tried to will her shaking to stop. Melia patted her leg with a warm palm and sang quietly. Parker couldn't understand any of the words to the song and couldn't even tell if the voice was male or female. The music was unlike anything heard in her day and not knowing how it could be there anytime Melia pushed a button was annoying.

"You having second thoughts?" Melia asked as the song ended.

Parker shook her head. She didn't want to reveal her weakness by admitting that she was afraid she would throw up if she had to move too soon. "The music, I just like to hear it," she lied.

Melia nodded her head as the next song started. "I was hoping you would. Why don't you let me bring the tape inside and we'll listen by the fire?"

"All right, just give me a minute, and I'll be there." Parker took a breath and dove into the truth. "I'm feelin' a little dizzy from the ride."

"I'll put on some coffee." Melia gave her leg one last pat and opened the door. She seemed to accept Parker's need to let the world stop spinning without explanation or judgement. It was so easy to just be human with her. The door slammed shut and Parker leaned her head against the seat. She'd barely closed her eyes before the sound of Melia's anxious voice reached back to her.

∩   ∩   ∩   ∩   ∩

"What the hell are you doing here? How did you get into my house?" Melia's voice sounded more than angry. There was a strong suggestion of fear and, even if she wouldn't have wanted to admit it, Dana liked the sound.

"I came to talk to you." Dana straightened from her slouch against the living room wall and walked slowly toward

Melia. She hadn't taken three steps before realizing the growing shadow in the doorway was an approaching figure. Her eyes widened as a tall, wiry woman stepped up to Melia and put her hand on her shoulder. The touch was protective, possessive. A red film passed briefly over Dana's eyes. Her fists clenched and she couldn't help but think that this time, Melia had gone too far.

"Who the fuck are you?" Dana growled.

The woman had the nerve to smile. Her jaw was tense and her eyes serious as premeditated murder, but she smiled. Dana's anger flamed into rage.

"You'd better just turn around and leave," Dana warned. "I don't know you, and I don't think you want to know me."

"But I do know you, Dana." The smile never faltered. She took a step forward and partially blocked Melia's body with her own. "And if you think I'm gonna turn my back on you, you're stupider than you look."

The words were more fuel for the fire raging inside Dana. The woman had spoken in a soft, slow drawl. She affected a western accent to match her outfit. She looked so ridiculous that Dana was tempted to discount her, but the readiness of her stance and the sense of controlled power in her body made Dana think twice. Pushing down the scathing remark that sprang to her lips, she struggled to give the woman one more chance to get out of her way.

"I've got no quarrel with you. I just want to talk to my girlfriend and it's none of your business."

Melia caught the woman's arm and looked up into her face. Dana hated the expression she caught crossing the woman's face as she turned her eyes to Melia.

"Listen, Parker. Maybe it would be better if you waited in the car for a few minutes," Melia suggested. Tension rasped in her voice. "I'll be okay."

"Ain't no way that's gonna happen." The woman, Parker, removed Melia's hand from her arm. She gently pushed Melia back against the wall and took another step toward Dana. She turned her attention back and Dana was taken aback by the coldness in her eyes. "Besides, you'd have a quarrel with me, if you knew who I am."

"Why don't you tell me who you are, if you think it will impress me?"

The smile still hadn't left her face. Dana wanted nothing more than to slap it off of her. Parker reached up and pushed her hat back from her forehead. Her every movement ground on Dana's nerves.

"That bruise on your head, I put it there. And if she didn't stop me," Parker tilted her head back in a gesture to mean Melia. "I would'a smashed your skull like a rotten apple."

"You're fucking crazy. You have no idea how I got this bruise." Dana could return the smile. It came easy now that she knew Parker was full of shit and nothing more. "It happens that I fell down in an elevator."

"An elevator in Melia's office buildin'. Yesterday, bout three o'clock. And you didn't fall." Parker took a step forward as she spoke. And another. Dana felt the cold of fear lining the pit of her stomach. No way the woman could know what happened to her, no way. She barely managed to keep herself from backing down from the level look of hate the woman was burning into her.

"You didn't see me. You were in the bathroom and you attacked her." Parker's lips twisted and continued to pound the words out at Dana. "You were gonna beat her or rape her or I don't know what. But I was gonna kill you before that happened. You're breathin' just because she stopped me."

Dana shook her head. It was not true. It was impossible. She would remember something like that and she had gone to see Melia with the best of intentions. There was no way she would have let it get so out of control. She took her eyes from Parker and looked at Melia. "That didn't happen. Tell me—tell her that never happened."

Melia never looked away from Parker's back. "It's true, Dana. Parker stopped you, she hit your head against the wall."

Dana's breath left her sharply like she'd been punched in the stomach. She lifted her hand and held it out to Melia. Parker stepped to the side and blocked Dana's path.

"You ain't touchin' her."

It was too much. The fear, the confusion, the rage. She had no memory of attacking Melia, but she couldn't doubt Melia's voice and the expression on her face. Maybe she was going crazy, but she had to have Melia. Just to talk to her, to hold her, to get her to straighten out this whole ugly mess. Melia was the only person who had ever accepted Dana for who she was, not how much money she had. She meant to get Melia back. No one was going to stand in her way.

"Back off, you fucking cow-poke, or I'll kill you."

The woman's face turned as pale as frozen milk. Six feet away, Dana could feel the rage welling up from inside her. She would have to strike fast, before the woman's fury gave her an advantage. Dana dropped her body several inches, flexing and relaxing her knees before aiming a roundhouse kick at the woman's head.

Her foot connected hard with Parker's jaw. She never saw it coming. Dana followed it with a straight right jab, landing in the same spot her foot had struck. Parker staggered backwards, struggling to keep her balance. Dana was amazed that she didn't raise her hands to protect herself or to hit back. Parker put her hands behind her as Dana matched her steps, her fist again poised to strike. Dana didn't want to hesitate, to lose the upper hand, but something in the woman's movement made her pause. When Melia screamed and tried to reach for Parker's arm, the realization came tearing into her mind with a force that sent her staggering backwards. Time bent and fractured.

Dana saw Parker's right hand pulling forward and she saw the black metal that filled her fist. Watching the movement coming as if frame by frame, Dana had plenty of time to know what was going to happen to her. Strangely enough, she herself seemed to be frozen by time and couldn't run away or even close her eyes. When Parker fired, she never heard the shot, but she would swear she heard her bone explode as the bullet plowed through her thigh.

She fell backward onto the coffee table, then dropped to the floor. There was a sudden roaring in her ears that increased as she looked down at the blood gushing from the small hole in the front of her jeans. The faded blue was rapidly turning black and the blood kept coming, running over to soak into the carpet. Dana tried to sit up but her muscles seemed to be wired all wrong. All she could manage was to turn to her side and pull her leg up. At that moment, she realized Parker could shoot her again. Her body jerked in an automatic response to the fear and she closed her eyes. Digging her elbow into the carpet, she tried to pull herself under the coffee table. The roaring still distorted her hearing, but she could pick up the sound of Melia and Parker arguing.

Dana opened her eyes and looked for the women's feet. They were standing by the door, Melia's feet right in front of the sharp pointed toes of Parker's boots. They continued to yell. As long as they fought each other, Dana was safe. She turned her head to try and judge how far it was to the kitchen door and if she could make it before they noticed her. A loud slam brought her eyes back. Parker's feet were gone and Dana realized that she'd heard the bedroom door closing hard. She knew that sound, she had caused it so many times herself.

The coffee table slid away, exposing her. Dana twisted her body again, trying to protect herself. But it was only Melia, and the appalled look on her face gave Dana hope that she would survive this, that Melia would protect her and not let Parker kill her. Melia put her hand to Dana's leg, pressing hard against the flow of blood.

"Jesus, Dana," Melia whispered, her voice full of shock and revulsion. "I'm so sorry. I didn't mean this—"

Dana grabbed her hand, her fingers slipping in the blood that already stained the cuff of Melia's sleeve. "Melia, we've got to get out of here, before she comes back. She can kill us both."

"She wouldn't . . . she wouldn't do that."

"Melia, goddamn. She shot me." Dana gestured at the wound, it was beginning to throb with a pain so intense it was hardly believable. "She shot me!"

"She didn't try to kill you. She aimed right for your leg, I saw it."

"You're fucking defending her? A fucking psychopath shoots me, and you defend her?"

"Dana, you don't understand!" Melia yelled right down in her face and Dana was shocked into pulling away. "You shouldn't have hit her, what did you expect her to do?"

"Hit me back? Fight with me? How in the fuck would I expect her to shoot me?"

"You don't understand," Melia repeated. She stared hard at Dana's face then quickly looked toward the bedroom door. When her eyes returned to Dana, she spoke in a low voice, her words clipped. "I can't expect you to get this, and I shouldn't even tell you. You'll think I'm crazy, too. But you've got to accept what I say. This is not her time. Where she's from, shooting someone to defend yourself is the normal thing to do."

The pounding of her heart and the roaring of her ears made it hard to comprehend Melia's words. "What the hell are you talking about? It's not like she's from the old West." Clutching Melia's arm, Dana tried to sit up. "We got to get out of here."

Melia pushed her shoulder and Dana fell backwards. Her expression was terrifying.

"No, Dana. It is exactly like she's from the old West. She's traveled through time."

Dana stared. Melia was serious. The look on her face, the look in her eye, she was dead serious. "Oh, my god, Melia. You don't believe that."

"Yes, I do."

"Fuck. No, Melia. You can't believe that. What the hell has she done to you?"

Melia looked away, turning her attention to Dana's thigh. The blood was still pouring out and Dana hoped that the chill she felt was from Melia's words and not the amount of blood she was losing.

"Melia, listen to me. She's crazy. She's got you believing her, but look at what she did. She's insane."

"No, Dana," Melia said again. It sounded so final.

Dana looked at her profile, her jaw was set firmly and she would not look up. She again pressed her palm to the wound, trying to hold back the flow. The realization of what was happening and why hit Dana with a shock stronger than the force of the bullet. She herself had driven Melia to this point, to the place that she would believe anything from anyone who was kind to her. The sense of guilt and responsibility was something she had not often felt, but she knew without a doubt, this whole situation was her fault.

"God, Melia, whatever I've done to you, I'm so sorry. But you got to listen to me. You can't stay here with her."

Melia put her fingers onto the hole the bullet had torn in Dana's jeans and tried to tear the material apart. The movement caused the blood to pump out even faster and Dana felt like she was going to pass out. At that instant, the bedroom door swung open and Parker strode into the room. She threw some clothing and Melia's backpack on the couch above Dana's head.

"I brought some of your jeans and shirts. Pack 'em. We're gettin' the hell out of here."

"I can't leave her, Parker. I have to call for an ambulance. She's going to bleed to death if we—"

"Let her. I didn't ask for this, she did." Parker stood at Dana's feet, her fists clenched and her eyes cold. She was now wearing a holster and the gun hung in plain sight on her hip.

Melia stared up at Parker, her look pleading. "I can't—"

"Pack the bag," Parker ordered. "Or we go without it."

"Parker, I know what you want me to do. I will, but not until we get her some help."

Parker's face darkened, Dana could see that she was ready to explode. She wanted to do something, to fight back, to save Melia and herself, but she was paralyzed by fear. She was weak, she was a coward. All her life, she had believed that to be true but had fought to keep it hidden from herself and the world. It was out in the open now. She was humiliated. Parker took two steps and knelt down between Dana and the couch.

"If she's all you're worried about, I'll put a stop to your worries. Right now." Parker slid her pistol from the holster and smoothly placed it on Dana's temple. The metal was unimaginably cold and set Dana to shivering. She wanted nothing more than to close her eyes, but she could not.

"Parker," Melia whispered, her voice a perfect match to the feeling in Dana's chest. "Please, don't do it."

"Pack the bag."

"Give me time."

Parker cocked the gun. Melia's hesitation disappeared. She got to her feet and started to stuff the clothing into the backpack, her hands leaving smears of Dana's blood on the fabric.

"No," Dana forced the word past her chattering teeth. "No, Melia. Let her kill me. Don't go."

Parker laughed. Dana had never heard anything so terrifying. "She's goin', don't matter if you're dead or alive. You see, this has nothin' to do with you. You're just in my way."

Dana tried to ignore Parker and the increasing pressure of the gun barrel against her head. "Melia, get away. Don't worry about me."

Parker grabbed a handful of Dana's hair and jerked her head up, before slamming it back to the floor. She was grinning, her lips pulled back, her face a wolf's mask. "You tellin' her to save herself? She's not in any danger, stupid. Just you are, and your talkin' ain't helpin' my temper any."

"Shut up, Dana," Melia snapped. "For once in your life, just shut up."

Dana closed her mouth and bit the inside of her cheeks to keep it closed. Her whole body shuddered with fear. Each breath she took was a struggle, a sob. Tears flowed from her eyes as she watched Melia shove the last of the clothing into the bag. Parker's presence was forgotten as she watched Melia, thinking how much she did love her and how terribly wrong she'd been.

"Jesus Christ, hurry up," Parker ground the words through her teeth. "I can't stand this."

"I'm ready." Melia hitched the pack onto her shoulder and stood uncertainly between them and the door.

"No!" Dana cried. The women ignored her. Parker eased the pressure of the gun against her head.

"Get that telephone thing and put it where she can reach," Parker commanded. Melia rushed to the end table and grabbed the phone. Dragging the cord over Dana's body, she put it on the floor within reach. Dana tried to take her hand. The pressure of the gun barrel returned until she dropped her hand.

"I'll be okay," Melia whispered. "I know I'll be okay."

Parker stood and returned the gun to its holster. She gestured for Melia to go. Dana tried again to sit up, but her strength had bled away through the hole in her leg.

"Melia, don't go. I'm so sorry. I promise, I'll never try to see you again." Dana begged, hoping that Melia could understand that she was finally telling the truth. "It doesn't have to be this way."

Melia paused in the doorway. Parker turned and burned one last look of hate into Dana's eyes before shoving Melia out into the night.

"No!" Dana screamed uselessly at the closing door.

She couldn't stop them, she had only one chance remaining to save Melia. Dana used the last of her energy to roll over and slap the receiver off the phone. With a shaking hand, she held it to her ear. Quickly, she read the list of names Melia had programmed into the speed dial. She pushed Chris' button and prayed that she would be home.

Seventeen

The night was engine noise and vibration and the endless sweep of headlights in her eyes. Parker leaned forward in her seat, the strap of the belt cutting across her chest. Shivering although heated air blew constantly on her feet, Parker felt like she was going to come apart at the seams. Melia hadn't said a word, she hadn't pushed the button for music, nor had she turned her eyes toward Parker's face. Lighted numbers on the dash held Parker's stare, Melia had explained during their drive that afternoon how the numbers told the time. They were deep into the mountains and it had been two hours since she'd forced Melia out of her house and left Dana lying on the floor. Dying. She'd seen that look before.

Parker took a breath, sucking it through her teeth, wishing for fresh air. Guilt settled its heaviness in her chest and pressed her lungs, making it impossible for her to take a decent breath. Her head wouldn't clear. She was wrong to shoot Dana, wrong to prevent Melia from helping her, and wrong to have left her lying there in her own blood. Since when had Parker's own life become so important that she felt she had the right to do such things? Even considering her hatred for Dana, she didn't understand the things she'd done.

But Dana had surprised her, kicking her right in the face like that. Parker didn't know how to fight that way or how to protect herself from someone who did. Pulling her gun was by reflex, bringing the gun sight down from Dana's forehead to aim at her leg was sheer willpower. It hadn't been easy. She wanted to destroy that mind, to erase the thoughts of a person who could be so cruel and violent to someone as defenseless as Melia. There could be nothing worth saving in a body like that. But she knew Melia was behind her, watching and afraid, and there was no way she could force Melia to witness something as ugly as death by a bullet to the head. Parker had brought her hand down and satisfied herself with the look of horror and pain that filled Dana's eyes.

Parker had expected Melia to be upset, angry even. She knew she had to be demanding, to keep pushing her advantage, to take control of the situation before Melia lost her nerve. Before Melia had time to question if going with Parker was the right thing to do. What she'd done could be considered kidnaping, she supposed, but Melia was her only hope and she couldn't take the time to talk it out. Or ask nicely.

It hadn't gone quickly enough. Melia had put up more resistance than Parker expected. Her concern for Dana was frustrating and alarming. Putting the gun to Dana's head had been the lowest, most sickening thing Parker had ever done. No one deserved that, to lie gun shot and bleeding, waiting for the next bullet to come. It was too much fear, too much pain, and when Dana had shown disregard for her own life in hopes of saving Melia, Parker wanted nothing more than to run from the room. She was no better than Dana, probably worse. Here she was, forcing her will upon Melia, no different from what Dana had done before her.

"Oh." The small sound escaped her lips as she closed her eyes to the night and the lights of the approaching cars. Her fists clenched and pulled in to press against her stomach.

"Parker?" Melia finally looked her way, just when Parker wished she wouldn't. "Are you all right?"

She was rocking in the seat. It wasn't from the motion of the car. She couldn't stop herself, she couldn't breathe, and no matter how hard she tried, she couldn't hold down the feeling rising in her chest.

"Are you going to be sick?"

"Yes." Parker found the word and forced it out. "Yes. Yes."

"Okay, hold on. Hold on," Melia encouraged as she abruptly pulled the car to the side and braked hard. Parker's head bent down almost to the dash and still she whispered, "Yes, yes, yes."

The door opened and a gust of incredibly cold air filled the car. Parker gasped, then jumped as Melia jerked open the door beside her. Pushing her back into the seat, Melia leaned over her and unlatched the seatbelt. Parker tried to turn and put her feet out on the ground, but Melia had already grabbed her by the shoulder of her coat and half-dragged her from the car. Parker let herself go and fell out onto the hard surface of the roadway. Melia helped her to her hands and knees and guided her to the edge of the road.

A gritty snow bank edged down from the darkness and ended in the gravel ditch. Parker crawled to it and leaned her forehead against the icy crust. Melia tried to pull her away.

"You'll freeze that way, Parker," she warned.

Parker didn't care, she wanted to shove her whole head down into the snow and freeze away the thoughts that crowded her mind. The cold wind was like a river washing over her, stripping away her skin and muscles, leaving nothing but bones. Bones and the hot pressure in her chest that wouldn't be relieved by the cold. There was only one way it could come out. The first tears felt like fire streaking over her cheekbones, so hot, she felt they would scar her face permanently. Melia misunderstood her shaking.

"Just do it, you'll feel better after," she encouraged.

The soft concern in her voice made Parker cry harder. She leaned deeper into the snow and tried to keep the sobs from breaking from her lips. Her knees crunched in the gravel as she pulled herself into a ball. She wanted her hat, she needed to pull it low and hard on her head and feel its tightness helping to hold in her thoughts. Melia rubbed her back for a moment then stopped suddenly.

"Parker, are you crying?"

Parker shook her head, snow and ice crystals tangling into her short hair. Melia tried to pull Parker away from the snow bank, but Parker held herself firm. Melia wouldn't let it go, she grabbed Parker's hair and pulled her head back. She touched Parker's cheek and felt the wetness of her tears. Using the weight of her whole body, Melia shoved at Parker until she fell sprawling onto her side in the gravel. Parker folded her arms over her face.

"Don't be ashamed." Melia crawled up to her shoulder and gently tried to pull her hands away. When Parker wouldn't budge, she leaned down and shielded Parker's body from the night air with her own. "Oh, Parker. You can cry."

Parker fought it as hard as she could, but it was a battle she could only lose. Melia's caring intensified her feelings of guilt. "I'm sorry," she managed to whisper before the emotion overwhelmed her. "I'm sorry," and it meant sorry for crying, sorry for hurting Melia. Sorry for shooting Dana, for being so damn selfish, and for just being alive in this time way beyond her own. Melia said nothing more, but brushed away her tears with warm fingers.

Parker stared over Melia's shoulder at the stars that hung so low in the black sky. They looked as bright as the headlights that had burned into her brain all evening. They tore at her eyes and every time she blinked a fresh wave of tears would flow out to catch on Melia's skin. Parker cried until all the heat within her was gone, replaced by the frigid mountain air. Her body was cold, too cold to even shiver. Melia felt her go still and responded instantly.

"Come on, get back in the car." Melia lifted herself from Parker's chest and pulled at her collar. Parker didn't move, she felt frozen to the ground. "You're not going to lie here and freeze to death. Not after what you've done to get here."

Those were cold words. Parker grabbed at them and took them in. That was what she needed to hear, she didn't deserve compassion, she needed the cold to fill her veins with ice water. She needed to be as cold as the mountain air. Melia pulled at her again, dragging her a few inches through the gravel. Parker tried to fold her stiff legs and rise to her knees, but her body wouldn't comply.

"Parker," Melia yelled in her ear. "I can't drag you to the car. You have to help me."

Parker mumbled past her chilled lips, "Give me a minute."

"We don't have a minute, you're just going to get colder." Melia took a deep breath, then slapped Parker's face.

"Ahh!" Parker shouted. She felt like her cheek had shattered into a hundred slivers of ice. Melia raised her hand again and Parker could barely move to block the blow. But blood was flowing again, a pounding, red heat that blurred her vision. She gripped Melia hand and rasped, "Don't do that again."

"I'm sorry. I just don't want you to die here."

"I'm not dyin'." Parker rolled to her side and, with Melia's help, managed to get to her hands and knees. It was only a short distance to the car, ten or fifteen feet, but Parker was determined to walk it. She didn't want the further humiliation of crawling back.

Melia knelt beside her and helped Parker push herself to her feet. Parker's legs felt like old, wooden stilts, but they managed to get her to the open car door. Falling inside, she was instantly warmer, just to be out of the wind increased her body temperature. Melia checked that she was in and slammed the door.

Melia ran around the car and got in, closing her door quickly behind her. She grabbed the steering wheel with both hands, holding tight as she shook violently. When she reached down to turn the key, her fingers fumbled and couldn't hold it. Parker leaned over and slid the base of the key between the knuckles of her first two fingers.

"Which way?"

"Right," Melia directed through her chattering teeth.

Parker turned the key and the engine came to life immediately. Melia sighed as warm air began to fill the car. Parker still felt too frozen to shake, like a thick lump of ice inside her would have to melt before she could begin to feel anything.

"Up ahead, about fifteen miles, there's a gas station. We're going to get some coffee and sit and talk about what's going on here, and what you expect from me." Melia stared out along the black roadway almost invisible in the blackness of the night. Her body relaxed as it warmed, Parker could see the stiffness easing from her arms. But the expression on her face didn't change. "I need to know what you expect from me."

Nodding, Parker dropped her head and stared at her boots. She hoped that fifteen miles was enough distance for her to figure out what she did expect.

It was not.

A cluster of lights huddled in the fold of a small canyon ahead. Melia slowed the car and let it drift onto the road that circled down to reach the few buildings. Everything was brightly lit, although only the gas station that Melia pointed out seemed to be open. Melia drove up to the side of the building and stopped the car. Enormous sheets of glass made up three walls of the place and Parker could see right through to the night beyond. She pitied the man standing at the counter inside, exposed to whatever eyes might be peering in from the darkness.

Melia led her inside and pointed her to a table in the corner. Parker sat on the hard, slick seat and watched as Melia crossed the room. The lights were too bright for her mood and had that sick, bluish tint that seemed to be everywhere these days. It sharpened the corners on everything and when she looked at her hands, her skin appeared papery and discolored. The tabletop had the look of wood grain but it was unnaturally hard and slippery. Knocking it with her knuckles, Parker tried to figure out why it was so cold.

"Are you warming up?" Sliding a cup of coffee in front of Parker, Melia sat down across from her. She cradled the cup in her cold hands and waited for Parker to nod. After a moment, Melia reached out to take off Parker's hat and brush the hair back from her forehead. "It's still wet."

"Do you think she's alive?"

Melia twisted her lip and looked as if Parker had slapped her. "I don't know. Do you really care?"

"Of course, I don't want to be a killer."

"You already are," Melia shook her head and made a sound like a laugh stillborn. "Already were, whatever."

"I told you, I had to do it, he didn't give me no choice." Parker hunched her shoulders and dropped her chin down, level to the edge of her cup. The coffee had tasted bitter and burned all the way down to her stomach.

"Like Dana? Like she didn't give you a choice?"

"I'm not blamin' her. That was all my doin', maybe that's why I hope she didn't die."

"Where was this concern when we could have actually done something to help her?"

"I'm sorry, Melia. What can I say to you?" Parker fought the desire to raise her voice. The man who worked behind the counter stared at them without trying to disguise his interest. "I was scared. I shot her 'cause I was scared for you."

"Oh, please don't try that. Don't try to blame this on me." Melia voice was even more bitter than the coffee.

"I told you, this was my doin'." She had to fold her hands in her lap to keep from crushing the thin-walled cup in her fists. Melia was not willing to listen to what Parker was trying to say, but she deserved that. It was up to her to convince Melia she wasn't as cold-blooded as it seemed. "But I couldn't have beat her fightin'. If she got me out, what would'a happened to you?"

Melia lifted her chin, but didn't answer.

"I did want to hurt her, and when I think about what she's done to you . . . yeah, I want to kill her. But I really don't think I could. Me holdin' the gun to her head and threatenin'? Well, that was all bullshit. I could'a no more pulled that trigger than fly."

"You're telling me the truth?"

"Jesus Christ. I've done a lot of stupid things, but where's the good of lyin' to you?"

Melia studied her face. Parker waited. There was nothing more she could say. If Melia decided she needed to turn around and head back to Denver, Parker wouldn't argue. Melia didn't owe her a damn thing. Maybe Parker could stay here and hope someone traveling her way would be willing to give her a ride. She hoped it wouldn't come to that, the thought of leaving Melia was getting more painful every moment they were together.

But the past was waiting for her. When she found that hole, she was going to step through it. No question anymore, she couldn't stay here. She would be leaving Melia, one way or another.

"Is it okay if I call a friend, just to check on her?" Melia sat forward in her seat and touched Parker's arm lightly.

Parker wrinkled her forehead. "Why you askin' me? I ain't runnin' this show."

"Aren't you?" Melia leaned back and again examined Parker. "You're the one with the gun."

Slapping her side, Parker shook her head in disgust. "You can see I took it off."

"Shit. It's still there. And it wouldn't matter if it wasn't. Do you really think you won't get your way?" Melia's tone was hard to read, but Parker understood the words well enough.

Taking her hat from the table and jamming it on, Parker stood. Her anger shook her to the core. Keeping her voice down was impossible. "All right, I deserved that. I been nothin' but trouble for you, so we'll just put a stop to it now. We can part ways right here. You go back to Denver. Go back to her."

"Go back to who? The dead woman on my living room floor?"

Parker took a step toward Melia before she could catch herself. She struggled to keep down her angry reply. Melia was clearly baiting her. What the reason for it was, she didn't know. But how could she blame Melia for being so upset?

"Listen, you got nothin' to gain from pushin' me. I told you, I'm sorry. I told you, I didn't mean it. I told you, we can part right now." Parker's words were like little fists. She couldn't hold them back. "You want to know what I expect from you? Nothin'. I don't want nothin' from you. Just what do you expect from me? I got nothin' you want."

"Shit, Parker. If that was true, I wouldn't be here."

"Well, what do you want?"

Melia sighed and Parker suddenly saw the fatigue in her face. She looked so thin, so pale, so tired. A wave of guilt rushed over Parker. She'd turned Melia's life upside down and it had been none too stable to begin with.

"Parker, I just want to have the time to talk to you. It seems like since the minute we met, one thing or another has been pushing us on. I want to talk. I want to get to know you and find out . . . where we're going."

The pause before her last words was revealing. Obviously Melia didn't mean the direction they would be driving. Parker fought to suppress the hope that tried to leap up into her chest. How much time did they have together? Maybe two days? Melia must not realize that she meant to go, not just check out the possibilities. A strange voice startled her out of her thoughts.

"Hey, you girls are gonna have to pay for that coffee." The man had come from behind his counter and approached their table. Parker glared at him and he stopped where he was.

"No shit, asshole. You think we're gonna walk out?"

Melia jumped to her feet and took Parker's arm. "Parker, sometimes people do." Melia dug in her pocket and smiled encouragement at the man. "She's not from here, she just never thought of doing something like that."

"Not from here?" The man returned Parker's glare, but couldn't resist the warmth of Melia's smile. "Well, she sure has the English down."

"That's the first thing they all learn." Melia laughed, a light sound. "The swear words."

The man's laughter joined hers as he took the money Melia offered. Parker turned her back on them and tried to ignore their words. But what Melia said next caught and held her attention.

"Is there a hotel near here?"

"Yeah, about twenty more miles down the freeway. But it's pretty expensive."

"Well, thank goodness for plastic, then."

The last comment had no meaning for her, but the thought of Melia's intentions was enough. Maybe they did have only two days, and maybe it was time to make the most of them.

∩   ∩   ∩   ∩   ∩

There was dried blood on the cuff of her shirt. Melia's eye was caught by the dark stain as she parked the car under the yellow neon of the hotel sign. Parker was a silent shadow in the seat beside her, wordlessly waiting for Melia's lead. Melia dropped her hand, hiding the discoloration from both their eyes. She didn't want to deal with it, not yet. She didn't have the strength and nothing she could say would take back the shooting anyway. Parker couldn't be sorrier and Melia couldn't help but feel Dana had pushed Parker into it. It was the fault of her environment. There was nothing she could have done differently.

There had been no answer at Chris' house or her own. Melia had stood in the cold phone booth outside the gas station praying, wanting to believe that Dana had called 911 and got the help she needed. There was no time to call every hospital, the bookstore was already closed, and the only option she had left to her was calling Langley. Melia couldn't make herself do it. Lang hated Dana too much, and Melia knew what she thought of Parker. Involving Langley would be a stupid mistake. Melia had run back to the car, hoping that she would think of another option during the drive to the hotel. She hadn't been that lucky, but at least here she could use the phone in a warm room and maybe she would call every hospital.

"I think you should stay here until I check us in," Melia suggested. Parker was stretched about to her limit and was not responding well to people. She wasn't surprised to hear Parker's hasty agreement. They both needed some quiet and good night's sleep.

Melia buttoned up her coat and prepared herself for the rush of cold air when she opened the car door. The night was growing colder by the hour, none of the early spring warmth that had begun to creep into the valleys below survived this altitude. She ran to the door with the small red vacancy sign and pushed through it.

The desk was deserted. Melia lifted a tiny, silver bell from the counter and rang it politely. In the small room beyond Melia could see a large TV screen. The music of the ten o'clock news show's introduction competed with her bell ringing. A body lifted from an overstuffed chair parked in front of the screen and lumbered toward her.

"I bet you're wanting a warm room." The man spoke through a bushy, gray beard that shrouded the lower half of his face. Melia could tell he was smiling only by the twinkle in his eye.

"Darn right," Melia spoke, managing a weak grin. The man slid the register to her and she could feel him staring with curiousity at the bruises on her face as she quickly wrote down her information. "Sorry to interrupt your news."

"Ah, it's a Denver station. They never show anything that affects us up here." He turned and bent his head to read her name and address. "We're praying for cable."

"I've heard it's not much better."

"You need to write down your license plate number, do you know it?"

"Um, surprisingly enough, no." Melia pulled her coat together again and started to turn for the door.

"Stay there, you're cold. I think I can read it from the window." The man picked up the registration book, rounded the counter, and shuffled to the plate glass window. "Ain't no surprise to me anyway, most people don't know."

Melia smiled and turned back to the counter. Her smile froze as she looked across the room and saw her own face looking back from the television screen. The picture was one she'd given Dana last year. Melia hadn't even thought she'd keep it. She leaned forward, holding her breath as the voice of the announcer carried to where she stood.

"Melia Ellis, 32, was abducted from her home this evening by an armed assailant. Her roommate was shot in the attack and remains at St. Luke's Hospital in critical condition. Police are on the lookout for Ms. Ellis' 1989 Honda—"

"Someone else with you?"

Melia spun around at the sound of the hotel manager's voice. She stared at him, wondering how much he had heard and if he would recognize her name when he looked down at the ledger in his hand.

"Are you okay, hon? It doesn't matter if you have someone with you. We don't ask any questions here."

"Listen, um, I think maybe I've changed my mind. I guess I'm not as tired as I thought."

The man returned to the counter as she spoke. Melia fought her desire to grab the paper with her name on it and run from the building. He put the register down and, following her worst fear, glanced at it before he answered. "Look, Ms. Ellis. I said we don't ask any questions."

"No, it's not that. I really just want to keep driving. I'm sorry to have bothered you."

He smiled and shook his head. "Now, that's all right.

Pretty girl like you is never a bother." He took his pen and wrote the word VOID across the registration sheet.

"May I have that paper?" Melia tried to make the question sound casual, but the strain in her voice was apparent.

"I can't do that, I have to keep . . ." His voice faded as the television continued to blurt out her story.

"—friends describe Ms. Ellis as five feet one, brown hair and eyes."

"Hold on a minute." The man twisted his body to look at the screen. Her picture was again plastered across it. Before he could turn and compare her face to the picture in his living room, Melia ripped the paper from the ledger and ran out the door.

Eighteen

The humming of the machines standing vigil by the bed and the sterile late-morning light that glared from every angle of the room drove Dana crazy. The endless drip of the fluid in the IV made her want to shred the plastic hose and bag with her teeth and nails. Her leg was propped up high in a fat, shiny-white cast and blood had been restored to her veins. She was burning with the need to move. But the doctors wouldn't let her go and she suspected at least half the reason for that came from advice from the police.

Parker's bullet had shattered her femur, breaking it completely in half. The police told her that they couldn't identify the slug. Dana couldn't give them any help with a description of the weapon, besides that it was long and the hole in the barrel had looked outrageously large. The bitch must have been packing an elephant gun. Dana shifted on the cool sheets. Her leg didn't hurt anymore and that infuriated her. She demanded they stop giving her pain medication, but the nurses just looked at her and shook their heads. They didn't understand. If it hurt, and hurt bad, she could almost forgive herself for letting Parker take Melia. Without the pain, she couldn't accept her inaction. She shifted again, trying to wiggle her foot, trying to bump the cast against the metal rails around her bed.

"For some reason, I think it would be better for you to lie still."

Dana felt no guilt at the sound of the voice. She glared at the door and prepared herself for another tirade against the pain killers. The words died on her lips as she recognized Chris standing in the doorway. They stared silently for a moment, both wary and uncomfortable at being on the same side for once.

"Any news?"

"Nothing." Chris slapped her hands on her thighs and looked around the small room. "Mind if I come in?"

"Oh, sure. Sorry." Dana shifted again as she pointed to the metal chair beside the bed. The way Chris looked at her leg embarrassed her.

"It hurts a lot?"

"No, not at all."

Chris raised her eyebrow and Dana could see that Chris thought she was trying to be tough. No one would even try to understand. The silence that filled the room was beyond deadly. Chris noticed the dripping of the IV and focused her attention on that. The sound was like a ticking clock wired to a time bomb. Dana grabbed at and discarded thirty things to say before Chris finally spoke again.

"So this woman . . . you really think she's a psychopath?"

"Well, she shot me. She kidnaped Melia. And somehow she convinced Melia that she's from the old West. What would you say?"

"I'd say I don't want to believe it." Chris rubbed her eyes with her thumbs. "But, now that it's too late, I can sure see that Melia was primed for someone like this."

"What does that mean?"

Chris pushed back her chair and stretched her legs under Dana's bed. Her expression filled with contempt as she crossed her arms over her chest. "You really want to get into this? You really want the cold truth?"

Dana bit her lip. Her hands immediately began to sweat. Whatever Chris felt she needed to say, Dana was not ready to hear it. Besides, she had already thought it all herself.

"I didn't think so." Chris twisted her mouth. Her contempt was painfully clear. "So where did this woman come from? Where did Melia meet her?"

"I don't know. I didn't even know she existed until she walks in shooting."

"Fuck, I should have listened to Langley and gone to see Melia yesterday."

"Who's Langley?"

"Jesus, Dana. Do you know anything at all about Melia's life? Or just how you wanted her to fit into yours?"

"I'm sorry." Dana knocked her leg against the rail and the hollow tube rang like a bell. It didn't hurt. The goddamn thing would not hurt.

"I don't know why I should care, 'cause I don't think there's anyone in the world I hate as much as you, but I think you should try to hold that leg still."

Dana leaned her head back on the pillows and watched the room swim around her head. Her eyes were filling with tears and any movement was likely to send them spilling down her cheeks where Chris would see them. She held her breath and kept her eyes fixed wide open, staring at the ceiling. Her voice was a dry monotone as she answered the thoughts she knew were screaming to get out of Chris' head.

"Chris, I know." Dana had to swallow and breathe hard a few times before she could continue. Chris waited. "I know what you're thinking. I know, because I'm thinking it, too. I treated her like shit. I never knew what it was she needed and I didn't bother finding out."

Dana tilted her head carefully and looked into Chris' eyes. "God, Chris, if you would have seen this woman. She was playing the part so hard. She looked like she walked straight out of one of Melia's stupid books. I don't know how she did it, but she must have known just what to say, just how to say it. But, if it wasn't for me, my stupidity and my temper, she couldn't have done it. You're right, I primed Melia for this. I set her up and then I laid there and watched her fall."

Chris jumped up from her chair and took two steps toward the door before stopping herself and taking two back. Her fists were clenched and she looked like she needed to run, or to scream. She came to the bed and gripped Dana's arm with fingers like steel bands.

"Dana—" Chris licked her lips before continuing. "Do you think she will . . . kill Melia?"

The tears came again and this time Dana could not stop them. It was her answer.

Chris bared her teeth and Dana was afraid. Taking the collar of Dana's shirt in both hands, Chris half-pulled her up from the bed. She leaned down until her face was only inches from Dana's.

"You worthless piece of shit. I wish I could kill you right now. I wish I would have killed you a year ago."

Dana was shaking, her whole body trembled in Chris' hands. It took all the strength she had just to respond. "I wish that, too."

Chris dropped her back to the bed with a look of disgust. Turning to face the wall, she ran her fingers through her hair repeatedly. "I've got to find her," she said without looking at Dana. "Did they say anything?"

"No. She made Melia pack some clothes. It felt like they weren't staying around here."

"Where would they go? Did this Parker say anything about where she was from?"

"No, we didn't really chat." Dana closed her eyes and tried to picture Parker, there had to be something that would give her a clue. "She did have some kind of accent. I don't know if it was southern or Texan, it sounded fake to me."

"Is there anything else? There's got to be something."

"I told the police everything. There's nothing we can figure out that they can't."

Chris dropped back into the chair and put her head in her hands. "But they don't know Melia. We do. I do. Maybe I can come up with something if you just think."

Dana grasped for straws. She didn't think it would do any good, but clearly Chris needed it. "Parker wanted her to do something. Melia said she knew what Parker wanted and she seemed willing to do it. She told me she knew she'd be okay."

"Melia said that? How could she say that when the woman is standing there with a smoking gun?"

"I don't know, Chris. Melia just doesn't think she's insane. She defended Parker for shooting me." The thought still grated on Dana. Even with accepting the whole situation as her own fault, that point burned her. If only she would have hit Parker harder when she had the chance. Suddenly her memory was jolted. "Oh, she was at Melia's office building. What day was that ... uh, Wednesday. Do you think she might work there, too?"

"Her office?" Chris lifted her head but she was looking somewhere beyond the walls of the room. "Melia's been having some trouble at her office. Someone stealing her books, watching her."

"Shit. That's how she knew Melia was a Western freak. God, she must have planned this out."

"Okay, calm down. This might actually help us. I know Melia's supervisor." Chris stood and unconsciously rested her hand on Dana's shoulder. "I can go down there and find out what he knows about a woman named Parker. Did you tell the police this?"

Dana held very still, not wanting to draw Chris' attention to her gesture of tenderness. She'd be furious at herself for extending compassion to Dana and Dana knew it. "No," she whispered. "I just remembered it."

"I'll tell them, after I talk to Bob."

There was a quiet knock at the door. Chris stepped away from the bed as the door swung open. A crop-haired young woman stood nervously in the doorway.

"Hey, Dana. I just stopped by, am I interrupting anything?"

"No, Benny. Come on in. This is my—this is Chris."

Chris looked at Benny and shook her head slightly. Dana hoped that Benny didn't catch its meaning. "I'd better go," Chris stated, her voice toneless.

"I don't mean to chase you off," Benny protested. She was so uncertain, in her voice, in her movements. At work, at the bar, Benny could be a real smart ass, but in private she didn't seem to know what to be. Dana wondered how Benny had the nerve to hang around her. "I just brought you a book."

Chris laughed aloud at the look on Dana's face. She went to the door and took Benny by the arm. "You come right in here and sit down. I think what Dana needs is for you to read it to her." She led Benny to the chair and smiled encouragement. Dana kept her mouth shut. "Oh, and make sure she doesn't hit her cast on the railing."

Before Benny sat and opened the book, she took a pillow from behind Dana's head and tucked it carefully between her leg and the rail.

"Chris." Dana stopped her before she could leave the room. "One thing I need to know, who is Langley?"

"She's a friend of Melia's, a good friend. More importantly, as far as you're concerned, she's the only person who can back up your story that this Parker even exists."

"Maybe I—"

"Dana, if you are lucky, you will never meet Langley. She's not even as forgiving as I am, and she hated you long before this happened."

Ω   Ω   Ω   Ω   Ω

Langley couldn't wait for Chris to come to the door. As soon as she saw Chris' car pull up in front of the bookstore, she rushed out onto the sidewalk. Nervously, she rapped her knuckles on the hood while Chris got out and walked around to her.

"The police called."

"Jesus, let's go inside."

"It's not bad, not all bad." Langley let Chris take her by the arm and lead her back into the bookstore. Chris was handing it so well, Langley wondered where she found her strength.

Locking the door behind her and flipping the sign to "closed," Chris pushed her on toward the back room. Langley took a seat on a box and waited for Chris to sit down in her desk chair.

"Okay, Melia was seen last night, in the mountains. There's a gas station on I-70, about two hours from here."

Chris leaned forward, her elbows on her knees and her eyes burning into Langley's. "Was she all right?"

Langley nodded her head, but the gesture was less than convincing. "She was with Parker, they stopped for coffee. The clerk said . . . well, he said they seemed to be fighting. And

Parker was really belligerent. He thought she was going to hit him because he asked her to pay."

"Fuck."

"But he said Melia smoothed it over real well. Said that Parker was from another country or something."

"What? That's dumb. Dana—uh, I heard she has a southern accent."

"Texan, maybe. But Melia said she wasn't from here. She was probably just trying to cover for Parker somehow."

Chris wrinkled her forehead. "Wasn't from here? Or was from another country?"

"I'm sorry, Chris. I don't remember exactly what they said. Maybe I'm confused with what she told me. She said that Parker was out of her element. I don't know, it's like she's trying to excuse her behavior."

"God, how many times did she do that for Dana?" Chris rubbed the wrinkles out of her forehead. Langley could feel that she was trying to piece together things that she'd heard, there was surely an answer there somewhere, but it was no good trying to get it out of her before she thought it through.

"There's more."

"Oh," Chris shook her head and reached out to touch Langley's thigh. "Go ahead."

"About a half hour later, Melia went into a hotel to rent a room. The manager said she seemed nervous, but friendly. She wrote down her name and address. He read the name and went to get her license plate number. He noticed that someone else was in the car and that's when Melia got really nervous. When he came back to the counter, he hears her name on the TV and turns to see her picture on the screen. That was when she grabbed the ledger sheet and ran out."

"This makes no sense at all. If there's a fucking lunatic in your car and they let you get away long enough to rent a room, why do you run back to them the minute you could get help?"

Langley had asked herself the same thing. She hadn't thought that her stomach could sink any lower, but it did. Nausea had gripped her since the night she left Melia's house, since she'd left Melia alone and defenseless with Parker. "She's got her," she breathed, the words almost soundless. "She doesn't need a gun, she doesn't need to use force. She's got her fingers right inside Melia's brain and she knows every button to push."

"How could she?" Chris screamed the words. Langley almost fell backwards from her box as Chris leapt to her feet and kicked a stack of books across the narrow room. "How in the hell could she get inside Melia so quick, when we can hardly reach her? What the fuck has she got?"

Langley thought back to Parker standing before her, her hand relaxed at her hip, her stance powerful and composed. The look in those too cool eyes, the seduction imminent in those lips. What did she have?

Apparently, exactly what Melia had been searching for.

∩ ∩ ∩ ∩ ∩

The desert air was hot and soaked into Melia's skin like bath water. She was lying on her side in the warm sand, watching Parker on the flats below her, gathering wood. They wouldn't need a fire for light or heat for hours to come, so Melia suspected that Parker just needed the physical activity. Her eyes burned as she watched, she couldn't think clearly enough to calculate how long it had been since she'd slept, but she didn't want to close them. She wanted to wait and ask Parker to lie down beside her before she fell asleep.

Parker looked right at home in the desert. It had been hours since they'd passed a car and many miles since seeing any sign of civilization other than the narrow, red-dirt road they traveled. Melia had driven slowly while Parker scanned the cliffs for a cave or overhang they could use as shelter while Melia caught up on her sleep. She'd nodded at the wheel as they inched along, Parker's shout had caused her to slam on the brakes and practically fling Parker up on the dash. But they had found their shelter and a jumble of boulders not far from the road that they could hide the car behind.

Scouting the trunk, Parker had discovered her winter survival kit and dragged the whole thing, blankets, energy bars, kitty litter and all, up the hill and under the lip of sandstone that hung over a smooth sand floor. Melia had stumbled along behind her with the water jug, mindlessly admiring the strength in Parker's legs, and collapsed as soon as she reached the shelter. Now she couldn't sleep, or wouldn't sleep, until Parker returned. Every few minutes, her view of the desert would warp and shift and she would have to stretch her eyes open wide to get things back in focus.

"You still awake?"

Melia had lost sight of Parker, not realizing until she spoke that she'd climbed back up the slope to sit in the sand next to her.

"I waited for you."

"I'm not sleepy."

"Oh." Melia wondered if she sounded petulant, but couldn't really care. She propped herself up on her elbow, her head in her hand.

Parker pushed the toe of her boot through the sand and grinned as she nudged Melia's thigh. "I remember now, you don't like to sleep alone."

"That's right." Melia's head rolled forward and she almost fell over into the sand. Parker laughed and Melia giggled like a fool.

"Come on, get down here."

Parker pushed Melia toward a blanket she'd spread across the sand. It looked so comfortable, no bed had ever held such promise. Melia scooted over to it and stretched out, gratefully accepting Parker's invitation. Parker slid up behind her and cradled Melia's body with her own. She put her arm over Melia's waist and Melia grabbed her hand, pulling it forward to hold it under her chin.

Parker laughed again as Melia sighed deeply. Her breath was warm in Melia's ear.

"I love this," Melia mumbled, too far gone to come back any time soon. "I love you."

When Melia woke her, face was heated by a small, dancing campfire, but her back was cold. Sitting up, she held the blankets around her shoulders and looked for Parker. Melia spotted her sitting just outside the circle of firelight, her back to the warmth and her face turned up to the night. Melia followed her gaze and was astonished by the number of stars that swept across the sky. There seemed to be layer upon layer of tiny suns spread out across the heavens and they felt so close they could almost brush against her fingers if she stood and raised her arms.

But even that splendor could not hold her interest long. Her eyes were soon drawn down, returning to study the back of the woman sitting beyond the fire. Melia wanted her. More than she'd wanted anything or anyone in the world. It was like a taste she craved, like a cloth so soft her fingers couldn't stop returning to it, like a breath that kept filling and expanding her lungs until she thought she would burst from it. As if the intensity of her emotion was a hand that could reach out and caress Parker's shoulder, she turned and looked into Melia's eyes.

"You all right?" Parker asked as she stood and came to lean over Melia. The map of the desert taken from Melia's fax machine was crumpled in her hand. "Did you sleep well?"

Melia nodded. Parker's shadow covered her face and she hoped it hid the longing she couldn't erase from her expression. "I'm a little cold. What time is it?"

"I guess it's along after midnight. Don't you have your little clock?"

"Oh yeah." Melia pressed the light button on her watch and had to blink as it flashed on. "It's twelve forty. Not a bad guess, how did you do that?"

"The moon moves along. You can learn to judge it like the sun."

A fingernail moon nestled up among the stars. The night was so dark that Melia could clearly see the unlit mass of the moon blocking the stars behind it. A shower of red sparks flew up to join the stars as Parker tossed more sticks onto the fire.

"Weren't you cold, sitting over there?"

Parker looked over to where she'd sat outside the fire's glow. She shrugged. "The fire makes it hard to see out there, I try to keep my back to it."

"But weren't you cold?" Melia pushed.

A quiet laugh, almost a sound of exasperation, came from Parker's lips. "Yeah, I was cold," she admitted.

"Then you should come down here and let me get you warm." Melia held the corner of the blanket up and gestured for Parker to slide under. After a moment's hesitation, Parker kicked off her boots, peeled off her coat, and sat next to Melia. She unbuckled her gun belt and leaned to put the pistol above Melia's head, within easy reach. Melia hooked her finger into Parker's front pocket and pulled until Parker followed the pressure and worked her way under the blankets.

Parker shivered once, hard, then was still. Melia hesitated for the space of five heartbeats before she pulled Parker even nearer and wrapped her leg across Parker's thighs.

Parker lifted her right arm and Melia snuggled in close to her side, her head resting on Parker's strong shoulder. Parker put her arm behind Melia, her hand pressing softly against the small of Melia's back.

"Better?"

"The best."

"Are you getting warm?"

"I'm well on my way."

They were quiet and the desert was quieter still. The only sound was the crackling of the flames as they devoured the dry branches Parker had fed them. Melia could, for the moment, believe that they were both out of the pull of time and the world would spin on without them. But she knew tomorrow would be different and time might undo her heart completely. She took the map from Parker's left hand.

"You found out where to go?"

Parker sighed before she spoke. "There are two close by, if I'm readin' that right. Probably just a few minutes in that car of yours."

"Can we drive right to them?"

"No, I s'pose we'll have to hike a ways."

Melia closed her eyes and pushed her face closer to the warmth of Parker's chest. Her voice was muffled by the blankets. "Are you sure this is what you want?"

Parker lifted her hand and touched Melia's cheek with cold fingers. She tilted Melia's head up, but still Melia couldn't see her eyes in the shadows. "It's what I gotta do. You know I don't fit here."

Melia bent her neck, forcing Parker's fingers to slide away from her face. She put her head down again.

"Don't think it ain't hard," Parker said suddenly, her voice harsh against the night's stillness. "Don't think I ain't regrettin' everything."

"Everything? Meeting me is included in that?"

"Hell, yes. What do you think? I can leave here and not know what I'm leavin'?"

"But aren't you doing just that?"

Parker once again tried to lift Melia's face, but she stubbornly would not be moved. "What are you talkin' about?"

Melia pushed herself away from Parker and moved to lie on her back. She stared up into the sky, the stars now seemed distant and cold. "I want to *know* you, Parker. And I want you to *know* me. But you've been pushing me away, you've rejected every move I made to you."

"That's not true."

"Well, then your truth is different than mine."

"It's always that way."

"Then, that's the way you want it? You want to leave here with *this* between us? Without ever lifting your stupid hand to take what I'm trying to give you?" Melia struggled to get free of the blankets and raise herself from the sand. Parker grabbed the front of Melia's shirt and had her jerked back to the ground before Melia could get away. She twisted her body until she was leaning over Melia, using her forearm to hold her down.

"I'll tell you how I want it. I'll tell what I been thinkin', sittin' out there in the dark, what I wanted to do to you. You're not gonna like it," Parker's face was dark with anger. "I was gonna lead you right up there, and when I was ready to step through that hole, I was gonna grab you and drag you along with me."

Parker's fist tightened and she shook Melia's body with every word. "Do you think I'm proud of that? Do you think I want to admit to wantin' you that bad?"

The fear that had exploded in Melia's chest as quickly drained away. Parker's hand was shaking and her body was stiff with tension. Melia slowly put her hand on Parker's and, with gentleness, pulled Parker's fingers from their grip. She slid her fingers around the back of Parker's hand and pulled her palm down to brush over her breast. Parker's shaking increased and she groaned with the stress of holding herself away.

"Parker," Melia whispered. "Please, don't make me wait any more."

"But every last time we talk, it seems like we're in a fight. It don't seem right to go on and do this . . ."

Melia smiled and stroked Parker's cheek. "You do this, and I guarantee things will go better. I promise it will be easier to talk to me. We'll be closer without this pressure building between us."

"Oh, Melia. I been wantin' you for so long." Still, she held herself away. But her hand remained, cupping the softness of Melia's breast.

"What can I do?" Melia frowned as she thought of what had restrained Parker in her bathroom. She was no more ready or able to express her feelings than she'd been before. "Do you still need me to tell you what I feel?"

The smile that crossed Parker's face was like a light in the darkness. Just looking into the joy of that expression gave Melia a sense of freedom, a promise of a future.

"I know, Melia. I already know." The words seemed to release Parker from whatever bound her. Her shaking stilled and her body relaxed. She leaned down and gently kissed the tip of Melia's nose.

Melia laughed and pulled her face away. "I'm gonna need a little more than that."

"I reckoned you would."

The accent still charmed Melia. The words were so foolish, nobody "reckoned" anymore. But Melia loved the sound of her voice. She touched Parker's lips with her fingertip, then let her touch glide down over her chin and throat to stop at Parker's collar. One-handed, she smoothly began to unbutton Parker's shirt. When she reached the end of the shirt, she continued, pulling apart the metal buttons on the fly of Parker's jeans. Turning her hand, she slid her palm across Parker's tight belly, easing her hand down to curl her fingers in the soft hair. Parker's hips pushed against Melia's touch and she released a long breath.

"Has it been awhile?" Melia teased.

"Oh, more than a hundred years, I'd say." Parker's eyes never left Melia's face. "And I remember wantin' it, but never this bad."

"Move over." Melia pushed Parker's shoulder until she shifted to lie on her side away from Melia. "And take off your shirt."

Melia watched to see that Parker obeyed. When she was satisfied that Parker was really going to do this and not back down, Melia began undressing. She worked her way out of her shirt and jeans, managing to keep herself under the blankets. The desert air held a chill, nothing like the sharp cold of the mountain air, but enough of a bite to keep Melia under cover. Parker leaned on her elbow, her upper body completely exposed, and did not seem to notice the cold. She smiled as Melia removed her bra and underwear, reaching out a bare arm to fling them onto her growing pile of clothing.

"I'd like to see you."

"You can, tomorrow morning when the sun comes up." Melia clutched the corner of the top cover.

"I don't think so."

Parker took Melia's hand and loosened her fingers from their grip on the blanket. Slowly, she pulled it aside, letting the cloth flow away to reveal Melia's pale skin in the orange glow of the firelight. Melia tensed, ready to curl her body inward, to protect herself from the exposure. Parker shook her head, the slightest movement of a command, and Melia opened and let herself be seen. Parker's expression seemed to say that it was too good to touch, the view, the lines and shadows that outlined Melia's body. Melia looked down at herself. Her breasts were small, her ribs too close to the skin, her waist curved in, impossibly slender. Parker seemed all brawn, wiry muscles and hard bones, but soft skin covered that strength and Melia ached to feel the force of her power pressing against her.

Refusing to lie passively under her stare any longer, Melia touched Parker's shoulder and slowly, carefully, pushed her onto her back. On her knees, Melia let her hand drift down to Parker's waist before straddling Parker's hips. She lowered herself, her hair tangling in Parker's buttons as Melia brought her body forward to rest first her belly, then her breasts, then her lips against Parker's warm skin.

Parker wrapped her arms around Melia and they savored the heat of the kisses Melia traced across her shoulder. Melia could feel a fire building inside her, it rapidly warmed her skin. Where their bodies touched, she could feel the cold fading away. Parker rubbed her hands down Melia's back, her touch strong, and growing stronger as she held Melia's hips and pulled her tight against her stomach.

Melia lifted her head. Parker's lips were open slightly, Melia could see the gleam of the fire on her teeth. It was such a primal sight, Melia felt a thrill of fear course through her veins. The possibility of danger inflamed her desire. Parker moved one hand to the back of her head and slowly, insistently brought Melia's lips down to her own.

The kiss was deep. Parker held nothing back and Melia felt as if she was being drawn into the woman's soul. Her lips caressed, her tongue teased, and her teeth bit soft gasps of desire from Melia's mouth. Melia closed her eyes and lost all sense of direction. One moment, she was above Parker, her hair flowing down to curtain them in darkness. The next moment, Parker was looking down at her, moving her mouth away just far enough to make Melia strain to reach and plead for another taste of her lips. Parker held her chin in a grip like steel and turned her head to the side. Melia stared wide-eyed into the flames as Parker bit her earlobe, the sound of her teeth clicking against Melia's earrings sending a chill over both of them.

"I waited for you." The words came so low, deep from Parker's throat.

"I'm sorry," Melia whispered, too easily and instinctively trying to soothe her lover's anger. Her mind unaware, her body tensed for the anticipated pain.

Parker raised her head. She could feel the change somehow and her response to Melia's reaction made Melia realize what she'd done. Holding her breath, she hesitated, with no idea how to behave.

"It ain't gonna be like that." Parker's voice threatened kindness. Her body pressed Melia down in the sand, holding her there like she was planning to torture her with gentleness. "You're not gonna be afraid." She moved her lips to Melia's throat, shifting her body downward as her kisses moved lower. "You're not gonna hurt." Kisses outlined Melia's collarbones. "You're not gonna think about no one but me." Her lips reached Melia's breast and paused for an agonizing moment before closing around her nipple.

Melia gasped and clenched her hands in Parker's hair, again expecting pain without expecting to, again overwhelmed by the gentle pressure that was just as stimulating. She spread her legs apart and Parker immediately accepted the invitation. Her hand slid down, touching the heat, her fingers becoming instantly wet and welcomed into Melia's body.

Melia was on fire. She was as hot as she'd ever been and as hot as she would get. Parker needed to spend no more time on arousing her, she was ready and aching for release. "Parker, I need you. Right now."

Parker didn't change her movement, didn't attempt to increase the pressure or pace of her touch. Melia raised her hips, trying to drive Parker deeper inside. Parker moved with her, refusing to be anything but gentle.

Melia tried again, panting. "I don't know if I can come— uh, have an orgasm this way. It's so soft, I don't think—"

Parker put her fingers across Melia's lips. Her other hand kept up its movement, the smooth strokes continuing despite Melia's words. "You don't think so? I think you're wrong."

Melia shook her head, pressing it down into the sand. The touch was driving her mad, it was torture. She squeezed her eyes shut tight and silently begged for Parker to hurt her, to somehow force the feeling to come from her. She knew what she needed, what she was used to and this lightness, this playing would never be enough.

"Look at me."

Finally, the demand was there in Parker's voice, the hint of anger, of real passion. Melia opened her eyes and looked. There was something in Parker's eyes, but it was not violence. It was not anything she'd ever expected to see.

"Forget about what I'm doin'," Parker whispered. "Forget about what you think you need. Forget your body. There's a feelin' inside you, reach for it."

"I don't understand. I can't—" Her eyes filled with tears of frustration and she tried to turn her face away.

"Look at me." Parker was actually smiling. Her fingers were tireless. "Let go, and think for a minute when you were fallin' asleep today. What did you say to me?"

Melia tried. She held her breath and tried to remove herself from the demands of her desire. She remembered the comforting strength of Parker's body, the security of her arm around her. She remembered . . . "I—oh, my god."

"Yes." The sound hissed through Parker's teeth. "I'm here. Feel it."

"Oh, my god—" Melia's body shook and suddenly, everything connected. She could feel the cold sand on her toes, the heat of Parker's body against her side, the rush of Parker's breath on her cheek, the pressure building inside from the delicious stroke of Parker's hand. The mad, wild beating of her heart, the sudden taste of Parker's mouth holding back the words that Melia wanted to repeat again and again. "Oh, my god," she said one last time against Parker's lips and her explosion of passion wiped the stars from the sky.

Nineteen

"I'm going with you." Melia cut past Parker and began throwing their things into the trunk of the car. Parker took two steps backwards and leaned her shoulder against a sandstone outcropping.

"I don't care to hear anything you have to say unless it's wonderful, I was hoping you'd say that.' " Melia wadded the blankets into a ball and stuffed them inside. Several of the shirts she'd ruined with Dana's blood were jammed in next to the spare tire. Slamming down the lid of the trunk, she glared at Parker over the top of the car. "I'm going."

Parker returned the stare. "So, why do you sound pissed when you say it?"

"Because I know you're going to argue with me."

"How do you know I wasn't gonna spend the day beggin' you to come?" Parker spoke just loud enough for the sound to carry across the space that separated them. She tilted her head lower, her hat brim blocking out the sight of everything but Melia.

"Because I don't believe your bullshit. There was no

way you were going to drag me along, or beg me, or even ask me to join you."

"How could I?"

"Christ, Parker. How couldn't you?"

Parker sighed and looked past Melia to the desert beyond. Already the sun was causing ripples of heat to rise up from the ground. She'd hate to be stuck here when summer came around. She looked back to Melia, to the expression of anger that twisted her face. "I thought you said we'd get along better after we made love."

"Well," Melia started, then paused. She searched for the right words, then finally threw up her hands in frustration. "Well, I couldn't know it would be like that."

"What did you want it to be?" Parker pushed away from the stone and paced off the distance between them. She came within inches of Melia's face and spoke bitterly. "Did you think I'd hurt you? Degrade you? You got the wrong woman." Parker turned to walk away.

"No, I don't," Melia shouted, grabbing Parker's arm and pulling her around. Parker was surprised at her strength as she pushed Parker up against the car and blocked her escape. "I've got the right woman. I've finally got the right woman, but you're leaving me. If I don't go with you now, I'll never see you again. And I am going."

"Melia, you ain't thinking this out."

"Yes, I am. I did last night after you went to sleep. I couldn't think of anything else." Melia's shoulders sagged. Her anger fell away and she let her body lean forward against Parker's. Melia rested her check on Parker's chest, her voice sounded as if it was coming from far away. "A friend gave me some advice not long ago, I don't think I really believed it until last night."

Parker put her arms around Melia and waited for her to go on. She was glad to have the solidity of the car behind her, her legs were shaking and had felt weak since Melia informed her that she was going. Letting the metal hold her, she held Melia and hoped there was an illusion of strength in her embrace.

"She told me when it's love, I'd feel it. That I would go to the ends of the earth to be with someone. That no book could compete for my attention. I see that now. I don't need . . ." Melia lifted her head and looked into Parker's eyes. "I don't need anything but you."

"Melia, it's a hard life," Parker warned.

"Do you need me? Do you want me?"

"Of course I do," Parker tangled her fingers in Melia hair and held her tightly to her chest. "But I can't—"

"Will you keep me with you?"

"Yes."

"I don't need anything else."

Parker dropped her head to bury her face in Melia's hair. "Oh, Melia. This changes everything. I can't just—we got no horses, no money. Can you walk across the desert until we find a town?"

"I can do anything you need me to do."

"Things are gonna be different."

"I know. I'm glad." Melia put her arms around Parker's waist and squeezed her hard. Parker laughed and with the laughter came the strongest, most incredible feeling of joy she'd ever experienced. She leaned back and yelled to the sky.

"Let's go! Let's do it!"

Melia poked her in the ribs. "Not so half-cocked, cowboy. We're going back to town and getting some supplies. I told you I thought about this last night. I'm going to need clothes. Most of the stuff you grabbed for me is covered with Dana's blood. Also we need packs and—"

"But the law is lookin' for you. For us," Parker reminded her. The thought of heading back to any town for any reason upset her. Melia had explained that she couldn't get
money because as soon as she showed her identification the
computers would recognize her. Parker couldn't imagine anything so frightening. "How are we gonna buy what we need?"

"Nobody knows who you are, they don't have pic-
tures of you. I'll cover my hair, keep out of sight. We'll go into
Moab and you can trade your gold coins for cash."

"But we're gonna need money over there, too."

"Over there?"

"My time. The past. Wherever it is we're going."

"We have to have food before money. And clothes. We
can't just drop down in the middle of the desert with nothing."

Melia was right, and Parker knew she couldn't argue.
But going back among people seemed so dangerous. She did-
n't want anything to happen that would jeopardize her
chance to get back to where she belonged. Melia looked up
into her face and Parker knew her doubt was visible.

"Moab is a small town, but a lot of tourists visit. We
won't stand out." Melia ran her hands down Parker's back and
slipped them into her back pockets. Parker held her breath as
Melia pulled her pelvis forward to press against Melia's belly.
"And if we have enough money left, we could rent a hotel
room for one last night. Take a bath, watch TV, flip the light
switch on and off a few times just for the memory."

"Anything else?"

"We might have time for something else."

Parker was melting from the heat of the contact
between their bodies. She thought of the bath, the ready hot
water, so hot it could steam up the room, and thought of
undressing Melia and lowering her into the tub. Since Melia
had come into the bathroom that first time Parker had

bathed, she'd thought of making love there. Now, imagining the pressure and push of the water, the heat that made her heart pound, the slickness of skin, her decision was made. Suddenly, the danger had no meaning, it was nothing worth giving up her last chance at a fantasy that would never again be so easy to fulfill.

"Let's do it."

Ω   Ω   Ω   Ω   Ω

Ripping the hotel letterhead off of three sheets of paper, Melia sat down at the small table and debated the wisdom of writing to Chris. It wasn't that she didn't think she needed to give her best friend an explanation of what she'd done and where she was disappearing to, it was just the matter of finding the words to make it all sound real. Chris would never believe this, she was too level-headed. Maybe Langley would understand, she could let her mind go to explore any possibility, but Chris was the one person Melia felt she owed an explanation to. The thought gave her a momentary twinge of guilt. Dana surely deserved an apology, but Melia knew she wouldn't write it. She had tried to explain and Dana had shut her down. There was no way she could write anything that would have meaning to Dana, even if Dana bothered to read it.

"Hey, I'm gonna put water in this tub," Parker shouted from the bathroom. "You 'bout ready for a bath?"

"Yeah, go ahead." Melia smiled. What Parker had in mind made it infinitely harder to concentrate on what she needed to write. Maybe she could put this off until morning . . . Melia shook her head and forced herself to start the letter. She managed to write the date and "Dear Chris," before losing it. Sighing, she pushed the paper away and tapped the pen on her chin. "If I had a computer, this would be easier," she said aloud.

"You talkin' to me?"

"No," Melia shouted back. "I'm just trying to write. It's not coming very easily."

Parker padded out of the bathroom on bare feet, the knees of her jeans soaked with water. She stood behind Melia and rubbed her tight shoulders. "You gotta do it?"

Melia nodded. "I think so, she's a good friend."

"All right." Parker bent over and put her chin on Melia's shoulder. She turned her face so her lips brushed against Melia's ear as she spoke. "I'll be in the bath tub. I'll give you fifteen minutes to write. If you can't do it now, you can always try later, when you might be more relaxed."

Melia laughed softly, the sound turning to a sigh as Parker measured her neck with soft kisses. "All right," Melia consented. "Fifteen minutes."

Parker hesitated, as if she already regretted giving Melia so much time. She knelt by Melia's chair and put her hand under Melia's shirt. Melia's stomach muscles tightened as Parker eased her palm upward, over her belly and across her breast. Her heart beat hard and she could feel it pounding between her legs. Parker circled her fingertip around Melia's nipple and Melia could not prevent herself from pushing her body forward, trying to encourage a more intense touch.

"Fifteen minutes." Parker withdrew her hand and stood before Melia could protest. "I'm taking your time piece."

Melia unhooked the band and dropped her watch into Parker's waiting palm. She glanced at the digital clock on the television to compare the time and nodded. Parker smiled and brushed her lips against Melia's before walking away. The bathroom door closed behind her.

The paper waited. Melia thought of Chris, probably worried out of her mind right now, and felt guilty at the pleasure she had planned for herself. How could she think of spending the next eighteen hours satisfying her desires while her friends could be wondering if she was even alive?

"God, you are a selfish asshole." Digging her toes into the deep pile of the carpet, she forced herself to pull the paper back before her. She wrote the letter I' and stopped.

Melia turned and looked at the bathroom door. The sound of running water was muted, the thick door blocking the noise until it sounded like nothing more than a distant hiss. When she turned back around, her eyes went straight to the telephone. Without thinking, her hand lifted the receiver. Melia bit her lip and hesitated.

It was the right thing to do. She had her phone card so she wouldn't have to go through the office switchboard, and no one could know where the call was coming from until it was too late. Clicking her fingernail against the plastic, Melia debated who she should call and what she could say. Anxiety burned in her stomach. The hesitation made calling as difficult as her attempt at writing had been. Melia closed her eyes and began pushing buttons, impulsively dialing Dana's apartment with no clear reason why, except that the number had come to her on its own accord.

The phone rang five times. When it picked up, Melia expected the answering machine.

"Dana's house."

Melia waited for the message to continue, then realized that the pleasant voice was live and now waiting for her response. Before she could answer, the woman spoke again.

"This is Benny, can I help you?"

The name was not said with certainty or comfort in answering Dana's phone. Melia felt a moment of panic, thinking the woman might be with the police. "I just called, to ask about Dana. How she's doing."

"Oh," the voice brightened and Melia was somehow convinced she was not a cop. "Well, she's doing really good. But she's not here right now, she won't be back until tomorrow afternoon."

"Oh, that's okay. I just, I just wanted to say how sorry I am about this happening to her. And I hope there's no permanent damage." Melia's face flushed and she found it hard to put her sentences together. She should have thought out what she meant to say. "I mean, that her leg will heal right and all."

There was a moment of tense silence on the line. When Benny spoke again her voice was quiet and intent. "How do you know what happened? Nobody knows, except . . . who are you?"

"Just a friend, I heard—"

"Don't bullshit me. The police didn't release the details about Dana's injuries. You're Melia, aren't you?"

"Listen, I don't know what you're talking about. I just—would you please tell her—" Melia sighed and put her finger on the disconnect button. "Just forget it."

"No, wait. Please don't hang up. I'll give you her number at the hospital. She really needs to hear that you're okay."

"No. I really don't know what you're talking about. I only called to check on her."

"Come on, maybe you can give me your number and . . ." Benny stopped herself as if she knew her question was useless. She sounded sincerely concerned. Melia wondered who she was. "Well, can you tell me that you're okay? I mean, really okay? I'd like to be able to tell her that."

"I don't . . ." Melia dropped her head. It was stupid not to give her that much. "Yeah, I'm okay. Really okay."

"Can I help you, at all? Can you come back?"

"No, I'm not coming back. I've got to go." Melia ignored the woman's protest and punched the button. Her hand was shaking and her finger was slick with sweat. It seemed impossible to get a full breath of air, but the water continued to run in the bathroom and she had to do it one more time. Before she could think, before she could talk herself out of it, she dialed Chris' number. The answering machine picked up with an audible click and she jammed the disconnect button again. She couldn't leave a message on the machine. It was just too cold. The burn in her stomach intensified and her eyes were already filling with tears as she rapidly dialed the next number.

"Woman to Woman."

"Langley," Melia whispered, suddenly finding it impossible to voice the words she'd meant to say. The full meaning of what she intended to do slapped her in the face. Her tears poured down as she remembered the love she had last seen in Langley's eyes.

"Melia! Oh my god, Melia. Where are you?"

"Lang, I can't say. I just wanted to tell you, I love you. I love Chris and Molly, tell them that, please."

"Fucking Christ, Melia, don't do this to me." Langley's voice was low, the pain was unbearable to Melia's ears. "Tell me where you are, we can help you. You got to try."

"No, Lang. You don't understand, she didn't force me to come. I want to be with her."

"Listen Melia, I don't know what she's told you. Maybe she's said a lot of things, maybe things you really needed to hear. But you can't trust her, you don't know her. Melia, we all love you, we'll help you." Langley spoke quickly, Melia could imagine the intent look on her face, the lines that framed her mouth when she frowned. She was so young, but already too serious.

"I don't need help. You don't understand. I wish I could explain."

"Melia, hang on, let me get Chris. Let her talk to you—"

"No," Melia interrupted. Her voice was as firm as she'd ever made it and Langley could not miss the authority of her command. "I'll hang up if you try to switch me."

"Melia, please, then let me help you. Is she there? Is she listening?"

"No, she's not."

"Okay then, just get out. Wherever you are, just get out and call the police. They'll help you. They're looking for you and they'll protect you. From her and from Dana."

"Lang, goddamn it. I do not need help. I know what I am doing and it is my choice."

"What *are* you doing, Melia? Tell me what you're doing. Just tell me, and tell me the truth, am I ever going to see you again? Alive?"

Melia's stomach sank and a fresh wash of tears burned in her eyes. How could she say this? How could she not? The letter, if she could ever write it, would explain the things she couldn't say, but it would not help Lang understand what she was going to say right now.

"Mel?"

"No, Lang. You won't."

There was a stricken silence at Langley's end. Then Melia heard the sound of pain and she felt it like a knife stabbing into her heart. She'd never known Langley to cry.

"Melia, god, don't do this. Whatever—"

Melia lost the words as the receiver was jerked from her ear. She looked up into Parker's dark scowl and felt fear. Parker pulled the receiver from her hand and put it to her head. Her face grew even darker as she listened to what

Langley was saying. Melia tried to push her chair away from the desk, but Parker shot her hand out and grabbed Melia's shoulder, holding her forward until her stomach pressed against the table.

"Shut up!" Parker yelled into the phone. "Just shut up a minute and wait." Parker turned to Melia, her fury pulling her lips back from her teeth and distorting her face. "Tell me who you're talkin' to," she demanded.

"It's Langley," Melia whispered. "Just Langley."

Parker narrowed her eyes. She let go of Melia's shoulder, but instantly grabbed her hair and pushed her face down to the table top. The pressure was painless, but firm. "She the kid with no hair?"

"Yes, I just had to—"

Parker shook Melia's head, silencing her and ignoring her speech beyond the affirmation of Langley's identity.

"Listen, Langley. This is Parker. Can you hear me?" Parker paused just long enough for Melia to know that Lang had answered with a single word. "Now, I told you that I was not meanin' to hurt her. And I'm not. But you don't interfere with me, you don't fuck with me, 'cause I never made no promise 'bout anybody else. She made her decision. You try to stop her when she ain't willin' and I'll kick your ass. She changes her mind, she can go home. But it's gonna be her decision alone."

There was another pause. Melia felt Parker's hand release some of the pressure against her head, but she kept her cheek pressed to the cool wood. Parker squatted down and her face was level with Melia's, their eyes locked in a cold stare.

"Jesus Christ. You don't need to say nothin'. I already know how you feel about her, but you gotta let her go and follow her own heart." The anger that had begun to fade from Parker's expression returned at Langley's response. She took the phone from her ear and held it back to Melia's face. "Tell her goodbye."

"—chicken—shit mother fucker, I'll kill you!" Langley was screaming in rage and Melia had to call her name twice before Langley heard.

"Goodbye, Lang. I'll try to write and explain everything," Melia promised, hoping that Parker would still allow her to. "Tell Chris, tell Molly—"

Parker took away the phone and hung it up before Melia could finish. Melia closed her eyes, expecting a storm of rage to hit her. Parker dragged her from the chair, forcing her to stand, to face her.

"Did you tell her where to find us?"

Melia shook her head.

"Did you ask her to take you back?"

"No," Melia denied. "No, I want to be with you."

"Then what are you doin'? Why you takin' a chance like that?" Parker shoved her, pushing her toward the bathroom door. "Why did you try to hide it from me?"

"I just had to talk, I didn't know if you'd be angry. I just wanted to say goodbye." Melia stumbled in the doorway. Her voice quavered, but she forced herself to go on. "Didn't you wish you could have said goodbye?"

Parker followed Melia into the bathroom and slammed the door shut behind them. Melia sank to her knees and clasped her hands together to stop them from shaking. Parker knelt down in front of her and Melia again closed her eyes. She didn't know what to expect, what kind of pain Parker would have to inflict to relieve her anger, and the touch, when it came, was nothing she could have prepared herself for.

Parker took Melia's face in her hands, and kissed her. Melia gasped and opened her eyes. Parker's face was open and kind, the anger gone.

"Oh, god. Parker, I'm so sorry."

"Now, don't be. You gotta learn to talk to me and tell me what you're doin'. I wouldn't a been mad if you said good-bye." Parker put her thumbs under Melia's chin and tilted her face up. "You just scared me, I thought you were givin' me up."

"No. Never," Melia hung onto Parker's wrists as if she would fall without that grasp. "I just got you, and I ain't done with you yet."

Parker smiled and Melia let herself be pulled forward, into Parker's arms, her head against her heart. She listened to the warm, comforting sound and thought how different this encounter would have been if Dana was in Parker's place. Melia realized with a shock that she no longer knew the rules, and what jolted her harder yet was the realization that she could begin to make them herself.

Melia drew back from Parker and studied her face. Parker waited.

"Oh," Melia sighed. A broad smile curved her lips. "Oh, this is going to be good."

Parker raised her eyebrows. Melia knew she was well ahead of Parker, but doubted it would take long to catch her up. Melia got to her knees and shifted forward to straddle Parker's thighs. Parker put her arms around Melia and tried to pull her close. Melia braced her hands on Parker's shoulders and resisted the pull. Parker looked puzzled, but released her and again waited with patience.

"Do you think I'm too forward?"

Parker shook her head slightly. "I don't know what you mean."

"Um," Melia squinted her eyes and thought for a moment. "Maybe I can show you. Is this your favorite shirt?"

"No—"

Melia grabbed the collar and tore the shirt open.

There was a sound of ripping cloth and buttons flew and skittered across the tiles. Before she could even catch a glimpse of the look on Parker's face, Melia leaned forward, using her weight to push Parker backwards to the floor. She bit Parker's neck, locking her teeth lightly in the skin just above her shoulder. Pulling Parker's open shirt away from her body, Melia yanked the sleeves down to entangle Parker's arms, preventing her from lifting her hands.

Parker laughed. The sound stopped abruptly as Melia bit her again on the firm muscle of her chest. Melia slid her body lower, slowly, letting Parker feel the pressure of Melia's hips as she rode her body down. Melia's chin brushed Parker's nipple and Melia lifted her head to bring her mouth over Parker's breast. She licked it once, teasing.

"Anything I do . . ." Melia paused to swirl her tongue around the hardening bud. ". . . that you don't like . . ." Her lips tugged at it gently. ". . . you just tell me . . ."

Parker groaned as Melia bared her teeth and bit her nipple lightly, holding just firmly enough to keep it from escaping the touch of her tongue. Between her legs, Melia felt Parker's body tensing. She continued. ". . . and I'll stop." She removed her mouth from Parker's breast and waited. Parker didn't respond, except to shiver when Melia blew a cool breath over her wet nipple. "Of course, I'll just find something else to do . . ." She proved it by dropping her head again and roughly sucking the nipple back into her mouth. She bit harder this time and Parker's hips lifted, pressing against Melia's. She could feel her own wetness and it drove her on.

Melia rested her weight on her elbows and drew her knees up to pin down Parker's sleeves and hold her immobile. Straightening her back, she held Parker's eye. The desire so clear on Parker's face made her weak, but she kept her weight on Parker and hoped she wouldn't decide to really struggle against her. Melia would lose. She kept pushing her mental advantage.

"I'm gonna ride you, cowboy," she whispered, her fingers slowly unbuttoning her own shirt. The warmth of the room and the steam from the bath caused a sheen of moisture to cover her chest. Pulling her shirt away, she leaned forward, her breasts held firm in the confines of her bra. Parker's gaze left hers and focused on Melia's cleavage. A drop of sweat rolled down her forehead. Melia touched her fingertip to Parker's lips. "I'm gonna ride you, I'm gonna break you."

Parker swallowed and her lips parted. Melia pushed her finger inside, to Parker's teeth. When she met that barrier, she hooked her fingernail on the edge of the lower teeth and forced Parker's jaw down. When her mouth opened, Melia slid her finger inside and under Parker's tongue. Melia held her that way, one finger inside and the others holding her jaw firmly as she brought her lips down to cover Parker's mouth. She ran her tongue over Parker's lips and teeth and tasted the saltiness of her own finger. Kissing her deeply, Melia felt Parker breathing careful, shallow breaths through her nose. Melia knew from experience that breathing that way would quickly make Parker lightheaded. She also knew, from experience, how that could be used to an aggressor's advantage. She sucked Parker's tongue into her mouth and bit it lightly. Parker's arms strained against the bounds of her shirt.

Melia instantly moved her mouth away and withdrew her finger. Still clenching Parker's chin, she pushed it to turn her head away. She pushed until she knew Parker's neck muscles were strained, then leaned down and whispered a sharp command in Parker's ear. "Turn over on your stomach and don't move."

Melia lifted her weight and Parker immediately turned her body to press her stomach to the cool tiles. Melia put her left hand in the middle of Parker's back and leaned against it, half to brace herself, half to continue to prevent Parker from taking a deep breath. She unbuttoned her jeans and kicked them off of her legs. Releasing the pressure on Parker's back, Melia slid her hands beneath her hips, lifting her enough to reach the buttons on her jeans. A dizzying sense of deja vu swept over her as she remembered Parker holding her this way in the crawl space when she took off Melia's belt to bind her hands. Melia wished Parker wore one other than her gun belt, which was too wide for the purpose. It would be a nice reversal to make Parker experience what she had done to Melia. Melia satisfied herself with jerking Parker's shirt down farther and twisting it tight to pull her wrists together.

Roughly, she yanked at Parker's jeans, not allowing Parker to help by her movements, pulling them down over her long legs and off. Shoving at Parker's side, she made her turn back over, pinning her hands beneath her. Melia briefly hoped that it didn't hurt, but the look on Parker's face was anything but pained. Melia let her take several deep breaths before she swung her leg over Parker's body and lowered herself onto Parker's hips, rubbing herself softly on Parker's mound until their hair tangled together. Melia arched her back, letting Parker see the length of her body, the depth of her desire. She freed her breasts from her bra and caressed them before Parker's eyes.

"Don't you wish you could touch me, cowboy?" Melia continued to tease, with her voice, her hands, her wetness still rubbing rhythmically against Parker.

"Yeah, I do." Parker's voice was a deep growl of desire and Melia could feel the vibration of it right down to where their bodies touched together. Her passion almost betrayed her ability to dominate.

"That's a shame," she whispered, her voice nearly as rough as Parker's had been. She moved her hips in a slow circle and let the pleasure of the contact show in her face. Parker growled again, this time without words.

Melia closed her eyes and gave herself over to the wet heat of the friction her movements produced. After only a few moments, Parker found it unbearable. She tried to push with her hips, to control Melia's movements. Melia put her hands on Parker's hipbones and held her still.

"I said this is my ride," she warned. "I decide where we go and how fast we get there."

"Jesus Christ, I can't do this." Parker's shoulder muscles strained and the sweat was now running from her forehead. "Let me . . . let me go."

Melia knew she wouldn't be able to hold Parker much longer. She wished for Parker's strength, for Dana's, to be her own. But what she couldn't control with brawn, she could command with brains. Parker closed her eyes.

"Don't do that," Melia commanded. "Look at me and tell me what you want."

"I want to touch you—"

"We're touching." Melia moved her hips again to prove her point.

"I want to make you come—"

"I will," Melia interrupted her again. "I'm so close."

"No, I mean—"

"You want some control? You want to decide how I come, cowboy?"

"Yeah," Parker groaned.

"Well . . ." Melia pretended to hesitate. "Maybe I could let you taste me. Would you like that?"

"Oh, yeah." Parker was again breathing too shallow. Melia smiled, her control regained. She put her hand up, waiting for Parker's eyes to follow it, then slowly moved it down between her legs, letting Parker see as she dipped her fingertip into her own wetness. This time, when Melia brought her finger back to Parker's lips, she didn't have to force her mouth open. Parker licked the length of her finger slowly, the expression on her face pushing Melia dangerously close to the edge.

Melia's breasts brushed Parker's as she leaned forward. She let her upper body rest on Parker's so she could shift her weight and bring her leg from over Parker's body. When Parker felt her moving to the side, she thought that Melia was going to let her go. Melia laughed and put her left forearm high across Parker's chest, again using her weight to keep Parker on the floor. She lifted her knee once more and used it to push Parker's legs apart, in the same instant, she plunged her fingers deep inside Parker's body.

Parker's breath caught in her chest. Melia pushed the moment, using hard pressure and deep strokes to keep Parker high. Parker struggled to release her arms, to push Melia aside.

"Let me go," she moaned.

Melia lifted her body from the floor, forcing all of her weight to one knee and the arm across Parker's chest. She never relented in her control of Parker's passion, but kept driving into her, her fingers pushing deep, the heel of her hand rubbing hard against the outside.

"Jesus, let me go." Parker struggled harder, almost bucking Melia off onto the floor. Melia silently prayed for the strength to hold out, Parker was almost there. "Please," they both asked in the same breath. Melia kissed her hard to silence her.

Parker suddenly hooked her leg around Melia's and pulled, drawing Melia off balance, making her fall over onto Parker's body.

"Let me go."

"Let yourself go," Melia demanded and finally, Parker did. She came loud, hard, lifting her hips and pushing against Melia's hand. Melia stayed with her, continuing her thrusts, waiting for the relaxation that would signal the end of Parker's passion. It never came.

Before Melia knew what was happening, Parker braced her leg and shoved Melia off onto the tiles. Raising herself to one knee, she shrugged down the shirt, separating her arms. The cloth tore away and Parker's hands were free. She grabbed for Melia as Melia tried to kick herself away. Her foot slipped on the steam-dampened tiles and Parker caught her leg. Half laughing, half panicked, Melia screamed as Parker growled, her eyes wild and out of control.

As if Melia suddenly weighed nothing, Parker pulled her toward her and held her to the floor. It seemed that Parker had actually gained strength from her orgasm. Melia screamed again as Parker effortlessly lifted her and stood. Parker laughed. "You're gonna get the law here if you're not careful."

"Am I going to need them?"

"Only if I can't satisfy you."

"Oh, god you do. You already did." Melia squirmed until Parker let her turn to wrap her legs around Parker's waist. Parker lifted her, pressing her wetness against her stomach.

"Oh, no. You ain't gettin' off that easy. Not the way you tormented me." Her voice held a threat, a promise. Melia's fear was gone, her desire multiplied. "And that taste of you was just enough to stir my appetite."

"You want more?"

"I want it all." Parker took a step toward the bathtub.

Melia couldn't help but test the power she held in this relationship. The idea was just so new. "Wait, I want to do it on the bed."

Parker sent one glance of longing at the water before turning and carrying Melia to the doorway. Melia rested her head on Parker's shoulder. "We'll get back there," she promised. "We have time."

Twenty

Here was the streetlight where Melia had stood, her fingers freezing cold, while she worried about the snowflakes falling on Langley's head. Here was where things really started spinning out of control. Here was where Langley should have taken a stand. The expression on Melia's face that night had said it all, she was afraid, she'd been crying, but Langley turned away and allowed Dana to take Melia home. Every day she walked to work and passed that streetlight and remembered.

The bookstore was worse by far for memories. How many hours had Melia spent there, lending her spirit to the place, keeping Langley distracted from the needs of her other customers? Every time Langley broke open a case of books and saw the cover of a Western, she would remember that last night at Melia's house, when she had her at the door and again turned away. That was the hardest feeling to face, knowing that she could have stopped it there. Right there. It was her last chance and she let it, and Melia, slip away.

She'd almost lost her mind when the news came. The television kept going on and on about the police finding

Melia's old Honda abandoned in the desert, about the blood-stained clothing in the trunk. Looking up at the stars every night as she walked home, she wondered if they were the last things Melia had seen. She prayed that it had been easy, Melia's last night, that the cold-eyed woman who had captured her soul had possessed enough human decency to make it easy. To make it quick. Langley dwelt on that thought too much and wished for the chance to see Parker again some day. For some reason, she knew the police would never find her.

Chris had not let her quit the bookstore. Langley tried, afraid of spending each day with the memories so near. But the work had been a blessing and the people were so kind. Her first shift back, after spending days in a black well of emptiness, she'd looked up from the counter realizing that all that was left of Melia was right there in the building, surrounding her. Now, although it still hurt to be there, Chris could hardly get her to go home.

Then one day, after Langley had been back to work about a week, she was behind the counter, just kneeling down to drop a disc in the CD player when the bell rang above the door.

Langley lifted her head to look through the glass of the display, and at first, could not believe her eyes. But her shock did not immobilize her for long. She was up, over the counter, diving toward the woman who stood just inside the door, reaching her before the woman knew she was there.

Langley clenched her fist and slammed it into Dana's face. Dana staggered, losing control of her crutches and smashing into the bookcase lining the wall. Langley watched her fall and drew back her foot to aim at Dana's head. Her rage had her speechless. Suddenly, before she could connect with the kick, someone jumped on her from behind. She spun around, crashing into the door and driving the woman on her back into the wall. Langley ignored her as she fell away and returned to Dana, who hadn't attempted to get up from the floor.

"All right, all right, you fucker," Langley's voice had returned, if not her vocabulary. She again drove her fist at Dana's face. Dana ducked and caught the blow on the side of her head. Langley grabbed her hair with one hand and her throat with the other, trying to pull her into the middle of the room so she could swing her fist without hitting the wall. There was a commotion behind her, but all of her awareness was focused on the face in front of her.

"You killed her, you cock-sucker. You!" Langley shouted the words into Dana's face as she dragged her forward. Dana didn't look away from her eyes as Langley threw her to the floor.

"I know," Dana whispered. "I'm so sorry."

Langley couldn't stand to be mocked. She again grabbed Dana's throat, cutting off her air, shutting her up for good. Someone behind her took a fistful of her jacket and pulled her away from Dana like she was nothing more than a poodle in a dog fight. Langley struggled, still kicking out at Dana as she was dragged away. Chris pulled her down to the floor and held her still.

"Goddamn it, Chris, don't you dare stop me!" Langley screamed, not believing that Chris would really keep her back.

"You stop it, Lang. I'm serious."

"That bitch killed Melia." Langley glared at the young woman who was helping Dana back onto her feet. "Did she tell you that? She's a fucking murderer? Don't think you won't be next."

"Langley!" Chris grabbed Langley's chin and turned her face away. "That is enough!"

Langley looked up at her in shock and confusion. "Chris? How can you—"

"I asked her to come here. She's not here to hurt you, or me, or anyone." Chris let go of Langley, but stood between her and Dana until it was clear that Langley was not going to rise from the floor. She turned to Dana. "Well, Dana, this is Melia's friend Langley. I believe you once said that you wanted to meet her."

"Well, you were right. It's pretty clear she hates me as much as you do."

"More," Langley spat.

Chris nodded. "More. But she's young. She hasn't got a clue about how we're all in these things together."

Dana shook her head. Blood ran into her eyebrow from a deep cut in her scalp. Langley hoped it hurt. The woman holding Dana upright used her sleeve to tenderly wipe the blood away.

"I know, you don't have a clue either. That's why I asked you to come."

Langley sat up and closed her eyes. She couldn't stand to see someone showing Dana kindness, or even to see Dana here, in the place Melia had come so many times as sanctuary from Dana's abuse. It sickened her that Chris would ask her to come. Chris led Dana past, helping her navigate the narrow path to the back room. Langley felt a gentle touch on her leg and she slapped it away without bothering to open her eyes.

"My name's Benny," a soft voice informed her. "I'm sorry you're hurting."

"What the fuck do you care?" Langley lashed out bitterly.

"A lot more than you could know." Benny touched Langley again, encouraging her to open her eyes and look at her. "See, I love her. And every night, I get to share her nightmares. I guarantee you, there's nothing you can do to hurt her any more than she already hurts."

"Is that supposed to make me feel sorry for her?"

"No."

Langley did look, finally. She studied Benny's face. She looked, pointedly, at Benny's throat and at her arms.

"No," Benny said again, the simple word saying volumes.

"So what makes *you* the lucky one?"

Benny shrugged. "It isn't always easy for her, and I haven't always been so lucky. Especially at first. But I love her, and she's beginning to love me."

"And it's worth it?"

"Haven't you ever been in love?"

Langley looked away and tried to mask her expression. The pain could not be hidden so easily.

Benny sighed. "I was afraid it was like that. Why you could hate her so much. I'm very sorry."

"Forget it. It's over."

"It's not over. Not just yet." Chris stood behind Langley and pulled on the back of her jacket. "Come on, we need to talk."

"With her? Go to hell."

Chris smiled. "I'm gonna forget you said that." She pulled harder and as she lifted Langley from the floor, Langley drew her feet under her and stood. Chris held her arm and led her into the back. Sitting her down across the room from Dana, Chris ignored the look of hatred Langley burned into Dana's eyes. She took a deep breath. "Okay, you both know they finally found Melia's car. And you know, just as well, that they found some of her clothes with blood stains on them, and they've pretty much decided she's dead."

Breathing out slowly through her teeth, Langley fought to hold back her tears. No way could she cry now. Her stomach burned and she focused on what she'd like to do to Dana if Chris would only leave the room for a few minutes.

"What you don't know is that Melia sent me a letter. I got it the day after they found her car." Disregarding the looks on their faces, Chris lifted a folded sheet of paper from her desk and opened it carefully. "I wasn't going to tell anyone about it. I didn't think it would be right to let you read it, I thought that it would just hurt the two of you even more."

Catching sight of the fine lines of Melia's handwriting, Langley wanted to rip the paper out of Chris' hand. How could Chris be so selfish as to keep anything of Melia from her?

"I see what you're thinking, Lang. But trust me, I knew this was nothing you wanted to hear."

"Let me be the judge of that."

"I will. I'll read it to you now." Chris bent her head and read the words quietly. Dana and Langley both leaned forward, not wanting to miss a word.

Dear Chris, (and Lang)

I'm writing this from the balcony of my hotel room. All right, I'm exaggerating, it's more of an over-blown window ledge with a rickety railing. But I can see the desert from here, all red rocks and sand, and I'm looking forward to the heat that tomorrow's sun will bring. I want to take a whole page or two to describe how beautiful the sunset is, and how long it lasts, and how I think the rocks have been stained the color they are by millions of years of sunsets bleeding down on them. But I know it's just my desire to avoid what I really need to write to you. It's harder because I know this is my last opportunity to ever talk to you and I have to say everything I'm ever going to say in these lines. You can imagine the pressure, can't you?

Before this starts sounding like a suicide note (or something worse) I have to tell you that I'm completely safe and I've never been happier. Parker is wonderful. Chris, I finally understand what you meant about love, I'm so glad to know you have it with Molly. And I know that Lang will find someone who will make her feel this way. I hope then she can forgive me for what I'm doing now. I wanted to tell you both about Parker. I meant to, but I just ran out of time.

And now, tomorrow, Parker and I are going to drive out into the desert. I don't think we'll be coming back. I hope not anyway, because if we do, Parker will be very unhappy. You see, she doesn't belong here and really, neither do I. Both of us are in the wrong time. Me, just because I was born here. Parker, because of a strange twist of fate. What we'll do tomorrow is go twist fate again. Hopefully, we'll go back to where she came from and Parker can pick up her life again and I can finally begin to live. I don't even want to think of failure or what will happen if we go the wrong direction and end up in the future. I guess it's one of those blind faith ventures. I would ask you to wish us luck, but if all goes well, we will be long gone before you read this.

I need to go. I should have explained this better, but I know you think I'm crazy or deluded or deceived. There's no way I can convince you that this is real and I am happy, so I will just tell you how much I love you and that I hope when the emotion of the moment wears away you can forgive me and be happy for me. Parker asked me to thank you both for taking care of me until she came and she's very sorry she was angry with Lang on the phone. And please, tell Dana she didn't want to shoot her. Things sometimes just happen.

Please remember me. The time I had with you, I'll cherish for the rest of my life.

I love you,
Melia

There was a timeless moment of silence in the room before Langley lost her composure. Unable to speak, she leaped up and tried to rush past Chris. Chris put out her hand and shoved Langley back down into her chair. Her voice was much gentler than her touch. "I didn't think you'd like it. Bear with me a little more." She reached into a box and took out two books, tossing one to both of them.

"Seen that face before?"

"What the hell are you talking about?" Langley leaned forward, her arms crossed over her stomach. Dana was sitting, frozen, her face reflecting the feeling of nausea that gripped Langley. "What are you do—"

"Lang. Shut up and look at the picture."

Langley felt her anguish quickly becoming fury, but the only way out of the situation was to humor Chris. She looked down at the book cover and, slowly, a spark of recognition flamed into remembrance. Langley looked up at the same time Dana did and they stared at each other in shock.

"It's not just me? You think . . . it looks like her?"

Langley nodded. Then her anger burned even hotter at agreeing with Dana on anything. "So, it's a weird coincidence."

Chris nodded. Pulling out her desk chair, she turned it around and straddled it. "Yep. It's a coincidence. Coincidentally, I gave this book to Melia. She loved the cover."

"Ah." The quiet sound of pain escaped before Langley could hold it back. God, she didn't want to cry in front of Dana. Clenching her teeth, she whispered, "I don't need to hear this."

"I do," Dana said quietly.

"Yeah, I think you both do." Chris was smiling a bittersweet smile. "I know the artist who did this picture and I mentioned to her how much a friend of mine liked it. I was thinking of a painting or something for Melia's birthday, before she left."

Langley found herself trying to push her thumb through the image.

"Finally, yesterday, this artist comes back with a copy of the photograph she based this cover on. It's dated 1865. This woman was real and her name was Parker. Parker McCallem."

"No." Langley shook her head. "No, don't start that time shit again. Melia was deluded, she was murdered, and her body . . . dumped out there in the desert. Alone. I'm not going to play these stupid games."

"It's a game all right, Lang." Chris agreed. "But one Melia apparently learned to play."

Chris held a copy of an old, sepia-colored photograph out to Langley. Reluctantly, she took it and held it, shaking, to the light. Her eyes stung, but she looked.

Parker sat astride a tall black horse, her hat pulled low and her eyes barely visible through the black shadow that covered half her face. Her mouth, her sensual lips, were in fine detail, same as the painting on the book Langley held. What was different—what was meaningful to this whole experience—was the woman who was not in the painting, but was in the photograph. Standing in a way so familiar, with her hand on Parker's stirrup and her face turned up, she was smiling. Her dark hair framed her eyes and her smile was so full of love, so full of happiness that Langley's heart almost broke all over again to see it.

She had never seen Melia's face so full of joy, so sure of belonging.

About the Author

Beverly Shearer has spent all of her life in the West. From helping to herd cattle on her father's ranch in Northern Idaho to being part of the herd in Denver, Colorado's rush hour, she has learned that the spirit of the West is eternal. The Western love of independence and freedom knows no gender and knows no age. The characters that people her books—the good guys and the bad guys—can still be found in the small towns and big cities from Washington to New Mexico, from Wyoming to Nevada.

In addition to writing novels, Ms. Shearer works as a newspaper copy editor and a freelance Internet content writer.

ALSO BY BEVERLY SHEARER

And Love Came Calling

Rising Tide Press brings you the best in lesbian fiction and nonfiction. We publish books to stir the imagination for women who enjoy ideas that are out of the ordinary.

We are committed to our community and welcome your comments.

We can be reached at our website:
www.risingtidepress.com

More Fiction to Stir the Imagination
From Rising Tide Press

CLOUD NINE AFFAIR   Katherine E. Kreuter

Christine Grandy—rebellious, wealthy, twenty-something—has disappeared, along with her lover Monica Ward. Desperate to bring her home, Christine's millionaire father hires Paige Taylor. But the trail to Christine is mined with obstacles, while powerful enemies plot to eliminate her. Eventually, Paige discovers that this mission is far more dangerous than she dreamed. A witty, sophisticated mystery by the best-selling author of Fool Me Once, filled with colorful characters, plot twists, and romance. $11.99

THE DEPOSITION   Katherine E. Kreuter

It is April in Paris and the Deposition's loopy narrator, G.B. is plotting the caper of capers. This provocative and hilarious novel by the author of the Paige Taylor Mystery Series resonates with gasps and guffaws. $12.00

STORM RISING   Linda Kay Silva

The excitement continues in this wonderful continuation of TROPICAL STORM. Join Megan and Connie as they set out to find Delta and bring her home. The meaning of friendship and love is explored as Delta, Connie, Megan and friends struggle to stay alive and stop General Zahn. Again the Costa Rican Rain Forest is the setting for another fast-paced action adventure. Storm fans won't want to miss this next installment in the Delta Stevens Mystery Series. $12.00

TROPICAL STORM   Linda Kay Silva

Another winning, action-packed adventure featuring smart and sassy heroines, an exotic jungle setting, and a plot with more twists and turns than a coiled cobra. Megan has disappeared into the Costa Rican rain forest and it's up to Delta and Connie to find her. Can they reach Megan before it's too late? Will Storm risk everything to save the woman she loves? Fast-paced, full of wonderful characters and surprises. Not to be missed. $11.99

CALLED TO KILL   Joan Albarella

Nikki Barnes, Reverend, teacher and Vietnam Vet is once again entangled in a complex web of murder and drugs when her past collides with the present. Set in the rainy spring of Buffalo, Dr. Ginni Clayton and her friend Magpie add spice and romance as Nikki tries to solve the mystery that puts her own life in danger. A fun and exciting read. $12.00

AGENDA FOR MURDER   Joan Albarella

A compelling mystery about the legacies of love and war, set on a sleepy college campus. Though haunted by memories of her tour of duty in Vietnam, Nikki Barnes is finally putting back the pieces of her life, only to collide with murder and betrayal. $11.99

ONE SUMMER NIGHT   Gerri Hill

Johanna Marshall doesn't usually fall into bed with someone she just met, but Kelly Sambino isn't just anyone. Hurt by love and labeled a womanizer, can these two women learn to trust one another and let love find its way? $12.00

BY THE SEA SHORE   Sandra Morris (avail 10/00)

A quiet retreat turns into more investigative work for Jess Shore in the summer town of Provincetown, MA. This page-turner mystery will keep you entertained as Jess struggles with her individuality while solving an attempted murder case. $12.00

AND LOVE CAME CALLING   Beverly Shearer

A beautifully told love story as old as time, steeped in the atmosphere of the Old West. Danger lights the fire of passion between two women whose lives become entwined when Kendra (Kenny), on the run from the law, happily stumbles upon the solitary cabin where Sophie has been hiding from her own past. Together, they learn that love can overcome all obstacles. $11.99

SIDE DISH   Kim Taylor

A genuinely funny yet tender novel which follows the escapades of Muriel, a twenty-something burmed—out waitress with a college degree, who has turned gay slacker living into an art form. Getting by on margaritas and old movies, she seems to have resigned herself to low standards, simple pleasures, and erotic daydreams. But in secret, Muriel is searching for true love. $11.99

COMING ATTRACTIONS
Bobbi D. Marolt

Helen Townsend reluctantly admits she's tried of being lonely...and of being closeted. Enter Princess Charming in the form of Cory Chamberlain, a gifted concert pianist. And Helen embraces joy once again. But can two women find happiness when one yearns to break out of the closet and breathe free, while the other fears that it will destroy her career? A delicious blend of humor, heart and passion—a novel that captures the bliss and blundering of love.
$11.99

ROUGH JUSTICE
Claire Youmans

When Glenn Lowry's sunken fishing boat turns up four years after its disappearance, foul play is suspected. Classy, ambitious Prosecutor Janet Schilling immediately launches a murder investigation, which produces several surprising suspects-one of them, her own former lover Catherine Adams, now living a reclusive life on an island. A real page-turner!
$10.99

NO CORPSE
Nancy Sanra

The third Tally McGinnis mystery is set aboard an Olivia Cruise. Tally and Katie thought they were headed out for some sun and fun. Instead, Tally finds herself drawn into a reunion cruise gone awry. When women start turning up dead, it is up to Tally and Cid to find the murderer and unravel a decades old mystery. Sanra fans new and old, won't be disappointed.
$12.00

NO ESCAPE
Nancy Sanra

This edgy, fast-paced whodunit set in picturesque San Francisco, will keep you guessing. Lesbian PI Tally McGinnis is called into action when Dr. Rebecca Toliver is charged with the murder of her lover Melinda. Is the red rose left at the scene the crime the signature of a copycat killer, or is the infamous Marcia Cox back, and up to her old, evil tricks again?
$11.99

NO WITNESSES
Nancy Sanra

This cliffhanger of a mystery set in San Francisco, introduces Detective Tally McGinnis, whose ex-lover Pamela Tresdale is arrested for the grisly murder of a wealthy Texas heiress. Tally rushes to the rescue despite friends' warnings, and is drawn once again into Pamela's web of deception and betrayal as she attempts to clear her and find the real killer.
$9.99

DEADLY RENDEZVOUS
Diane Davidson

A string of brutal murders in the middle of the desert plunges Lt. Toni Underwood and her lover Megan into a high profile investigation, which uncovers a world of drugs, corruption and murder, as well as the dark side of the human mind. Explosive, fast-paced, & action-packed.
$9.99

DEADLY GAMBLE
Diane Davidson

Las-Vegas-city of bright lights and dark secrets-is the perfect setting for this intriguing sequel to DEADLY RENDEZVOUS. Former police detective Toni Underwood and her partner Sally Murphy are catapulted back into the world of crime by a letter from Toni's favorite aunt. Now a prominent madam, Vera Valentine fears she is about to me murdered-a distinct possibility.
$11.99

RETURN TO ISIS
Jean Stewart

It is the year 2093, and Whit, a bold woman warrior from an Amazon nation, rescues Amelia from a dismal world where females are either breeders or drones. During their arduous journey back to the shining all-women's world of Artemis, they are unexpectedly drawn to each other. This engaging first book in the series has it all-romance, mystery, and adventure.
$9.99

ISIS RISING
Jean Stewart

In this stirring romantic fantasy, the familiar cast of lovable characters begins to rebuild the colony of Isis, burned to the ground ten years earlier by the dread Regulators. But evil forces threaten to destroy their dream. A swashbuckling futuristic adventure and an endearing love story all rolled into one.
$11.99

WARRIORS OF ISIS
Jean Stewart

The third lusty tale is one of high adventure and passionate romance among the Freeland Warriors. Arinna Sojourner, the evil product of genetic engineering, vows to destroy the fledgling colony of Isis with her incredible psychic powers. Whit, Kali, and other warriors battle to save their world, in this novel bursting with life, love, heroines and villains. *A Lambda Literary Award Finalist*
$11.99

EMERALD CITY BLUES Jean Stewart

When comfortable yuppie world of Chris Olson and Jennifer Hart collides with the desperate lives of Reb and Flynn, two lesbian runaways struggling to survive on the streets of Seattle, the forecast is trouble. A gritty, enormously readable novel of contemporary lesbigay life, which raises real questions about the meaning of family and community. This book is an excellent choice for young adults and the more mature reader. $11.99

DANGER IN HIGH PLACES Sharon Gilligan

Set against the backdrop of Washington, D.C., this riveting mystery introduces freelance photographer and amateur sleuth, Alix Nicholson. Alix stumbles on a deadly scheme, and with the help of a lesbian congressional aide, unravels the mystery. $9.99

DANGER! CROSS CURRENTS Sharon Gilligan

The exciting sequel to Danger in High Places brings freelance photographer Alix Nicholson face-to-face with an old love and a murder. When Alix's landlady turns up dead, and her much younger lover, Leah Claire, the prime suspect, Alix launches a frantic campaign to find the real killer. $9.99

HEARTSONE AND SABER Jacqui Singleton

You can almost hear the sabers clash in this rousing tale of good and evil, of passionate love between a bold warrior queen and a beautiful healer with magical powers. $10.99

PLAYING FOR KEEPS Stevie Rios

In this sparkling tale of love and adventure, Lindsay West an oboist, travels to Caracas, where she meets three people who change her life forever: Rob Heron a gay man, who becomes her dearest friend; her lover Mercedes Luego, a lovely cellist, who takes Lindsay on a life-altering adventure down the Amazon; and the mysterious jungle-dwelling woman Arminta, who touches their souls. $10.99

LOVE SPELL Karen Williams

A deliciously erotic and humorous love story in which Kate Gallagher, a shy veterinarian, and Allegra, who has magic at her fingertips, fall in love. A masterful blend of fantasy and reality, this beautifully written story will delight your heart and imagination. $12.00

NIGHTSHADE Karen Williams

Alex Spherris finds herself the new owner of a magical bell, which some people would kill for. She is ushered into a strange & wonderful world and meets Orielle, who melts her frozen heart. A heart-warming romance spun in the best tradition of storytelling. $11.99

FEATHERING YOUR NEST:

An Interactive Workbook & Guide to a Loving Lesbian Relationship

Gwen Leonhard, M.ED./Jennie Mast, MSW

This fresh, insightful guide and workbook for lesbian couples provides effective ways to build and nourish your relationships. Includes fun exercises & creative ways to spark romance, solve conflict, fight fair, conquer boredom, spice up your sex lives. $14.99

SHADOWS AFTER DARK Ouida Crozier

While wings of death are spreading over her own world, Kyril is sent to earth to find the cure. Here, she meets the beautiful but lonely Kathryn, and they fall deeply in love. But gradually, Kathryn learns that her exotic new lover has been sent to earth with a purpose—to save her own dying vampire world. A tender, finely written story. $9.95

SWEET BITTER LOVE Rita Schiano

Susan Fredrickson is a woman of fire and ice—a successful high-powered executive, she is by turns sexy and aloof. From the moment writer Jenny Ceretti spots her at the Village Coffeehouse, her serene life begins to change. As their friendship explodes into a blazing love affair, Jenny discovers that all is not as it appears, while Susan is haunted by ghosts from a past that won't stay hidden. A roller-coaster romance which vividly captures the rhythm and feel of love's sometimes rocky ride and the beauty of life after recovery. $10.99

HOW TO ORDER

TITLE	AUTHOR	PRICE
☐ Agenda for Murder	Joan Albarella	11.99
☐ And Love Came Calling	Beverly Shearer	11.99
☐ Called to Kill	Joan Albarella	12.00
☐ Cloud Nine Affair	Katherine Kreuter	11.99
☐ Coming Attractions	Katherine Kreuter	11.99
☐ Danger! Cross Currents	Sharon Gilligan	9.99
☐ Danger in High Places	Sharon Gilligan	9.95
☐ Deadly Gamble	Diane Davidson	11.99
☐ Deadly Rendezvous	Diane Davidson	9.99
☐ Dreamcatcher	Lori Byrd	9.99
☐ Emerald City Blues	Jean Stewart	11.99
☐ Feathering Your Nest	Leonhard/Mast	14.99
☐ Heartstone and Saber	Jaqui Singleton	10.99
☐ Isis Rising	Jean Stewart	11.99
☐ Love Spell	Karen Williams	12.00
☐ Nightshade	Karen Williams	11.99
☐ No Escape	Nancy Sanra	11.99
☐ No Witness	Nancy Sanra	11.99
☐ No Corpse	Nancy Sanra	12.00
☐ One Summer Night	Gerri Hill	12.00
☐ Playing for Keeps	Stevie Rios	10.99
☐ Return to Isis	Jean Stewart	9.99
☐ Rough Justice	Claire Youmans	10.99
☐ Shadows After Dark	Ouida Crozier	9.95
☐ Side Dish	Kim Taylor	11.99
☐ Storm Rising	Linda Kay Silva	12.00
☐ Sweet Bitter Love	Rita Schiano	10.99
☐ The Deposition	Katherine Kreuter	12.00
☐ Tropical Storm	Linda Kay Silva	11.99
☐ Warriors of Isis	Jean Stewart	11.99

Please send me the books I have checked. I enclosed a check or money order, plus $4 for the first book and $1 for each additional book to cover shipping and handling.

Name (please print) _____

Address: _____

_____

City: _____ State: _____ Zip: _____

Arizona residents please add 7% sales tax to total.

Send to: Rising Tide Press
PO Box 30457, Tucson, Arizona 85751

Or visit our website: www.risingtidepress.com